## Praise for Bentley Little, "THE MASTER OF THE MACABRE"*

"*The Walking* is wonderful, fast-paced, rock-'em, jolt-'em, shock-'em, contemporary terror fiction with believable characters and an unusually clever plot. Highly entertaining."
—Dean Koontz

"Bentley Little's *The Walking* is the horror event of the year. If you like spooky stories you must read this book."
—*Stephen King

"*The Walking* is a waking nightmare. A spellbinding tale of witchcraft and vengeance. Bentley Little conjures a dark landscape peopled by all-too-human characters on the brink of the abyss. Scary and intense."
—Michael Prescott, author of *The Shadow Hunter*

"The overwhelming sense of doom with which Bentley Little imbues his . . . novel is so palpable it seems to rise from the book like mist. Flowing seamlessly between time and place, the Bram Stoker Award–winning author's ability to transfix his audience . . . is superb . . . terrifying. [*The Walking*] has the potential to be a major sleeper."
—*Publishers Weekly* (starred review)

*continued . . .*

## *The Ignored*

"This is Bentley Little's best book yet. Frightening, thought-provoking, and impossible to put down."   —Stephen King

"With his artfully plain prose and Quixote-like narrative, Little dissects the deep and disturbing fear of anonymity all Americans feel. . . . What Little has created is nothing less than a nightmarishly brilliant tour de force of modern life in America."   —*Publishers Weekly* (starred review)

"Bentley Little offers an entertaining but relevant take on contemporary society. . . . *The Ignored* is a singular achievement by a writer who makes the leap from the ranks of the merely talented to true distinction with this one. This one may become a classic."   —*Dark Echo*

"Inventive. Chilling."   —*Science Fiction Chronicle*

"A spooky novel with an original premise."
—SFSite (Web site)

"Little is so wonderful that he can make the act of ordering a Coke at McDonald's take on a sinister dimension. This philosophical soul searcher is provocative."   —*Fangoria*

"*The Ignored* is not average at all."   —*Locus*

## *The Revelation*
## Winner of the Bram Stoker Award

"Grabs the reader and yanks him along through an ever-worsening landscape of horrors. . . . It's a terrifying ride with a shattering conclusion."    —Gary Brandner

"*The Revelation* isn't just a thriller—it's a shocker . . . packed with frights and good, gory fun. . . . A must for those who like horror with a bite."    —Richard Laymon

"I guarantee, once you start reading this book, you'll be up until dawn with your eyes glued to the pages. A nail-biting, throat squeezing, nonstop plunge into darkness and evil."
    —Rick Hautala

## *The Store*

"*The Store* is . . . frightening."    —*Los Angeles Times*

"Must reading for Koontz fans. Bentley Little draws the reader into a ride filled with fear, danger, and horror."
    —Harriet Klausner, *Painted Rock*

## *The Mailman*

"A thinking person's horror novel. *The Mailman* delivers."
    —*Los Angeles Times*

## *University*

"Bentley Little keeps the high-tension jolts coming. By the time I finished, my nerves were pretty well fried, and I have a pretty high shock level. *University* is unlike anything else in popular fiction."    —Stephen King

# THE
# ASSOCIATION

## BENTLEY LITTLE

A SIGNET BOOK

SIGNET
Published by New American Library, a division of
Penguin Putnam Inc., 375 Hudson Street,
New York, New York 10014, U.S.A.
Penguin Books Ltd, 27 Wrights Lane,
London W8 5TZ, England
Penguin Books Australia Ltd,
Ringwood, Victoria, Australia
Penguin Books Canada Ltd, 10 Alcorn Avenue,
Toronto, Ontario, Canada M4V 3B2
Penguin Books (N.Z.) Ltd, 182–190 Wairau Road,
Auckland 10, New Zealand

Penguin Books Ltd, Registered Offices:
Harmondsworth, Middlesex, England

First published by Signet, an imprint of New American Library, a division of
Penguin Putnam Inc.

First Printing, September 2001
10 9 8 7 6 5 4 3 2 1

PUBLISHER'S NOTE
This is a work of fiction. Names, characters, places, and incidents either are the
product of the author's imagination or are used fictitiously, and any resemblance to
actual persons, living or dead, business establishments, events, or locales is entirely
coincidental.

This book is dedicated to my son, Emerson Li Little, with the hope that he will never have to deal with the petty stupidity of a homeowners' association.

Special thanks to Keith Neilson
for the gate and the robes.

# ONE

"It's perfect!" Maureen announced.

Barry agreed, but he was glad the real estate agent wasn't there to hear it. She already had them pegged as a couple of suckers, and if she heard Maureen's unequivocal enthusiasm, she'd know that all she had to do was reel them in. They'd have no room at all to negotiate.

But the agent—or "Doris," as she'd insisted they call her—had gone back to her car to gather the paperwork on this property (and, Barry suspected, give them time to talk), and the two of them were left alone to discuss matters between themselves.

He and Maureen walked around the house's upper deck. The view was spectacular. They'd looked at other houses, newer houses, bigger houses, but none that had a location to match this one. It was on the side of a hill overlooking the town, and breathtaking scenery stretched all the way to the mountains on the horizon, taking in miles of forest and canyon in between. Even in this, the hottest part of the day, a slight breeze was blowing, rustling the pine needles in the tree on the deck's west side, ruffling the hair that he had combed so carefully in order to give himself a more respectable appearance.

"We could expand the deck," Maureen said. "Wrap it around the front of the house, maybe put in one of those misters to cool it off during the day. I see, like, a little patio set—some chairs and a table—where we could have lunches or romantic dinners. And, of course, I'll put a lot of plants up here."

"The deck's way down on the priority list," he told her.

"That's true," Maureen admitted.

Barry shielded the sides of his face with his hands and peered through the screen door into the house. The interior was hideous. The previous owners had had no taste whatsoever, and every room was carpeted in bright orange, with walls and ceiling covered in the darkest paneling. It was like being in a cave, and the tacky 1970s furniture did little to dispel the air of tired sadness that hung about the rooms.

No doubt that was why the house had not yet sold, why it had been on the market for so long with no takers, and it was why Barry felt confident that, if they did not tip their hand, they might be able to get the seller to drop the price.

He looked away. "Tear off the paneling," he told Maureen, "repaint the walls, install new carpet, junk the furniture, no one would even recognize this place."

"I like the windows," she said. "Whoever built this house planned it smartly."

That was true. The trilevel house seemed to have been constructed in order to take full advantage of the breathtaking scenery. There were three bedrooms: a huge master bedroom with an adjoining deck directly below them that offered a view only slightly less spectacular than the one they were enjoying now, another smaller bedroom on the same floor, and, directly above that, on the top floor, the third bedroom, which had French doors opening on to a small balcony overlooking the driveway. The living room, through which a person entered the house, was the sole space on the middle floor, and the ceiling here was two stories high, with extra-tall windows facing the empty and heavily wooded lot on the up side of the hill. Twin carpeted stairways led either down to the bottom level or up to an open dining room/kitchen area on the top.

"I want to make an offer," Maureen said. "This is the house."

"Just don't appear too eager. We need some wiggle room here."

Maureen nodded. "I know."

"They're asking a hundred and ten thousand."

"We can probably get them to knock off ten or fifteen."

From down in the driveway, they heard Doris' car door slam, and Barry motioned for Maureen to be quiet as they waited for the real estate agent to return.

"Found them!" she announced cheerfully, entering the house and climbing the steps to the upper level.

Barry opened the sliding screen and walked back into the house, and Maureen followed. The real estate agent spread a packet of papers across the top of the ugly dining room table. "As I told you before, they're asking one-ten. There's a new septic system, installed just last year, that incorporates the latest technology, meets all federal standards, and has a service agreement that remains in effect until you pay off the mortgage. You have a quarter of an acre, and of course the ridge behind the neighborhood as well as all of the land on the west side, out to the highway, is national forest land. So no one can build. Your views will remain unobstructed. The house itself has a ten-year termite warranty, with free yearly inspection and, if necessary, fumigation. There's also a ten-year warranty for all plumbing and electrical wiring, which, believe me, is a godsend." She looked up. "You want me to go on?"

"We're interested," Barry told her.

Doris' face lit up, her already animated features suddenly invested with a new and even greater enthusiasm. She continued running down the attributes of the house and lot, the specifics of all attendant deal sweeteners, before Maureen finally stopped her and said, "I think we're ready to make an offer."

Barry nodded.

The agent smiled widely. "Let's go back to the office, then, shall we?"

They went downstairs and outside, Barry and Maureen walking around the edge of the driveway, looking around at the pine trees and manzanita bushes on the property while Doris locked up the house.

"Whoever buys this house is getting one heck of a good deal," the agent said as they got into her car, Maureen slipping into the passenger seat in front, Barry sitting in the back.

"Well, not *that* good a deal," Barry said. "The house has been on the market for quite a while and no one's wanted it. If it was a real bargain, someone would've snatched it up."

"The market's soft right now. But that's changing. This thing'll be worth two hundred next year." Doris guided the car down the sloping road, through the trees. She smiled. "Beautiful here, isn't it? Smell that air? Smell the pine? Nothing like it."

They reached the wrought-iron gate blocking the foot of the street, slowing as they waited for hidden machinery to swing the gate open.

Maureen looked out at the sandstone sign flanking the gateway, where the name of the development, "Bonita Vista," was spelled out in green copper letters.

"That's the only thing I don't like," she said, turning back around. "It seems sort of . . . snobbish. I don't really like the idea of living in a 'gated community.'"

"The homeowners' association only recently put that in," Doris admitted. "And there are quite a few people who don't like it. On the one hand, it offers you privacy and keeps up property values. But the fire chief opposed its installation because it blocks access. Although," she added quickly, "you should have no trouble escaping if there's a forest fire. The gates open outward, and you don't need to punch in a code to leave."

Barry leaned forward. "There's a homeowners' association?"

"Yes. I'm afraid you are required to pay homeowners' association dues. That's usually around a hundred or two hundred a year. I know a lot of people don't like associations, but in an area like Bonita Vista, they're a necessity."

"Why?" Maureen asked.

"Because it's unincorporated. You're outside the town limits, and since the county maintains only dirt roads, the association is responsible for paving the streets and all improvements like ditches, abutments, what have you. It's the association that put in the street lights, that maintains all ditches and storm drains, that will put in any sidewalks or signs."

"What if someone doesn't want to join?"

"It's not an option. If you buy in Bonita Vista, you are required to belong to the association. But there are other benefits, too. There's a communal tennis court for members, and they're talking about putting in a clubhouse and swimming pool."

The road wound between two low hills covered with old-growth ponderosas before hitting the highway. Doris waited for a roofing truck to pass before turning left and heading into town.

Barry smiled. He liked the idea of having to go *into* town, of it *being* a town instead of a city. Hell, he liked the whole damn thing. When they'd first started talking about moving out of southern California, when they'd looked at their options and discussed their preferences, this had been exactly the type of place he'd imagined, and he could hardly believe their good fortune at having discovered such a picture-perfect location.

Truth to tell, Corban wasn't *much* of a town. The population was somewhere around three thousand, and while there were a few restaurants and gas stations, a rundown hotel, a couple of shops, and a market, there was no Store, no fast-food franchises, no tourist traps, none of the usual amenities that made rural America palatable to city dwellers like themselves.

But he liked that.

And he knew Maureen did, too. This wasn't Aspen or Jackson Hole or Park City, one of those co-opted communities that had turned into playgrounds for Hollywood's elite and the ultra-rich. This was a genuine small town in a nontrendy part of Utah, where real people had real jobs, a place where the wave of service industries cresting over the rest of the nation had not yet reached.

The real estate office was a doublewide trailer across the street from a converted house that served as the Corban library, and Doris swung into the microscopic parking lot, braking to a halt with the skid of fat tires on gravel.

Barry got out of the car and looked up at the hill where their house was.

*Their house.*

He was already starting to think of it as theirs, though they had not even made an offer. He wasn't sure if that was good or bad.

The three of them walked up the rickety outside steps into the office, where an overweight man and an underweight woman sat at desks in the larger of the trailer's two rooms, unhappily staring into space.

"Good afternoon all!" Doris announced cheerfully, and falsely happy expressions appeared on the faces of her coworkers. The man immediately picked up his phone and started dialing, the woman began shuffling papers.

"Let's go into the conference room." Doris led the way past the desks and into the trailer's other room, a smaller space dominated by what looked like a dining room table.

The agent closed the door as they sat down. "All right," she said. "As you know, the asking price is one-ten."

"The price is a little steep," Barry said.

"Especially for a house that ugly," Maureen added.

"It needs a lot of work."

"A complete makeover."

Doris laughed. "I understand. How about I offer a hundred?"

"How about you offer ninety-five?"

"I have to tell you: there's no guarantee the seller will come down at all, let alone fifteen thousand. But let me make a few calls and see what we can do." She motioned toward a coffeepot and a pile of Styrofoam cups placed on top of a low bookshelf at the opposite end of the room. "Have some coffee if you want. I'll be back."

They waited until Doris left, closing the door behind her.

"How high are we willing to go?" Barry asked.

Maureen met his gaze. "I like that house."

"It's not a bad price even at full." He stood and started pacing around the room. "But it's a big decision. Should we be rushing into it like this? Maybe we should take a few days, think about it."

"We have thought about it. And we've been looking for a while now. This is exactly the kind of place we wanted and, as you said, it's a fair price. And if we can get them to lower it even more . . ."

Barry looked out the small window. "You're right." He walked over to pour himself some coffee and grimaced as he took a sip. "How much you think they'll counter with?"

Maureen shrugged. "Who knows? I'm hoping, after all the wrangling's over, that we'll at least be able to knock four or five off."

He sat back down at the table and they waited for Doris' return.

A few minutes later, there was a knock, and Doris

pushed the door open, walking in. "I called the seller," she said, "and offered ninety-five."

"And?" Barry prodded.

Doris smiled. "You've got yourselves a deal."

# TWO

The first thing Barry unpacked was the stereo.

He wasn't used to the quiet, to the absence of cars and sirens and soccer game screams—the sounds of a city on a Saturday—and the silence of the country made him nervous. Besides, he thought, it would be nice to hear some tunes while they unpacked, and he set up the various components while the others continued bringing in boxes from the truck and van.

He still had cartons of vinyl albums from his college days, and he put on something they could all agree upon—Jethro Tull's *Thick as a Brick*—cranking up the volume and facing the speakers toward the door before walking back outside.

"Whoa!" Dylan said, grinning. "Head music!"

Maureen rolled her eyes. She elbowed Barry's side as she headed into the house carrying a pile of clothes. "Thanks a lot."

She was not thrilled with the fact that Jeremy and Chuck had left their wives back in California, or that Dylan had come at all, but they'd elected to rent a giant U-Haul truck rather than hire movers, and there was no way the two of them could have loaded and unloaded everything themselves.

Jeremy pulled a dripping six-pack out of the ice chest in his now nearly empty van. "Unpacking fuel!" he announced. "Get it while it's cold!"

The rest of them took a break while Barry made up for lost time and started unloading the U-Haul, carrying out lamps, chairs, and cartons of kitchen items. Maureen remained inside, trying to find the box containing the pots, pans, and cans of soup she'd intended to heat up for lunch.

In the driveway, Dylan, Jeremy, and Chuck had finished their beers and were tossing cans back into the van.

"That hit the spot," Chuck said.

"Sure you don't want one?" Jeremy called out.

Barry shook his head, and Jeremy closed the lid of the ice chest.

"Cool!" Dylan said. "Look at this!" He pointed over at the house's mailbox, a rural rounded red-flagger situated on top of a short pole. Like Barry, Dylan had probably only seen such mailboxes in movies, and Barry watched as his friend walked over, flipped the little red flag up and down, then leaned forward and pulled open the metal door.

He leaped back. "Jesus!"

"What is it?" Barry asked, hurrying over.

Dylan didn't answer, but Barry immediately saw for himself. A dead cat had been shoved into the mailbox, and its twisted head and crooked paws were facing outward, the blood-matted fur crawling with ants. A line of the insects was marching into the empty hole that had been the animal's right eye. The smell was disgusting, and he instinctively stepped back, covering his nose.

Jeremy and Chuck showed up behind them and peeked in.

"Probably just kids," Chuck said.

Jeremy whistled and shook his head. "Pretty sick kids."

Barry looked around, saw that Maureen was still in the house, and quickly closed the mailbox door. "Don't say anything to Mo," he said. "She'll freak about this. I'll just clean it out later. I don't want to stress her out on our first day here."

Chuck and Jeremy nodded as Dylan saluted smartly. "Yes, boss," he said.

"Come on. Let's finish unpacking."

With all three of them working, they were able to pull out the big furniture—the couches and dressers and bookcases and beds—swearing as they attempted to maneuver the bulkier objects through the house's front door. They stopped for lunch, eating soup and crackers on the upper deck, then went immediately back to work, but the dead cat remained at the forefront of Barry's mind. He had no idea how he was going to get the animal out. The mailbox was too small to handle a shovel—his preferred method for disposing of dead animals—and the only thing he could think of to do was put on a pair of rubber gloves and pull out the body. He had no idea if the dead cat had any diseases, if handling a rotting corpse like that would spread contamination, and he decided he would do it this afternoon, have one of his friends help him while the other two kept Maureen occupied.

But Maureen was with them throughout the rest of the day, carrying the smaller boxes, jumping into the back of the truck to decide what would go into the house and what would go into storage, directing them where to put what.

They made an effort to put the bigger items in their permanent places, but the rest of the stuff they simply piled against various walls, making sure there were still walkable pathways as the piles grew out into the centers of the rooms. The leftover furniture that had come with the house was shoved into the two small bedrooms. It would be sold at a garage sale eventually, and whatever didn't sell would be donated to Goodwill or Salvation Army or whatever thrift store they had in this town. Maureen told Dylan, Chuck, and Jeremy that if there was anything they wanted, they should feel free to take it.

The remaining boxes and furniture they took to the storage unit Barry had rented in town. Maureen stayed home since there wasn't enough room in the truck cab for all of them. A sour old man in a Deer-o paint cap let them in the gate of the storage facility, and they pulled the truck in front of the dented metal door marked SPACE 21, unloading everything fairly quickly. As Barry closed and locked the door, he could feel a dull soreness in his leg and arm muscles that he knew would explode into full-fledged pain by tomorrow. It had been a long time since he'd done any heavy manual labor, and between last week's packing and today's unloading, his neck and back already hurt.

"Miller time!" Jeremy announced. He'd brought his ice chest, placing it by his feet in the cab, and he reached up and opened it, then started tossing out beers.

Barry popped open the can he caught and took a long swig. The four of them stood in front of the storage unit, drinking, celebrating the end of a long and tiring day.

Chuck looked around at the surrounding scenery. "Why Utah?" he asked Barry. "I mean, it's beautiful and all, but, shit, it's so far away from everything. What are you going to do out here in the middle of nowhere?"

"The same thing I did back in California: write."

"You know what I mean."

Barry shrugged. "I never did all that much to begin with. I mean, hell, a big night out for us is dinner and a movie."

"But there's no movie theater here."

"There's a video store. And we can always drive over to Cedar City if we have to. It's only two hours away and it has movie theaters, a college, a Shakespeare festival, pretty much anything you could want." He finished downing the last of his beer. "But that's small stuff, that's not important. The reason we're out here is because this is where we want to live, this is the type of environment we want to spend the rest of our lives in. We're not getting any younger, you know. It's time to start talking permanence, it's time to start setting down some roots."

"Your roots are in California."

"We want a transplant."

Jeremy shuffled his feet awkwardly. "How are you guys set for money? Your books pulling in enough?"

"Yeah. And Mo'll be working, too."

Dylan snorted. "In this town? Where, the gas station?"

"She can pretty much hang out her shingle anywhere and get tax work. And a lot of her old clients are staying with her, so she won't exactly have to start from scratch."

"Staying with her? How's that? They're going to drive through three states just for an accountant? I know she's good, but . . ."

"Fax. E-mail. Telephone. She doesn't have to actually meet with her clients to get their financial information." He grinned. "It's the age of the telecommuter, dude. Get with the program."

Chuck shook his head. "You really think you're going to like living in a small town?"

Barry laughed. "It's the yuppie dream."

They had dinner that night at a steakhouse in Corban where they were the only customers and the waitress looked like Flo from the old TV series *Alice*. They drank a lot and talked politics and culture, Maureen admonishing Jeremy and Chuck for abandoning their wives at home and depriving her of some much-needed female allies.

Back at home, they tried to figure out the sleeping arrangements. The old beds had been dismantled, and only their bed in the master bedroom had been set up. It was decided that Dylan, Chuck, and Jeremy would sleep on the floor in the dining room area—the only part of the house that wasn't completely overrun with unpacked junk.

Jeremy, always prepared, had brought along a sleeping bag, but Chuck and Dylan hadn't, and they spent twenty minutes pushing cartons and furniture aside, digging through boxes looking for blankets and pillows.

"Sleep tight," Maureen said after they were all settled. "Don't let the bed bugs bite."

"*Are* there bed bugs here?" Chuck asked.

"We don't know *what* kind of critters there are," Maureen said cheerfully. "Good night."

"You're vicious," Barry told her as they walked down to the master bedroom. "Vicious."

In the morning, he was awakened by the sounds of movement from upstairs. He got out of bed without waking Maureen, quickly slipped on his jeans, and went up to the dining room, where Jeremy was rolling up his sleeping bag, and Chuck and Dylan were putting on their shoes.

Barry yawned, looking toward the kitchen. "I'm sorry we don't have any breakfast for you. I should've gone to the store yesterday and picked up some doughnuts or bagels or something."

Jeremy waved him away. "Don't worry about it. We'll grab something to eat on the road. We have a long trip today, and we need to get started early anyway."

It occurred to Barry for the first time that it might be a while before he had a chance to see his friends again. He felt sad all of a sudden, but it was a strange sadness, one tempered by a sense that though his old life was over, a new one was beginning.

"You guys want to take a shower or something first?"

Chuck shook his head, grinning. "No reason to. It's just us."

Jeremy picked up his sleeping bag. "Say good-bye to Mo."

"Say good-bye yourselves."

Barry turned around to see Maureen standing at the bottom of the stairs, bundled up in her bathrobe.

"Bastard," she said with a smile. "You weren't even going to wake me up."

"Sorry."

She stepped aside while Jeremy, Chuck, and Dylan walked down the steps to the living room. "See you guys," she said. "Thanks so much for all your help. We really appreciate it."

"No problem," Jeremy told her.

"You're welcome to come and visit anytime." She smiled. "Even you, Dylan."

He laughed. "A little out of the way for me, but thanks. It's the thought that counts."

"You got everything?" Barry asked.

"Didn't bring anything in," Chuck said. "It's still in the van."

Barry followed Jeremy, Chuck, and Dylan outside, while Maureen remained in the doorway. "Good-bye!" she called. "Have a safe trip! Drive carefully!"

"Always do," Dylan said.

"You planning to drive all the way back to Brea today?" Barry asked.

Dylan shook his head. "I think we're going to take an extra day. I want to stop off in Vegas on our way back. Pull a Willie Nelson."

"*Electric Horseman*?"

Dylan grinned. "You got it."

Barry reached into the right front pocket of his jeans, found the wadded five that he'd shoved in there after getting the change from dinner last night. "Well, while you're kicking back, why don't you actually *play* some of that Keno. I'll split the take with you."

"Deal."

Jeremy tossed his sleeping bag in the back of the van and closed the tailgate. None of them were huggers or touchy-feely kinds of guys, but this seemed to call for more than a mere wave and a quick "Good-bye," and they stood around awkwardly, not ready to part but not willing to make that leap and share a genuinely emotional moment.

"Well," Chuck said, shuffling his feet, "I guess we'd better shove off."

"Yeah," Jeremy said.

Dylan nodded.

"Thanks again, guys. I really appreciate it." Barry looked back at Maureen, still standing in the doorway. "Both of us do."

Jeremy smiled. "What are friends for?"

*Friends.*

Barry realized that he would have to start from scratch and make new friends here. Neither he nor Maureen knew anyone within a five-hundred-mile radius or had relatives in any of the Four Corners states.

Jeremy and Dylan got into the van, and Chuck climbed into the U-Haul's cab. Barry had given Chuck the truck's keys last night, as well as the rental paperwork, and he poked his head into the window of the cab. "It's not due back until Thursday, and it's unlimited mileage, so if there's anything you need to haul or you need a truck for anything, feel free to keep it."

Chuck grinned. "Don't worry. I will."

"Call and let me know when it's back safe. And send me the receipt so I can double-check and make sure they're not ripping me off."

"You got it, chief."

Jeremy started the van, stuck his head out the window, and waved. "Good luck!"

"You're going to need it!" Dylan shouted and cackled.

Barry glanced over at the mailbox, and thought of the dead cat still shoved in there. He walked out to the edge of the driveway, waving, as Maureen yelled "Good-bye!" from the porch.

He watched the truck and van head down the hill, and he continued to stare down the street long after Jeremy's van was gone and the whine of the U-Haul's engine had faded into nothingness.

# THREE

They held their garage sale the next weekend, taking out an ad in the local newspaper, the *Corban Weekly Standard*, and spending all day Friday pricing furniture and household items stored in the small bedrooms. They kept a few things—a clock radio, a punch bowl, a kerosene lamp—but most of the stuff that had come with the house was ugly as sin, and they were happy to clear it out. Barry had originally wanted to wait a little longer, so they'd have a better chance to sift through it all and see if there was anything they could use, but Maureen correctly pointed out that they had no room in either their house or the storage unit for all this crap, and the sooner they dumped it the sooner they could start fixing the place up.

"Nothing over ten dollars," she said as Barry placed a strip of masking tape on a hideous formica table and wrote down the price. "Our goal is to get rid of this junk, not make money."

"Yes sir," he said.

Saturday morning, they got up before dawn and started setting things up, laying out some of the smaller junk on metal folding tables that were also for sale, displaying the rest flat on the asphalt of the driveway. The furniture they arranged in such a way as to block off access to the lower deck and the steps that led up to the front door.

The classified ad clearly stated that the garage sale did not start until seven, but cars and trucks were parked on the road in front of the house two hours beforehand, hunched shapes visible in the half-light of the dawning morning, looking at street maps, reading newspapers, sipping thermos coffee. One obese woman, smoking an ash-heavy cigarette and carrying a huge canvas sack, actually got out of her car and walked up the driveway, intending to look over the sale items, but Maureen, putting last-minute prices on an old mop and bucket she'd found in the kitchen closet, told the woman firmly that the garage sale was scheduled to start at seven and it would not open a minute earlier. She could either leave and come back later or go to her car and wait.

It wasn't a garage sale really—they had no garage, not even a carport—but they were putting out quite a bit of stuff, and neither the woman nor any of the other early arrivals left. Instead, they waited patiently. Barry found it hard to believe that all of the ugly furniture and useless household goods that they wanted out of their home, this junk that they were willing to give away for free if necessary, could be of such interest to people.

There was the sound of a high-pitched meow, and Barry looked down to see a black cat bumping against his leg, looking up at him.

"Hey, Barney." He reached down to pet the cat. "How're you doing?"

The animal purred.

Barney had shown up on their lower deck midweek, yowling loudly, and Maureen had fed the cat milk and a can of tuna. The animal looked as though it was starving, and it was so grateful for the food that it had remained even after feeding, hanging around the porch, rubbing against their legs, purring whenever either of them walked out. Since then, it had spent each day hanging around, using the juniper tree next to the house as a ladder to climb from the lower to upper deck, sleeping on the welcome mat outside the front door. Barry had named it Barney, after Fred's best friend in *The Flintstones*—a name to which it seemed to be responding.

He guessed that meant the cat was their pet.

He looked over at the mailbox, its metal glinting in the pink rays of the rising sun, and thought of the other cat.

The dead one.

He'd disposed of the body while Maureen was taking her shower last Sunday evening. Jeremy, Chuck, and Dylan had departed in the early morning, and he'd assumed he'd have time to himself during the day when he could take care of the problem, but he and Maureen had been together all morning and afternoon, and it wasn't until she took her shower before dinner that he had the opportunity to sneak out by himself. Necessity, as they said, was the mother of invention, and for all his worrying about how he was going to get the animal's body out of the mailbox, when the time came and he realized that he would have maybe ten minutes at most to solve the problem, he wrapped his hands in a Hefty garbage bag, shoved them in the mailbox, yanked out the dead cat and turned the bag inside out. He quickly scrubbed out the inside of the mailbox with a sponge drenched in Lysol, and tossed the sponge into the bag as well, leaving the mailbox door open to air out. He quickly tied the Hefty bag shut and dumped it in the metal garbage can beneath the bottom deck before hurrying back inside, washing his hands in the upstairs bathroom and sitting down on the couch. He turned on the TV just as Maureen emerged from downstairs to make dinner.

Two days later, the new cat showed up.

There was nothing connecting the two. The dead one had been white, this one was black. But their new pet was a constant reminder to him, and when the mail started mid-week and he began going out to collect it every afternoon, he found himself thinking about that bloody carcass, about the ants crawling in the empty eyesocket.

He also found himself wondering *why* he hadn't told his wife about the dead animal. She wasn't a dainty flower, it wasn't anything she couldn't handle. Hell, she was the bug buster of the family, the one who killed every insect that crept into their house. She was the one who chopped up chicken fryers and gutted fish. She probably had a stronger constitution than he did.

So why had he kept it from her?

Why was he *still* keeping it from her?

He didn't know.

Barry sat down on a metal folding chair behind one of the tables and broke open the rolls of quarters, dimes, and nickels that he'd gotten Thursday from the bank, putting them in his cleaned-out tackle box. Barney curled around his feet, purring.

Maureen went inside and made some coffee while he made last-minute adjustments, and she soon brought him out a doughnut and a cup of decaf.

The sun was up now, and there was a crowd milling around in the street and at the foot of the driveway. Barry looked at his watch, glanced toward Maureen, then waved them in. He was taken aback by the sudden frenzy that greeted his simple invitation, and for the rest of the morning it was all he could do to keep up as garage salers came and went, most not buying anything, some picking up a few items, several trying to bargain him down from the marked price. One old man bought all of the tools for sale. One woman purchased all of the kitchenware. Another woman paid for the garish dining room set, told him that her husband would be by later to pick it up in his truck, then returned after a half hour and asked for her money back.

The man with the clipboard showed up just after ten.

It was a thick crowd, with cars parked on the street half a block in either direction and the yard filled with intense-looking bargain hunters, but the man immediately distinguished himself from the pack by his utter lack of interest in the items for sale. Tall and thin, with a prim face and the brand-name casual clothes of a dyed-in-the-wool yuppie, he seemed more interested in the house, in their car, and in the people milling around.

Barry glanced over at Maureen and caught her eye. She'd noticed, too, and he waited until the man had come near the table before calling out, "Hey there!" and motioning him over.

There was no smile on the man's serious face as he stopped writing, looked up from his clipboard, and focused on Barry. "Is this your house?" the man asked.

"Yeah. I'm Barry Welch. What can I do for you?"

The man nodded. "My name is Neil Campbell. I'm from the Bonita Vista Homeowners' Association. I'm writing you up."

Barry frowned. "Writing me up?"

"Garage sales, yard sales, sales of any sort are prohibited within Bonita Vista. The guidelines are very clear on this point."

"I didn't know," Barry said. "No one told me."

"You have not gotten your copy of the C, C, and Rs?"

"I don't even know what that is."

The man smiled thinly. "You can be excused *this* time, since you have not yet received our C, C, and Rs, but in the future you will have to abide by the same rules and regulations the rest of us follow." He made a little note on his clipboard. "I'll suggest to the board that you not be fined but merely issued a written reprimand. That should satisfy the requirements and the sticklers on the board." There was another thin smile, as if Campbell was trying to suggest that he was one of the more liberal and lenient members of the homeowners' association, but the smile suggested no such thing.

Then a woman wanted to pay for a pair of pink pillows,

and a teenage boy wanted to buy a beanbag chair, and by the time Barry had taken the money and counted out the change, Campbell was gone.

"What was that all about?" Maureen asked.

"Apparently, we're in violation of the homeowners' association's bylaws. That guy was here to write us up and issue a fine, but we got off with just a warning,"

"A fine? What does that mean? Can they do that?"

Barry shook his head. "I don't know. I guess we'll have to look into it."

"I knew it was bad news when I heard there was a homeowners' association. Remember Donna and Ed in Irvine? They couldn't even put up a basketball backboard on their garage." Maureen frowned. "I was hoping it'd be different out here. Doris said that the association just paved the roads and did, like, maintenance work."

"She's a real estate agent. And she was trying to sell us the house. What did you expect, honesty?"

"Silly me."

People came in waves after that. There would be ten minutes with no activity, then suddenly four cars would arrive at once and the driveway would be overrun with parents, children, and single adults all searching through different boxes for different things.

As the crowds thinned and the furniture began to be loaded onto pickups and hauled away, Maureen went inside, leaving Barry to handle things alone.

It was during one of the slow times that a burly older man walked up and started sorting through a box of odds and ends. Friendly looking, with a ruddy face, thick white mustache, and round wire-framed granny glasses, he did not seem to be particularly interested in the few leftover items for sale, and after a quick cursory glance at the box's contents, he wandered over to Barry's table. "Howdy," he said. "You just move in?"

"Last weekend," Barry told him.

The man smiled. "Had a visit from the association yet?"

Barry nodded wearily. "Yeah."

The man laughed, held out his hand. "I'm your neighbor. Ray Dyson. Sworn enemy of the Bonita Vista Homeowners' Association."

"My name's Barry. Barry Welch." He shook the proffered hand.

Two cars pulled up on the street and parked. Three elderly women emerged from one, a tired-looking man with a scrawny overalled boy got out of the other.

Barry turned his attention back to his new neighbor. "So you're not a fan of the association either, huh?"

"To put it mildly."

"Thank God. At least I'm not *all* alone here."

"Oh, hell no. There are quite a few people who have run afoul of those assholes. Most of 'em are too intimidated to say anything, but they're with you in spirit. I can tell you that much."

"Most of the people today have seemed nice," Barry admitted.

"Oh, they're not from Bonita Vista. They're from town. You're not going to get anyone from Bonita Vista brave enough to buck the rules and actually attend a yard sale." He chuckled. "Except me."

Barry looked out at the two cars. "But how did they get through the gate?"

"Someone broke the gate last night. It's open now until they get it repaired. Happens every month or so. Some contractor or roofer who's working on a job here forgets the entry code, gets ticked off, and rams the gate." Ray nodded at his fellow garage salers. "That's the only reason they're here. If everything was normal and the gate wasn't busted, you would've come out here today and waited and waited and not a damn person would've shown up."

"Except you."

"Except me."

Barry sighed. "We just got here. We haven't even finished unpacking. I don't want to tick anybody off just yet. Maybe we should just lay low for a while, try to get on the association's good side and hope they don't bother us."

"The association's good side?" Ray chuckled. "No such thing. And these bastards are so used to having things their way that they don't even *pretend* to be nice. The problem is, the courts always take their part. I threatened to sue once, and I found out that no one would take my case because I had no legal grounds. It seems unconstitutional to me, but apparently homeowners' associations have the right to make you pay dues, to make you conform to their standards, to trespass on your property in order to ensure compliance. They can require you to join and force you to abide by their rules even if it's against your will. That's especially ironic since we're in what they call a 'right to work' state. Which means that even if you work in a union shop, you can't be compelled to join the union. Exactly the opposite of the situation here." Ray leaned forward. "In case you can't tell, I'm an old union man."

"Where are you from?" Barry asked. "I mean, originally. I assume you're not from Corban."

"New Jersey. I'm a retired transit worker. We moved out west because of my asthma. Besides, my wife has family in Salt Lake City."

"But you like it here, right? I mean, overall?"

Ray shrugged. "Sure, I guess. The scenery's beautiful, we have four seasons a year, I live in a great house, and I've met a lot of nice people, made a lot of friends. It's a wonderful place to retire."

"But?"

"But the association is way too intrusive, and it's such a . . . pervasive influence here. I blame the board. The association's board of directors is made up of old busybodies with no hobbies and no lives who get their jollies harassing people and snooping around to make sure everyone's conforming." He nodded at Barry. "Who'd they send after you? Who came out this morning?"

"I don't know. The guy introduced himself, but I forgot his name."

"Youngish? Short hair? Serious face? Prissy?"

"Sounds like him."

Ray nodded. "Campbell. He's fairly new, just moved in last year, but already he's their little toadie. Hopes to be elected to the board once one of those geezers croaks."

"If the association's so bad, why don't people elect some new board members? Or just disband the organization entirely?"

"Maybe I gave you the wrong impression. Don't get me wrong, there are people like me who don't like them. But we're very definitely in the minority. Most of the homeowners here love having an association. They *want* to live in a gated community where there are strict maintenance standards and everyone's forced to keep up their property values." He smiled. "Welcome to Bonita Vista."

"Great."

Ray laughed. "So what do you do for a living?"

"I'm a writer," Barry said.

The thick eyebrows shot up. "Really?"

"I write horror novels. You know, like Stephen King."

"Stephen King, huh?"

"Well . . . not exactly. I say that so people will understand the type of books I write. I used to just say 'horror' and leave it at that, but people were introducing me as their friend the science-fiction writer or their friend the mystery writer, and I don't write science fiction or mysteries. The Stephen King comparison seemed to clear that up."

Ray shook his head. "A writer. That's pretty exciting. I don't think I've ever met a real writer before. Where can I get your books?"

"Around here?" Barry chuckled. "I doubt if you can. But they're at most of the big chains. I'll give you a copy of the newest one next time I see you."

"Autographed?"

"Sure."

Ray leaned forward. "You know, this might work in your favor. I'll spread the news, play up the fact that you're a big-name celebrity, a rich and famous writer. It might intimidate the board into leaving you alone."

"You think so?"

"Can't hurt."

Barry nodded. "Feel free to lie. You can tell them I *am* Stephen King, if you want to. Anything to keep them off my back."

"No guarantees, but I'll spread the word."

Two new cars pulled up, twin families emerging from the four-doored vehicles. One of the elderly women who'd been looking through the displayed junk stepped up to Barry's table with a vase and a set of placemats in hand, and Ray waved good-bye as Barry tallied up the woman's total. "I'll stop by later in the week," Ray said, "once you guys've gotten settled."

"Nice to meet you, Ray." Barry waved, then turned his attention back to his customer.

It arrived in their mailbox the next day. *The Bonita Vista Homeowners' Association Declaration of Covenants, Conditions, and Restrictions*—the promised C, C, and Rs. Thicker than the Corban phone book, it was a perfect-bound document filled with nearly a hundred single-spaced pages of text, all written in dense legalese. Barry sat down, tried to read it, got through about half a page, then tossed the booklet over to Maureen. "Here you go. Some light reading material."

She glanced through a few pages, then threw it onto one of the unpacked boxes. "It looks pretty thorough," she said.

"I assume that means that loopholes will be hard to come by."

"Then thank God I'm a rich and famous writer who will be treated with deference and respect and won't be bound by the petty rules of mortals."

She laughed. "Dream on."

"I think that's a song cue!" He rushed over to the stereo and quickly put on an old Aerosmith album. Turning up the volume, he held out his hands, and soon they were dancing through the living room, weaving between the boxes and twirling around the furniture to the music of their adolescence.

# FOUR

**The Bonita Vista Homeowners' Association Covenants, Conditions, and Restrictions** Article III, Land Use Classifications, Permitted Uses and Restrictions, Section 3, Paragraph A:

*No yard sales or garage sales may be conducted in, on, or from any Lot or any portion of the Properties.*

# FIVE

Maureen was not sure she liked Bonita Vista.

It was not something she would ever admit to Barry. And it wasn't a strong feeling or a definite mind-set. It was more a vague recognition that perhaps her impression of the neighborhood wasn't as favorable as she'd expected it to be.

Part of it was the snotty letter they'd received from the homeowners' association about their garage sale. Written in a formal yet clearly judgmental manner, it stated that they were in violation of the C, C, and Rs, which plainly declared that yard sales or garage sales were forbidden. The letter went on to say that they would be excused this time because of their ignorance of Bonita Vista rules and regulations, but in the future any such infraction would be punishable by a fine.

The letter wasn't all of it, though. Not even most of it. There was something else.

Only she didn't know what.

Outwardly, everything was fine. The few people she'd seen walking or jogging along the road seemed to be nice, the area was beautiful, and despite all of the work that remained to be done, she loved their house.

Except . . .

Except those elements didn't gel the way they were supposed to. The nice neighbors, the beautiful environment, the perfect house, all of these were separate components, isolated attributes that were entirely unconnected.

And the whole was less than the sum of its parts.

But she refused to acknowledge any of this to Barry. She did not want to dampen his obvious pleasure with her unfounded impressions.

Besides, the feelings would probably pass.

They spent the next few weeks working on the house: repainting, wallpapering, transforming the dead dark space of their predecessors into a light, airy home that complemented their own furniture and did justice to the magnificent surroundings outside the generous windows. They ripped out what paneling they could, papered over the rest, replaced the heavy brown drapes with white miniblinds, and pulled up the stained and rotted carpet in the bathrooms, sanding and buffing the hardwood floors underneath. Maureen had brought most of their houseplants from California, even the ones she knew wouldn't survive the winter, and once the palms and ficuses were in place, once the spider ferns and hanging baskets were positioned in the corners and near the windows of the various rooms, the house looked 100 percent better.

It was Barry who discovered the sealed envelope in the master bedroom.

He was in the process of painting the inside of the closet and was dusting off the top shelf before applying his brush to it when he suddenly stopped and said, "What's this?"

Maureen looked over from where she'd been painting the window frame next to the bed. "What?"

He walked over, carrying a sealed business-size envelope. It was covered with a layer of dust and addressed to "New Homeowners." She took it from his hand. There was definitely something inside, a document or letter, and she held it up to the window, trying to see if the backlight would illuminate the envelope's contents.

"What do you think we should do?" he asked.

"I don't know. You think this was meant for us?"

Barry shrugged. "We *are* the new homeowners. Although this thing definitely looks like it's been sitting around for a while."

"Let's open it." She ripped one end of the envelope and used a fingernail to pry open the stubborn paper. Inside was a note on plain white stationery, black ink in a man's sloppy, hurried hand.

*We are not leaving voluntarily,* the note said. *You need to know that. We are being forced out of our home. It could happen to you, too. For your own protection, write down EVERYTHING!! Names, dates, witnesses.* They're *doing it, they're keeping track of all of it. Don't think they aren't. You'd better, too.*

*Don't let them see this letter. Burn it after you read it.*

The note was neither signed nor dated, and Maureen looked up at Barry as she finished reading the message. It was confusing and didn't make a whole lot of sense, but the obviously earnest and paranoid tone gave it urgency and immediacy despite the layer of dust on the outside of the envelope. The feeling within her was one of unease. "What *is* this?"

Barry shook his head, baffled. "I don't know."

"I don't think it was meant for us. It's obviously been sitting up there for a long time."

"Maybe kids left it. You know, when we were little, my sister and I buried a fake treasure map before we left Napa, hoping that whoever dug it up later would think it was real and try to search for the treasure. Maybe this is something like that. A prank."

"Maybe," she said doubtfully.

"Well, what do *you* think it is?"

"I have no idea. But it seems totally serious to me. I don't mean that *we* should take it seriously, but it seems like whoever wrote it was dead serious and was trying to get across what he thought was important information."

Barry took the note from her, glanced over it again. "What do you think we should do with it?"

"Throw it away," Maureen told him. She knew it was stupid, knew it was superstitious, but the idea of having that scribbled warning sitting in their house spooked her a little. "It's old, and it's not even ours. There's no reason to keep it."

Barry nodded. "Yeah. You're right." He wadded up the envelope and note and tossed them both into the plastic garbage sack in the middle of the floor.

"Weird," he said, walking back to the closet. "Very weird."

Other than that, the remodeling proceeded smoothly. The combination of high altitude and manual labor tired them out and led them to bed each night well before their usual time of eleven, but their days were full, they got a lot of work done, and gradually the house began to take shape.

Outside, they cleared brush, trimmed dead branches off the trees, and planted flowers and shrubs that Maureen bought at Corban's only nursery, a mom-and-pop operation adjacent to the Shell station. Under the lower deck, Barry found not only a working wheelbarrow but part of an antique plow, which Maureen strategically placed in the patch of dirt next to the driveway in order to give the front of the house a more rustic look.

It was their third Friday in their new home, and they'd been working on the sloping section of the lot on the north side of the house and were returning from one of their numerous trips to the dump when Ray Dyson flagged them down. The old man was walking down the hill as part of his afternoon constitutional, and Barry slowed the Suburban, rolling down his window. "Hey, Ray."

The old man nodded. "Barry. Maureen. I was wondering if you two would like to come by for dinner tonight. Liz and I would love to have you."

Barry looked over at Maureen, who glanced down at her

filthy clothes, at the work gloves she'd tossed on the floor. She shook her head.

Barry smiled. "I don't think so. Some other time maybe."

"Come on. It's not anything formal. Hell, come as you are and wash your hands in our sink if you want. There's no standing on ceremony with us. It's just that Liz is making a batch of her spaghetti sauce, and we thought it'd be nice to have you guys over." He looked at Maureen through the open space between Barry and the steering wheel. "Save you from having to cook tonight. No work, no dirty dishes afterward. Come on. It'll be fun."

That did sound tempting, she had to admit, and when Barry looked back at her once again, she nodded. "All right."

"Great! What time can we expect you?"

"What time do you want us?"

"Six?"

Barry nodded. "Sounds good."

"You know which house is ours, right? The redwood one you can see from your driveway. Twelve-twelve Ridge Road. Number's on the mailbox."

"We'll find it."

"See you at six, then." Ray nodded to them, waved, and continued his walk down the hill.

Barry had been planning to start on a stump that needed to be dug out, but the afternoon was getting late and they were both tired, so they went inside to clean up. Maureen took a bath in the downstairs bathroom while he took a shower upstairs. He finished well before she did, and when Maureen emerged dressed and refreshed, she found him lying on the couch dead asleep, CNN blaring loudly on the television.

She quietly grabbed a few magazines from the coffee table and went upstairs to read on the deck, letting him rest.

They left the house at quarter to six. Barry had wanted

to drive, but there was the beginning of a beautiful sunset, and Ray's house was close, less than a block away. "You have to get out of that California mind-set," she told him. "There's no reason to drive everywhere. Especially on a gorgeous day like today." She motioned west, toward pink clouds that ringed the setting sun.

"You're right," Barry admitted. "Habit."

Even after all of their yard work the past week, both she and Barry were pitifully out of shape, and they were huffing and puffing as they walked up the hill to Ray's house. They slowed the pace for the last couple of yards, trying to catch their breath, and finally stopped to rest at the edge of the Dysons' gravel driveway.

"Jesus," Barry said. "This altitude's a killer."

Maureen took his hand, pulled him forward. "Come on. My throat's dried out. The sooner we get in there, the sooner we can get something to drink."

Ray had stopped by a couple of times to chat while they were working in the yard, but this was the first opportunity for either of them to meet his wife. Liz Dyson was a petite elderly woman with a sophisticated demeanor who seemed an odd fit with the earthier Ray, but after only a few minutes with the couple, Maureen could see how the two complemented each other, and she thought them a good match.

After some obligatory introductory chitchat, Liz brought glasses of wine, and Ray led them all on a tour of the house.

Which was spectacular.

The Dysons' place was like something out of a home decorating magazine. Maureen thought *their* house had quite a view, but it was nothing compared to their hosts'. The sun had still not set completely, and the fire-red sky illuminated hundreds of miles of forests and canyons, little opalescent glints in the landscape marking tin-roofed ranch houses, miner's shacks, and windmills. Below them, the town of Corban was shrouded in shadow from the surrounding hills and mountains, and lights were blinking on in downtown buildings. It was a breathtaking panorama that put to shame any postcard shot she'd ever seen, and the line of windows that made up the south-facing wall of the Dysons' living room and overlooked this magnificent vista curved gracefully in an almost perfect half-circle. The room itself was furnished rustically with lodgepole-pine tables and chairs, a southwestern print couch, and a glass-topped coffee table with a tree stump base.

They went from there to the kitchen. It was huge, with an indoor grill built into the Mexican-tiled island between the refrigerator and sink. A greenhouse window faced the side of the property and a terraced garden. There was a gigantic pot of spaghetti sauce simmering on the stove, and the entire room smelled deliciously of garlic and onion and spices.

The master bedroom, guest bedroom, and den were sparsely and tastefully furnished, and Maureen found herself wondering where Ray and Liz kept all their . . . stuff. Where were the photographs of friends and family, the collected knicknacks, the tangible personal effects that represented their past? Had the two of them simply thrown out the accumulations of their East Coast life when they moved out here? It didn't make any sense, but it seemed so. She and Barry had more junk in one room than the Dysons seemed to have in their entire house, and it was hard to believe that two such homey old people were so completely unsentimental.

But it was not her place to wonder, and as they walked back out to the living room, she complimented their hosts on having such a beautiful house.

Liz smiled graciously. "Thank you."

Ray grinned. "Sure beats Hackensack." He patted Maureen's arm, motioned for Barry to come and look at his new widescreen TV, and as the two men started talking electronics, Maureen followed Liz into the kitchen.

The older woman removed a checkered apron from a

hook on the pantry door and put it on, and Maureen had to
smile. She'd never seen anyone actually wear an apron outside of movies and early television programs, and the gesture seemed quaint and endearingly old-fashioned.

Liz stirred the spaghetti sauce and looked over at her.
"So do you have a job outside the house, or are you a full-
time homemaker?"

"I'm an accountant."

Liz's face lit up. "Really? Me too! I was an auditor back
in New Jersey. Doyle, Bell, and McCammon. Thirty years.
What's your specialty?"

"Taxes, primarily, although I handle some payroll and
related accounts. I'm an EA, although that's not something
that often comes up."

"I bet it helps to lure in the clients, though."

Maureen laughed. "It doesn't hurt."

"Well, well, well. Another accountant." The older
woman shook her head, smiling. "It'll be nice to have
someone to talk to who speaks the same language."

Maureen had been thinking exactly the same thing. She
liked Liz, and it was a load off her shoulders that the first
woman she met in Utah was not some backward small-
town hick but worldly, smart, and sophisticated. She'd had
visions of having to condescend to her companions, feign-
ing interest in church bingo games and soap operas in order
to have someone to talk with, and the fact that she'd met
someone who was not only intelligent but had a background similar to her own filled her with relief.

The older woman walked over to the refrigerator, took
out a head of lettuce and several plastic bags filled with
vegetables, and Maureen asked if she could help. She was
assigned the job of peeling cucumbers, and the two of them
stood side-by-side in front of the long counter, preparing
salad to accompany dinner—or "supper," as Liz called it.

They talked of trivialities, the safe subjects broached
tentatively by two people just starting to get to know each

other and not wanting to offend unfamiliar sensibilities. Despite the difference in age, they were more alike than not, both of them gardeners, both avid readers, both hardcore fans of the Home & Garden channel, and Maureen found herself opening up. She asked Liz about their predecessors, the people who had lived in the house before she and Barry moved in, but Liz said she hadn't known the couple very well. No one had. They weren't there long, less than nine months, and they kept pretty much to themselves. They'd come and gone without making a ripple, and the house had been empty for over a year since then.

The family before that was something else entirely. The Haslams—a husband, wife, and two sons—had been one of the first families in Bonita Vista, well known and well liked, and their departure had caused a stir. The family had practically disappeared, moving out suddenly in the middle of the night. They'd never returned, never called, never communicated with anyone else in the neighborhood again, something entirely out of character for them, particularly for the mother, Kelli, whom Liz knew quite well. Maureen thought to herself that it was a scenario consistent with the panic and paranoia of the note they'd discovered in the closet, and she told Liz about the warning, describing the way Barry had come upon it while cleaning and the creepy feeling she'd gotten reading the hyperbolic words. Ray walked in at that moment to refresh his and Barry's drinks, and he frowned as he listened to Maureen's description.

"That doesn't sound like Ted or Kelli."

"No, it doesn't," Liz said. "But Maureen's right. It fits in with their disappearance. Or at least it sounds like something that people fleeing in the middle of the night would write." She turned back toward Maureen. "You didn't save the note?"

"No. It was over a week ago, and I had Barry throw it away. I didn't want it in the house."

"You think Ted was doing something . . . illegal?" Ray asked his wife.

Liz shrugged. "You knew him better than I did. I was close to Kelli and the kids, but I didn't know Ted that well."

"He was into computers," Ray explained. "He had some type of job with a defense contractor, debugging systems. Wasn't home that much. Spent a lot of time in Salt Lake City." He finished pouring the drinks and picked up the glasses. "I suppose that kind of job would make anyone paranoid. It just . . . doesn't sound like Ted."

"Just because you're paranoid doesn't mean they're not out to get you."

"Maybe they *were* out to get him."

"Who?"

"I don't know. The government? Maybe he was selling secrets or something. Who knows?"

Maureen turned toward Liz as Ray left the kitchen and returned to the living room. "But why would Ted or his wife try to warn *us*? If he'd done something wrong and the authorities were after him, it doesn't follow that the next residents of the house would be in danger."

"None of it makes any sense. The whole thing's strange."

Maureen recalled the spooky feeling she'd had reading the fervent words of the note. "Yes," she said, "it is."

They finished making the salad, Liz put a pot of water on the stove to boil, and the two of them walked back out to the living room to join the men.

"How would you feel about a party?" Liz asked, sitting down on the couch. "Sort of a 'get acquainted' get-together with some of our neighbors. Some of our more *normal* neighbors."

Maureen looked over at Barry. "That would be fun. We don't know anyone here, except you and Ray, and it'd be nice to meet people."

Barry nodded.

"Good. We'll set it up."

The rest of the evening passed by quickly, and Liz called the next day to find out if the following night was too short notice for the party. "We're kind of informal here, and nearly everyone has their evenings free—I don't know whether you've noticed, but Utah is not exactly a hub of exciting nightlife—so if you don't mind, we could have a potluck tomorrow night to welcome you two to Bonita Vista."

"That would be fine."

Maureen volunteered to bring soft drinks, and Liz said that she'd work the rest of the details out with the other guests; all they had to do was show up at six.

The next night, Maureen and Barry were once again walking up the road to the Dysons', this time carrying plastic grocery sacks filled with Coke and Sprite and Diet Pepsi. There were several cars in the driveway and on the street, and Barry, as she'd known he would, began making noises about ducking out early and leaving the party as soon as possible.

Maureen stopped in her tracks. "We're staying," she said simply, "until *I* say it's time to go. We have a chance to start out on the right foot here, to make some friends and get to know our neighbors, and I don't want you being your usual boorish antisocial self. There's time enough for that later. *Next* time you can bail. But right now we're going to make a good impression."

It looked like he was about to argue, but the expression on her face must have conveyed her seriousness, because he sighed. "You win," Barry said, resigned. "I'll be on my best behavior and we'll stay to the bitter end."

As it turned out, he had a fine time, and he *wanted* to stay until the bitter end. Ray and Liz had chosen their guest list wisely, and the house was filled with a variety of people: some old, some young, some middle-aged, some married, some single. Nearly all of them had homeowners' association horror stories, tales of run-ins they'd had with bureaucratic members of the board of directors, and Barry was in his element, railing against authority and conformity and exhorting them all to band together into a single voting block in order to oust the association's current board.

Afterward, they walked home tired, happy, and a little drunk. The night was moonless, and the black sky was filled with more stars than Maureen had ever seen in her life. Every so often, a meteor streaked across the heavens.

She liked the Dysons. They were nice. And most of the other people seemed nice, too.

But despite it all, Maureen still wasn't sure she liked Bonita Vista.

# SIX

Barry felt guilty. He had never gone this long before without writing, and while moving in and fixing up the house could be blamed for the first month of literary inactivity, this last week was entirely his own fault. He'd read, watched C-Span and CNN, viewed a couple of old horror flicks that he'd taped but had never gotten around to watching . . . and he didn't write.

There was no fear of writer's block, no worry that he'd run out of ideas, but the rhythm just wasn't there, that routine he'd established since becoming a full-time author, and he found it hard to simply jump back into the grind after so much time off. He would have to get busy soon, he knew—the next book was due in six months and he hadn't even started on it yet—but for now, he seemed compelled to slack off. It was as if he was still in vacation mode, as though either his brain or his body had not adjusted to the fact that this was their new home and was waiting for him to return to California before once again settling down to work.

He sorted through the mail, separating the bills, tossing the ads and credit offers without even bothering to open the envelopes. There were no royalty checks, though they should be coming in any day now, but he had received one small press magazine and two postcards advertising upcoming horror novels. He glanced over the postcards before throwing them in the trash pile, then perused the magazine. There were several short stories, some out-of-date movie reviews, and numerous letters to the editor from other writers either defending or attacking an up-and-coming author who had apparently made disparaging remarks on the Internet about one of the horror field's old guard. The letters were uniformly vitriolic, and Barry shook his head at such petty infighting.

It was why he didn't socialize much with other writers, why he assiduously avoided workshops and conventions and professional get-togethers.

The only author with whom he had any sort of relationship was Phillip Emmons, a suspense writer who had specifically looked him up at the lone horror convention he had attended because he had so enjoyed Barry's debut novel *The Leaving.* The two of them still corresponded, and Phillip had been sort of a mentor to him over the years: helping him choose a new agent; letting him know he was getting ripped off in a multibook contract; suggesting that he start retaining electronic as well as audio and movie rights to his work. Barry not only admired Phillip's fiction, he admired the man himself, and in many ways he was still trying to emulate the other author's personal style.

He remembered the way Phillip had handled hostile criticism the one time the two of them had done a signing together. It was at a bookstore in downtown L.A. soon after the convention. There was a lull in the crowd, and a middle-aged, morbidly obese woman with a bitter, disappointed face confronted Phillip at the table and demanded to know why he wrote about such disgusting topics in such graphic detail. He was going to hell, she informed him, and he should cease writing such filth because it was corrupting his readers and society. God did not approve of what he was doing.

Phillip looked at her calmly. "The Good Lord has seen fit to make me rich, happy, and successful," he told her. "He has made you ugly, grotesquely overweight, and miserably unhappy. It seems to me that He has smiled upon me and shit right in your face. Maybe if you were a nicer person, He would have treated you better, but from where I sit, God has made His displeasure with you pretty plain. So fuck off and quit bothering me." He smiled at her and turned to Barry. "The Lord works in mysterious ways, my friend. The Lord works in mysterious ways."

Barry himself could never have reacted in such a manner. But, damn it, it was *cool*. And he admired Phillip all the more for how he handled the woman.

Afterward, they had talked of God, and Phillip said seriously that he believed in God but disbelieved in religion. "The Bible is God's word. Why can't I just read it for myself and let Him speak directly to me? Why do I have to have an interpreter between us? That's all organized religion is: a buffer between me and God. I'm sorry, but my faith doesn't need a bureaucracy to administrate it. Besides, every time you confront one of these fundamentalist wackos with a real question, they can't answer it. Ask a preacher why your mama died of cancer or why your little boy was hit by a car, and you'll get an 'It's God's will,' or 'The Lord works in mysterious ways.' In other words, they don't know. But they *do* know that God wants you to vote Republican and He's against raising taxes and for raising the defense budget and, despite the fact that it's His own creation, he desperately hates marijuana."

Phillip made a lot of sense. He was an intelligent guy. He was also very giving of his time, helping out quite a few other young authors besides Barry, and Barry had often thought that if other writers were as real and unpretentious and unconcerned with image, the horror field would be a hell of a lot better off.

He tossed the magazine aside. Maureen came up from

downstairs, holding a stack of papers. "I'm done. The computer's all yours."

Barry shook his head. "That's okay. I think I'm just going to read this afternoon. You can have the computer."

"I thought you were going to start writing again," Maureen said.

"Maybe tomorrow," he said. "Maybe I'll start tomorrow."

He awoke to the sound of Maureen's fax machine.

Barry squinted over at the clock and was surprised to see that it was almost eight. The light outside, seeping between the cracks of the miniblinds, looked too dark for eight, looked more like six, and he nudged Maureen next to him. "Get up. It's eight o'clock."

"What?" She opened one sleepy eye.

"It's late."

They'd both overslept, and it was the sound of the fax machine more than his prodding that made Maureen get out of bed and face the day. He turned onto his side and watched her bare buttocks as she padded naked over to the bathroom. Even after all these years, she still looked damn good, and if she didn't have so much work to do this morning and the fax wasn't prompting her to get started on it, he would've lured her back to bed and spent the next hour engaged in some dirty, nasty sex that was more than likely illegal here in the state of Utah.

But instead, he got up, slipped into his jeans, and went upstairs to put on the coffee. He took out the Friskies box and pulled open the shades on the sliding glass door, intending to feed Barney breakfast on the top deck, but the cat was nowhere to be seen. Barry walked back downstairs to the bedroom, where Maureen was already dressed and making the bed, but when he pulled the drapes open, there was again no sign of the cat.

"Huh," he said.

"What?"

"I can't find Barney."

"I told you we should make that cat sleep inside. There are coyotes, skunks, and who-knows-what out there. You'd better make sure he's okay."

Barry slid open the door, slid open the screen, and walked outside, shaking the Friskies box.

"Barney!" he called.

Nothing.

"Barney?" He shook the box again.

There were no noises in the bushes or in the tree that the cat used as a ladder between the upper and lower decks, and, frowning, Barry walked down the wooden steps off the deck and around to the front of the house.

Where he stopped.

The flowers they'd planted had been ripped out and thrown into the driveway between the Suburban and the Toyota. Uprooted rosebushes lay littered on the asphalt. Geraniums and impatiens, clods of dirt still sticking to their roots, draped the Suburban's white hood. Iris bulbs were strewn about like golf balls on a driving range.

Someone had sneaked onto their property in the middle of the night and destroyed their fledgling garden, had negated all of their hard work, and his first reaction was one of anger. He wanted to beat the shit out of whoever had done this. But there was unease mixed in there as well, and while it was probably just kids—

*Pretty sick kids*

—he couldn't help feeling slightly disturbed by the fact that their house was the target of this vandalism, that they had been specifically chosen to be the recipients of this attack. His gaze shifted to the various areas they'd landscaped, and he saw that every last plant they'd put in had been pulled out of the ground or trampled. Their property looked as though a mini hurricane had hit it, and only pine trees and manzanitas seemed to remain standing.

And there was still no sign of Barney.

His gaze alighted on the mailbox.

With a sinking feeling in his gut, he walked around the Suburban. He stepped up to the mailbox and paused, then reached out and pulled open the rounded metal door.

There was nothing inside.

He let out a sigh of relief, unaware until that second that he'd been holding his breath. He'd been almost certain that he'd find the cat mutilated, its body stuffed into the mailbox, and he had never been so thankful to be wrong. He turned back toward the house, intending to bring Maureen out here and show her the damage, when he saw a glimpse of fuzzy black amidst the light green stems and deep magenta flowers that had been tossed onto the driveway between the cars.

He knew without looking closer exactly what that fuzzy black was, but he moved forward nevertheless, bending down to examine the object more fully.

Barney.

The cat was lying atop two discarded plants, and its dead open eyes were staring upward at the bumper of the Toyota. White foam was dripping from the animal's mouth onto the asphalt, where it had already puddled into an irregular pool. He wasn't an expert on these things, but he was pretty sure that Barney had been poisoned, and he hurried into the house, dragging Maureen away from her fax to show her the damage outside.

"My God," she breathed. She looked around the property at the upturned vegetation and the dead cat. "Who do you think did this?"

Barry shook his head, completely at a loss. They didn't know anyone here other than Ray and Liz and the other people they'd met at the Dysons' party, and his gut reaction was that it was probably an act of random vandalism perpetrated by bored teenagers looking for a thrill, but whether they were teenagers from town or the kids of parents who lived in Bonita Vista he had no idea.

*Pretty sick kids.*

"Do you think we should . . . call the police?" he asked.

"Hell yes," Maureen said angrily. "I want the assholes who did this prosecuted. We spent almost a hundred dollars on those new plants—not to mention all the work we put into clearing brush. And they can't get away with killing Barney. I mean, what kind of creep would poison a defenseless little animal like that?"

He had no idea, but it made him furious as well. They hadn't had Barney long enough to feel real sadness at his loss, but they felt rage at what had been done, and he, too, wanted justice, his indignation fueled and amplified by Maureen's righteous anger, pushing aside his earlier uneasiness.

There was no police station in Corban, but he called the sheriff's office to report the vandalism, and twenty minutes later a tan Dodge with the sheriff's insignia painted on the doors pulled into the driveway. The deputy who emerged from the vehicle was not the stereotypical redneck he'd been expecting but a skinny unassertive kid who looked as though he were still in high school.

Barry and Maureen met him in the driveway.

"I'm Wally Addison," the deputy said, nodding. He was trying to look authoritative but didn't have either the face or the years to pull it off. He withdrew a metal clipboard from the front seat of the car. "I understand you've had some vandalism on your property. You need this reported for your insurance?"

"No," Maureen said. "We want whoever did this caught."

"Caught?"

Barry frowned. "Of course."

"I'll be honest with you," the deputy said. "There's a lot

of vandalism around these parts—people shooting up stop signs, tipping over cows, batting mailboxes, what have you—and unless there's an eyewitness, we hardly ever catch the people who do it."

Maureen looked at him levelly. "What does that mean? You're not even going to try?"

"No, no," he said nervously, trying to assure her. "We'll do our best to apprehend the culprit. I just wanted you to know that the odds of doing so are not in our favor."

"Well, we don't care about your past track record," Maureen said. "We expect you to find out who killed our cat and tore up our yard, and we expect you to arrest him."

"Of course, ma'am. Of course. Now if I can just get some information from you good people, we can get started . . ."

Barry described how he'd looked for the cat, going through his discovery step-by-step. Maureen stated that the last time she'd seen Barney had been after dinner, when she'd fed him some leftover chicken on the top deck. Neither of them had had any run-ins with neighbors or had seen any mysterious individuals lurking about; neither was aware of any grudges held against them or any reason why they would be targeted.

The deputy dutifully took everything down, and with an uncertain glance at Maureen stated that it sounded to him as though this was a random attack, probably carried out by troublemaking teenage boys. But, he added hurriedly, the sheriff's department would do everything in its power to solve this case. He gave Barry a carbon of his report and a business card with his beeper number, promising to call as soon as there was any information to report.

Ray showed up before the deputy left, and he remained silent, staying unobtrusively in the background until the tan car pulled out of the driveway and headed back down the road. Maureen headed back inside the house, and Barry walked over to where Ray stood waiting.

"I saw the hubbub from my window," Ray said. "What's going on?"

Barry gestured around. "Take a look for yourself. Someone poisoned our cat and tore up Mo's plants."

"And you called the sheriff?"

"Of course. What did you expect me to do?"

"What I mean is: are you sure this was illegal? Did the sheriff or whoever that guy was give any indication that this *wasn't* a crime?"

"What are you talking about?"

"The sheriff's office has been known to . . . assist the homeowners' association in disputes with individuals."

"You think someone from the homeowners' association killed our cat?" Barry asked incredulously.

Ray shrugged. "I'm not saying anything. I'm just pointing out that, under the bylaws, pets are prohibited in any residence within Bonita Vista." He was quiet for a moment, tilting his head. "Hear that? No dogs barking. I don't know if you've noticed, but there are no domestic animals of any kind within Bonita Vista. No dogs or cats, no hamsters, no goldfish." He met Barry's eyes. "No pets."

"But—"

"It's in the C, C, and Rs."

Barry thought of the dead cat in the mailbox and found that he could not dismiss the idea entirely.

"What about the plants, though? This is vandalism. This isn't enforcement of regulations."

"You're supposed to get approval from the architectural committee before any landscaping changes are made," Ray said quietly.

He didn't believe it, not really, but the idea sent a quiet chill down his spine. Was it possible that someone from the homeowners' association had come to their house in the middle of the night and, while they were sleeping, poisoned their cat and dug up their garden?

He recalled Neil Campbell, the man with the clipboard, and it didn't seem all that far-fetched.

"But . . . people wouldn't put up with this, would they? I mean . . ." He shook his head. "Even in someplace like Utah—*especially* in someplace like Utah—it seems like people would be more . . . individualistic, like they wouldn't want to get involved in things like homeowners' associations."

Ray snorted. "For people who are so antigovernment and antiregulation, they're pretty well sold on this association crap. I mean, hell, most of them are NRA members who pitch a shit fit every time there's so much as a whisper of trigger-lock legislation. But they have no problem with making a homeowner come before one of their damn committees if he wants to trim a tree or plant a flower. On his own property!"

"NRA members, huh?"

Ray waved his hand. "Don't let that scare you. I kicked one of 'em off my lot just last month. They're tough when they're sending out memos or holding a meeting, but one-on-one, they're pussy-boys. Pardon my French."

"What happened? Why were they harassing you?"

"I put up a storage shed. It isn't even visible from the street, but apparently someone saw me unloading the materials from my truck and turned me in. It's like the goddamn Third Reich around here. Everyone's an informant."

"Ray! Barry!"

Barry looked toward the street, where Frank Hodges, one of the men he'd met the other night at Ray's house, was walking toward them, waving.

"I saw the sheriff's car. What happened?"

Barry went through it again, told how he'd been looking for the cat to feed it breakfast and had discovered the animal's dead body along with the uprooted plants.

Frank shook his head sympathetically.

"Ray says there's a prohibition against pets."

Frank nodded. "Yeah. The association doesn't want—" He stopped, frowned. "Wait a minute. Are you—?"

Barry gestured around at the damage. "We were wondering if this could be . . . policy."

"No." He shook his head. "They might be jerks and uptight assholes, but they wouldn't do this. Destruction of property is the *last* thing they would authorize. The problem with the association is that they're *too* strict about upkeep of property, about making sure everyone conforms to their standards. There's no way they would deliberately vandalize a lot in Bonita Vista. They might clean it up for you and send you the bill, but they wouldn't damage it."

He had expected support from Ray, corroboration, but the old man was silent, and the expression on his face was one that Barry found unreadable.

*Everyone's an informant.*

Now he was just being paranoid.

He looked over at Frank.

Wasn't he?

He'd been planning to confide in the other man, share his thoughts openly, attempt to forge an ally, but instead he nodded absently and said, "Yeah, you're probably right." He did not look at Ray again.

He told the others that they were welcome to hang around and watch—or help, if they so desired—but he needed to get to work. There was a lot of cleaning up to do.

"Take pictures first," Frank suggested. "This is all probably covered under your homeowners' insurance."

"Good idea," Barry said. "Thanks."

Ray and Frank walked away, waving, and he watched them for a moment before heading around the side of the house to find a shovel and bury Barney.

# SEVEN

**The Bonita Vista Homeowners' Association Covenants, Conditions, and Restrictions** Article III, Land Use Classifications, Permitted Uses and Restrictions, Section 3, Paragraph C:

> *No animal, fish, or fowl shall be kept, permitted, or maintained on any Lot. No Owner shall remove, alter, or interfere in any way with any shrubs, trees, grass, or plants without the written consent of the Association having first been obtained. No improvements, alterations, or other work which in any way alters the exterior appearance of any Property shall be made or done without the prior approval of the Architectural Committee.*

# EIGHT

The adjustment was easier than she'd expected.

Maureen had worried that she'd go stir crazy working at home rather than in an office, dealing with her clients over the phone, through E-mail, and by fax, but in truth it was liberating. Her life had been pared down to its essentials, and she loved it. Now, she could take time off in the middle of the day to watch a movie or read a book. If work became too frustrating or overwhelming, she didn't have to take a sick day, she could just opt out for a few hours, go outside, and dig in her garden. True, it was a little hard to get used to the lack of human contact and interaction, but Barry was always around, and anytime she wanted, she could walk up to the Dysons' and visit with Liz.

It was a good life, and despite the vandalism of their property, her initial reservations about Bonita Vista faded away with the passing of days.

As expected, the sheriff had failed to find whoever had killed Barney and dug up their yard, but luckily it had not happened again. They'd bought new flowers and shrubs, replanted, and for the past two weeks everything had been fine. Barry still seemed half-convinced that it was part of some sinister plot on the part of the homeowners' association, but she had never put much stock in that theory and as the days and weeks passed, it began to seem more and more ludicrous.

She'd taken to walking each morning, going on a brisk twenty- to forty-minute stroll through the neighborhood, getting to know the area, acclimatizing herself to the altitude and engaging in some much-needed exercise. The more she explored, the more she liked Bonita Vista, and the more sure she was that they had made the right decision by moving here. The houses, spaced far apart on large lots, were uniformly well-kept yet distinctively individual, and the view in every direction was spectacular. Although she enjoyed the scenery to the south, that breathtaking panorama in which forest segued to desert canyonland and the horizon was so far away that you could see the curve of the earth, in truth she preferred the view to the north, and it was when she was walking up the hill, facing the heavily wooded plateau directly behind Bonita Vista, that she felt most at home, that she felt a part of this place.

Maureen strode purposefully down the sloping street that went around the back of their hill. Most of the houses here were vacant vacation homes, but even the residences that were obviously occupied year-round seemed empty, their owners either gone to work or off on errands. From somewhere in the muffled distance came the faint sound of pounding hammers, the noise of construction, and here and there in the brush random bird cries rang out in the still morning air. Other than that, the world was quiet.

There were no dog barks or cat yowls. Barry was right about that—domestic animals were not allowed in Bonita Vista—and she thought of poor Barney, buried on the east side of the house. It had been nice to have a cat, even for a few weeks, and while she didn't believe that the homeowners' association had anything to do with the animal's death, she still resented the organization for disallowing pets.

The houses grew farther apart as the road rounded the

back side of the hill and dipped into a narrow area between the hill and the plateau. Many of the lots here remained unsold, and rusted real estate signs were posted next to the white lot-number stakes. She passed a small empty A-frame with a chain blocking the driveway, and a rustic log cabin with a three-car garage. The road turned again, heading into a copse of tall ponderosas. There were no homes on this section of road, only the uncleared forest pressing in, and though it was midmorning, the positioning of the hill and trees kept most of the route in shadow.

Ahead, she thought she saw something, a still figure that was not a bush, not a tree, not a road sign.

A man.

He stood by the side of the road, unmoving, and Maureen was grateful that he was not close enough to hear her surprised intake of air.

She halted for a moment and bent down, hands on her knees, pretending she'd been running and was only taking a small break from regimented exercise. She counted to ten, then broke into a jog, keeping to the side of the road opposite the unmoving figure, ready to bolt should he make any movement toward her.

It was probably nothing, she told herself. Years of L.A. living had simply made her paranoid, fearful of strangers. He was probably just a fellow resident of Bonita Vista, one of her neighbors out for a stroll. There was no reason for her to assume that he was in any way a threat.

But he was just standing there, not moving.

Better safe than sorry. Following through on her "serious exercise" ruse, ready to ignore him completely or smile in a friendly manner, depending on his reaction to her, she jogged by.

"Fuck you," the man said.

His voice was deep and raspy, sickly sounding, and there was something menacing in not only the words but the tone in which they were spoken. She was afraid to look at the man's face, afraid of what she might see there, and she sprinted faster, her heart pumping with fear as well as exertion.

There were houses ahead, and whether or not they were occupied, she was grateful to be once again in the vicinity of human habitation. The road headed up the side of the hill, and though her muscles were starting to ache, and her mouth was painfully dry from breathing so hard and heavily, she ratcheted up the intensity a few notches and managed to maintain her speed as she ran toward the crest of the incline.

She stopped at the top to catch her breath and casually turned around to look behind her.

The man was striding purposefully up the road toward the spot where she stood.

Panic flared within, and all Maureen could think was that she was being chased, that this man was after her. He seemed even more frightening in the full sunlight. She had not gotten a good look at him before, but she saw now that he was tall and hairy, with a wild mane and bushy beard. The weather was warm, but he wore a flannel overcoat, and even from this distance his heavy boots made a staccato slapping sound on the pavement, the noise absurdly loud in the stillness.

"Fuck you!" the man yelled, his voice echoing.

And he started to run.

Crying out, Maureen sped forward as fast as her feet would carry her, ignoring the protestations of her leg muscles and lungs, wanting only to get away from this psycho and his irrationally dogged pursuit.

She raced the rest of the way up the hill to Liz and Ray's house and fairly flew over the gravel of their driveway, pounding furiously on the door, praying to God that they were home. She glanced back over her shoulder to make sure the man was not coming onto their property after her, already planning how she would make her escape if he was.

Liz opened the door almost immediately, and Maureen pushed breathlessly past her into the house, shutting the door and fumbling frantically for the lock.

Some of her panic seemed to have transferred to Liz. "What is it? What's wrong?"

Maureen held a hand up, shaking her head, trying to catch her breath, then moved over to the window, looking out. The man was there, on the road, standing at the edge of the driveway, and she pointed. "That guy," she managed to get out. "He's following me."

"Who is he?"

"I don't know."

Liz frowned, peeking out. "Ray's at the store. Check that door and make sure it's locked. I'm calling the sheriff."

"Wait!" Maureen said. "Look!"

Outside, on the road, a car had pulled up next to the man, and two other men were getting out, one approaching her pursuer from the left side, the other from the right.

Liz moved away from the window. "That's Chuck Shea and Terry Abbey." She quickly unlocked and opened the door. "Chuck! Terry!"

They looked over, saw Liz, and waved. "Hey there!" the taller man called out.

"That guy's been chasing my friend Maureen here! I was just about to call the sheriff."

"Call!" the tall man said. "We'll hold him!" He turned to his friend. "Told you this joker was up to no good."

Liz retreated to the kitchen, where Maureen heard her dialing the phone and giving the person on the opposite end of the line a quick rundown. Outside, Chuck and Terry were making sure the bearded man wasn't going to go anywhere. Their car was behind him, and they stood on both sides, effectively blocking off all escape routes.

"Fuck you!" the man yelled. He looked toward the house, toward Maureen. "Fuck you!"

"They're on their way," Liz said, returning.

They didn't have long to wait. Five minutes later, they heard a siren in the distance, and two minutes after that, a sheriff's car was pulling to a stop in front of the Dysons' driveway. She and Liz had remained inside, just in case, but with the arrival of the law, they walked out.

This time, the sheriff himself showed up. An older fellow with the hard, sinewy look of a reptile and the improbable name of Hitman, he brought with him another deputy, this one young but seriously overweight, and the two of them forced the bearded man into the back of the car. They didn't even try to talk to him, apparently intending to ask questions later.

Maureen was the one who had been chased, and she described her encounter, telling the sheriff how she'd run past the man, how he'd yelled out an obscenity, and how he'd followed her up the road.

"I don't know if he was chasing me. I mean, I don't know if that would technically be considered chasing, but I felt—"

"Don't worry about it," the sheriff told her. He nodded to the deputy, who'd been writing everything down. "Johnson. You get all that?"

"Yes, sir." The deputy looked around at the gathered group. "I just need your names, addresses, and daytime phone numbers."

He took down the necessary information, and Terry, after giving his stats, took the sheriff off to the side for a moment and peeled off a business card, handing it to him. The two of them conferred quietly. A few moments later, with the man in the back seat yelling "Fuck you! Fuck you!" the sheriff and his deputy got in the car and drove back down the road toward town.

Maureen watched the car head down the hill. She shook her head. "Sheriff *Hit man*?" she said incredulously.

They all laughed.

Chuck moved next to her. "Are you all right?" he asked. "You want a ride home or something?"

She shook her head. "No. But thanks for asking."

"All in a day's work," he said with an exaggerated southwestern drawl. "Ma'am."

Liz smiled. "Thanks, Chuck. Thanks, Terry. You're good guys—no matter what anyone says."

"Yes. Thank you," Maureen said gratefully.

"No problem. That what homeowners' associations are for."

"I—" She reddened, caught off guard. "What—"

"You don't have to say it." He laughed and looked over at Liz. "I know our reputation around these parts."

"Don't blame me."

Terry chuckled. "Comes with the territory."

"A lot of people bristle at the restrictions," Chuck admitted. "But in an unincorporated area like this, an association is the only means we have of taking care of basic needs. You want to be hard-nosed and cynical about it? It helps maintain order. And things like the gate keep out most of the riffraff. But the other side of the coin is that it also fosters a sense of community. You've seen the courts, right? The tennis courts?"

Maureen nodded. "We haven't used them yet, but, yeah, I've seen them."

"There you go. We're also going to be building a community pool, maybe a clubhouse. We have our own little world here, a world that's better than the one surrounding it, and if that means that our standards need to be a little higher, that our rules need to be a little more strict, that we need to put out a little extra effort . . . well, that's a price that most of our residents are more than happy to pay." He smiled at Liz. "*Most* of our residents."

"Some of the townies—" Terry gestured down the street, where the sheriff's car had disappeared. "—resent us for that. Chuck and I are on the security committee, which means that it's our responsibility to keep an eye out for unfamiliar faces or suspicious behavior. We don't get too many outside disruptions here, but when we do, it's usually some local yokel who's ticked off at us about something. We have better houses or better cars or better jobs or better retirement plans. I don't know what this particular guy's story is, but nine times out of ten it's something like that."

"This has happened before?" Maureen asked.

"Oh no," Chuck said quickly. "Nothing like this. But there've been . . . breaches in security, let's say. And like Terry explained, it's usually some teed-off townie."

"Teed off or drunk."

"Teed off or drunk," Chuck amended.

"You know," Maureen said, "someone vandalized our house a couple weeks ago. Well, not our house really. Our yard. And they killed our cat. Although it wasn't really our cat. It was just a stray and we were feeding it. We'd sort of adopted it."

Terry frowned. "Did you file a complaint with the association? I don't remember hearing about this."

"Oh no. We just called the sheriff."

"You should've filed a complaint. In fact, not to be too much of a stickler, you're *required* to file one according to the C, C, and Rs." He held up a hand. "I'm not blaming you. You're new and you didn't know. But we like to keep up with what's happening here. Particularly if it's something like vandalism, something that could happen to any of us. It helps us know what to keep an eye out for."

Chuck nodded. "I wouldn't even be surprised if this guy was involved. He seems to have been targeting you, and maybe he picked you out as a symbol or something. You're young, good looking, and, probably to him, you're rich. In his eyes, you're probably the perfect candidate for harassment."

"Don't worry," Terry said. "The sheriff's going to phone me once he has a chance to interview this loser. I'll call and let you know as soon as I hear anything." He opened the passenger door of the car and Chuck walked around to the driver's side. "You sure you don't need a ride home?"

Maureen shook her head. "Thanks, but I'm going to stay and talk to Liz for a while."

The two men got into the car, waving as they drove down the hill, and Maureen turned to Liz. "They don't seem that bad," she said.

"No," her friend admitted. "Sometimes they're not."

Barry was on the couch when she returned, reading over the pages he'd written that morning, and though the immediacy of what happened to her had faded during the half-hour visit with Liz, seeing him comfortably ensconced in the living room, knowing that he'd been sitting here alone and happily self-absorbed while she'd been running up the road in fear for her life, irritated her somehow.

He looked up. "Hey, what took you so long?"

"I was chased down the street by a psycho and the police—I mean the sheriff—had to arrest him and take him away."

Barry stood quickly, dropping his papers, and rushed over to her. "What?"

She explained it all, from the beginning, going into more detail than she had with Hitman, emphasizing the way she felt, the menacing feeling she'd gotten from her hairy pursuer. Barry kept interrupting with exclamations of "Jesus!" and his genuine expressions of worry and concern softened the resentment she'd felt. They ended up hugging, and she found herself reassuring him that it wasn't really that bad, that she was never in any real danger, that it sounded a lot worse than it was. His first im-

pulse was to drive down to the sheriff's office and confront this guy, make sure that charges were pressed, but
she convinced him to wait, to let law enforcement authorities do their jobs.

They walked upstairs together to the kitchen. He poured
himself some orange juice, while she had the last of the coffee.

"Kind of ironic that it was two homeowners' association
guys who helped you out."

She shrugged. "Maybe we've been a little too hard on
them."

Barry looked at her incredulously. "Too hard? They tore
up our yard and killed our cat!"

"I don't think they did."

"Really? What proof did you suddenly discover that—"

"What proof do you have that it *was* them?" She shook
her head. "Jesus, Barry, for someone who prides himself
on being fair and open-minded and willing to think outside the lines, you sure can be a rigid, linear son of a
bitch."

"I'm sorry. I don't mean to dismiss what happened—"

"Even though that's exactly what you're doing."

"—but don't go giving credit where credit isn't due.
These two guys are part of the association. Fine. They
helped you out. Fine. But that's it. They didn't do anything
anyone else wouldn't do. Liz is the one who let you in her
house, she's the one who called the sheriff."

"Would you have stopped to help someone you didn't
even know?"

"The way you described it, I got the impression that they
didn't stop to help you, that you were in Ray's house and
they just stopped to check on this guy because he looked
suspicious."

"That's true. It was like a neighborhood watch. Which is
even better. They weren't just looking out for me, they were

concerned about what this character might do to *anyone* in the neighborhood. Would you do that?"

Barry smiled. "No. But I'm an egotistical, self-obsessed writer focused only on my own career."

"You're only *half* joking."

"Half? I'm not joking at all."

The phone rang, and Barry quickly moved to pick it up. "I'll get it," he said. They'd left the cordless on the dining room table, and he grabbed the handset and pressed the Talk button. "Hello?"

He handed her the phone. "It's for you."

It was Chuck Shea. He'd heard back from the sheriff, and the man who'd been harassing her had confessed to the killing of their cat and the destruction of their plants. He had apparently vandalized several other homes within Bonita Vista, vacation homes whose owners had not yet been by to discover the damage, and the sheriff was in the process of compiling a list of acts and addresses.

The man, Deke Meldrum, had some sort of grudge against the neighborhood, although the reasons for that remained vague. "Probably a disgruntled handyman or something," Chuck opined. "Last year, the association con- tracted with a local maintenance company to provide all groundskeeping services for the greenbelts and communal property, and it ticked off some of the freelancers when we did that. I think this guy was one of them. There's some- thing vaguely familiar under all that hair."

"So what's going to happen? Has he been arrested?"

"Oh yeah."

"He's not just going to turn around and get out . . ."

"Don't worry," Chuck assured her. "The association will press charges and make sure that he is prosecuted. He'll be in jail for quite a while."

"Is there anything I need to do?"

"We'll take care of everything. You probably won't even

have to testify. With so many Bonita Vista properties involved, the association will be the complainant, and the most we'll need from you will be a statement. Terry and I are going down to the sheriff's office right now, and we'll let you know if anything else comes up."

"Keep us informed,"

"Don't worry. We will."

Maureen thanked him for the information, said goodbye, and put the phone back down on the table, breathing an audible sigh of relief. "Thank God."

"What?"

"That was Chuck. He said the sheriff called and the guy who chased me is the guy who killed Barney and trashed our plants. His name's Deke Meldrum, and he's some kind of gardener or handyman. Apparently, he vandalized several other houses, too—vacation houses—and they're going to get him for all of them."

"Do we have to go down and swear out a complaint or something?"

"No. The homeowners' association is pressing charges."

Barry was silent.

"Come on. You can't have a problem with that. What, you think there's some sort of vast conspiracy and now that you and Ray are on to them they're trying to pin everything on a psycho gardener? That doesn't sound ridiculous even to you?"

He said nothing, but she saw the look of embarrassment on his face and pressed forward. "The association is not the bad guy here. They're the ones going *after* the bad guy. Whatever else they do, however much they cramp your style, they're on our side in this case."

"I just don't like them."

"You can't admit that maybe you've been a little harsh and unyielding, that there's a slight possibility you *might* be wrong?"

He looked at her, took a deep breath. "All right," he said. "I might be wrong."

She nodded. "Okay."

"I *might* be."

"You are," she told him.

And she found that she believed it.

# NINE

The Gordon Lightfoot album ended and Barry continued typing. He didn't like to write without music, but he was on a roll, and for once the silence didn't seem to affect his concentration. Ten minutes later, however, he hit a creative brick wall, and though he tried to keep going, leaving increasingly longer spaces between words with the intention of filling them in later, it was obvious that he was stuck, and he finally gave up, wheeled his chair back from the desk, and walked over to the stereo.

He sorted through his pile of vinyl and put on an old Joni Mitchell record, staring out at the view. There was something about those folkies of the late sixties/early seventies that complemented nature, that understood the rural lifestyle. There was a wistfulness in the music as well, a tinge of melancholy that somehow bridged the hopes of that era with the reality of today and subtly pointed out the disparity.

This was music that spoke to him.

Of course, Joni Mitchell herself was no longer the Joni Mitchell of those early albums. The last time he'd seen her, on VH1 at one of those charity concerts, she'd been droning on in a cigarette-ravaged voice, stopping in midsong to lecture the crowd for not paying close enough attention to her lyrics. She'd seemed angry and bitter, a far cry from the open, giggly young woman captured on the live *Miles of Aisles*, and it had been depressing and dispiriting to realize how much times and people changed.

With the music on, his creative energy returned, and he quickly got back to work. He wrote for another hour or so, then stood and stretched. Maureen was gone, meeting with the manager of the only bank in town, trying to drum up some business locally and get to know some of Corban's financial movers and shakers, and he was alone in the house. He walked upstairs to the kitchen and got out a can of Coke. He'd been cooped up in here almost all week, and he felt more than a little restless. The writing had been going well, but being indoors so much was stifling, and Barry walked downstairs and outside, grateful for the fresh air.

He headed out to the end of the driveway and looked across the street at the forested lot next to the greenbelt. He glanced up and down the road, thought for a moment, then on an impulse went back inside, wrote a quick note to Maureen, and carefully shut the front door behind him. Walking down the hill, he turned on the first street to the right and slowed down, looking for the wooden post that marked the entrance to the east bridle trail.

Even without the post, Barry would have seen the wide swath of open dirt that wound between the trees and away from the road, and he stepped happily from pavement to ground, feeling the delicious crunch of pine needles beneath his tennis shoes.

It was one of the things he liked about Bonita Vista, the fact that it had greenbelts and bridle trails, though he hadn't availed himself of their use until now. He should come here every day, he thought, an hour or so to get some exercise and stop the spread of middle-age paunch that had materialized since he'd become a full-time writer. Maureen had been after him to walk with her, particularly after her run-in with that lunatic, but she wasn't a hiker, she only liked to stroll up and down streets, and he found it boring and pointless to simply traverse their neighborhood. After a few obligatory efforts, she'd given up on him and had started going out with Liz and one of Liz's other friends each morning, leaving him to veg on the couch and watch *The Today Show*.

But he liked hiking, liked walking on trails and being surrounded by trees and brush and the earthy smell of nature. Hell, maybe if he could convince Maureen to come with him, they *could* walk together.

The trail curved down into what looked like a natural gully, following the contours of the land, winding between heavy copses of manzanita and a spread of wild holly bushes. The trees here were tall, much bigger than the ones on their lot or next to the road, and since no homes were visible from this vantage point, he had no trouble feeling as though he were in the middle of some dense, unexplored woodland.

There was a sudden noise in the bushes off to his right, and though it was morning and a bright sunny day, a bolt of instinctive fear shot through him. He wasn't an outdoorsy guy, a nature guy, and unexpected sounds in unexpected places never failed to unnerve him. One of the hazards of his profession. As a horror writer, he always thought of the worst possible scenario: a mountain lion that would rip his lungs out, a bear that would tear him limb from limb. He wasn't the kind to ascribe benign causes or motivations to situations he encountered, and he stopped and looked around, listening, trying to determine where the noise had come from.

There was the rattle of underbrush.

And a sound.

He froze, and it came again. A moan that almost sounded like a word. Whatever was causing it was definitely human, and the hackles rose on the back of his neck. He could not tell from which direction the sound originated, and it was not until he saw the movement of leaves and branches off to his right that he was able to determine how close the source was.

From under the bushes crawled an armless legless man, a dirty, tanned, and heavily bearded individual who pushed himself forward through spastic undulations of his disfigured form. The man's eyes were wild and unfocused, and the slurred incomprehensible noises he made indicated to Barry that he was mentally retarded. He was wearing nothing but a muddy, blood-stained diaper, and when he opened his mouth, all of his teeth were missing.

A chill passed through Barry, and though he knew that such a reaction was childish, that he should be feeling pity and concern rather than fear and horror, he could not help being spooked by the hideous figure before him.

The man flopped into the center of the path, looked up at him, and shrieked.

"It's okay," Barry said. "I'm not going to hurt you." He looked around to see if there was anyone else about, but the trail was deserted. "Do you need any help, any—"

The man shrieked again and began jerking convulsively on the ground, his limbless body moving up and down in obvious agitation. Barry had the feeling that the man was trying to communicate with him, was trying to say something, but whether the sharp cries and ragged movements meant that he wanted Barry to get the hell away from him or that he needed some sort of assistance was impossible to determine.

The bearded face twisted upward on the corded neck, eyes bulging hugely, toothless mouth opening impossibly wide.

Barry crouched down. "Do you want something?"

The figure jerked, screamed at him.

"I'm sorry. I don't—" He broke off, unsure of what to say, not knowing how to respond.

The man cried out again, his flopping becoming ever more frantic.

Barry backed away. Should he just continue on, pretend as though nothing had happened? He looked ahead. The trail before him seemed dark and forbidding, and he immediately turned around, hurrying back the way he'd come. He had no plan, no specific course of action, but he knew that he had to tell somebody, had to try and get the man some help. As bizarre as the incident was, as much as it creeped him out, he understood that underneath the horror-show grotesquerie, this was a real person with obviously real problems and that it was his responsibility to make sure that the authorities were alerted and made aware of it.

He was jogging by the time he hit the road, and when he reached the intersection of his own street, he saw Frank driving by in his pickup. Barry held up his hands, waved him down, and the vehicle slowed to a stop.

"Barry. You look like you've seen a ghost."

"You're not far off." He was breathing heavily from the altitude and exertion. "I was hiking along the east bridle trail, and I ran into . . . a man. A man without any arms or legs who couldn't talk and was sort of slinking along the ground in a diaper."

"Oh, that's just Stumpy," Frank said, chuckling. "He lives on the trails."

Barry didn't know what he'd expected, but this certainly wasn't it. He'd been prepared to run back down the bridle trail with Frank to show him the limbless man, even to help carry the poor unfortunate back to the truck so they could take him into the doctor's office, the sheriff's office, or wherever assistance could be found. But he was not prepared for this cheerful recognition that there was a hideously deformed person living in the forest surrounding them, this open acknowledgment that there was a freak who spent his days skulking along the greenbelts of Bonita Vista—and that apparently everyone knew about it. It seemed surreal, like something out of one of his novels, not like something that could happen in real life, and for once

Barry was at a loss for words, uncertain of how to react or what to say.

Frank must have misunderstood his silence. "Stumpy's harmless. Don't worry."

"I wasn't worried *about* him. I'm worried *for* him. He's . . ." Barry took a deep breath. "He's all muddy and bloody. I mean, shit, the guy doesn't have any arms or legs and he's inching along on his belly in the middle of the woods—"

"That's our Stumpy." Frank smiled sympathetically. "Look, I know you want to help and all, but there's nothing to do. It's his choice. This is how he chooses to live. Who are we to deny him that and dictate what he's supposed to do with his life? He's an adult, it's a free country. Live and let live."

"I don't think he wants to be there," Barry said. "He was howling like he was in pain, and I think he was trying to tell me something."

"Oh, that's just the way he is. Don't sweat it."

Obviously, Frank did not understand his anxiety, could not comprehend why the sight of a filthy limbless man crawling along the ground might give him cause for concern, so Barry dropped the subject. He nodded as the other man talked, pretended that everything had been cleared up for him, and said good-bye, watching the pickup continue down the road toward the gate.

He walked back up the street feeling at once disturbed by what he'd seen and learned, and at the same time oddly disassociated from it. The fear he'd felt was real, and a vestige of it remained with him, but his concern for Stumpy's well-being was more intellectual, less emotional, and did not hit him at the same gut level.

The Suburban was not in the driveway, so he knew Maureen was still gone, and Barry continued up the street, past his house and directly to Ray's. Liz was outside, weeding, and she told him to go on in, Ray was on the deck.

He let himself in through the unlocked front door, walked through the entryway and into the living room. He could see through the windows that Ray was on a chaise lounge, reading a book.

Barry opened the sliding glass door, and Ray looked up at the sound. "Hey," he said. He held up the copy of *The Coming* that Barry had given him. "I'm reading your book. It's pretty damn good. I'm impressed."

"Thank you," Barry said awkwardly. He never knew how to handle compliments about his writing, and while he wanted people to like his work, praise made him uncomfortable.

Ray sat up, put the book facedown on the small table next to him. "So what brings you up here to disturb my reading?"

"Stumpy."

The old man chuckled and stood. "So you heard about Stumpy, huh?"

"Heard about him? I saw him. I was out walking on the east bridle trail, just taking a break from writing to stretch my legs a little, and all of a sudden I heard weird noises in the bushes. A minute later, this man with no arms or legs came squirming toward me, shrieking like a lunatic. Scared the hell out of me. I tried to talk to him, but he seemed retarded and he obviously couldn't speak. When I went back to get some help, I ran into Frank, who told me that it was just Stumpy, and that he lives out in the woods and, apparently, everyone knows about it."

"Yeah," Ray confirmed. "Stumpy lives out there. I think he probably has a hutch or a lean-to or something, but for the most part he just crawls around wherever he wants to."

"And the people who live here don't care? They just put up with it?"

"Well . . . yeah."

"You don't think that's a tad bit peculiar?"

"Of course it is. But he doesn't live *in* Bonita Vista. He

lives in the national forest next to it. We've sort of agreed to let him roam the trails. I mean, who's going to prosecute someone like that for trespassing? Even the homeowners' association isn't that hard-hearted. Stumpy's been around here longer than we have, and I think most of the people have a sort of live-and-let-live attitude toward him. We don't bother him and he doesn't bother us."

"But isn't it sort of irresponsible to turn a blind eye to someone like that? I mean, he was wearing a bloody diaper, for Christ's sake. Shouldn't there be someone who at least makes sure that he's all right, that he . . . I don't know, has access to running water and a toilet, that he has at least the minimum necessities of life?"

Ray smiled sadly. "I'm ashamed to say I never really thought about it that way." He sighed. "Live here long enough, you get hardened to anything."

"So you think I should call someone? Social Services or whatever kind of indigent help the county has?"

Ray thought for a moment, then slowly shook his head. "I'm not a knee-jerk, if-it-ain't-broke-don't-fix-it guy, but in this case, maybe it would be best to let things be. Liz and I have been out here nine years now, and in all that time Stumpy hasn't needed any help, hasn't asked for any help—"

"He was screaming though, crying out like he was trying to talk."

"That's the way he *does* talk. He's always that way. I admit it's a little unnerving at first, but . . . well, like I said, you get used to it. I don't think he was upset or in pain or trying to enlist your help. More than likely, he wanted you to get off his trails and go somewhere else. He doesn't much like company, and he seems to be pretty possessive and territorial."

"So there's nothing we can do?"

"There's nothing *to* do. Stumpy may be handicapped, but other than that he's like any recluse or eccentric. If he had arms and legs and could talk, he'd still be living out in the woods, only you wouldn't think anything of it. You'd think he was some crazy survivalist and never give him another thought. Well, that's exactly how you should think of Stumpy."

"What if sometime he really does need help?"

Ray shrugged. "I guess he'd make his way to someone's house and try to get their attention somehow."

Barry thought of that horrific shriek, of the way the limbless man had looked as he strained his thickly corded neck and opened his toothless mouth. A chill passed through him as he imagined waking up in the middle of the night to find such a sight waiting for him on his doorstep. Maybe it was just his line of work, the fact that he spent his days dreaming up horrors of the flesh and terrifying images of the supernatural, but he could not seem to summon the sort of understanding and acceptance that he knew he should have, and despite his well-intentioned sense of outrage, his real gut reaction to Stumpy was one of fear and disgust.

Ray offered him a beer, but Barry said that he'd already been away from the word processor for too long and he'd have to take a rain check.

He walked back down the hill toward home. The Suburban was back in the driveway, and Maureen was just clicking off the phone as he walked through the door.

"Oh," she said. "That was for you. Where've you been?"

"Out for a walk, Who was it?"

"Your old pal Neil Campbell from the homeowners' association."

"Jesus Christ."

"Apparently, someone complained that you were playing music too loud this morning. Neil wanted to inform you that Bonita Vista does have noise restrictions and the rules state that music cannot be played so loud that it can be heard from someone else's lot."

"Too loud? It was *Ladies of the Canyon*, for Christ's sake. And you could barely hear it downstairs, let alone outside of the house."

"I guess sound carries here."

"Is he calling back? Or does he want me to call him back?"

She shook her head. "He'll send you a memo."

"This is getting ridiculous." Barry looked at her. "They're your friends, couldn't you tell them that we like to listen to music, that it doesn't harm anyone, and, by the way, mind your own damn business?"

"No one's trying to cramp your style, hon. They just want you to show a little more respect to your neighbors. It's not an unreasonable request."

"It is if it infringes on my rights. I live here, too, you know. And I should be able to live my life in my own house and do what I want on my own property without someone else trying to dictate and regulate my behavior."

"They're only infringing on your rights at the point where your rights begin to infringe on other people's."

"What kind of double-talk crap is that?"

"It means that, yeah, you live here, but you're not alone. Other people live here, too, and we have to take into account their feelings."

"Shit." He looked at her disgustedly, and they probably would have gotten into it then and there, but at that second the phone rang, and Maureen pressed the Talk button as she brought it to her ear. "Hello?"

The expression on her face brightened instantly. "Hey, how are you? . . . Yeah . . . It's great . . . Uh-huh . . . No, not at all . . . Yeah, hold on. He's right here." She handed Barry the phone. "It's Jeremy!"

He took the telephone from her hand.

"Dude!" Jeremy said. "Long time no hear!"

Barry smiled as he heard his friend's voice, and for a brief second he was back in California, back in the real world, far away from Bonita Vista and deformed men and homeowners' associations and pending memos about excessive noise. "Jeremy, you loser! It's about time!"

"Yeah. How goes it out there in the boonies?"

He took a deep breath, and though he was still annoyed, still upset, he found himself chuckling at the absurdity of it all. "You're not going to believe it, bud. You're not going to believe it."

# TEN

**The Bonita Vista Homeowners' Association Covenants, Conditions, and Restrictions** Article III, Land Use Classifications, Permitted Uses and Restrictions, Section 3, Paragraph M:

*Without limiting the generality of any of the foregoing provisions, no exterior speakers, horns, whistles, bells, or other offensive sound devices, except security devices used exclusively for security purposes, shall be located, used, or placed on any Lot. In addition, any noise generated from the interior of a home, including but not limited to the sound from television, radio, audio reproduction, or live instrumentation, must conform to agreed-upon noise levels. No sound that is determined by general consensus to be a nuisance or that is audible from the Lot of another Resident will be permitted to emanate from any Property during any time of day.*

# ELEVEN

"I don't know, Ray. I just don't know."

The two of them sat on canvas butterfly chairs next to the barbecue on the Dysons' deck, while the women remained inside talking. Past the town, past the hills, past the trees, the canyonlands were a brilliant orange, sandstone cliffs dyed bright pop-art colors by the setting sun. Barry looked over at his friend. "You'd think that in a place like this, out in the middle of nowhere, they wouldn't have rules and regulations and homeowners' associations. Tracts and subdivisions in southern California, yeah, I'd expect it. But out here?" He shook his head. "Whatever happened to living out in the country with broken washing machines on the back porch and cars on blocks and angry dogs tied up in the yard?"

Ray stood and flipped over the burgers. "Yuppiedom's gone national. It's everywhere, from sea to shining sea. You can't escape it." He pointed with his spatula toward Corban. "You want your white-trash houses, your mean dogs and broken cars and junky appliances, buy a place in town. You want good views and big houses and cable TV, then you're stuck with Bonita Vista." He sat down again. "That's the problem. All these city people like us, longing for a rural lifestyle, all us retired people and telecommuters, we want the comforts of home. We want fresh vegetables and gourmet food in the stores, we want fax machines and cellular phones. And we're willing to pay for it. But when we bring that shit out here, we bring the rest of it, too. The gated communities and homeowners' associations, the need for conformity and exclusivity. Turns out that we didn't really want to live the rural life at all. We wanted our city life with nicer scenery."

"You really think so?"

"Tell me," Ray said. "Why did you buy a house in Bonita Vista? You liked the homes, right? You liked the landscaping and the views. If this hadn't been here, if the only homes for sale in this area had been the ones in Corban, you would've moved on, found some other town to live in. You wouldn't've wanted one of those small dirty houses with dusty yards or one of those broken-down trailers in the pines. The thing that attracted you to Bonita Vista is that it's clean and well-maintained. What you liked about this neighborhood is what the homeowners' association has made of it." He paused. "Me, too."

"So we're hypocrites, huh?"

"No. But we were lured here, trapped, misled." He motioned around him, at his house, at the other houses beyond. "We thought this was all natural and organic, we didn't think it was an artificially maintained environment. Now we're living in this safe little bubble that's completely cut off from the rest of the town."

"I was talking to my friends back in California, and they were shocked when they found out we have so many restrictions here, so many do's and don'ts."

"You were, too, weren't you?"

Barry nodded.

Ray sighed. "So was I," he said quietly. "So was I."

They ate inside, but after dinner, all four of them retired to the deck. Liz lit citronella candles to keep away the bugs, and they sat on the wing chairs, staring out at the sky and the millions of stars visible on this new-moon night. One star seemed to be moving, heading straight across the heav-

ens at an even pace, and Ray pointed it out. "That's a satellite," he said.

"I didn't know you could see those with the naked eye,"
Maureen admitted.

"You can out here. Back in New Jersey you couldn't.
And probably not in California either. But out here, there's
no light pollution, no air pollution, and if you stay out here
long enough and your eyes get adjusted, you can see some
pretty amazing things."

They were silent for a moment, looking.

"I wonder why we never went back to the moon," Barry
said.

Maureen groaned. "Not this again."

"I'm serious. When I was little, we were supposed to
have colonies up there by this time. What the hell happened?"

"He was so brainwashed by all that NASA propaganda
in the sixties," Maureen explained, "that he feels cheated
and personally insulted that he can't take a flight up to the
Lunar Hilton on his vacation."

"Space travel's important," he insisted.

Ray nodded. "The future's arriving at a much slower
pace than everyone thought. My father went from a world
of horse-drawn carriages to a world of cars and planes and
rockets and televisions. I think everyone thought that pace
would be maintained. And it hasn't."

"Don't complain," Maureen said. "We may not be
*Things to Come*, but we're not *Escape From New York*, either."

"Or *Farenheit 451* or *1984* or *Brave New World*." Liz
sipped her wine, smiled. "Contrary to what Ray may think."

"Only because the homeowners' association doesn't
have the technology," he said. "Not for a lack of willingness or inclination."

Liz wrinkled her nose mischievously. "See what I have
to live with?"

Barry laughed and was about to chime in with a defense of Ray, when, out of the corner of his eye, he saw colored lights and movement. For a brief crazy second, he thought it was a UFO, but he recognized almost immediately that the strobing red and blue lights were on the ground, coming from some sort of law enforcement vehicle. In the dark and through the trees, the lights seemed amplified, illuminating trunks and branches, the side of a house.

"What's going on?"

"I don't know." Ray stood by the railing, squinting into the night. "But whatever it is, there's at least two or three patrol cars down there."

"How come we didn't hear any sirens?" Maureen asked.

"Beats me." Ray turned away from the railing. "I'm going to check it out." He nodded to Barry. "Want to come along?"

"Sure."

"I guess the little women will stay home," Liz said loudly to Maureen. "Since we can't accompany the men on their manly mission, maybe we can go back to the kitchen and make them a nice dessert for when they return. They'll probably be hungry."

Ray looked at her, surprised. "You want to come, too?"

She smiled. "No. But it would be polite to ask."

"Sorry."

Barry looked quizzically over at Maureen, who shook her head. "You boys go have your fun. We'll just stay here and gossip about you behind your backs." She turned toward Liz. "Now, if you want to know what he's like in bed . . ."

The two women burst out laughing.

"Very funny," Barry said.

Ray motioned him toward the door. "Come on. I can tell when we're not wanted."

"Don't worry," Liz told him. "We'll have all the world's problems figured out by the time you return."

There must have been some residual heat from the barbecue on the porch, because when they walked up the driveway and out to the road, the temperature dropped. Goose bumps popped up on Barry's arms, and he suddenly wished that he'd brought a jacket.

He and Ray walked down the hill, passing Barry's house and stopping for a moment to get their bearings since the lights could not be seen from ground level. They ended up going down the street that led to the east bridle trail, and there, right before the post that marked the trail's entrance, stood a small crowd of people and two sheriff's cars, patrol lights on and flashing.

Barry's first thought was that it was Stumpy, that the limbless man had crawled onto the road and been run over by a car or something. But there was no car in sight other than the sheriff's vehicles, and the tarp-covered body by the side of the road appeared to be full-sized.

Wally Addison, the young deputy who'd taken their vandalism report, was standing next to a mean-looking older man who could only be Sheriff Hitman. Several neighbors had walked either up or down the street from their houses to see what all the commotion was about and were milling around, talking in low, hushed voices. There was no police ribbon up, no authorities ordering people to stay back, but the onlookers seemed to be observing an invisible barrier, and they remained behind the cars, far away from the side of the road where the covered body lay in the dirt.

Ray walked past that invisible line and directly up to the sheriff.

"Saw your lights from up the hill," he said. "What happened?"

Hitman nodded toward the tarp. "Dead body. Annie Borham found him. Looks like he fell in the ditch and hit his head on a rock. Probably bled to death."

Indeed, there did seem to be a lot of blood on the dirt and

stones of the culvert, and Barry could only imagine what
the man looked like under the tarp.

"Who is he?" Ray asked. "Anybody know?"

"Deke Meldrum. We arrested him up here recently for
harassing a young woman."

The deputy said something to Hitman in a low, inaudible
voice, and the sheriff raised his eyebrows, looking over at
Barry. "I guess that was your wife."

Barry nodded, his stomach tense. The second he'd heard
the name he recognized it, and he was glad that Maureen
had decided not to come with them. He tried to speak, but
no sound came out, and he cleared his throat. "I thought
Meldrum was locked up."

"Oh, he made bail day before yesterday. Court date's set
for next month when the circuit judge comes through, but
until then he's out on his own recognizance." Hitman
paused. "Or was."

The sheriff turned away, obviously not intending to answer any more questions, and Ray went over to talk to some
of the gathered residents. Barry followed. Around them, the
pine trees seemed taller than they did in the daytime, the
black bulk of their closely grown forms blocking out all but
a thin strip of stars. The flashing red and blue lights created
a sort of shield about them, boxing them in against the darkness of night, and the faces of the crowd, bathed in the
strobing colors, were unreadable.

The scene was surreal, made even more so by the realization that Stumpy was probably hiding out there in the
woods, watching this, taking it all in. Barry scanned the
lower bushes and the beginning of the bridle trail, looking
for a telltale glint of eyeshine, and though he saw nothing,
he shivered.

Ray was asking Russ Gifford, a young man Barry had
met at the Dysons' party, what he thought had happened.

"You got me. I just saw the lights and came out to in-

vestigate. I thought it was probably an accident or something, maybe a burglary. I didn't expect anything like this."
He nodded toward the bearded man on his left. "Hank says
he heard the guy was creeping around, casing the neighborhood, and he tripped and cracked his head open."

"Is that true?" Ray asked.

The bearded man shrugged. "I don't think anyone was
actually there to see it, but that's what I heard Annie told the
law. And she was the one that found the body."

Annie Borham, a fitness freak of the first order, had apparently been on one of her nightly jogs when her flashlight
had illuminated Meldrum's feet poking out of the ditch.
She'd run home and dialed 911.

"She never came back out here, though," Hank said. "I
guess she was pretty freaked out about it, didn't want to see
it again. They probably interviewed her at her house."

A middle-aged woman standing next to a young man
who could have been her husband, could have been her son,
said that she heard Meldrum had been hit in the head *with*
a rock, and that that had knocked him into the ditch, where
he hit his head on another rock and died. The retiree next to
her said that it was kids, that teenagers from town had been
hiding in the brush, throwing rocks at passing cars, and
they'd accidentally hit Meldrum, taking off and running
back to the highway so they wouldn't get caught.

Rumors were rampant. No one in the crowd seemed to
really know anything—most of them had simply been
drawn by the lights the way they themselves had—and after
waiting for the ambulance and watching it take away Meldrum's dead body, lights and siren off, Barry and Ray
started back up the hill the way they'd come. They had
company until they reached Barry's street, but then their
silent companions headed in the opposite direction, and the
two of them continued on alone.

Neither of them spoke for a moment.

"Did you see all the blood?" Ray said quietly.

Barry nodded. "Yeah."

"Looked like an awful lot for someone just tripping and falling on a rock."

"You think those guys were right? You think he was hit before he fell?"

Ray didn't respond.

"What?" Barry said.

Ray shook his head.

"Come on."

"You don't want to hear what I think. *I* don't even want to hear what I think. I'm just a paranoid old buzzard who should be on the Internet all day spreading conspiracy theories."

"Tell me."

"Forget it."

"Come on."

"You really want to know?"

"Of course."

Ray stopped walking and turned toward him. "I think the homeowners' association bailed him out. I think they did so because they knew he'd return here and they could get a little vigilante group going and run him out of the county, maybe out of the state. But I think something went wrong. I think they meant to just scare him but somehow things got out of hand and they ended up accidentally killing him."

Barry laughed. He couldn't help it. "That's wild," he said.

Ray shrugged and started walking again. "Told you."

The laughter faded, and despite the outrageousness of the claim, Barry found that he was unable to dismiss it entirely. While he didn't exactly believe it, he *could* believe it. Such a scenario was within the realm of possibility.

That in itself was frightening.

They walked in silence for a moment.

"Is there any way to check, to find out for sure who bailed him out?"

"I don't know," Ray said. "But I'm going to call the sheriff's office tomorrow."

"What if it's true? What if the association did bail him out and now his dead body's found up here in Bonita Vista? You think the sheriff'll look into that? You think he'll see a connection?"

Ray shook his head. "I told you before. He's in their pocket. I don't know whether he's getting actual kickbacks or whether this is just the usual law enforcement kowtowing to moneyed interests, but he's beholden to them, and there's no way he's going to upset the applecart by investigating them."

"You think Meldrum has family in town?"

"I don't know."

They trudged up the hill.

"If that *is* what happened," Barry said, "if the association did bail him out because they knew he'd return here, and then they killed him, and no one investigates it and the case is closed . . . that means that they'll get away with murder."

Ray didn't answer.

They walked the rest of the route without speaking.

Maureen and Liz were no longer on the deck. The bugs had apparently grown immune to the scent of citronella, and the two women had come inside to avoid being eaten alive. They seemed to be in a good mood, but when Barry and Ray gave them a rundown of what they'd seen, it put an end to any hope of finishing the evening on a high note, and Barry and Maureen went home soon after.

In bed, getting ready to fall asleep, he told her Ray's theory, that Meldrum had been bailed out of jail by the homeowners' association specifically because they knew he would return here, and that they'd gathered together a vigilante group to scare him, but things had gotten out of hand and he'd ended up dead.

"That's ridiculous," she scoffed.

He had to admit that here in bed it didn't sound quite so logical, but when he thought back to the scene on the road, the black trees illuminated only by the flashing lights of the patrol car, the covered body on the ground, the blood on the dirt, the staring crowd, he could not help feeling a twinge of queasiness.

They were both silent for a while.

"I'm glad," Maureen said quietly.

He'd thought she'd fallen asleep—he was about to doze off himself—and though the words came out of nowhere, had no context, he knew exactly what she was talking about.

She rolled onto her side, facing him. "I'm glad he's dead," she said.

Barry said nothing, not knowing what to say.

"Does that make me a horrible person?"

"No," he told her, and leaned over to kiss her forehead. "No it doesn't."

# TWELVE

They came over while Liz was taking a bath.

Ray didn't know if that was intentional, but the idea that the house was under surveillance, that his and his wife's movements were being monitored, made him both uneasy and angry. He was near the entryway, and he opened the door at the sound of the knock. Neil Campbell stood on the welcome mat, Chuck Shea and Terry Abbey just behind him. As always Neil carried a clipboard, and he nodded brusquely in his annoyingly officious manner. "We need to talk to you alone for a few minutes, Ray."

"Alone?"

"Yes."

"How do you know I'm alone?"

"What do you mean, Ray?" The innocence was a little *too* innocent.

"Where do you think Liz is?"

"I'm sure I don't know."

"She's in the bath. So I *am* alone. Pretty damn convenient."

"All I meant was that we would like to speak to you outside of the presence of your wife. I thought we might chat behind a closed door in some room of your house. But, yes, the fact that Elizabeth is bathing at this time is quite fortuitous."

The uneasiness increased. "What do you want?"

"May we come in?" Neil asked.

Ray favored him with a tight smile. "No you may not."

"Then we will conduct our business here on the porch."

"I have no business with you," Ray said. "As I've told you assholes before: get off my property."

They made no effort to move, and Chuck's mouth curved upward in an amused smile. "You know very well that we're not trespassing. We have the right to be here."

"Why?"

"The association has been informed that you spoke with Sheriff Hitman," Neil said, "and attempted to discover the identity of the person who bailed the late Deke Meldrum out of jail."

"So? What business is that of yours?"

"When behavior of an individual reflects badly on Bonita Vista, the homeowners' association naturally takes an interest. As you know, it is our goal to avoid tarnishing the reputation of our community and to do everything within our power to make sure that property values are maintained. Needless to say, the death of a man, even a transient, even by accident, is cause for concern."

"What does that have to do with my trying to find out who bailed out Meldrum?"

"We are simply trying to stave off potential embarrassment. It is clear from the questions you asked and from your past behavior that you are somehow trying to place blame for this man's death on the association, and we're here today to . . . dissuade you from that course of action."

"Got something to hide, Campbell?"

Chuck stepped forward. "Ray, Ray, Ray. You still haven't learned that sometimes you need to just leave things alone, let them be."

"Yeah? Why is that?"

They moved fast: Chuck grabbing him by the left arm and pulling him out onto the porch, Terry stepping quickly behind him and yanking on his right arm. The two of them held him, while Neil thwacked his genitals with the clipboard. There was a sudden sharp flare of pain, pain so intense that he wanted to cry out and clutch his balls, but he refused to give these bastards the satisfaction of a response, and he willed himself to remain stoic.

Neil grinned, and there was real enjoyment in it. Malice and pleasure, a lethal combination. For the first time since he and Liz had moved to Utah, Ray was scared. Really and truly scared. A line had been crossed, and it was impossible to go back again, to pretend it hadn't occurred.

Neil lovingly stroked the clipboard as he paced in front of the stoop. "You're not a team player, Ray. Bonita Vista is a community, and you are part of that community. You and your wife are not hermits or recluses, living on your own. You live here, with us, in respectable, civilized society." There was steel in his voice, in his eyes. "You need to play ball."

"Tell your goons to get their hands off of me."

Neil punched him in the stomach and Ray doubled over. He remained standing only because Chuck and Terry were holding him up, and he was humiliated to hear that the sounds he made while trying to suck in air sounded like sobs.

"Bonita Vista is your home, and you'd better start showing it more loyalty, more respect. The reason you have such a nice house in such a nice neighborhood is because of the standards maintained by the homeowners' association, because of our vigilance in going after those who do not follow the rules and regulations. Your life is easy because we have made it easy. Yet you are ungrateful, always looking for the cloud behind the silver lining, always imagining nefarious schemes behind perfectly innocent efforts to improve life in our neighborhood."

"It's a free country," Ray reminded him.

Neil smiled. Behind him, Chuck and Terry laughed harshly.

"A free country? Do you know *why* we have a home-owners' association?" Neil asked. "It's because we are not under anybody's rule. The federal and state governments do not concern themselves with our petty little problems, and the county, even if it wanted to, doesn't have the means. We're in an unincorporated area, so there is no local government that has jurisdiction. We are on our own. We have been forced to provide for ourselves, to take care of ourselves, to look out for our own. And you're right, we *are* free. Free from government interference and meddling and micromanagement. But it is only our self-sufficiency that makes it so."

It sounded like a militia attitude, particularly in the fervency of its delivery, and that was as scary to Ray as anything he had yet heard.

"*This* is true democracy," Neil said. "It's not representative government but direct participation. We, the people, are the ones making decisions and carrying them out. We're not relying on others, on outside assistance. And we're doing a damn good job of it. A homeowners' association is more efficient than a government agency. More efficient and more responsive. This," he said, gesturing to the neighborhood around him with the clipboard, "is the wave of the future. The decentralization of government that people have been fighting for for years? We have it."

"I'm a liberal Democrat," Ray said. "I like big government."

Neil punched him again.

The patina of politeness, the attempt to convert through persuasive argument, was gone, and Neil's voice was annoyed and angry. "You're a slow learner, Ray, and we're not going to put up with this forever. Get with the program. We're here today as a courtesy call, to give you some friendly advice before you really get yourself into trouble."

Ray could not breathe, but he managed to croak out a message of defiance: "Fuck you!"

Chuck kicked him in the shins, Terry punched the back of his neck. Without the support of their hands, he crumpled to the ground, gasping. Neil said something he did not catch, and then all three of them were walking away, back up the driveway toward the road. He tried to stand up, and was only able to do so by balancing himself against the doorjamb. He ached all over. They'd hurt him, he realized, in a way that would not show, and even if there were some law enforcement agency he could go to, there was nothing he'd be able to prove. He was filled with a deep furious desire for revenge, but it was tempered by fear, by the more realistic assessment that these people were willing to go to any lengths to achieve their ends.

Their ploy had worked, Ray realized.

He had not been afraid before.

Now he was.

He was grateful at least that he had shown no fear, that he had been able to keep up his defiant bravado in front of those assholes, and he moved slowly and painfully back into the house, locking the door behind him and limping into the living room. He sat down hard on the couch, still trying to catch his breath.

A few moments later, Liz emerged from the bathroom. "Did someone stop by? I thought I heard voices."

Ray shook his head. "No," he said. He tried to smile. "It was just the TV."

# THIRTEEN

**The Bonita Vista Homeowners' Association Covenants, Conditions, and Restrictions** Article III, Land Use Classifications, Permitted Uses and Restrictions, Section 3, Paragraph L:

*Any member of the Architectural Committee, any member of the Board, or any authorized representative of such, shall have the right to enter upon and inspect any Lot within the Properties for the purpose of ascertaining whether or not the provisions of this Declaration have been or are being complied with, and such persons shall not be deemed guilty of trespass by reason of such entry.*

# Fourteen

Whatever it was that had initially turned her off to Bonita Vista seemed to have finally and completely died with Deke Meldrum. Maureen pulled the hose around the right front tire of the Suburban as she watered the replanted irises. She looked out at the road, looked up at the sky. She no longer had any reservations about being here, and contrary to expectations, she found that she liked living in a gated community, enjoyed the security such an extra layer of protection provided. She felt safe—not because they were in rural Utah, away from the smog and the gangs and the high crime rate of the major metropolitan areas, but because they were living in Bonita Vista, an enclosed world, a hermetically sealed environment, shielded against all that lay outside. Her reservations had been turned on their head, and what she had originally thought of as drawbacks now seemed like attributes.

Barry said that it was her "accountant side" coming out, and though he'd meant it as a joke, perhaps there was some truth to that. She was neater than he was, more fastidious and methodical, more concerned with order and organization. It was a trait common to those who enjoyed working with numbers, just as comfort with chaos and disorganization seemed to be de rigueur for liberal arts people like Barry, and she had to admit that there was something reassuring about living in well-regulated surroundings.

Usually, she was big on first impressions. And as old-fashioned and superstitious as it sounded, she was a firm believer in "women's intuition." Or at least her own intuition. She trusted her gut instincts, and it was rare that she changed her mind once an opinion had been formed.

But change her mind she had, and it was Meldrum's death that had been the catalyst. It was as if he'd been the conduit for the negativity she'd had toward this place. And with his sacrifice, all of that had disappeared.

*His sacrifice?*

She didn't know where that had come from, but she didn't want to think about it. That was a remnant of those disgraced first impressions, a holdover from before, and she refused to acknowledge that it had any validity. There was nothing untoward about Bonita Vista, and neither the neighborhood nor the homeowners' association had anything to do with that lunatic's death. It was an accident, pure and simple.

Barry walked out of the house, sipping Dr. Pepper from the battered plastic Batman cup that had been his sole contribution to their kitchen supplies. "What are you doing?" he asked.

"Watering."

"No, I mean after that. Are you busy?"

"Not really. Why?"

"I thought we could check out the tennis courts, get in a little exercise. We're paying for those courts with our association dues. We should at least get our money's worth."

It had been a long time since they'd played tennis. In the early days, when they were dating, when they were poor, they spent many a Saturday afternoon on the courts of the high school next to her old apartment. Neither of them were particularly athletic, however, and time and inclination had led them away from outdoor recreation. But playing tennis again sounded like fun, and she nodded enthusiastically. "Let's do it."

"All right, then."

"Do you know where the rackets are?"

"I put them in one of the garage boxes we have in storage. I'll cruise down and pick them up while you finish your watering."

"Okay." She smiled and pulled on the hose as she moved to the next group of plants. "Prepare to meet your doom."

"You never beat me once," he reminded her. "And I don't think ten years of inactivity have improved your tennis skills."

"Famous last words," she said. "Famous last words."

She finished watering, and after Barry returned with the rackets and a can of balls, they walked down to the tennis courts. Located near the entrance of Bonita Vista, the better to impress outsiders and passersby, the twin courts were perfectly maintained and surrounded by a high green chain-link fence meant to prevent balls from flying into the forest and to keep out nonresidents. Inappropriately large stadium lights were mounted on streetlamp-sized poles in order to illuminate the courts at night and allow evening play.

They stepped up to the gate. An electronic lock with a small keypad was mounted above the latch.

"Guess we should've read our handbook before coming down here," Barry said derisively. He handed Maureen the can of balls and bent forward to look at the metal square. "There aren't any instructions." He punched in the entry code for the community gate, but there was no response.

"Try our address," Maureen suggested. "Or our lot number."

The lot number did the trick, and the framed chain-link rectangle swung smoothly open.

"Keeping track of who uses it," Barry said. "Nice."

Maureen laughed. "You're as paranoid as Ray." She walked onto the green court, felt a slight give beneath her feet as she headed toward the net. It was a far cry from the faded lines on concrete that had defined the school court on which they used to play, and she was impressed that Bonita Vista had such a professional, state-of-the-art facility.

She touched the taut net and walked around it to the other side. "Didn't Mike and Tina say that they played tennis?"

Barry nodded. "Yeah."

"Maybe if we practice up a bit, we could play doubles with them."

"Sure. In a year or two."

"Speak for yourself." Maureen threw up a ball and hit it over the net to him. He returned the ball, but that was the end of their volley. She missed, swinging against air, and the ball bounced harmlessly, dead ending at the fence. For the next several minutes, they took turns serving and missing, managing only an occasional return.

"Still think we're good enough to play the Stewarts?" Barry called.

"Let's get into it, writer boy. Four out of seven. You serve first."

They started playing. An actual game, not just random volleys. She noticed that he kept looking away from the court, out into the forest behind them, that he kept peering through the chain-link fence into the underbrush each time he picked up a ball. "Looking for Stumpy?" she teased him.

He glanced up quickly, guiltily, as though she'd read his mind, and it was obvious that she'd hit the nail on the head.

She'd been joking, of course, but she should've known better. Although he hadn't said much about Stumpy since that first day, she should have figured out that he'd be obsessing about it. A deformed man living in the wilds? That was right up his alley, and no doubt he'd conjured up some outrageous scenarios involving underhouse crawl spaces and perverse voyeurism, and pets that had been stolen and eaten.

The truth, as she understood it, was not nearly so melodramatic. The limbless man was not malevolent but harmless. Almost everyone seemed to have a Stumpy story, and most of them were pretty damn funny. Barry was right; it was sad that someone actually lived like that in this day and age. But on the other hand, from everything she'd heard, it was his own choice, he preferred to live that way, and apparently it made him happy.

Barry picked up the tennis ball, and moved back into place.

"You think he's spying on us? Is that it?"

"I think he *watches*," Barry said. "And I think he knows a lot. Stumpy has access to everything. He can go where he wants when he wants. If he could talk, I bet he'd have quite a story to tell."

Maureen shook her head. "Just serve," she told him.

He beat her three games to one, and despite the fact that they were only playing for fun, her natural competitiveness would not allow her to go down without a fight. She walked forward. "Switch. The sun's in my eyes."

"A likely story."

Still, he let her trade sides, and she actually won the next game despite the fact that he was serving.

Then it was her turn and she let fly a not particularly effective serve, but Barry did not even try to return the ball. Instead, he let it bounce behind him and moved toward the net, motioning for her to do the same. They met in the middle of the court. "Don't be too obvious, but look across the street. There's an old lady spying on us."

She turned. On the other side of the road from the tennis courts was a house, a two-story residence of wood and glass with twin front windows facing the road. She saw the curtains move, saw an elderly face peer out.

"So? Old people are always nosy. It gives them something to do: gossip about their neighbors."

"It's not just that. She's been watching us *intently*, keeping track."

"Maybe she's a tennis fan."

Maureen turned back, saw the curtains move once more. On the road in front of the house, an equally old couple was walking by, taking a stroll. The woman smiled, waved at them, but the man spent too long looking, did not turn away, and it was clear that he was watching them, studying them.

"See?" Barry said. "There's something weird going on."

"What? Face it, hon, this place isn't exactly a hotbed of activity in the middle of the week. We're probably the day's excitement."

"It's not just that." He glanced around, as though searching for something. "I feel like we're under surveillance." His gaze traveled upward to the top of the fence, to the light pole. He frowned, moved around the pole, looking up. "Check that out," he said.

"What?"

"Up there. Look."

She followed his pointing finger. Mounted atop the light pole, aimed down, was what appeared to be a video camera, the type of security device found in banks and convenience stores.

"See?"

"See what? It's obviously an antivandalism measure. A perfectly appropriate one considering what happened to my flowers."

He walked around the pole again. "Where does it go?" he wondered. "Where's the monitor that it's attached to?"

"There probably isn't one. It's probably just a VCR."

"But where? In the president's house?" He glanced up at

the camera. "You telling me that thing doesn't have a zoom on it, that whoever's monitoring it doesn't use it to peek down babes' tennis blouses?"

"Now you're just being crazy." She looked at him. "Or is this some story idea you're trying out on me?"

"It's not a bad idea for a story, but no, I'm being serious."

"You're overreacting."

"Am I?"

"It's called security, and I have no problem with it. We have security gates here, security cameras. It's why our crime rate is almost nonexistent. It's why people like to live here."

"You sound like an advertisement."

"Barry?" She shook her head, thought of saying something else, didn't. "Let's just play tennis."

But he wasn't ready to let it go.

"What about that old lady peeking at us from behind her drapes? What about the people walking by?"

"I think it's nice," she said. "They're watching out for us."

"They're spying on us."

"Isn't this what people are trying to recapture, this sense of community, this idea that everyone looks out for everyone else? Isn't that what they mean by the 'good old days'?"

"But that was natural, it evolved on its own. It wasn't imposed on people."

"We had a 'Neighborhood Watch' in California, for Christ's sake! It's the same exact thing!"

"No, it's not the same thing." He walked over to where she had put the Voit can and dropped his ball inside. He picked up the can. "Let's go home," he said. "I don't want to play anymore."

"I do."

"Fine. Then play by yourself. But I'm going back. I'm not going to stay here to be monitored and spied on."

"You're an asshole," she said.

They left together, walking in silence back up to the house. Maureen checked the mailbox on the way in, but it was empty. There was a piece of pink paper attached to the screen door, however, that was fluttering in the slight breeze and drew their attention. It was tucked into the top of the grating that covered the door's lower half, and they walked up the porch steps. Barry pulled out the paper and held it so they could both read.

It was a form, obviously a duplicate of an original, and the heading at the top read *Exterior Maintenance Review.*

Beneath the heading was a short paragraph explaining that the Bonita Vista Homeowners' Association Architectural Committee had conducted a review of the property and had determined that the subsequent maintenance was required. There followed a list of actions, two of which had check marks next to them: "Paint chimney/chimney cap" and "Clean pine needles and cones."

They'd been gone only half an hour or so—forty-five minutes at the most—and it was hard to believe that in that time someone had inspected their house and lot for all of the possible violations listed on the form. It was also a little disconcerting. While she knew it was legal, she didn't like the fact that people had been on their property while they were gone, snooping around. There seemed something sneaky about it, something wrong. Why couldn't the inspection have been conducted while they were at home?

But she didn't want Barry to know she felt that way. He was no doubt furious and incensed at such a violation of their privacy, and as petty as it was, she was glad. It served him right.

He stared at the form. "Pinecones?"

It was rather small and silly, she had to admit, and she had half a mind to call up Chuck or Terry and ask why they were being harassed for such minor details, but she was mad at Barry and wanted him to be irritated and annoyed.

"I guess you're going to have to do some yard work," she said.

# FIFTEEN

The day was beautiful, the blue sky filled with gigantic white clouds that drifted lazily from east to west, and Barry decided to write outside on the deck rather than coop himself up in the house in front of the computer. If he came up with anything good, or anything usable, he could type it up later.

He picked up his notebook, defiantly cranked up the stereo volume despite the fact that the music playing was an undefiant James Taylor, and pushed open the sliding glass door.

"Turn that down!" Maureen yelled from the bottom floor.

"I won't be able to hear it outside!" he shouted back.

"Buy a Walkman!"

Barry ignored her, went outside onto the deck, and settled into a chair; but he was not surprised when a moment later the music was abruptly cut off. There was a tap on the glass, and he glanced over to see Maureen grinning at him.

"Thanks a lot," he said.

"My pleasure."

She returned downstairs to where she'd been working on the computer, and he turned his attention to the page before him.

The blank page.

He stared at the lined paper. Ever since they'd moved here, he'd had a scene from the movie *Funny Farm* stuck in his brain. In the film, Chevy Chase moves out to the country because he wants to write a novel, and in the initial tour of the new house with his wife, he finds a perfect room for his studio where there's a bird cheerfully chirping on a branch outside the window. Later, he's sitting at his writing desk in front of his typewriter and a blank roll of paper, completely blocked, and this time when the bird chirps happily outside, Chase throws a cup of hot coffee at it.

That had been Barry's greatest nightmare, that he would be unable to write in these gorgeous surroundings, and even today, as he sat on the porch, pen in hand, there was the small nagging fear at the back of his mind that he wouldn't be able to come up with anything, that the creative juices wouldn't flow.

But he needn't have worried. As always, he had no problem tapping his imagination, and soon his pen was flying, describing the feelings of a young boy forced by his psychotic sister to eat cereal made from the bone dust of their cremated mother.

A woman walked by on the road in front of the house, and he caught her eye and waved. She gave him a thin smile, waved back, then hurried on, obviously eager to be away from him.

So much for small-town friendliness.

He looked at her retreating back. Now that he thought about it, the sociability quotient of their neighborhood seemed to have gone down over the past week or two, the dinner invitations they'd received upon first arrival no longer extended. He wasn't complaining—they had friends here now: Ray and Liz, Frank and his wife, Audrey, Mike and Tina Stewart—but still it was odd, and he wondered why it had happened, whether they'd broken some unwritten code and made some hideous social faux pas, or whether their newness and novelty had worn off and everyone who wanted to meet them had done so.

The woman rounded a bend in the road, disappearing behind the pines, and Barry looked down at his notebook, flexed his fingers one more time, and resumed writing.

The weather changed quickly, as it often did here in Utah. He'd been sweating in the June heat, then suddenly thick white clouds blocked the sun, and there was a measurable drop in temperature—a full eight degrees according to the Sierra Club outdoor thermometer Maureen had installed on the wall next to the door. The sweat cooled on his skin. If what Ray said was true, July would bring the monsoons, and then they'd *really* see some schizoid weather. Barry was looking forward to it. As a native southern Californian, his exposure to different seasons had been through movies, books, and television, entirely secondhand, and it was nice to finally experience for himself the vagaries of Mother Nature.

He broke off for lunch some six pages later, his right hand starting to cramp. He felt good about what he'd written this morning. If it went this well every day, he'd be able to write for six months out of the year and take the other six off. Or crank out two books a year instead of one. Probably the latter. Writing was a notoriously fickle and unstable business, and no matter how well he was doing, there was always the possibility that he could be stone cold in a year and find his fiction unsalable. It was the nature of the beast, and even if he hadn't had a borderline-obsessive work ethic, he would still feel the need to strike while the iron was hot.

But inspiration wasn't that consistent, and although there were days when he finished twenty clean pages, there were others when he eked out only a single paragraph that more often than not had to be rewritten the following day.

This morning had been productive, though. Walking inside, he dumped his notebook on the dining room table and went into the kitchen, searching for something to eat. He opened the cupboards, looked through the refrigerator, but the house seemed to be devoid of snacks and he was too lazy to actually make anything. He finally settled on an apple, chomping it as he walked downstairs. Maureen was in the bathroom, but on the table next to the computer were several stamped envelopes addressed to the IRS, entreaties on behalf of her clients no doubt, and he called out between bites, "Hey! You want me to take these letters out to the mailbox?"

"Go ahead!" came the muffled response.

Anxious to be walking, on the move, doing something physical after sitting on his butt all morning, Barry tossed his apple core into the wastepaper basket, picked up the envelopes, and headed outside. At the mailbox, he flipped up the red flag and opened up the rounded metal door to drop off Maureen's outgoing correspondence.

But he saw immediately that the box wasn't empty. Today's mail had not yet been delivered, so there were no bills, no letters, no postcards. But there was an unstamped envelope bearing his name and, in the upper left corner, the printed initials "BVHA."

*Bonita Vista Homeowners' Association.*

He ripped open the envelope, angry before he even knew what was in it. There was no form this time but a typed note on letterhead stationery. He read the message. Read it again.

*Dear Mr. Welch,*

*It has come to our attention that you have been using 113 Pinetop Rd. as your place of business as well as your primary residence. Bonita Vista is a strictly residential community and all commercial or business activities are prohibited. No homeowner may practice his or her occupation on any of the Properties.*

*The Board has only recently learned of your specific situation, and after careful review we have determined that as per the Bonita Vista C, C, & Rs you are required to secure an alternate site at which you can conduct your writerly vocation within thirty days of this notice.*

*If you have any questions or concerns, please do not hesitate to call me at 555-7734. I would be happy to assist you in any way I can.*

*Sincerely yours,*

*Boyd R. Masterson*
*Committee Chair*

The paper in his hand was trembling, he was so angry. Barry shoved Maureen's envelopes into the mailbox and shut the door.

*Writerly vocation.*

In his mind, he was revising and rewriting the letter: a pointless exercise but one that he often did when confronted with adversarial documentation. Too many people in this world were unable to compose an effective missive, and it always gave him a boost to realize that his opponents were not as adept at composition as he was. It diffused the threat somehow, gave him, at least in his own mind, a psychological advantage.

There was the sound of a vehicle coming up the road, and he looked up to see a red Jeep rounding the corner and starting up the hill. It was Mike Stewart. Mike worked in town at the Cablevision office and was obviously on his way home for lunch. He gave a honk and a wave as his Jeep passed by. But something in Barry's demeanor must have alerted him that something was amiss, because a second later Mike braked the vehicle and coasted back down, stopping in front of the driveway. "Anything wrong?" he called out.

Barry walked up to the Jeep, holding out the letter. "What do you make of this?"

Mike reached out the driver's window and took the paper from his hand. He started to read, then snorted. "Those assholes."

"You know anything about this rule?"

"No, but that's only because it doesn't apply to me. If they say it's in the C, C, and Rs, you can bet your mama's cooze that it is."

"But don't you think this rule was probably made to keep people from selling stuff out of their house, or setting up some sort of manufacturing unit in their garage, or doing things that would disrupt the neighborhood? I mean, I write, for God's sake. I type. That's it. It doesn't harm anything. No one would even know I do it if I hadn't told them."

Mike sighed. "You're probably right, but these are letter-of-the-law guys. Intent doesn't mean shit to them. They're just into throwing their weight around and enforcing their rules, and the more infractions they find, the more people they can crack down on, the happier they are. They're grateful you slipped through that loophole and they could pounce."

"God *damn* it!"

"You know," Mike said, "it's my goal to win the lottery. There are quite a few empty lots up here, and if I won, I'd buy them all. Not just to keep the open space, but also because for each lot you own you get one vote in the association election. I'd have a massive voting block, probably more than all the existing residents put together." He grinned. "I haven't decided whether I would vote to disband the homeowners' association or just vote myself president and exempt myself and my friends from all existing rules while enforcing them to the max for everyone else."

"That," Barry said, "sounds like a plan."

"Lottery's every Wednesday and Saturday."

Barry smiled. "I'm a friend, right?"

"Damn straight. And I'll make those bastards pay for this." He handed back the letter.

"But until then?"

Mike grew more sober. "I think you're screwed." He held up a hand. "Don't go by what I say, though. I'm no expert on this shit. You should talk to a lawyer or something."

"Yeah."

"Hey, I gotta get home and eat lunch. I only get a half hour, and fifteen minutes're gone already. I'll call you later."

"All right. Thanks, Mike." Barry waved good-bye as the Jeep took off up the hill, and, still clutching the letter in his fist, headed up the driveway and into the house.

Maureen, after he'd told her, after she'd read the letter, didn't seem all that upset. At least not as upset as he thought she should be. She agreed that it was unreasonable to force him to stop writing at home, but she admitted that she understood the logic behind it. "They can't very well let you off the hook and make you the exception. They're obligated to apply the rules fairly and evenly, not pick and choose who they're going to harass. That would be selective enforcement and there'd be lawsuits galore after that. I know it sucks that you fell through the cracks, but I don't think it's intentional, I don't think they're after *you*, I think they're just trying to enforce their regulations—as unfair as they are—in a way that proves they're not singling anybody out for prosecution *or* favors."

"Jesus Christ."

"It's not the end of the world."

"Thanks for the support."

Maureen shrugged. "All I'm saying is that it might not be all that bad for you to get an office, at least not from a tax perspective. The rent's deductible—"

"That's not the point."

"I know that. I'm just saying that we're doing pretty well

these days, and your business expenses are almost nonexistent. That's why we took such a big hit last year on taxes.
But if you got yourself an office . . ."

"Stop trying to be practical and calm me down. I'm
pissed off here, and, goddamn it, I have a right to be. Knock
off the every-cloud-has-a-silver-lining crap."

Her mouth tightened.

"If I was retired, I could sit here all day and write crank
letters to the newspaper or the government or whatever, and
I wouldn't be breaking any rules. But because I make my
living writing, I can do the exact same thing for the same
amount of time and suddenly I'm in violation of the regulations. Don't expect me to be happy about that."

A thought suddenly occurred to him, and he took the letter from her hand, read it over again. "You know what?" he
said. "It only mentions me. What about you? You're using
this as your office, too. I'm not the only one working out of
the house here."

"And what's that supposed to mean? You're going to
turn me in?"

"Of course not."

"What, then?"

"Nothing."

"Then why'd you bring it up?"

"Because they're *not* applying the rules fairly, because
they *are* singling me out."

"So what are you going to do? Sue them over it?"

"Threaten them with it at least. You're right, it is selective enforcement. And maybe if I play my cards right I can
get a waiver."

He had Maureen call Chuck Shea, her association buddy,
to feel him out, to see if something could be arranged, a sort
of don't-ask-don't-tell policy that would allow him to continue working at home, but Chuck said the work rule was
hard and fast. The only exceptions were those explicitly
spelled out in the C, C, and Rs; specifically real estate

agents and accountants, who were not allowed to meet clients at home but were allowed to do paperwork—which was why Maureen had not been cited in the letter. Barry was the first writer to live in Bonita Vista, and it was conceivable that there could be an exception made for his occupation in the future, but Chuck said the matter would have to be brought before the voting membership at the annual meeting in September. Until then, he would have to abide by the rules.

"Not selective enforcement after all," Maureen told him after relaying the message, and wasn't that a hint of triumph in her voice?

No. He was being paranoid. He was angry at her, though he didn't really have any right to be, and he went upstairs to the kitchen to get himself something to drink and to calm down before he said something he might later regret.

Afterward, he called Ray, who was of the same opinion as Mike: underneath all the sympathy and sincerity and heartfelt offers of assistance, the association people were loving this.

"Think I should talk to a lawyer?" Barry asked.

He could almost hear Ray's shrug over the phone. "It's your call. But if I were you, I'd save my money. These C, C, and Rs have been challenged in court too many times to count, and they've survived every attempt made on them. You might go over the regs yourself with a fine-tooth comb, see if you can figure out a loophole, but my guess is that they've got you on this one."

"What are they going to do if I refuse, if I just ignore the letter?"

Ray chuckled grimly. "You're opening up a whole other can of worms there. What they'll do first is hit you up with fines. That'll go on for quite a while, until the total is an outrageous sum that's almost impossible to pay. Then they'll call in their lawyer and put a lien on your property—"

"Can they do that?"

"Oh yeah."

"Are you speaking from experience?"

"They haven't done it to me. Not yet. But it's been done around here and I've known the people. Believe me, it's not pretty. If you can't find a legitimate loophole or find some way to argue your way out of this with the board, I suggest you start office hunting."

Barry spent the rest of the afternoon poring over their copy of the C, C, and Rs but to no avail. He called Mike that night, who called someone else who supposedly knew someone on the board, and though neither waivers nor petitions of appeal were mentioned in the association handbook, he was hoping to find someone in authority willing to let him slide.

No such luck.

He went to bed that night angry and frustrated. If he'd known he wouldn't be able to write in his own home on his own property, they never would have bought a house in Bonita Vista, he told Maureen. No matter how beautiful the scenery might be, this defeated the entire purpose of moving here, and if they hadn't already sunk so much money into it, he'd put the damn place up for sale and put Utah in his rearview mirror.

She didn't argue, didn't agree, remained silent, and they fell asleep on opposite sides of the bed, not touching.

In the morning, Barry once again tried to wade through the dense doublespeak of the C, C, and Rs, hoping the fresh perspective of a new day might grant him insight and allow him to see something he hadn't before, but if anything, the association's case looked even more airtight than before.

Maureen put a hand on his shoulder. "Find anything?" she asked.

He touched her hand, gave it a squeeze, last night's simmering hostility forgotten. "Not yet," he said.

"So what's the plan?"

He shook his head. "I don't know."

Jeremy was a lawyer, and Barry considered calling his friend for some free advice, but he thought about what Ray had said and decided to hold off for now.

He had a sneaking suspicion that he might be needing a lot of legal advice in the future.

Barry put away the handbook and stared out the window at the trees. He wondered if he might be able to set up a little office in their storage unit, and he drove down to Corban to check. As he'd known, the small space was completely full, piled high with boxes and furniture and all the extraneous crap they could not fit into the house. He stopped by the office on his way out and asked the old man behind the counter if it would be possible to rent another space and use it as a work room. The old man shrugged. "No law against it, I guess. But you'd have to keep the door closed except when loading and unloading. Company policy. And there's no lights inside and no electrical outlets. Gets pretty hot in there come June and July." He squinted as if visualizing something and shook his head. "Now that I think on it, maybe it ain't such a good idea."

Barry nodded.

"Not a bad thought you come up with, though. Storage units rented for office space. Somebody could make a fortune. Not here, though, not in Corban. Maybe in St. George or Cedar City . . ."

"Thanks for your time," Barry told him.

He got into the Suburban, looked out the dusty windshield for a moment, thinking. Realistically, there was only one option open to him, and he drove down to the real estate office, poked his head inside the trailer. "Is Doris here?"

The skinny woman seated behind the desk nearest the door called out, "Boss?" and a second later a familiar face peeked around the corner of the conference room.

Doris saw him and smiled. "Hey!" she said. "How's it going?"

"Fine."

"Give me a minute, will you? I'm sending a fax to one of the sellers. You can sit down at my desk there." She pointed. "Or you can—"

"That's okay," he told her. "I'll stand."

"I'll just be a minute."

Barry glanced around the office, saw an autographed photo of Pat Buchanan in a frame on one of the desks, amateur paintings of fish and wildlife on the paneled walls.

Doris emerged from the back room. "Sorry to keep you waiting. Is this business or pleasure?"

"Uh, business," he said, caught off guard.

"Just teasing. So how do you like living in Bonita Vista?"

"We love it," he said.

"No problems?" She smiled. "How do you like the homeowners' association?"

"Well . . ."

"Sorry I had to soft-pedal that, but it's my job."

"That's kind of what I'm here about."

"What can I do for you?" she asked sweetly.

"I need an office. The homeowners' association says I can't work at home, it's against their rules and regulations, so I have to find someplace else to write. I was wondering if there's a small room or something I can rent in town, maybe a—"

She put a hand on his arm. "Oh, I've got just the place! It's right in back of the coffee shop. Used to be a teapot museum, if you can believe that. Old Man Pruitt, who owned a lot of land in these parts some years back, had a wife who collected teapots. Antique teapots, china teapots, teapots from Russia and all over the world. Well, she got this idea in her head that she wanted to open up a teapot museum. I don't know who she thought would come to visit it. There aren't exactly a horde of tourists passing through here, and even if everyone in town came to see her collection—which not all of them did—it wouldn't take more than two days. But Old Man Pruitt built her a little building and set her up. It was hardly ever open, but she kept it until the day she died. That was back in the eighties. It's been empty ever since. Want to go over and take a look at it?"

"I'm not looking to buy anything," Barry told her. "I just want to rent."

"That's what I'm talkin' about, sugar. Bert from the coffee shop bought that property off Old Man Pruitt in case he ever wanted to expand or build a bigger parking lot or something. That little building's just been sitting there empty ever since, and I bet if we made him an offer he'd take it. He probably hasn't thought about it for years, and if he found out he could make a little cash on that shack just by doing nothing, he'd jump at the chance." She smiled, picked up her keys off the desk. "Come on. Let's go talk to Bert."

The coffee shop was only a block away, but Doris still wanted to drive rather than walk, and Barry figured that for an old real estate trick, an effort to ensure the customer would remain in her clutches and at her mercy until she decided it was time to let him go. But he got into her Buick without complaint, and the two of them drove down a narrow dirt backroad rather than the highway; a longcut it seemed to Barry, but one that allowed Doris the time to fill him in on Bert's eccentricities and convince him that it was smarter to stay silent and let her do all the talking.

It was midmorning, after breakfast but well before lunch, and the only customer in the coffee shop was a sour-looking old man eating eggs and toast at the counter. Doris waved to the teenage waitress. "Lurlene! Your daddy here?"

"Just a sec!" The girl disappeared into the kitchen and emerged a moment later with a short, skinny man sporting a crew cut and wiping his hands on a dishtowel.

"Bert!" Doris called out.

The man nodded, no discernible expression on his face. "Doris."

"I got a man here's interested in renting Pruitt's teapot museum from you."

"What?" He looked genuinely puzzled.

"I thought you were interested in making some extra money."

"Always."

"Well then. Mr. Welch here's a writer, lives up in Bonita Vista. The homeowners' association won't let him write at home, so he's looking for an office, someplace he can set up shop and work on his books. I knew you had that old museum sitting empty, and I thought the two of you might come to some agreement." She touched Barry's arm again in a way that seemed overly familiar.

Barry looked at her, and she smiled at him. There was a flirtiness that had not been there in Maureen's presence and which made him slightly uncomfortable. He should have brought Mo with him, was not sure why he hadn't, and he glanced quickly away.

"What're you thinking?" Bert asked. "Moneywise?" The question was addressed to Doris.

They hadn't discussed amounts, hadn't even speculated on a range, and before Doris committed him to something he was not willing to pay, Barry spoke up. "Why don't we look at the place first?"

"That's a fine idea," Doris agreed brightly. She turned her smile on Bert. "Want to let Lurlene hold down the fort for a few minutes while we go on back and check it out?"

Bert grunted noncommittally but put down his dishtowel.

"Don't worry, Daddy," Lurlene said, smiling. She nodded toward the old man at the counter. "I can handle this crowd."

They walked through the kitchen and out a back door.

The building was indeed small, Barry saw. The size of

their master bedroom. But it had windows, shelves, a built-in counter and electrical outlets. Most importantly, there was an adjoining closet-sized bathroom. Neither the water nor the electricity were turned on, and Bert said that Barry would have to pay for both, but at least they were hooked up. A giant cottonwood tree provided ample shade, and on the side of the building opposite the coffee shop, a green grassy meadow stretched all the way to a hill and the tree line.

"So how much would you say it was worth?" Bert asked.

Barry was about to say he'd be willing to pay a hundred a month plus utilities when Doris quickly stated, "Fifty a month." It was an offer, not a beginning bargaining point, and the flatness of her voice made it sound as though this were a take-it-or-leave-it proposition. She walked slowly around the room. "Lot of work to be done here, and Mr. Welch'll only be using it to write in. It's not like he's a lawyer or doctor renting a first-class suite with all the fixings."

Bert nodded. "Fifty a month's reasonable."

Doris held out her hand for Bert to shake. "Thanks, Bert. We'll go back to my office and discuss it, and I'll call you back. If everything's jake, I'll get some papers drawn up and we'll seal this agreement."

"I can kick you out anytime," Bert warned. "I bought that place because I want to expand, and if I need more parking lot or have to add on to the restaurant, I'll kick you out."

Barry nodded. "I understand."

"Okay then."

In the car on the way back to the real estate office, Doris laughed. "Kick you out. That's a hoot. Old Bert probably forgot he even had that place until we showed up and mentioned it to him."

"Thanks for stepping in there," Barry said. "I was about to offer a hundred a month."

"I thought you might go high." She smiled. "Didn't want you to cheat yourself. Even if it would've upped my commission."

"I can't commit to anything yet," he told her. "I have to call my wife first."

"Call her? Bring her on down! Look at it, think about it, discuss it. That shack ain't goin' anyplace. And no matter what Bert says, he has no other plans for that place. You're a godsend to him. Take all the time you need."

"Thanks," Barry said.

Doris winked at him. "Just doin' my job, sugar. Just doin' my job."

# SIXTEEN

In a way, the homeowners' association had done him a favor.

As much as Barry hated to admit it, working out of an office had opened up both his life and his work. He found that he liked spending his day in town, liked the contact with local characters and the sense that he was part of Corban's day-to-day life. His new novel had undergone a shift since he'd gotten out of the house, acquired depth and texture and a real-world sensibility. It was more mainstream now, more accessible, less insular and self-referential, and in an indirect way the homeowners' association was responsible.

He smiled wryly. Maybe he should thank them on the acknowledgments page.

Outside the window, a redheaded woodpecker swooped out of the cottonwood tree and disappeared into what looked like a microscopic hole in the eave of the coffee shop. It was a hot day, and the cicadas were out in force, their chirruping overpowering the fan hum of his computer and fading all other noise into background static. Inside, shaded by the massive cottonwood's thick foliage and giant branches, the air remained pleasant and temperate, but he could see shimmering heat waves distorting the air above the dirt road and knew that out in the open the temperature was anything but pleasant.

Barry saved what he'd written, shut off his computer, leaned back in his chair, and swiveled around. It was pretty neat having an office. He liked it. Ray Bradbury had an office. A lot of famous writers did. And there was something . . . official about it. He felt more professional, more successful, his writing suddenly seeming more like a vocation than an avocation.

Besides, he and Maureen were getting along better now that they were out of each others' hair.

And no longer had to share computers.

He checked his watch. Nearly noon—although his stomach could have told him that. Grabbing his wallet from the desktop, he locked up and walked across the field to the coffee shop.

He'd taken to eating lunch here each day rather than going home or bringing something he'd made himself. He was not the only one. The coffee shop seemed to be a favored hangout of many locals. And the food was not half bad. Besides, it couldn't hurt to patronize the business of his landlord. He might be able to stave off potential rent increases. Or get some free work done should the plumbing act up or the roof leak.

Barry pulled open the smoked glass door and felt the welcome chill of air-conditioning. The place was already starting to fill up, but his usual table by the restroom was free and he waved to Lurlene, grabbed himself a menu off the counter, and sat down.

He'd felt awkward the first time he'd come in here. He was not one for eating alone, was not one of those people who was comfortable without companionship in social settings. Being by himself in restaurants or movie theaters always made him feel self-conscious, as though everyone were staring at him, and though intellectually he knew that was not the case, he'd been sorely tempted to get his food to go and eat it in the office. But he forced himself to sit down at the counter and order lunch, and while he was fidgety and ill-at-ease, he managed to get through the meal unscarred.

He returned the next day. Barry was not good at meeting new people, at injecting himself into existing groups or conversations, but he was lucky enough this time to have Bert do it for him. He was seated at the counter, eating a cheeseburger, pretending to be proofreading a manuscript, and behind him, two old-timers were talking about *Kingdom of the Spiders*, a William Shatner horror movie that had been on one of the Salt Lake City stations the night before. The movie had been filmed in Camp Verde, Arizona, which was where one of the old-timers was from, and he was tearing apart the topography of the film, complaining that in one scene Shatner was driving *away* from the ranches he was supposedly heading toward, and that editing and selective shooting made the movie's downtown seem very different from what it was.

"It wasn't that they just shot the flick at Camp Verde," the old man said. "I could understand that. But they claimed it *was* Camp Verde. It wasn't supposed to be no made-up town or nothing. They were pawning it off as a real place."

"This guy here writes scary stories like that," Bert said from behind the counter, nodding toward Barry. "Maybe he knows why they do things like that."

Barry hadn't attracted any attention in the coffee shop on his first visit, had been ignored by the other customers as though he wasn't there. But all of a sudden the old man and his cronies took an interest in him, and Barry found himself the subject of serious attention. One old-timer even reached into his shirt pocket and put his glasses on in order to see better.

"I rent him the old museum out back," Bert went on. He sounded almost proud. "He writes his books back there."

The old man who'd been complaining about the movie squinted at him. "You a *famous* writer?" he asked.

Barry laughed. "I don't know how famous I am, but I make a living at it."

"What's your name?" one of the other men asked.

"Barry Welch."

There was shaking of heads all around.

"Never heard of him," someone said.

The complainer pushed his chair back, walked over to the counter, held out his hand. "Name's Hank Johnson. Pleased to meet you."

Barry smiled, shook the hand. "Likewise."

"So, as a writer, would you do something like that? Put in false stuff about a town even if you knew it wasn't true?"

"Writing is lying," Barry said. "We make things up, and if we put in real places or actual events, we change them to suit our story. We don't care about reality."

Hank nodded. "Makes sense. Ticks me off. But it makes sense."

"A helpful hint: don't watch *Kingdom of the Spiders* if you're looking for realism."

The old man chuckled. "You're all right, son. Come offa that counter there and eat with us. I got a lot a questions and I don't like standin' here this close to Bert. It's disturbing."

"Hey," Bert growled.

Barry picked up his plate and glass and followed Hank back to his table.

Ever since then, he'd been treated like one of the regulars, one of the gang, and that was another reason he was glad he'd been forced to rent the office. There was something gratifying about being a part of the workaday world rather than remaining apart and aloof, isolated in his hillside house in his gated community. It appealed to his egalitarian, democratic sense and made him feel as though he were a better person for it.

Lurlene came over and took his order—barbecued chicken sandwich and a Coke—and he nodded to Lyle and Joe over at the next table. "Where's Hank?" he asked.

"Can," Joe said simply.

Hank emerged a moment later, wiping his hands on his pants. He nodded at Barry, smiled. "Howdy, son. Hot enough for you?"

"Temperature's fine out in my little shack."

"Lucky bastard." Hank sat down in his usual spot at the adjacent table, gestured to Lurlene for some more iced tea.

At the next table over, Lyle cleared his throat. "Another dog got poisoned last night."

"No shit?"

"Bill Spencer's Lab, Bo. They found him facedown in his bowl, tied up right in the front yard. Guzman's going to do an autopsy on him this morning."

Hank shook his head. "Never liked Guzman. I take all my animals to Ryan. He's my pet and livestock vet."

"Yeah, but Guzman'll be able to tell what killed him."

"We already know what killed him. What's this make? Four dogs this year?"

"Somewhere around that."

"Six pets total if you throw in Abilene's cats," Joe offered.

"I never even heard about this," Barry said.

Hank nodded. "Been goin' on for a while. It's not regular, not consistent, but every month or two some dog'll be poisoned. Always happens in the middle of the night. It's bad enough for a man to come out and find his animal dead, but when it's kids that find the body, like with the Williamson girls . . ." Hank shook his head. "It just ain't right."

"And that walking piece of crap Hitman won't do a damn thing about it."

Hank snorted. "Hitman. There's a proper candidate for lynching."

Barry chuckled, but stopped when he realized that he was laughing alone. Hank wasn't serious, he wasn't proposing murder, but the sentiments behind the statement were anything but joking, and he understood, looking around the room, just how different he was from these people. This was a whole other world, and while he might be friendly with Hank and Joe and Lyle and some of the other regulars, he was just a visitor here.

A woman at one of the other tables spoke up. "Why don't the sheriff just arrest those bastards?"

"That's the sixty-four thousand dollar question."

Barry was incredulous. "You mean the sheriff knows who's doing this?"

"Everyone knows."

"Who is it?"

Lyle looked at him as though he were a moron. "Your homeowners' association."

The answer came as a complete shock, and Barry's first instinctive reaction was one of guilt by association—no pun intended. He was suddenly certain that everyone in the coffee shop held him at least partially to blame for the pet killings, but a quick look at the faces of his lunch buddies convinced him that such was not the case, that he was considered one of them—not one of *them*—and though he was filled with relief, he still felt at fault somehow, as if he had betrayed the people around him.

"The homeowners' association," he said dumbly.

Lyle nodded.

Hank spoke up. "It's true."

The expressions on the faces of the other men and women were grim.

Barry wished he could dismiss such a charge out of hand, but it was too easy to believe, and he had no trouble picturing a pet-killing committee dressed all in black, spreading out through Corban in the middle of the night to do away with dogs.

He thought of the dead cat in the mailbox, thought of Barney.

"But why would they do that?" he said aloud. "What's the point?"

Hank shrugged. "They're trying to extend their influence into town, trying to make us all into a part of their little kingdom. Corban's unincorporated, and they want to take over. We have no town council, so they figure they can call the shots."

"But no one's buying into it," Lyle said. "Their Master Plan just won't fly here."

Joe nodded. "So they're trying to *force* their lifestyle on us. *They* don't allow pets, so they start killing *our* pets."

"Next they'll be painting our houses for us, cleaning up our yards."

"Let 'em!" someone called from a booth near the door. "I'd appreciate some free maintenance work!"

There were scattered chuckles, even Lyle smiled, and the mood seemed to be broken. The tension that had been gathering over the coffee shop dissipated, and Lurlene brought over his Coke. "Sandwich's coming," she said.

"I'muna get me one of them motion detectors," Joe said. "Put it on in the backyard where I keep Luke tied up. Anyone comes snoopin' around in the middle of the night—blam!—all the lights'll go on, and I'll come out with my shotgun, blasting."

"Not a bad idea," Hank said. "Maybe everyone with a dog oughta do something like that."

Lyle nodded. "Maybe they should."

Barry walked back to his office after lunch feeling strangely unsettled, and though he immediately fired up the old computer and sat down before it, more than an hour passed before he finally started writing again.

He closed up shop late, time-fooled by the summer sun, but when he got home, Maureen was still down in her office, knee-deep in calculations. She was auditing the payroll expenses for Corban Title and Mortgage, and she informed him that she didn't have time to cook dinner and wasn't in the mood for any of the limited number of dishes *he* knew how to cook, so he was on his own tonight.

"No problem," Barry said. He went upstairs, microwaved a frozen pizza, and sat on the deck eating, watching the sun start its slow descent toward the canyons.

After depositing his plate and glass in the dishwasher, he told Maureen that he was going to go for a walk, get a little exercise, maybe stop by Ray's for a minute.

"Say hi to Liz for me," she said.

"Will do."

Barry hiked up the road to the top of the hill. It was still light out, but the world was suffused in an orange glow, and from this angle the Dysons' house looked like it was on fire, so bright was the reflection of the setting sun in the home's windows. Ray must have seen him walking up, because his friend was on the porch steps drinking a beer and waiting to greet him as Barry trudged across the gravel driveway.

Ray smiled. "Hey, stranger. What brings you up this way on a school night?"

"The homeowners' association."

Ray's smile faded. He nodded toward the front door. "In or out?"

"The weather's nice. Let's stay out here."

"Want something to drink?"

Barry shook his head. "That's okay. I just had dinner."

Ray took a sip of his beer, sighed. "So what's happened now?"

Barry told him about lunch at the coffee shop, the story of the poisoned pets and the conviction of the locals that the homeowners' association was responsible. "So what do you think?" he asked. "Do you think they're really killing off pets?"

Ray thought for a moment. "I doubt it," he said. "It's not that I think such a thing would be beneath them. It's just that I don't think they have any interest in things outside of Bonita Vista. The rest of the world could go to hell in a handbasket for all they care. As long as we're still safe up here, as long as the houses are painted the proper color and no one has an extra car in their driveway, all is right with their world."

"But like you said, they have the sheriff in their pocket. Maybe they want to expand their reach, take over Corban."

"Maybe," Ray said doubtfully. "But Hitman's in their pocket only when it comes to Bonita Vista matters. I'm not defending those assholes, you understand. But I really think that their interest lies here, that their only concern is what happens in our little area. They might kill *our* pets, but I don't think they'd cross the border and go outside their territory." He paused. "You know, it's not power they want, not specifically. It's power over Bonita Vista. It's hard to understand, at least for normal people like us, but they really do seem to have some sort of primal territorial feeling about this place, some sort of myopic localized interest that forces them to focus on Bonita Vista and Bonita Vista only. To the exclusion of everyplace else."

"The land under a gated community possesses evil energy and has some sort of hold over its residents, making them do horrible, unspeakable things." Barry smiled. "Sounds like the plot of one of my novels."

Ray nodded seriously. "You're right," he said. "It does."

"I was joking."

"I know."

But Ray was still not smiling, and he sipped his beer as he walked over to the side of the house and looked down on the town of Corban, where lights were beginning to flicker on against the coming darkness.

Barry watched him. His friend had been acting odd lately. Nothing specific, nothing overt, nothing concrete, but there'd be a vibe at strange moments, at strange times, that made Barry sense something was wrong. He'd hesitated to mention it before for fear that it was some sort of marital trouble, some problem between Ray and Liz, but that did not seem to be the case, and he cleared his throat and stood next to his friend. "Is . . . is there anything the matter?" he asked awkwardly.

"Nope."

He tried humor. "You don't seem your usual happy-go-lucky self."

Ray waved his hand dismissively, still not looking at him. "It's nothing. I'm just tired."

Barry let the matter drop. Maybe it *was* nothing. If it wasn't . . . well, no doubt his friend would talk to him when he was ready. It wouldn't do any good to push.

Ray looked away from the edge, glanced over at Barry. "Liz wants to have another party, a neighborhood get-together for all us outsiders. You and Mo game?"

"Sure."

Ray shook his head. "I'm getting too old for this shit. Never thought I'd say that, never thought I'd end up one of those old farts who just likes to sit on the couch and watch *Jeopardy*, but damn if that's not what I'm turning into." He sighed. "Getting old sucks. Don't let anyone tell you otherwise."

"I always knew it did," Barry told him.

His friend was silent for a moment, and when he finally spoke again, his voice was soft. "You don't want to cross them. The homeowners' association. There's no telling what they're capable of. The best thing you can do is just stay out of their way."

"Something *did* happen!" Barry said.

"No. Nothing did. Something could've. But nothing did."

"Then—"

"It's one thing for an old-timer like me to be defiant, have a high profile. They know me. I've been around for a long time, and . . . I'm tolerated. But someone new, some-one like you . . ."

"But nothing. I'm not afraid of those bastards."

"Maybe you should be."

"Why?"

Ray sighed. "Just try to stay out of their way," he said. "If they come after you, go at them full force. Use everything at your disposal to defend yourself. But don't go looking for trouble, that's all I'm saying. Don't put yourself in harm's way for no reason; for pride or stubbornness or principle. It's not worth it."

"Don't worry," Barry said. "I'm not stupid."

"I know you're not. I just want you to keep that in mind, though. Just keep that in mind."

They were late to the party. At the last second, Maureen got a call from a panicked client back in California who had just arrived home to find an IRS audit statement in his mailbox, and it took her ten minutes to calm him down and reassure him that there was nothing to fear, that everything for the past five years was in order, and that this was merely a random audit, not a red-flag situation. "Don't worry," she told him, "I'll take care of it."

She spent the next ten minutes quickly accessing computer records and looking through her file cabinets to make sure that what she'd told him was true.

So they were a half hour late getting to the Dysons'.

Liz answered the door. She gave each of them a big hug. "We were wondering what happened to you two!"

"Just some last-minute business," Maureen said.

Liz winked at her. "I understand."

"What does that mean?" Barry whispered as they walked into the living room. "Does she think we were fighting or fucking?"

Maureen hit his shoulder, gave him a stern look, then turned on her smile as she headed over to the punch bowl.

Barry felt a strong masculine hand slap his back. He turned to see Frank Hodges holding a Heineken and grinning hugely. "How goes it, bud? Haven't seen much of you since you took over the teapot museum."

"There aren't any teapots anymore. It's now home to perverted sex and violence."

Frank laughed heartily, slapped his back again. "Glad to hear it. That's the way things oughta be." He motioned across the room, where quite a few people seemed to be mingling by the windows. "Do you know Kenny Tolkin?"

The name didn't ring a bell. Barry shook his head. "I don't think so."

"Oh, you gotta meet Kenny." Frank led him through the crowd and around the couch. "He's the only person here with a job cooler than yours. Kenny is a career consultant to rock stars. Right, Kenny?"

The man standing before them elegantly holding a glass of red wine was tall, gray-haired, and distinguished look-ing—save for the gaudy blue patch over his left eye. He smiled. "'Artistic consultant' is what I'm calling myself now."

"Tell Barry here what you do."

Kenny laughed. "Frank . . ."

"Come on."

"I make pop stars into artists."

Frank nudged Barry with his elbow. "Listen to this."

Kenny shook his head and waved his hand, begging off. "No."

"Come on."

"I'd like to hear it," Barry admitted.

"Oh, all right." He smiled, paused, took a sip of his wine. "There comes a time in the career of most singers and musicians, if they're successful enough, when they want to be taken more seriously. When they have enough fame and fortune and start to crave critical respect. That's where I come in. For an outrageously inappropriate fee, I choreo-graph a media campaign, stage interviews, and go over lyrics in order to make rock critics think my clients are serious artists. Music journalists are probably the most gullible people on the planet, and they're desperately willing to buy into the fantasy. I remember one time Kurt Cobain showed up for an interview wasted and wearing a dress, and the interviewer wrote a glowing piece on how Cobain was 'challenging gender stereotypes.'" Kenny laughed. "So it's not as hard as you might think to con these people into believing that a twenty-two-year-old high school dropout is now making profound observations about the human condition."

"So how do you do it?" Barry asked.

Kenny smiled. "Trade secret. But I will clue you in on two important words: spiritual journey. It's my most tried-and-true method. I take some of that godawful drivel these kids are writing, slip in a few references to fate or a higher power, tell them to stay out of the limelight for six months and to inform everyone that they're 'recharging' their spiritual batteries. Voila! Instant artist. They return from their hiatus with a new respect from critics who now laud their artistic growth and ambition."

It was an interesting occupation, Barry had to admit, and one that he had not even known existed until now. One of those new entrepreneurial jobs that the high-techies were always talking about.

Still, it was Kenny's eye that had really piqued Barry's curiosity.

Horror writer-itis rearing its head once again.

He casually glanced at the blue patch. How many people lost eyes these days? And how many of them wore patches? It seemed anachronistic, slightly exotic, like something out of another era. But he knew it would be impolite to ask about, and he was resigned to the fact that neither Frank nor Kenny was likely to bring up the subject.

Hell, maybe the man's eye was fine. Maybe pirate chic was big in the rock world these days and Kenny was just riding the cresting wave of the trend.

Once again, he felt Frank's hand slap his back. "Barry here's a writer. Like Stephen King."

Kenny looked intrigued. "Is that so?"

"I'm a horror writer," Barry admitted.

"Published, I assume?"

He smiled. "I wouldn't call myself a writer if I wasn't. In fact, I wouldn't be calling myself a writer unless I was making a living at it."

"You're a rare breed. I know writers who've never even *written* anything."

Barry chuckled. "So do I."

"Have any of your novels been optioned for film?"

"Not yet, no."

"I have some contacts in the film industry," Kenny said. "I'll ask around for you. Put in a good word. If I'm not imposing or overstepping my bounds."

"Wouldn't you like to read one first to make sure I'm not a complete hack?"

"Hacks sell their stuff to Hollywood all the time. Hackdom's no drawback in the film industry. Not that I think you are one," he added quickly.

Barry smiled. "No offense taken."

"Besides, if Frank and Ray vouch for you, that's good enough for me. I'm always ready to help a fellow outcast."

Frank was beaming.

It seemed odd to Barry that someone with connections in the music and film industries would have a place out here in the middle of nowhere—but he was a novelist and refugee from California himself and should be the last person to generalize and stereotype about the type of people attracted to Bonita Vista. Again, he wondered about the patch, and he thought that maybe, despite the professorial appearance, Kenny Tolkin was like Norman Maclean, one of those outwardly cultured men with a rough-and-tumble rural background. It made as much sense as anything else.

"You know," Frank said, "with talents like you two, we

oughta be able to bring the fucking homeowners' association to its knees."

"I take it you're having a problem with the association?" Kenny derisively pronounced the word *ASS-ociation*.

"You could say that. I got a notice yesterday that I have to repaint the trim on my house. I just painted it last year, but apparently their inspectors found minute spots that are peeling on the south side, the side exposed to the sun. So either I try to find a massive ladder tall enough to reach the roof on the hill side and risk breaking my neck, or I shell out big bucks to have it painted."

Kenny shook his head. "That certainly sounds familiar. Last fall, I received notice that I was to resurface the asphalt on my driveway. I'd had it done only the month before."

"So did you?"

"Hell no. I hosed off the driveway, sprayed off the dirt, and it looked as good as new. I called up and told them I'd done it, and I haven't heard back from them since."

"Maybe I should just tell them I did it," Frank said. "Make them go up again and inspect it. *Then* have it done."

They all laughed.

Barry told how he'd gotten a notice to paint the chimney cap for their wood-burning stove and to pick up pinecones on the property. "There was one damn pinecone," he said. "One! And for that they gave me a written notice?"

"Did you paint your chimney cap?"

"I had to hire someone to do it. Some guy named Tom Peterman, who didn't even come out himself but sent his son up to do it. A week late."

"Be prepared to paint it again next year," Frank said morosely. "Peterman's the one who did my trim."

Kenny chuckled. "Welcome to rural America."

Gradually, other partygoers started gathering around, people with their own complaints, their own tales of confrontation and capitulation, and, like the previous party, it soon became a round-robin, with one homeowner relating a horror story while the others listened, and then another taking his turn after that. It was what they all had in common, this hatred of the homeowners' association, it was why the Dysons had brought them all together, probably why they had become friends with Ray and Liz to begin with. Barry had never been a joiner, had always had a deep fear and distrust of groupthink, but the tribal aspect of this made him feel surprisingly positive. It was empowering, knowing that there were others like you, that different people felt the same things you felt, had the same reactions to things that you did.

Greg Davidson dropped the evening's biggest bombshell.

"We're leaving," he said. "We can't afford to live in Bonita Vista anymore." He put an arm around his wife, Wynona.

The Davidsons had been quiet through most of the diatribes, not registering much interest or enthusiasm in the anti-association rants that had become the party's focal point. That was unusual. Barry didn't know Greg well, but from what he'd seen at the Dysons' earlier get-together, the man was not shy about speaking his opinion and was a very vocal opponent of the association.

Mike Stewart put a hand on Greg's shoulder. "What happened?"

Greg glanced around the room without meeting anyone's eyes. "It's the association. They've been targeting us for a long time, and . . . we just can't fight them anymore." He sounded as though he were about to cry.

"It's the gate," Wynona explained.

Barry was confused. "You can't afford to live here because of the gate?"

"They put that gate in to get rid of us."

Mike shook his head. "I don't think—"

"Hear me out." Greg took a deep breath. "We voted against the association on the last ballot. We knew it was a risk, but I couldn't justify supporting them anymore, and I didn't want . . . I was tired of just caving in." There were nods of understanding all around, but Greg must have seen the look of incomprehension on Barry's face. "You're new," he said. "You haven't been through one of their elections. Or one of the farces they call elections."

"No," Barry admitted.

"They coincide with the annual meeting on Labor Day weekend. You'll get a ballot, and on it will be the names of the current board members. Next to each name will be a box that says 'Approve.' And that's it. There are no other candidates running, there is no space to put in a write-in candidate, there's not even a 'Disapprove' box. So all you can do is ratify the existing board."

"It's true," Mike said.

"I don't know why they even waste time on such a charade, but I suspect there's some sort of legal requirement that homeowners' associations hold yearly elections and this is their way of getting around that. Anyway, I was tired of supporting those assholes. In the past, we just didn't bother to vote. We threw away our ballot. But this time, I made my own boxes next to the 'Approve' boxes, and I wrote in, 'Impeach.' Needless to say, it did not go over well. I received a threatening letter warning me to cease and desist from making libelous and disparaging remarks about board members. I wrote back that I could find no bylaw forbidding me from saying whatever the hell I wanted about board members, and I pointed out that my attempt to institute a free election was hardly disparaging or libelous."

"Then they put in the gate," Wynona said.

Greg nodded. "Then they put in the gate. Well, not right then. A few months later. But we knew the reason."

Barry looked over at Maureen, who was frowning. "I'm sorry," he said. "I'm lost."

Greg glanced around embarrassedly. "We don't exactly . . ." He sighed. "Bonita Vista is a little out of our

range. We loved this place and we wanted to live here, and
with a little creative financing we were able to swing it, but
we were always hanging on by a thread. The association
knew that. So they decided to just . . . push us over the
edge. They couldn't get us on any of their precious techni-
calities, they couldn't find a single rule or regulation that
we'd broken or even bent, so about six months ago, they
decided to turn Bonita Vista into a gated community." He
held up a hand. "I know they said it was for other reasons,
and, who knows, that might have been part of it. I'm sure
they did want to prevent vandalism and burglaries and keep
out the locals and prevent outsiders from driving on our fair
streets, but the timing of it . . ." He shook his head. "What
they really wanted to do was increase the property values of
the homes up here in order to increase property taxes. They
knew we couldn't afford an increase, that it would drive us
out.

"And now it has."

"We got our property tax bill from the mortgage company," Wynona said.

"And we owe nearly a thousand dollars. There's no way
in hell we can pay that. We're in debt as it is."

"Maureen here's an accountant," Mike offered. "Maybe
she'd be willing to look over your finances, see if there's
some way—"

"Sure," Maureen said quickly. "I'd be happy to."

Greg smiled painfully. "Thanks for the offer, but no. We
know when we're licked, and we're not about to get ourselves in deeper just out of spite. The game's over. They've
won. And we're going to turn tail and run as far away from
Bonita as humanly possible."

"But your job . . ." Mike said.

"I'm quitting. We're selling the house and starting anew
in Arizona. My brother lives in Phoenix and thinks he can
get me a job at Motorola." He looked out the window. "I
was born in Corban," he said. "So was Wy. And ever since

I was a teenager, all I wanted was to be able to afford a house in Bonita Vista. It seemed like a paradise to me, and I thought if I ever got in here I'd be happy, things'd be perfect. But it's been a hellhole." He turned to face the gathered guests. "You guys've all been great. But most of the people here . . ." He shook his head.

Ray emerged from one of the back rooms. He'd been MIA for the past hour, and Barry wasn't sure how much he'd heard, but he'd obviously heard some of it. Just as obviously, he'd had a little too much to drink. "Fuck the association," he said, walking into the center of the room. "Those bastards can kiss my ass!"

There were echoes of support: "Yeah!" "You tell 'em!" "Damn straight."

"You're not going anywhere," he told the Davidsons. "We'll all chip in and pay your property tax. Hell, I'll pay the whole damn thing myself if I have to!" He put a boozy arm around Greg's shoulder. "We can't let those bastards win."

Both Greg and Wynona were shaking their heads. "I can't let you do that," Greg said firmly. "Besides, we've made up our minds. We're leaving. We're through with this place."

But Ray was on a roll. "Civil disobedience. That's what we need here. If we *all* rebelled, if we *all* refused to follow orders and go along with their dictates, there's nothing they could do about it."

"There's more of them than there are of us," Mike pointed out.

"Then we'll kick their asses! I threw one of those peckerheads off my lot last month, and he went running home to Momma. They're cowards! I'm telling you, we get a group of men together, men who have something between their legs, and when one of us gets a notice or an ultimatum, we all march over to the board members' houses and beat the living shit out of them!"

"Yeah!" Frank said.

The rally went on from there.

Despite the Davidsons' depressing story, Barry walked home at midnight feeling pumped up. The ideas Ray and his increasingly drunk guests came up with for thwarting the homeowners' association were outlandish and ridiculous, but the spirit was there, and that made him feel good. Such sustained and unanimous hatred of the homeowners' association gave him hope.

It had been over a week since he and Maureen had made love, but they made up for it that night in a marathon session that brought to mind the early days of their marriage. By the time he finally settled down to sleep, he was dead tired, and in his dreams Neil Campbell arrived at his garage sale with his prissy mouth and his clipboard, and Barry beat the tar out of him.

# SEVENTEEN

Maureen awoke with nothing to do.

It was not something to which she was accustomed, and while she'd known that this was bound to happen, she was still not entirely sure how to deal with it. She was not a workaholic, not by any stretch of the imagination, but she was not a slacker either, and while Barry could easily sit around all day staring into space and contemplating his navel, she was not wired for sloth, did not know how to enjoy huge blocks of free time. She was used to having a job, a regular job with regular hours, and even her week-ends and vacation days had always been planned out, her leisure time structured.

But as of yet there wasn't enough work here to keep her occupied on a full-time basis. She'd known that and she'd told herself to stretch things out, but she wasn't wired for procrastination either, and, as always, she'd done the best job she could in the quickest time possible. The fiscal year-end was coming up for most of her California clients, and two weeks from now she'd be so busy that she wouldn't have time for sleep . . . but for now she had nothing to do. Even her gardening was all caught up. She'd watered and weeded yesterday, trimmed dead flowers and fed the plants, so unless she wanted to start repainting the house, she was out of luck.

Kicking off the sheet and sitting up, Maureen looked

down at her still-flat stomach. She and Barry had often discussed having children, and she couldn't help thinking that a baby would provide her with plenty of work to fill up these empty hours.

But she felt guilty for even *speculating* about having a child for such a selfish reason. It was as bad as those accountants—and she knew quite a few of them—who planned their children's birth dates in order to get the maximum tax credits.

She sighed. At least when Barry had been home, she'd had someone to talk with. But with him at his office, she was alone and on her own.

Maybe she'd go down and meet him for lunch, she thought. That might be fun.

And on the way back she could stop over and see Liz. Or drop in on Tina Stewart, who'd been asking her to come by and see the new roses she'd planted.

Maureen hopped out of bed, feeling better. There *were* things to do, she was not entirely at loose ends, and the gloom that had threatened to engulf her only a few moments before disappeared completely, replaced with a more familiar and welcome feeling of energized purpose.

As she ate breakfast and listened to Howard Stern, whose show they got on a powerful and remarkably clear radio station out of Las Vegas, she decided to start her morning with a little exercise. It was a weekday, the tennis courts were no doubt empty, and she thought she'd hit a few balls, practice her serve, start using this free time wisely and get into shape. Afterward, she'd take a shower, then pack a lunch and surprise Barry down at his office. Maybe they'd even go on a picnic.

Maureen changed out of the jeans she'd put on and slipped into a pair of shorts. She grabbed her racket and a can of balls from the closet and jogged down the hill to the tennis courts.

As she'd known, as she'd hoped, there was no one playing, she had the courts to herself, and she picked the left court, the one nearest the trees, standing in alternate corners and hitting balls into the opposite squares. Serving was the weakest part of her game, and although she and Barry were pretty evenly matched, if she could tighten up her serve, that might tilt the balance in her favor.

A red Mustang roared down the street, sliding to a late-braking stop in the small gravel parking space adjacent to the tennis courts. Beat-heavy music thumped from behind dark tinted windows, and a moment later two teenage boys hopped out of the vehicle, rackets in hand. One was blond, one had black hair, both were scruffy, and Maureen saw them and then looked immediately away, not wanting to make eye contact. She wanted to practice on her own, without interference, and she kept hitting balls, ignoring the newcomers.

But that soon grew hard to do.

The boys had brought several cans of balls with them, but she could see out of the corner of her eye that they merely hit the same ball lightly back and forth, not playing a real game, not even putting effort into a decent volley. They seemed more interested in their conversation, a disgustingly graphic and obviously exaggerated account of their sexual exploits that grew louder and louder with the telling.

Part of her wanted to tell them to either quiet down or take it somewhere else, but they looked like the kind of kids who'd talk back, and the last thing she wanted was to start a verbal volley with these punks and have to stand there and argue with them for the next twenty minutes. It was easier to just let it slide and try to ignore them.

As if reading her mind, they took the volume up another notch.

"She had one of those skanky pussies, man. Smelled like she'd been shitting out of *that* hole, if you know what I mean."

"Been there, done that."

"I ate her anyway, though. Just held my breath and chowed down for Old Glory."

There was a harsh laugh of recognition in response, and Maureen picked up one of her balls and casually glanced over at the next court. She was nonplussed to see that both of the teenagers were staring at her.

"I hear tell those bitches from California have twats of gold," the blond kid said. "Taste like honey."

He smiled in a way that made her feel as though she needed to take a shower, and Maureen looked quickly away. She glanced up at the security camera, grateful that it was there. She wanted to pack up her stuff and leave, but she didn't want those punks to think they were driving her off, that she was afraid of them, so she finished picking up her balls and moved to the next corner on her rotation, continuing to practice her serve. One ball went into the net and she walked forward to retrieve it.

A tennis ball flew over from the next court, smacked her square in the back.

She straightened up. "Hey!" she called out angrily. "Watch where you're hitting!"

The dark-haired boy laughed harshly, and the thought occurred to her that it had not been an accident.

She turned away, and two balls came whizzing over. One sped past her head close enough that she felt the breeze, and the other hit the back of her bare right calf with a loud slap. The pain was tremendous, she was sure there'd be a welt, and, furious, she picked up the ball and swung her racket, hitting the ball over the fence and into the trees. She walked purposefully over to where their other ball lay, intending to swat that over the fence as well, but two more balls came at her, each of them hitting her hard in the buttocks.

She'd had enough. She was leaving. And if either of those two shits tried to stop her or harass her in any way, she was going to take her racket and smash it across his smirky face. She grabbed her can from where she'd placed it by the fence and began picking up balls. Hers were easy to identify: dull old-fashioned grayish white as opposed to their fluorescent yellow-green.

The last one was caught in the chain-link fence near the border of the two courts, an attempted serve that had gone wild. Below it was one of their balls, and as she walked over, she saw that the blond kid was coming over to get his ball as well. She slowed her pace.

He slowed his.

Clearly, he intended to reach the spot the same time she did, and though she definitely didn't want to meet up with him, she also didn't want to show any fear.

Her grip tightened on the racket.

They reached the fence at the same time, and she ignored him as she pulled her ball from the chain link and dropped it into her can.

Blondie dropped to his knees to pick up his ball.

"Aren't you from California?" he asked. Smiling, he licked his lips suggestively and looked at her crotch.

Maureen felt violated, and she wanted nothing more than to take off the top of his scalp with her racket, but she pulled away in as dignified a manner as she could muster.

"Go to hell," she said coldly.

Both of the boys laughed, but neither tried to stop her as she walked back across the court to the exit.

She checked out the license plate of the Mustang and committed the numbers to memory. She'd call Chuck Shea when she got home, sic the association on those assholes. Or on their parents. Someone needed to take responsibility, and at this moment she didn't care who. If Chuck thought it best to fine the kids' dads or double their dues or kick them out of Bonita Vista entirely, well, they had her permission.

But on her way back up the hill, she saw something that made her change her mind.

Or rather some*one*.

He was standing across the culvert to her right, in front of a low wooden house with too few windows. She had not noticed the house before, so unobtrusive was it and so far back was it set, but she noticed it now because of the man. He was at least six-foot-five, with a shock of white Lorne Greene hair that seemed incongruous atop his unlined baby face. But it was the crutches that drew her attention. That and his missing leg. For he stood there watching her, supported by the tallest metal crutches she had ever seen, crutches that glinted in the sun and shined in her eyes. The long left leg of his tan pants was filled out with his remaining limb, but the empty right pant leg dangled there, swaying gently in the air, rather than being pinned up or cut off.

Maureen tried to smile, gave a wave and an anonymous, pleasant "Hi," but the man swung away and hobbled back toward the house more quickly than she would have thought possible. There was fear in his flight, a fear that she had glimpsed on his face in the brief second before he turned away, and she looked immediately behind her to make sure there wasn't an approaching bear or murderous criminal, but of course there was not. She was the only one on the road, and she watched him hop up the gravel driveway and disappear into the house.

A moment later, she saw his face at one of the small windows staring at her and scowling.

Despite his obvious fear, something about the man seemed threatening to her, and she hurried on up the road. Again she thought of the association, of telling them that this weirdo had been bothering her, trying to scare her, but she stopped herself. Where was this going to end? Was she going to run crying to the association every time life wasn't perfect, every time she encountered a minor inconvenience or saw something slightly out of the ordinary?

She had changed her mind about calling Chuck, and it took her a moment to realize why.

She didn't want to be beholden to the homeowners' association.

That was a strange way to think. She and Barry paid dues, and she had every right to expect that they be provided services for those dues. And the association had helped her out with that lunatic Deke Meldrum and had not asked for anything in return. But the feeling remained that by asking for help she would be calling in a favor, a favor that would be expected to be repaid at some time in the future.

As much as she tried to deny it, as much as she refused to admit it, she seemed to have bought into Ray's and Barry's paranoid mind-set. Of course, the fact that nearly everyone at the Dysons' party had had association horror stories lent their paranoia a certain amount of credence, but it was not logical arguments or recitations of actual events that swayed her, it was her own nebulous feeling that . . . that if she called on the association for help, she would *owe* them.

What if, she wondered (and here she was *really* edging into Barry and Ray territory), those two teenagers at the tennis courts had been sent over specifically to harass her, in the hopes that she *would* call the homeowners' association and thus be indebted to them?

That was ridiculous, but although her other thoughts were almost as ridiculous, she did not discount them, and she hurried up the last section of hill, feeling better only after she was safely back inside the house with the door shut and locked behind her.

# EIGHTEEN

•

Ray spent the morning sanding and re-staining the deck. It probably didn't need to be painted for another year, but he liked to keep on top of things, liked to have the house looking good. Besides, he knew it drove the homeowners' association crazy that they couldn't cite him for neglect.

Although they'd no doubt find something to jump on his ass about. They always did.

He took a shower afterward, scrubbing his arms with Ajax in an effort to get the redwood stain off his skin. He was reaching around, trying to clean off his elbow, when the shower door was pulled open.

He let out a startled cry.

Six men stood in his bathroom, staring at him.

It was not Neil and Chuck and Terry this time, not the underlings or the toadies, not the newcomers. It was the board. The old men who ruled and ran the association. They stood close together in the confined space, faces partially obscured by shower steam, draped in the absurdly decorated judicial robes that they used when presiding over meetings.

Ray shut off the water. "Get the hell out of my house," he ordered.

The steam was clearing, he could see their faces.

The treasurer looked at his shriveled, dangling genitals. "You call yourself a man?"

Ray's heart was thumping hard enough to burst, and he was filled with a deep consuming terror unlike anything he had ever known. He had never seen any of these men up close before—not this close, at least—and they were older than he'd thought, their skin wrinkled and almost translucent, like ancient parchment.

There was also . . . something else about them. Something strange and undefinable that he could not quite place but that frightened him to the bone.

The president stepped forward. He was not snickering, and there was no smile on his face, only righteous anger. "Neil warned you, told you to behave." His voice was quiet but growing stronger, tone and volume steadily mounting. "I thought he and his committee made it abundantly clear that we would not put up with any more of your *shit*!" One knuckled fist hit the side wall, causing Liz's perfume bottles to shake on their shelf.

The other men were nodding assent.

Ray wanted to step calmly out of the shower stall, dry himself with a towel, and put on his bathrobe as they lectured him. But they were all pressing closer, and he knew that would not be possible. His heart rate accelerated, and though he tried to respond, tried to say something, his mouth would not cooperate and all it did was cough.

The treasurer casually picked up Liz's can of hairspray. There was nothing casual going on here, though, and Ray steeled himself to be sprayed in the face, in the eyes.

Instead, the old man cocked his arm back and threw the metal can as hard as he could at Ray's midsection. The bottom rim connected solidly with Ray's stomach, drawing blood and a gasp of pain. The can clattered to the floor of the shower stall.

"I thought everything was made clear," the president said. "I thought you understood."

This was it, Ray knew. There was no way they could expect to get away with this sort of harassment, no way they could think that he would not turn them in to the authorities. They could not expect to shut him up after invading his house like this.

Not unless they planned to kill him.

And that's exactly what the feeling in his gut told him was about to happen.

He saw all the evidence he needed in the president's eyes.

The bathroom seemed to be getting smaller as the six black-robed men pressed forward, advancing on him. Ray looked around desperately, trying to figure out some way to get by them, some means of escape, but the only window was a small opaque one above the toilet, and the board members had taken up all available space between the shower and the door.

He was trapped.

They weren't wearing gloves, he noticed, and a wild optimism flared within him. They'd left their fingerprints all over the doorknobs and anything else they'd touched. So maybe they weren't planning to take this all the way.

At the very least, if worse came to worst they'd be caught. Even Hitman couldn't shield them from a murder rap, not with Liz on their backs.

"We heard that you were rabble-rousing, inciting rebellion, telling people to—" He inhaled deeply, grimacing, obviously having difficulty even speaking the words. "—ignore the C, C, and Rs."

There'd been a spy at the party, a traitor, and Ray quickly ran down a list of names and faces, trying to figure out who'd betrayed them.

Frank, he thought. It had to be Frank.

*Everyone's an informant.*

He should have heeded his own dictum, not been so open in his dissent, so free and easy with his opinions. He had not entirely trusted Frank since the man had tried to defend the association after Barry's cat had been killed, and

Ray should have been more circumspect around him. Hell, he shouldn't have invited him to the party.

But he had always been one to see the best in individuals, even those who belonged to organizations and institutions he distrusted, and he had given Frank the benefit of the doubt.

Ray looked into the angry eyes of the president. The smart thing to do would be to deny everything, to explain that he was drunk at the time, to bow down to the board and kiss their asses. But he had the feeling that nothing would make any difference, so he stood up straight. "I did," he admitted. "And I told them, 'Fuck the association!'"

"You worthless little shit." The president came at him. And pushed.

Ray slipped, fell backward, hit his head. There was a flash of horrendous pain, the warm feel of blood gushing from beneath his scalp, and he closed his eyes and lay there unmoving, hoping they would think they'd killed him, hoping this would be the end of it.

But people were that stupid only in movies. These six were not about to *assume* anything, were not about to walk away without checking whether their attempts to kill him had been effective, and as he lay there bleeding and in agony, trying to feign lifelessness, he was yanked out of the shower by his leg. His head hit the edge of the stall, and bleeding erupted from a new fissure behind his ear. He opened his eyes, but his vision was strobing and be could not see. There was only a moving blackness against a pale blurred background: the robed figures of the board encircling him.

Other hands grabbed his arms. He was pulled into a modified standing position and dragged out of the bathroom, into the hallway, into the kitchen. On the way, he was unceremoniously slammed against doorjambs and table edges and countertops.

The battering seemed to restore some of the clarity to his

vision. He could now see where he was, and he both saw and felt the vice president grab his right wrist and use it to swat the wall phone. Pain flared up his arm, and the receiver was knocked off the hook.

He was dragged out to the living room, his right knee forced into the corner of the coffee table, drawing blood, his shoulder shoved against a potted palm stand, knocking the plant over.

The vice president opened the door to the deck.

He realized what was happening now, he understood what they were doing. They were making it appear as though he'd slipped in the shower and hit his head. Suffering from a disorienting head wound, he'd then staggered out of the bathroom, made his way to the kitchen where he attempted to dial 911, but, baffled and confused, he wandered into the living room, then onto the deck.

Where he fell over the railing and died.

It would look like an accident, he realized. No one would know that he'd been murdered.

As much as he hated himself for it, he began to scream, and to his horror his screams were the high-pitched yelps of a frightened woman. The board members were laughing and joking about his manhood as they pressed his right palm against the sliding glass door and rammed his genitals against the metal door frame. He kept screaming, and there was no thought behind it. He was not trying to frighten them off or attract attention from possible passersby, he was screaming because he had to. It was an instinctive reaction, an innate response.

They pulled him onto the deck.

He wanted to remain cool; disdainful toward them to the end. He wanted to make cutting remarks that would wound and hurt them, that they would think about after he was dead, but he could not do that. He simply screamed those girlish screams as the men held his body and smashed it repeatedly against the railing until a just-painted two-by-four came loose.

He could feel nothing below the waist, but his arms were working and he could still see through the blood, and he attempted to break his fall as he flew through the air and landed with a bone-crushing thud on the rocky soil of the wooded sloping hillside.

*He was still alive.*

The realization filled him not only with hope and an insane glee but with the unshakable desire for revenge. Despite their best efforts, the board had been unable to eradicate him, and their ineffectiveness would be their downfall. He did not know if he could move, if he was paralyzed or simply badly injured, but he knew enough to remain still. They were no doubt watching from above, and it would be best to play dead for a while. He could check his vital signs later.

But there was no later.

He must have drifted into unconsciousness because in what seemed like seconds, he was squinting through half-closed lids and drying blood at the feet of the board members. They were implacable, and more than anything else it was their relentlessness that finally sapped the last of his will and hope. Ray opened his eyes, not caring if they knew. He saw the president accept a large rock from one of the other board members, place it on the sloping ground inches from his face, then methodically repeat the procedure.

He felt several sets of hands lift the top half of his body, and he understood what they were going to do.

Please, he thought. Let it be quick and painless.

But no death was quick, he realized, no death was painless. And in a second that seemed to last an hour, that realization was brought home to him in a very profound and personal way.

# NINETEEN

**The Bonita Vista Homeowners' Association Covenants, Conditions, and Restrictions** Article IV, General Provisions, Section 6, Paragraph A:

*Punishment for noncompliance with the terms of these Covenants, Conditions, and Restrictions is to be determined by unanimous consent of the Bonita Vista Homeowners' Association Board of Directors.*

# TWENTY

After the funeral, they all went back to Liz's, where even with the large gathering of people, the house seemed curiously empty. Maureen, along with Audrey Hodges and Tina Stewart, had made the food and organized the informal social. The three women were gamely trying to get Liz involved, to keep her occupied with small details and thus prevent her from dwelling obsessively on her husband's death, but even amid the low buzz of multiple conversations, Ray's loss was acutely felt, and Barry could not help thinking how lonely this house would seem once all the people were gone and Liz was by herself.

He stood with Frank and Mike, and the three men watched their wives shunt a zombified Liz across the living room to refill an hors-d'oeuvre plate. They were talking about road construction on the highway that had narrowed the route to Interstate 15 down to two lanes. They *had* been talking about baseball . . . and the weather . . . gas prices . . . anything except Ray. They didn't know each other well enough to open up, to be emotionally truthful and share their feelings, and the three of them had been assiduously avoiding the one subject they'd each been thinking about. Ray had been the catalyst between them, the one who enabled them to speak honestly in front of one another, and with him gone there was a stiltedness to their interaction. He felt the way he had when Todd Ingalls, his best friend from kindergarten through third grade, had moved away and he'd been forced to play with John Wakeman, a casual friend, a backup friend, someone with whom he eventually found out he had almost nothing in common. Now Frank and Mike were his backup friends, and while they seemed like good guys, it was not the same, not the same at all.

He hadn't realized how much he had come to rely on Ray, how close the two of them had become. There was deep sorrow within him when he thought about the old man, and as he looked out the windows at the crowded deck, it hit him that they would never again sit out there barbecuing and discussing the Big Issues. Or just shooting the breeze. It was as though a huge chunk of his life had simply been cut out and discarded, and what was left behind was a painful emptiness.

Along with the sadness, however, there was anger. He had not yet figured out how, but he knew in his gut that the association had been involved in Ray's death. Not directly, that's not the way they worked, but in a circumspect, roundabout way, not doing the deed themselves but bringing about the circumstances that allowed it to happen. From across the room, he caught the eye of Greg Davidson, who nodded a weary hello. Greg and Wynona, he knew, were moving out this week, priced out of their own home by Bonita Vista's gate. *That's* how the association operated. They were facilitators.

He thought about Deke Meldrum, lying dead in the ditch as a crowd gathered in the darkness.

Sometimes they were direct, though. Sometimes they did the dirty work themselves.

*There's no telling what they're capable of.*

Maureen and the other wives brought Liz by to say hello and accept condolences, and the three men reiterated what they'd said at the funeral, how sorry they were for her loss, how much they'd miss Ray, he was a great friend. Barry kept his words short and sweet. He was unnerved by the listlessness of Liz's gaze. It was like looking at a completely different woman than the one he knew, and he glanced at her for only brief seconds before turning his attention back to Maureen. It was pathetic and heartless and selfish and self-centered, but he felt extremely uncomfortable. He was not one of those people who was good with the sick or the troubled or the dying. He could *write* about it, but in real life he was a complete washout when it came to offering others emotional support. Thank God there were people like Maureen, who always knew the right thing to do and who had the constitution to follow through.

"Can you help us in the kitchen for a moment?" Maureen asked.

"Sure." He followed the women, leaving Frank and Mike to their own devices.

Audrey and Tina busied themselves at the sink and dishwasher, while Maureen led him over to the breakfast nook, where an old leather suitcase sat atop the table. She glanced toward Liz and lowered her voice. "Ray's books," Maureen said. "For some reason, she packed a whole bunch of them in this suitcase and then put the suitcase here on the kitchen table. I don't know how she even lifted the thing. We could barely move it."

Barry nodded. Grief did strange things to people, and somehow this irrational act, more than anything that had gone before, more than the words and the tributes and the funeral itself, brought home to him the enormity of Ray's passing. Liz had obviously loved him a lot.

"What do you want me to do with it?"

"Take it into his den," Maureen whispered. "Just get it out of the way. We'll figure things out later."

He nodded. Grabbing the handle of Ray's suitcase, feeling the heaviness of the books inside, the anger rose within him. "God *damn* that homeowners' association," he said. "I know those bastards are behind this."

He was speaking to Maureen rather than Liz, but it was Liz who reacted, who responded to his accusation. She strode over, her gaze hardened, suddenly focused. "I don't want to hear anything about that association stuff," she said fiercely. "That craziness was why he was out there on that deck to begin with. If he hadn't been so paranoid about those people, he'd probably be alive today."

Barry said nothing. He did not want to argue with her, did not want to cause her even more pain, and he picked up the suitcase and looked over at Maureen. His wife's expression was unreadable.

Walking out of the kitchen, he saw Liz revert, her body slump, the tension that had momentarily animated her giving out and disappearing as if vacuumed away. He carried the heavy suitcase down the hall. How *had* she lifted it? He was struggling with it himself. He found the closed door and placed the oversized piece of luggage on the floor of the darkened den. Glancing about, he saw the hulking shadow of Ray's empty desk in the otherwise spartan room and he quickly hurried back out to the hallway, unaccountably feeling as though he were intruding on the couple's privacy. He closed the door behind him.

Had the association *really* been behind Ray's death?

He wanted to think that was the case, but he realized that he was grasping at straws, ready to believe any conclusion save the logical one: his friend's death had been an accident.

Barry took a deep breath. He was turning into one of those conspiracy nuts, those loonies who saw government plots behind all ill events, who believed in Bigfoot and UFOs, who refused to believe in luck or chance or even fate and attributed even the smallest occurrence to the complex and illogical machinations of a group of ultra-organized human beings.

And he was forced to admit the possibility that Ray had been one of those people, too.

Sometimes, he thought, the simplest explanation was the real one. Sometimes what was obvious was what was true, and looking for elaborate reasons was just a waste of time.

Still, he was glad there was no one from the association who had come by to offer sympathy, that there'd been no official attempt at wishing Liz condolences. It would have been hypocritical at the very least and an insult to Ray's memory.

He walked back out to the living room. Frank had wandered off somewhere, but Mike was still in place, talking to a woman with a broken arm, and Barry grabbed a drink off the coffee table and joined them.

"Moira? Barry," Mike said by way of introduction. "Moira and her husband, Dan, live around the side of the hill in that stilt-job. Dan used to be a contractor, and he's the one helped Ray figure out how to build that famous storage shed."

"He couldn't make it today," Moira explained. "So I came alone."

"Barry's a writer. Hooked up with Ray because of their mutual hatred of the homeowners' association."

Already, that description sounded embarrassing, childish, and he found that he was ashamed to be identified in such a way.

"What happened to your arm?" Barry asked in an attempt to change the subject. He gestured toward the cast and sling.

The woman reddened, became suddenly taciturn, the openness of her expression closing down. "It was an accident," she said in a voice that didn't sound at all sure that that was the case.

Over her right shoulder, Mike was shaking his head, making a slashing motion across his throat that Barry interpreted to mean stay away from that subject.

Spousal abuse, he thought, and was surprised at how calm he was with it, how unshocked and unfazed he was. In his dreams, in his fantasies, he was one of those people who got involved, who alerted the authorities, who stepped in and put a stop to wrongs and made them right. But here he was confronted with a situation, and he did not rise to the occasion. Like Mike, he felt more comfortable staying out of it, minding his own business and tiptoeing around that five-hundred-pound gorilla in the middle of the room.

This day was just full of surprises.

The afternoon quickly wound down as people who'd put in a token appearance and performed their neighborly duty excused themselves and headed home. This wasn't a party, after all, no one was having fun at this extremely awkward gathering, and Barry could see the relief on people's faces as they expressed their condolences to Liz one last time and escaped out the door, claiming prior commitments and suddenly urgent household chores.

When Mike and Frank left, leaving their wives behind, Barry decided he might as well do the same. Maureen gave him her approval and walked with him to the front door. They'd driven to the Dysons' house—to *Liz's* house—directly from the cemetery, but Barry felt like walking home, and he told Maureen to drive the car back when she was through.

She accompanied him out to the porch, closing the door carefully behind her. "What do you think?" she asked, her eyes meeting his. "Do you think it was an accident?"

He was surprised that she was even asking the question. "Probably," he admitted.

She nodded, but there was not the certainty in her face he would have expected, and he wondered if she'd heard something or seen something that made her suspect this was not the case.

He didn't ask her, though, didn't want to know, not right now at least, and he said good-bye, gave her a quick peck on the lips, and headed up the gravel driveway.

The air was hot and unmoving, not leavened by even the hint of a breeze, and the only sounds on this still afternoon were the scratchy scuttlings of lizards in the underbrush abutting the road, the chirrups of unseen cicadas, and the occasional far-off rumbling of truck engines as Corban pickups headed on or off the highway.

Bonita Vista seemed like a ghost town, as though all of the people had suddenly disappeared, and while in one of his stories that would have seemed creepy, Barry found the absence of audible neighbors almost welcoming.

He felt better being outside, walking, even in this heat. Ray's house had been so close to the man, so filled with his memory, that it had been difficult to think, to sort things through. It was easier out here, alone under the wide blue sky, to remember the good things about his friend, to celebrate his life rather than mourn his passing.

Ahead, Barry saw the entrance to his own driveway and the brown shingle roof of his house above the line of trees. As he drew closer and more of the house became visible, he saw something else, something that made his jaw muscles clench and the blood pump faster through his veins.

A pink piece of paper attached to the screen door.

The association had been here.

He was filled with a rage entirely disproportionate to the offense, a rage he knew to be misplaced anger at his friend's death, but he felt it nonetheless, and he strode furiously up the driveway and up the porch steps. Those bastards had been here, snooping around, while he'd been at Ray's funeral, while he and his wife and their neighbors had been consoling the old man's widow. Did they have no shame? Did they have no respect?

He ripped the paper from the screen and read it.

The association was fining them fifty dollars because the string Maureen had used to tie up her drooping chrysanthemums was white instead of green. All lines or cords used by a homeowner to tie plants to stakes were required to be green in order to blend in with the foliage and not distract from the lot's natural state.

He felt the muscles of his face harden into a painful grimace, and he squeezed shut his eyes. "Fuckers!" he yelled at the top of his lungs. "Fuckers!"

Taking a deep harsh breath, tears stinging his eyes, he crumpled up the paper, balled it in his fist, and walked angrily into the house.

# TWENTY-ONE

July.

The monsoons came just as Ray had promised they would. With the turn of the calendar page, afternoon skies were suddenly filled with massive thunderheads, and short summer storms brought the nearly unbearable heat of mid-day down to a level that made for cool and pleasant evenings. From the deck, Barry could watch the buildup of the storms, see the coalescing clouds, watch the rain as it came up from the south and moved like a light white curtain over the canyonlands and through the hilly forest toward Corban and Bonita Vista. It was beautiful, and he wished he were writer enough to capture that ephemeral splendor, but his forte was the grotesque, not the sublime, and translating such a magnificent sight into words was beyond his abilities.

He sat with Maureen, drinking iced tea, staring out at the landscape. There were scattered showers to the south, squares of gray and white that touched the earth and looked like ghostly extensions of the more solid clouds above. Occasional spikes of lightning and the rumble of accompanying thunder belied the tranquillity of the scene but were nevertheless equally majestic, and at one point Barry saw three jagged bolts of lightning hit the ground at once.

From the road came the sound of a mufflerless engine, and Barry peeked over to see who it was. A second later, a pickup packed with sand came speeding up the road, the vehicle's driver obviously attempting to get a running start on the steepest part of the hill. Despite the driver's intentions, the grade proved too tough, and the truck stalled out just above their house. The pickup was blocked from view by a pine tree, but Barry heard the engine attempting to turn over, and after one false start, the vehicle slid back down the hill into view, braking to a hard stop directly in front of their driveway. He looked over at Maureen.

"Don't you even think about it," she said.

"The guy obviously needs help. And this isn't California," he pointed out. "It's not part of some scam. He's not going to shoot us and rob us."

"Never can tell."

He shook his head and was about to go downstairs and ask the man if he needed any assistance, when another pickup pulled up behind the first and stopped.

"Saved by the bell," Maureen said.

The man who emerged from the second truck was tall and heavy, wearing too-new jeans, a fancy western shirt, and the sort of shiny oversized belt buckle that had been fodder for urban comedians for decades. A shock of white hair over a ruddy bulldog face gave the man an air of impatient arrogance, and while Barry had automatically assumed that the man had stopped to help, he knew even before the cowboy opened his mouth that that was not the case.

"You got a permit?"

The driver who stuck his head out of the window to answer was dark and spoke in a thick Mexican accent. "Yes, sir. Of course, of course. I have my green card."

"I don't mean a permit to work in this country. I figure you got that. I'm talking about a work permit for Bonita Vista. Does your boss have a permit to do work in our neighborhood?"

Sound carried up here, but if there was an answer, Barry couldn't hear it.

"Y'see, you gotta get the permission of the homeowners' association before you can do any work in Bonita Vista. *Any* work. I don't care what the man hirin' you said, that's the way it is, *comprende*?"

There was derision in the Spanish word, derision and an aggressive hostility. Barry could hear it all the way up on the deck, and it was clear that the driver sensed it as well. His response was low and cowed, subservient. He immediately tried to start the truck again, and although the first two efforts were unsuccessful, on the third the engine caught and held.

The white-haired man thunked his hand on the door of the pickup. "Now you turn this baby around. And you tell your boss what I told you, you hear? No permit from the association, no work in Bonita Vista. Got it?"

Again, if there was an answer Barry didn't hear it, but the pickup did not try to continue up the road and instead backed around the other truck and headed down the hill in reverse, the loud engine fading into the distance.

The white-haired man returned to his own vehicle. He looked up at Barry as he walked, scowling, as if aware that his conversation had been overheard, and Barry quickly looked away, moving out of the man's line of sight, nervous for some reason, not wanting to acknowledge that he'd been listening.

The man got in his pickup and drove away.

"Did you hear that?" Barry asked Maureen.

She sipped her iced tea, nodded. "There are racist assholes everywhere."

That was not what Barry had gotten from the exchange, although it was undoubtedly true.

He had the distinct impression that *any* worker, regardless of his ethnicity, would have been questioned. It was not a race thing . . . it was an association thing. He looked out once again at the approaching storm, but the pettiness of the people on the ground had drained the majesty from the sky, and he was no longer able to enjoy the view the way he had before.

They sat there the rest of the afternoon, as the rain approached and overtook them, whipcrack thunder that sounded simultaneously with the flash of paparazzi lightning shaking the house and rattling the windows as though they were in an earthquake. They bore the brunt of the storm for a good half hour before it finally broke, and Maureen went back inside to start dinner.

Barry remained on the deck as dusk approached, ignoring the book he'd brought out to read, simply staring at the scenery. The sunset was dazzling. A section of the butte that stood like a sentinel at the far-off end of the forest where it segued into desert canyon was illuminated by a swath of light that lent the tan rock a brilliant fiery orange hue. The remnants of the afternoon's monsoon clouds dispersing across the western sky were transformed into what looked like puffy strings of cotton candy by the gradations of pink generated by the setting sun.

It was impressive, it was awe-inspiring.

But as hard as he tried to enjoy the view, he could not stop thinking about the cowboy and the Mexican worker and the homeowners' association.

The next day was the fourth.

The Fourth of July had never been one of their big holidays, and although they slept in, waking up over an hour later than usual, they made no special plans to celebrate. Maureen allowed him to barbecue fat-free hot dogs for dinner in a modified concession to tradition, but the remainder of their plans consisted of doing yard work during the day and watching TV at night.

The day passed uneventfully, and they stopped working when the rains came, Maureen grabbing the rake, clippers, and broom, with Barry taking the shovel and the half-filled Hefty bag, both of them running for the shelter of the lower deck. The storm quit in time for him to barbecue, and they ate in front of the television, watching the two Flint movies back-to-back on AMC. Afterward, they showered together, made love, and went to sleep early.

They were startled awake by a loud boom that sounded like a bomb going off in the air above the house but that Barry recognized instantly as the sound of fireworks.

Despite the recent rains, it had been an exceptionally dry spring, and the national forest sign at the edge of town still had Smokey the Bear pointing to a red flag, warning of high fire danger. Barry's first thought was to wonder who was stupid enough to set off fireworks under such conditions. He got out of bed, slipped on a robe, and walked over to the sliding glass door. He pulled aside the curtain and watched a fat raccoon scramble off the lower deck and down an adjacent tree.

Maureen, still naked, moved up behind him and leaned on his shoulder, yawning in his ear. "Were those fireworks?"

"Sounded like it. But I don't see—"

Another one went off, the trace appearing to originate from the bottom of the hill near the tennis courts. A weak blue burst temporarily lit up a close section of sky, sparkles falling onto the pines.

"Isn't that a fire hazard?" Maureen asked, suddenly more awake.

"It seems like it to me."

"You think someone's setting them off illegally? Maybe kids are—"

Barry shook his head. "These are professional fireworks. Kids don't have the equipment to shoot off skyrockets like this. You need launchers. Besides, these kinds of fireworks are expensive."

They waited for several moments but nothing else went up.

"Maybe they were illegal," he conceded.

"Maybe the police or the rangers or the firemen got to them already and put a stop to it."

"No." Barry pointed. Another trace went up, and an anemic burst of red exploded above the trees.

Maureen smiled. "If this is supposed to be professional, it's pretty pathetic."

"We're spoiled." In southern California, spectacular fireworks could be viewed every weekend at various tourist attractions, along with the ubiquitous nightly displays at Disneyland: consistently impressive shows that could be seen from the beach to the Fullerton hills.

They stood, waited, and a few minutes later another skyrocket went off.

"I'm going to bed," Maureen said, yawning. "This isn't worth staying up for."

Barry agreed, and they both went back to bed, falling asleep to the intermittent sounds of exploding gunpowder.

Barry awoke late. Maureen was already out of bed, and the smell of eggs and hash browns wafted down from upstairs. He dressed quickly, ran a hand through his hair, and headed up to the kitchen. It was a beautiful day. Maureen had opened all the drapes and windows, and morning sunlight streamed in from a cloudless blue sky.

"Breakfast'll be ready in a few minutes." Maureen pointed her spatula at a folded newspaper lying atop the dining table. "Check out the paper. Top story."

"Got any coffee?"

"Check out the paper first."

Barry walked over to the table, unfolded the newspaper, and stared down at the banner headline.

*Bonita Vista to Set Off Fireworks Despite Fire Danger*

He started reading.

The *Corban Weekly Standard* came out every Tuesday, its stories written the week or weekend before, so there was no reporting on last night's display, only a pre-event article that addressed the situation from the vantage point of a few days prior. But there was no mistaking the tone of the piece or the anger that quoted Corbanites seemed to feel toward the arrogance of the Bonita Vista Homeowners' Association, sponsors of the display.

Apparently, Corban was running short on water this summer due to the extended drought conditions of the previous winter, something of which Barry had not been aware. Several years before, a similar situation had arisen, and for two weeks in mid-July, before late monsoons once again raised the water table, tanker trucks from Salt Lake City had brought water to the town and people had been forced to line up with plastic containers in order to get drinking water. Such an extreme situation was not expected this year, but voluntary rationing was currently in place, and it was suggested that people with lawns not water them and that no one wash their cars.

The article went on to say that Bonita Vista had its own wells, so it was not tied to the Corban water supply and was not suffering the same shortage. But water district officials said that it was still callous, insensitive, and potentially devastating to the surrounding forest to put on the display. "Those fireworks could cause a fire that would require digging into our reserves and could completely deplete our water resources," the superintendent said. A representative of the Forest Service concurred, adding that it would take several weeks of consistent monsoons before the trees and brush were no longer dried out and the area was no longer considered at risk. The chief of the volunteer fire department said bluntly that his men should not have to bail out Bonita Vista because of their shortsightedness and stupidity . . . but that they would have to, since a blaze would endanger the town and surrounding countryside.

The homeowners' association didn't care about these objections and intended to continue with their display no matter what. The final quote in the story was from his old pal

Neil Campbell. "We're not just doing this for the benefit of Bonita Vista," Campbell stated. "These fireworks will be able to be seen for miles and everyone will be able to enjoy them. They're our present to the town of Corban and the people living in this area. Happy Fourth of July!"

Barry looked up and grimaced. "I need some coffee," he said.

Maureen motioned toward the coffeemaker. "I figured you would."

"Jesus. Not only was it stupid from a PR standpoint, but it was dangerous on top of that."

"And the fireworks sucked besides."

"According to Ray, we don't even have any fire hydrants up here. One of the few things the association's actually supposed to do, take care of public safety, they can't be bothered with. It's more important to fine us over the color of our garden ties than make sure we can fight off a forest fire."

"Typical," she said.

Barry poured himself a cup of coffee. "Are you still enamored with your precious homeowners' association?"

"I was never enamored."

"But you're a little less happy with them now than you used to be, aren't you?"

She scooped up a pile of hash browns, then placed a fried egg next to the potatoes on the plate. "Here," she told Barry. "Breakfast's ready. Eat."

# TWENTY-TWO

The writing had stopped.

Barry still went down to his office each day, still fired up the old computer, still sat in his chair in front of the screen and attempted to finish the novel that was rapidly approaching its deadline . . . but nothing came.

This time, he conceded, it might be writer's block.

His inability to progress any further with his story coincided precisely with Ray's death. He'd taken a few days off because he hadn't felt like working, then the weekend of the Fourth had arrived and he never worked on a holiday weekend. But when he finally went down to his office the following week, he discovered that the well had run dry.

He knew exactly what was going to happen next in the narrative—he'd plotted out in his mind the events that were to take place in the current chapter and all he really had to do was fill in the blanks—but he just couldn't seem to get from A to B. He was stymied, stuck.

And he'd been stuck now for almost a week.

Logically, there was no reason this should have occurred. He'd been under deadline two years ago when his mom had died, and he'd managed to finish that book on time. Hell, he'd found the writing process therapeutic, and he'd ended up finishing the novel ahead of schedule, focusing on it to the exclusion of nearly everything else. And his mom had certainly meant more to him than Ray.

But still the writing had stopped.

He'd said nothing to Maureen, had been pulling a Jack Torrence on her, but oddly enough he'd found himself confiding in Hank and Bert and the gang at the coffee shop. They'd been cool to him after the debacle of the fireworks, unable this time to completely divorce him from the actions of Bonita Vista, but he assured them that he was just as outraged as they were, and he described the way he and Maureen had been awakened by the blasts and had had no idea where they'd been coming from.

His explanation was accepted, but there was not the wholesale wholehearted forgiveness that had accompanied his protestations of innocence after the dog death. He'd been in the wrong place at the wrong time once too often, and it was clear to him that if it happened again, suspicion would definitely be directed his way.

It was not fair . . . but he understood it. He might not condone the actions of the association, but he lived in Bonita Vista, paid his dues, and bore some of the responsibility. And as much as he tried to disassociate himself from his neighbors and align himself with the townies, the fact was that there was no rationing in the gated community. The realities of the water shortage did not affect him, and he felt a little like a condescending nobleman assuring the poor populace that he sympathized with their plight and understood their feelings. Even now, over a week later, he still sensed some residual resentment—not on the part of Hank or Lyle or any of the core group, but from some of the casual coffee shop patrons—and while he didn't like it, he could not really blame them.

Once again, he spent the morning in front of his computer. He tried to concentrate on the unfinished novel before him, but as usual his mind wandered to other things: an old girlfriend, the movie he'd watched last night on HBO, the groceries he needed to buy on the way home today, what he'd do with the money if he sold his next novel for ten million dollars.

He usually ate lunch around noon, but nothing was happening here and he closed up shop shortly after eleven, heading over to Bert's. It hadn't rained yesterday—the first time in over a week—and the air was hot and dry. Grasshoppers jumped up from the path before him, and several bounced off his jeans.

Bert, his daughter, and a youngish, short-haired man Barry didn't recognize were the only ones in the coffee shop, but Joe arrived soon after Barry sat down and ordered his iced tea, and fifteen minutes after that, the regulars were all in place.

Lyle was the last to show up, and he had news. "Word is," he said, sitting in his usual seat, "that the water restrictions are going to be lifted if we have one more week of monsoons."

"Who told you that?"

"I was down at the office paying my bill and I overheard Shelly talking to Graham in the back."

Hank snorted. "About time."

"I guess," Joe said loudly, "that Bert can start serving water again without charging, huh?"

"Don't hold your breath," Bert called out from behind the counter.

Ralph Griffith glanced over at Barry. "You know, I was heading down the ranch road yesterday when I saw this Lexus come out of the gate at Bonita Vista, all shiny and just washed. There was water still dripping off the hood."

"Hey," Barry said good-naturedly, "I haven't washed my Suburban in months. You can go out back and check."

They all laughed.

"I wasn't saying anything against *you*," Ralph said. "I

was just commenting that some of those rich guys in Bonita Vista are washing their cars right before a rainstorm while I can't even fill up my little boy's plastic pool with water."

The laughter died down.

"Face it," Hank said. "There are selfish pricks everywhere. And if the situation was reversed and we had water and Bonita Vista didn't, you can be damn sure that there'd be people washin' their cars and waterin' their lawns and flauntin' it. It's human nature."

"But don't you think there are *more* of them in Bonita Vista?" Ralph pressed.

Barry jumped in. "Probably."

"Don't try to take it out on Barry," Hank said.

"I'm not, I'm not. I just . . ." Ralph shook his head. "It's just that those assholes make me so mad sometimes. I wanted to ram that guy's car yesterday."

"Any of you ever been up there?" Joe asked. He grinned. "Barry, you're excluded."

Hank shook his head slowly. "You know, I never have. Never cared enough to until they put in that gate. Now I *can't.*"

"I never been up there either," Lyle said. "Old Al the roofer told me every house has a view and the views are amazing, but I ain't seen it for myself."

"Why don't you all come up and take a peek?" Barry said.

Lyle looked surprised. "What?"

"Yeah. I'll get you through the gate. We'll head up to my house, have a few drinks. I'll show you what you're missing." He smiled at Ralph. "Give you a peek at the enemy camp."

The other man reddened.

"That's a mighty nice offer, but . . ." Lyle trailed off.

"But what?"

"Hell. Nothing, I guess." He glanced over at Hank. "What do you say?"

"Let's do it."

They left after lunch. Ralph and a couple of the younger men were working and had to get back to their jobs, but Hank and Lyle were retired, and Joe and Sonny were unemployed, and the four of them piled into Joe's battered Econoline and followed Barry out of town and up the highway.

Barry pulled up to the entrance of Bonita Vista and leaned out the window to punch in the code that would open the gate. The metal arm swung inward, and he sped through quickly. Joe was right on his tail, as he'd instructed, and the Econoline made it in just as the gate started to swing closed.

"We're in!" he heard Lyle shout out the window in mock heroic tones.

Barry led them up the narrow winding road to his house. Maureen was not home, and he was not sure if that was good or bad. She was definitely not a fan of uninvited guests, and if she'd been there when he'd traipsed over with a horde of strangers, he would have caught hell for it after they'd gone. On the other hand, he'd talked enough about his newfound buddies that she doubtlessly would have wanted to meet the gang from the coffee shop, although perhaps with a little more advance notice.

The four men got out of Joe's van and looked around.

"Al was right," Lyle said. "What a view." He stood at the end of the driveway next to the edge of the house, looking back toward Corban, a few of whose buildings could be seen through the trees.

"You think that's something? Check out the view from the upper deck." Barry walked up to the front door, unlocked and opened it. "Come on in."

"Nice place you got here," Hank allowed.

Barry led them upstairs and through the sliding glass doors onto the porch. "You think we have a great view, you ought to check out the scenery from that place up there." He leaned over the edge of the railing and pointed toward Ray's house farther up the hill. "Their living room's all glass, and you can see all the way to the desert."

"You make enough off your writing to afford this place?" Joe said.

Barry nodded.

"I'm gonna have to start showing you more respect, boy."

Barry laughed.

Hank turned back to face the door. "So the association won't let you write here, huh? Your own damn house and you have to rent an office in town to do your work." He shook his head. "That's craziness."

"Reason number two hundred why I hate those bastards."

Sonny cleared his throat. "Didn't you say something about drinks?"

Barry chuckled. "Coming right up." He opened the sliding door. "Beer okay? I got Bud and Miller Light. Or Coke if you'd rather have that."

"Bud."

"Bud."

"Bud."

"Bud."

It was unanimous, and he walked inside to get some cans out of the refrigerator.

The men stayed for another forty-five minutes, but the visit grew increasingly awkward, and Barry was soon sorry that he'd invited them up here. He'd intended for this to be an ice breaker, a way for them to get to know each other better. Maybe, he'd thought, they'd become real friends instead of just lunchtime acquaintances. But instead their visit seemed to widen the gulf between them, and he felt like a nouveau riche snob lording his possessions over the local yokels. That was not his intention, and he did everything he could to counteract it and make them feel at ease, but the nice house with the great view on the hill in the gated community still stood between them. He should have left well enough alone. They all got along fine at the coffee shop, but outside of that specific environment their differences were emphasized, and even beer could not engender the kind of camaraderie needed. He'd wanted to bring them all closer together, but his invitation had ended up pushing them farther apart.

They left early, dispiritedly, offering polite thanks and rather formal good-byes, and he decided to stay home and take the rest of the afternoon off. He wasn't going to get any writing done anyway.

He sat on the deck reading a Richard Laymon novel. There was no storm to the south today, no clouds anywhere on the horizon, only a deep blue sky and hot, still air. Great, he thought. Just what he needed. An extension of the water rationing in Corban. They'd *really* resent him now.

He sped through the book. He'd continued drinking even after the others had left, and the cans piled up next to his chair as he read. One. Two. Three. Four. By the time he saw Frank's pickup pull into the driveway shortly after four-thirty, he was feeling more than a little lightheaded, and he walked back into the house and stepped carefully down the stairs, holding tightly to the railing.

"Hi, Frank." He opened the door just as the other man was about to knock.

"Whoa. ESP."

Barry smiled. "I saw you from the deck."

"Mystery solved."

"You want to come in?"

Frank shook his head. "No, no. I just stopped by for a sec." He looked uncomfortable.

"What is it?"

"I was working up here today, and I ran into a couple of the board members." Frank looked down at his shoes, shuffled his feet awkwardly. "They wanted me to tell you that you're not supposed to be fraternizing with the locals. At least not in Bonita Vista. I guess they said you invited some locals over or something. I don't know. Anyway, they said it's cool if you go to *their* houses, but you can't hang with them here."

"What?"

"Outsiders aren't welcome in Bonita Vista."

"Now they're trying to tell me who I can be friends with and who I can't?" Barry stared at him incredulously. "I don't believe this shit!"

Frank held up his hands. "I'm just the messenger. I know how crazy it is, but I don't make the decisions. I'm just repeating what they told me to tell you."

"I can't invite friends over."

Frank shrugged. "Not if they're from Corban."

"They can't do that."

"It's in the C, C, and Rs."

"So what? Fuck the C, C, and Rs." He wasn't sure if it was the alcohol or simply righteous anger, but at that second he wanted nothing more than to find his copy of the regulations, rip it up, and send Frank back with a counter-message: shove these pages up your asses.

Frank glanced around furtively, obviously worried that they had been overheard. "Don't even joke about that." He looked back toward the road. "What if someone from the association hears you?"

Something about Frank's reaction didn't seem right. It felt too exaggerated, as though it were part of an act put on for his benefit, and a hint of Barry's earlier suspicions returned. He remembered the way Frank had insisted to him and Ray that the association could not be behind the vandalism that had been visited upon them. The fact that Frank had turned out to be right was beside the point. It was his attitude that was important. Looking over at him, Barry realized how little he really knew the man.

*Everyone's an informant.*

Frank seemed like a good guy, and Ray had obviously trusted him, but despite his accounts of occasional problems and run-ins and disagreements, he was not as anti-association as Barry would have liked him to be. That didn't automatically make him a stooge or a spy, but it was definitely cause for concern.

"This is my house," Barry said evenly. "I'll say whatever I want to say and talk about whatever I want to talk about. And if I want to say that I think the architectural committee eats out their own mothers' assholes, I'll do it."

Frank nodded, pretended to smile.

"And if I want to invite friends over, I'll invite them over. Is that clear?"

Frank held up a hand. "Hold on there, cowboy. I'm on your side."

"Yeah." Barry's tone of voice made it clear that he did not think that was the case, and Frank backed up awkwardly.

"Well . . . I gotta be heading back. Just wanted to tell you what they told me."

Barry nodded and watched him retreat to his pickup. He stood in the doorway as Frank waved and the truck backed out of the driveway and continued up the road.

Barry closed the door. He'd had no intention of asking the guys from the coffee shop up here again, but now he was tempted to invite them for lunch every damn day. He walked upstairs to the kitchen to get himself another beer.

Hell, maybe he'd even give them the code to the gate.

# Twenty-three

**The Bonita Vista Homeowners' Association Covenants, Conditions, and Restrictions** Article IV, General Provisions, Section 9, Paragraph D:

*No member of the Bonita Vista Homeowners' Association shall, within the boundaries of the Properties, socialize with any individual currently residing in the town of Corban. The only exception to this shall be if a resident of Corban owns a Lot within the Properties and is also a member of the Association.*

# TWENTY-FOUR

Maureen had an early meeting with Ed Dexter at the title company, for whom she was doing some freelance account auditing, and since the Toyota was at the shop getting a new water pump and they had only one vehicle, she offered to drive Barry into town and drop him off at the microscopic shack he called his office. He didn't usually leave until after *The Today Show* ended, but this morning she made him get ready early, and they were out the door before eight.

She drove carefully down the steep winding road, through the neighborhood toward the entrance of Bonita Vista.

The gate had changed overnight.

Maureen slowed the Suburban, feeling an icy tingle tickle her spine and then settle like a lump of lead in the pit of her stomach. She glanced over at Barry in the passenger seat, and he, too, seemed dumbstruck and thrown for a loop.

They'd come through the gate just last evening. In what turned out to be a futile effort to cheer up Liz and get her out of the house, they, along with Mike and Tina, had taken her to a late steak dinner in town. As they probably should have known, the last time she'd been to the restaurant was with Ray, and she'd spent the first part of the meal crying quietly, the second half silently staring at her almost untouched plate. They'd returned to Bonita Vista around ten, Barry driving, and he'd stopped in front of the gate as always, entered the code, and once the creaky metal had swung open, driven through.

Now, though, the old gateway was gone. In its place was an even more elaborate entrance: stone columns on either side of the road, massive ornate double gates that looked tall enough to block a semi.

And a guard shack.

She and Barry looked at each other, although neither of them spoke.

The road had been widened at this point, bifurcating around the small square structure, allowing for simultaneous entrance to and exit from Bonita Vista.

The Suburban coasted up to the gate and stopped.

Maureen rolled down her window as the trim middle-aged man staffing the booth stepped outside at the approach of their car, clipboard in hand. He was wearing the olive uniform of a security guard, and his close-cropped hair accentuated the militaristic appearance.

The guard walked up to the driver's window. "May I ask your name, sir?" He looked over at Barry in the passenger seat, ignoring her completely, acting as though she didn't exist.

Barry met Maureen's eyes and looked deliberately away from the guard, which caused her to smile. "*My* name is Maureen Welch," she said.

The man looked down at the list on his clipboard. "Welch . . . Welch . . ." He glanced up. "Here you are. Barry and Maureen." The humorless formality gave way to a fawning smile. "You are free to go. Sorry for the inconvenience."

"Free to go?"

She'd been about to put the car into gear, but Barry's words caused her to stop.

"You mean if our names had not been on that list, we

would *not* have been free to go? You would have forced us to stay here and not let us leave?"

"There've been reports of intruders, and one apparent burglary," the guard said. "My job is to make sure that only residents are allowed in or out of Bonita Vista. If a trespasser has managed to get in, then, yes sir, I am obliged to hold them here until the sheriff arrives to take care of the matter."

Maureen glanced over at Barry, wondering if he was as chilled by the fascistic tone of this exchange as she was.

"So they put up this new gate and this guard booth and hired you because there was a *burglary*?"

"As I understand it, too many people knew the entry code. It had been given out to plumbers and roofers and contractors; half of Corban knew it. So the old gate was no longer effective as a security measure. It was felt that new measures needed to be taken."

"Are *you* from Corban?" Maureen asked, thinking they'd hired a local man to staff the entrance.

The guard shook his head. "No, ma'am. I live here in Bonita Vista."

There was the sound of a car driving up behind them, and she glanced in the rearview mirror to see a red Saturn pulling up.

She put the car in gear, but kept her foot on the brake. "How . . . ?" Maureen did not know how to ask what she was really wondering. "How did this get put up so . . . fast?"

The guard shook his head. "I don't know, ma'am. I didn't build it, I just staff it."

There was tacit recognition that this was unusual, strange, but not acknowledgment that it was damn near impossible. The gate swung open before them, and she guided the Suburban through. She glanced at the stone columns as she drove by. The cement did not even appear to be wet. It was as if this whole thing had been here for months, years, and she realized how truly incredible this all was. There was no way that even a large crew of workers could have torn down the old gate, put up an entirely new one, widened the road, and constructed a guard shack between ten o'clock last night and eight this morning.

They headed toward the highway.

She glanced over at Barry. "What are you thinking?" she asked him quietly.

"The Davidsons," he said.

Maureen nodded. "Me, too." She had not been sure at the time that she entirely believed the couple's story about the gate being built to increase property values and thus drive them out with higher property taxes, but it seemed eminently reasonable now.

"You going to call Chuck Shea or Terry Abbey and ask them what's doing?"

Maureen shook her head.

"Why not?"

"I'm afraid to," she said quietly.

That shut him up, and neither of them said anything as they drove between the two pine-covered hills toward the highway.

She took a deep breath. "Who do you suppose they're trying to get rid of this time?"

She didn't expect an answer and she didn't get one, and they rode the rest of the way into town in silence.

The telephone was ringing when they got home that afternoon, and Barry dashed past her the instant she unlocked and opened the door, picking up the phone from the coffee table where they'd left it that morning. "Hello?"

Maureen closed the screen and threw her keys in her purse.

"I'm fine," Barry said into the phone.

The call obviously wasn't for her, so she took her purse downstairs and then went to the bathroom. He was still on the phone when she walked back up several minutes later, still standing in exactly the same position. There was a strange expression on his face, one that she could not read, and she could not tell if what he was hearing was good or bad.

Her heart started pounding.

"Barry?" she said.

He held up his hand. "Yes," he said into the phone. "Okay."

She touched his elbow.

"All right. Thanks. Good-bye."

"So?" Maureen asked.

He clicked off the Talk button, looking stunned.

"What is it?"

"A movie deal."

"What!"

"They want to buy the rights to *The Friend*," he said. "Half a million dollars."

# TWENTY-FIVE

It was still hard to believe.

Barry finished packing his suitcase and closed it up, fastening the straps. True, *The Friend* was one of his more commercial novels, though it was not the biggest seller. And he'd always secretly thought that it would make a good film. But never in his wildest dreams did he imagine that Hollywood would be interested, let alone shell out this kind of money.

He'd assumed at first that the offer had been made as a result of Kenny Tolkin putting in that "good word" for him, but further questioning of his agent had revealed that the artistic consultant had not been involved at all, that the impetus had come from the movie studio, where a midlevel executive had read the book on vacation, liked it, and decided to option it.

Still, he'd wanted to run this by Kenny, who had much more experience dealing with Hollywood than he did and who might be able to offer him some pointers or let him know which minefields to avoid. He'd written down the name of the executive as well as the studio agent in charge, wanting to see if Kenny knew them or could tell him anything about them.

He'd called Frank to get Kenny's phone number and was shocked when an obviously angry Frank said that the artistic consultant had left Bonita Vista suddenly and would not be coming back. It turned out that he had not owned the house in which he'd been staying, that for the past two years he'd been illegally camping in a home purchased by an out-of-state property owner for investment. Indications were that he had no Hollywood or music industry contacts, that he was a con man who had pulled similar stunts in other states and who had successfully scammed several Bonita Vista residents before disappearing.

Barry carried his suitcase up to the living room, where Maureen was waiting. She smiled at him and held up crossed fingers. "Good luck."

"I shouldn't need any. I think it's a done deal."

"Still." She kissed him, put her arms around his neck. "Drive carefully. Call me from the airport when you get there. And call me when you land."

"I will." He smiled.

"You know I worry."

"Are you sure you don't want to come? It's only overnight."

She shook her head. "If it was longer, maybe. But just overnight, it's a waste of money."

"Money?" He grinned. "I don't think that's really a problem anymore."

"Don't spend it before you get it."

"Spoken like a true accountant."

Maureen glanced at the clock. "You'd better get going. It's at least a two-hour drive to Salt Lake."

Barry put his arms around her, held her close, and kissed her. "I love you," he said.

She smiled, kissed him back. "I love you, too."

The drive up to Salt Lake City seemed long. Once he got through the mountains and onto Interstate 15, the landscape remained unchanged for over a hundred miles: farmland to the left, foothills to the right. Thank God for tapes. There were no decent radio stations, and he popped in a series of cassettes he'd made from various albums and CDs, keeping awake and alert by listening to tunes.

He found himself wondering if he could live off the royalties and resales of what he'd already written should it come down to that. He hadn't typed a single word on his new novel for the past two weeks, and he honestly did not see himself meeting the deadline. He wondered if he would be able to finish the book at all. It would be one thing if he was only stuck on *this* novel, but he had no other ideas either, and he had not even been able to crank out a short story.

This movie deal was a windfall, and if he could just sell *one* more book to Hollywood, they'd be able to pay off the house and live quite comfortably here in Utah for the next decade. Particularly if Maureen's client list kept growing.

The idea that he was dried up, that his creative life was over, scared the living hell out of him. He'd never wanted to do anything other than write, didn't know how to do anything other than write, and if that was taken away from him . . .

He prayed this was just a temporary setback.

Salt Lake City was nothing like he'd expected. He'd never been there before, had only seen photos in magazines and on postcards, pictures of quaint Victorian homes and a modern downtown backed by snowcapped peaks, but the highway passed by mile after mile of rusty train yards and ugly industrial buildings. The sight depressed him, and he was grateful for the clean, generic modernity of the airport.

He barely had enough time to make the promised call to Maureen and buy some cheapo flight insurance before the boarding call for his flight. He got on the plane, settled into his seat, and pulled out a book to read from his carry-on bag. Reading made the time go by faster, kept him from worrying about crashes and accidents and the possibility of a fiery death, and it usually served to stave off unwanted conversations with his aisle mate. Maureen always suggested bringing one of his own books to read, hyping himself that way, but he couldn't bring himself to be so shameless. Besides, the last thing he wanted to do was reread one of his novels. After writing it, proofreading it, going over the typeset version, and checking the galleys, he was pretty well sick of a book by the time it hit the shelves.

The trip was uneventful, the young woman in the seat next to him seemed to be as loath to talk as he was, and before he knew it the plane was taxiing down the runway at LAX.

X.

He'd always wondered where the hell that had come from. The official name was Los Angeles International Airport. How the letter *X* had come to stand for the word *International* was a complete mystery to him. Of course, it also seemed to stand for *Christ*, since a lot of people abbreviated Christmas as *Xmas*. And the Christ connection held on the highway, where road signs shortened the word Crossing to *Xing*.

None of it made any sense.

The rental car he'd ordered was ready and waiting for him, and he gave Maureen a quick call to let her know he'd landed safely while someone brought the vehicle around. Five minutes later, he was out of the airport and on the street, driving. He cranked up the air-conditioning and turned the radio to his favorite station.

Despite the smoggy skies, despite the traffic from the airport, despite the homeless guys on the street corners, it felt good to be back, and he was surprised to discover that he actually missed southern California. Next to him at the stoplight, a short-haired blond man in a red convertible had his car stereo up so high that Barry could hear the thumping of bass over the sound of his own air conditioner and radio, the yuppie apparently attempting to impress the drivers around him by playing music loudly.

Ah, Los Angeles.

It felt as though he'd been gone for years, not months, and he took the 405 to Wilshire Boulevard, intending to drive surface streets to see what, if anything, had changed in his absence. There was still an hour and a half to go before he was supposed to meet his agent for an early dinner, and although he hadn't planned on it, he stopped off at his favorite used-record store. The vinyl section had shrunk a little, the CD section had grown, but there were aisles and aisles of both, and he happily sorted through the albums, picking up an armful before deciding that it was time to get going.

He headed east down Wilshire, tried to figure out how long it would take to get from L.A. to Brea. He'd only be here overnight, but he'd arranged to meet his friends for drinks. The dinner with his agent probably wouldn't take more than an hour or so, and there'd be plenty of time remaining to hang and catch up on gossip.

Lindsay White was waiting for him at Canter's on Fairfax, their traditional rendezvous point. As usual, there were tables full of old men from the neighborhood as well as assorted Hollywood wannabes and usetabes. Lindsay was ensconced in a corner booth, and she waved him over as he crossed the room. He'd barely had time to sit down when, in her usual overassertive manner, she motioned for a waitress with an imperial flick of her wrist and snap of her fingers. "The service here is still slow as molasses," she said as the waitress walked up, "so I already ordered. Order what you want and then we'll talk."

He hadn't had time to even look at the menu, but he ordered a pastrami sandwich and an iced tea—the same thing he'd had the last time they'd met here.

The waitress left and Lindsay leaned across the table, patting his hand. "How are you, Barry? How've you been out there in the heartland?"

"Fine," he said.

"That's great," she told him before he could say another word.

She spent the next fifteen minutes or so trying to impress him, as she always did, and he gamely feigned interest in her newest trendy passion. She was what Maureen called a "Miramax intellectual," one of those people who wasn't particularly knowledgeable or well read but who followed the cultural trends generated by art-house films: reading Janet Frame after seeing *An Angel at My Table*, pretending to be an admirer of Pablo Neruda after viewing *Il Postino*, referencing Jane Austen in conversation after seeing the movies rather than reading the books. It was a tactic that worked well these days in polite society, this false familiarity with culture, although it never failed to set his teeth on edge, and it annoyed Maureen to the extent that she made a conscious effort to avoid casual conversation with Lindsay.

When the food came and they finally got around to business, the news was not good.

"I expected to have contracts for you to sign," Lindsay admitted. "But . . . there've been complications since we last spoke. To be honest, I think the deal might've fallen through. I haven't given up hope," she added quickly. "We still might be able to pull this off. But there's been a changeover at the studio, and you know how these things work. Anything associated with the old regime, the previous administration, is automatically suspect. Right now, that means us. But I hope to call a meeting with one of the development execs early next week and see if we can work something out. *The Friend* is a very salable property, a very *shootable* property, and I have no doubt that once I can divorce it from the context in which it was rejected, I'll be able to make them see that."

Lindsay tried to smile. "Want any dessert?"

It was still light out when he emerged from the restaurant, and Barry hurried over to his car, driving straight down Fairfax to the freeway in an effort to beat the after-work traffic out to Orange County.

He was ahead of the game for a while, but he got bogged down in rush-hour traffic on the Santa Ana Freeway, and he took surface streets from Santa Fe Springs on, avoiding the areas where he knew they were doing highway construction, the challenges of southern California driving serving to keep his mind off Lindsay's disappointing news. Once in Brea, he drove through his old neighborhood on an impulse. The street and sidewalks were carpeted with purple jacaranda flowers, the arching tree branches above having lost their blooms and given themselves over to summer leaves. Sunset had turned the smog a bright orange color, and he felt a slight twinge of nostalgia for California life.

And for a neighborhood without a homeowners' association.

Jeremy, Chuck, and Dylan were already waiting for him in the parking lot outside Minderbinder's, a hangout from their college days at UC Brea. Minderbinder's was still a college hangout, and the three of them were greeted with suspicion if not hostility as they commandeered a table near the entrance.

"Guess we look older than we are," Dylan said.

"No," Chuck told him. "You feel younger than you are."

"I know that's supposed to be a dig, but doesn't a youthful attitude help promote longer life?"

"The benefits of immaturity have yet to be proven."

A bored-looking waitress showed up, and they ordered beers all around.

"It's on him," Dylan said, pointing at Barry. "He's a rich and famous writer. Just sold one of his books to Hollywood."

The waitress suddenly seemed a little less bored. She smiled at Barry. "Celebrating?"

"No."

"Congratulations anyway." She walked away with an exaggerated swing of her hips, and Dylan burst out laughing. He waited until she'd passed out of earshot. "She's yours for the taking, bud."

"I told you, the movie deal fell through."

"She doesn't know that. Besides, what good's fame and fortune if you can't use it to get a little strange?"

"I'll tell Mo you said that."

"So how's life in the wilds?" Jeremy asked.

"It's not so wild after all."

"Yeah?"

"Yeah." He started describing the imposed restrictions and regimented rules of the homeowners' association. Halfway through, the waitress returned with their drinks, bending far enough over to show him her breasts as she placed his beer on the table, and he pointedly ignored her.

"Now they've put up a guard shack and a new gate to keep out the riffraff. I have to check in and out with this uniformed guard if I want to leave or enter my own neighborhood."

Chuck laughed. "No shit?"

"No shit."

"Are you supposed to tip him?" Dylan asked. "I mean at Christmastime and stuff. I've heard that about doormen and things in New York. Maybe this is the same situation."

"I don't know," Barry admitted. "But that's the least of my worries."

He hadn't intended to say anything more, hadn't planned to talk about the weirdness, the scary things, the things he was really worried about, aware of how ridiculous they would sound to outsiders. But Jeremy's quizzical expression prompted him to keep going, to open up. These were his friends—and if he couldn't tell them, who could he tell?

He took a deep breath. "There's more," Barry said. He told them *everything*, from Barney's death to Ray's, from Stumpy to Maureen's stalker. He then explained that the new gate had gone up in one night, had appeared fully formed as if by magic.

The three of them were silent for a moment, obviously unsure of what to say.

It was Chuck who spoke first. "You're not trying out some new plot idea on us, are you?"

"I wish I was. But I'm totally serious. This is what went down." Barry took a long drink of his beer.

"*I* believe you," Dylan announced. "There are more things, Horatio—"

Chuck bumped him. "Stop trying to impress the coeds with your misquoted Shakespeare. It's not becoming in a man of your age."

"A man of my age?"

"Told you you shouldn't've moved," Jeremy said.

Barry downed the last of his beer. "Yeah. Thanks."

"And I knew that dead cat was a bad sign."

Dylan shook his head. "There's really some freak with no arms or legs or tongue flopping around in the forest between the houses?"

"There really is," Barry said.

They had a thousand questions, but they were questions of incredulity, not questions of suspicion, and he realized gratefully that his friends were not trying to rationalize or explain away his interpretation of events but believed him fully.

Jeremy put a hand on his shoulder. "We're there if you need us, dude. The situation gets too hairy and you need some help? Give us a call. We're there."

"I may take you up on that."

"Hell," Dylan said. "I could use a vacation."

It was nearly midnight when they parted, and though Jeremy offered to let him stay at his apartment, Barry had already passed the cancellation cutoff time for his hotel. "I'm paying for it anyway," he said. "I might as well use it."

Jeremy shook his hand, a strangely adult gesture for his friend and one that felt unfamiliar but at the same time reassuring. "I'm serious," he said. "If shit starts to go down, give out a shout. We're there."

Barry grasped the hand and squeezed it gratefully. "I will," he said. "You can count on it."

He'd opted to book a hotel in Orange County rather than near the airport, and he was glad of that. His plane wasn't scheduled to leave until eleven, and while he would have a long drive tomorrow morning during the tail end of rush hour, at least he didn't have to drive tonight. Fifteen minutes later, he was checked in and sacked out, and he did not stir until the phone next to his bed rang with the seven o'clock wake-up call.

He grabbed a quick Egg McMuffin for breakfast and headed back to L.A. Between the unexpected traffic and having to turn in the rental car, he barely made it onto the plane in time, but once in the air he relaxed and looked out the window at the receding megalopolis below. He realized to his surprise that he was happy to be returning to Utah, that, despite everything, it felt like home. California was a fun place to visit but he was no longer a part of it. He was glad he'd come, though. He felt better for talking to his friends, for unburdening himself, and he felt stronger on the return flight, as though he now had the strength to stand up to anyone or anything.

Even the homeowners' association.

They landed in Salt Lake City shortly after one. A small crappy lunch had been served on the flight, and he was still hungry. It would be after three by the time he finally reached Corban, so Barry stopped at a Subway and bought a sandwich and an extra large Coke before starting off.

Keeping one hand on the wheel, he sorted through the box of tapes on the seat next to him, finally popping in Jethro Tull's *A Passion Play*. He smiled to himself as the familiar strains of the music filled the car, and he cranked up the volume, feeling good.

If he had a hero it was Ian Anderson. Not only had the Tull leader created consistently good music over the past several decades, he had done so uncompromisingly. Barry admired the undiluted artistic ambition that had led Anderson to write and record an album such as *A Passion Play*, the willingness to buck the critics and buck the fans and follow his own muse, consequences be damned. It was what he himself aspired to, that sort of freedom and daring, and while he might not have the talent to carry it off, he at least hoped he had the guts and integrity to try.

An hour and a half later, he was off the interstate and on the two-lane highway that led to Corban. The semitrucks and out-of-state cars that had been whizzing by him disappeared, and only an occasional Jeep or pickup passing in the opposite direction let him know that he was not alone out here.

Why, he wondered, did television news anchors always refer to semis as "big rigs"? There didn't seem to be any "*small* rigs" or even just plain "rigs." They were always "*big* rigs." It sounded like trucker lingo to him, CB slang, and he wondered how such a phrase had garnered mainstream legitimacy.

The road was rising, high desert chaparral giving way to pinion and juniper forest, and he rounded a hilly curve to see a white Jimmy pull out from an almost invisible side road. He slowed to let the vehicle onto the highway, and the Jimmy accelerated quickly and roared away, rounding the next curve before Barry was even back up to speed.

He encountered it again ten minutes later, stuck behind a silver Lexus and honking furiously. He was still a good half mile back, but even from this distance it was obvious that the Lexus driver was playing games. He would speed up and slow down, brake nearly to a halt, then, when the Jimmy tried to pass, veer into the opposite lane to block the vehicle.

Finally, the Jimmy driver had had enough. He swerved

onto the narrow dirt shoulder and attempted to pass on the right. The Lexus increased its speed, preventing the other vehicle from getting back on the road. There was a dry streambed up ahead, a fairly deep gully that the highway crossed with a bridge. The shoulder disappeared at that point, and dirt flew as the Jimmy shot forward in a desperate effort to pull in front of the Lexus.

The Lexus kept pace.

It was only at the last moment that it seemed to become clear to the Jimmy driver that his rival would not pull back and let him in, that this was some bizarre game of chicken the Lexus driver refused to lose. The driver slammed on his brakes, but it was too late, and the Jimmy slid headfirst down the steep incline into the dry streambed.

Barry had closed the gap between himself and the other vehicles considerably and had a clear view of the accident. He braked to a halt on the last stretch of shoulder, got out, and ran toward the embankment. Ahead, he saw the Lexus' passenger window roll down, heard the driver yell something down at the victim. The car sped away. Barry tried to get the license number, but the back end of the Lexus was in shadow, and by the time it was again in full sunlight, it was too far away for him to read.

He slid down the slope in a crouch. The Jimmy had not rolled, but it had crashed headfirst into the sandy streambed, and the driver had apparently been thrown free of the vehicle through the open door.

Barry ran up. "Jesus! Are you all right?"

The man nodded, touched a hand to his bruised forehead, brushed sand and leaves off his shirt.

"You need some help? Want me to call an ambulance or the police?"

"No!" the man practically shouted. "No police!"

"Are you kidding? That guy ran you off the road. I saw it. I'm a witness."

"I'm not pressing charges. I don't want . . . I'm just . . ."

He shook his head as if to clear it. "Look, you offered to help. All I want is a ride up to the Shell station in Corban. Buck there'll come back with his tow truck and get the car."

"Sure," Barry said. "Anything you want. But you need to get the police out here. For the insurance report, if nothing else."

"No!"

Barry held up his hands. "Okay, okay."

The man pressed various spots on his face, looking at his fingers.

"I don't see any blood," Barry offered.

The man took a tentative step forward.

"You need some help?"

He shook his head. "No. I can make it."

"What an asshole," Barry said. "I saw him playing games with you, not letting you pass—"

"I'd rather not talk about it," the man said shortly.

Barry nodded.

The two of them made their way up the steep incline. Barry took it slow, in case the man needed assistance, but he made it to the top without help.

"You from Corban?" Barry asked as they walked toward his Suburban.

"Yeah."

"Me, too. I live in Bonita Vista."

The man's voice was quiet. "Me, too."

And though Barry tried to engage him in conversation, the man did not say another word until they reached the Shell station in town.

Barry did not even learn his name.

# TWENTY-SIX

Russ Gifford came home from work to find his girlfriend gone.

He probably would have thought she was at the store or down on the tennis courts or out for a jog along the bridle trail, if not for the pink piece of paper that had been slipped between the metal supports of his screen door and was fluttering noisily in the strong post-monsoon breeze.

It was an official notice from the homeowners' association.

Russ read and reread the form, his hands shaking, his stomach churning with an unidentifiable emotion that could have been anger, could have been confusion, could have been fear. His name had been illegibly scrawled on a blank line reserved for that purpose, and a box next to the statement *Action has been taken to rectify noncompliance* had been checked. On the open lines that comprised the bottom half of the form was written the chilling and cryptic note: "Unmarried couples are not allowed to live in Bonita Vista (see Article IV, Section 9, Paragraph F). Tammi Bindler has been removed to ensure compliance."

What the hell was going on here?

He read the form yet again.

*Not allowed to live? Removed?* The ambiguously threatening words and phrases could be interpreted to mean she'd been killed, although he knew that couldn't possibly be the case. Of course, the other alternative was equally unbelievable and almost as disconcerting—that she'd been kidnapped and forcibly taken elsewhere.

He hurried inside, called Tammi's sister in St. George and her mother in Kingman, hoping that Tammi had called at least one of them to explain what had happened, but neither of them had heard from her.

On an impulse, Russ ran into the bedroom to check the closet. Her clothes were all still there. In the bathroom, her toiletries were in place.

He stood, stunned into stupidity, unable to think of what he should do, the next logical step he should take.

The law, he thought.

He walked over to the phone and immediately dialed 911, but hung up before anyone answered. He'd seen enough cop shows to know that Tammi wouldn't officially be a missing person until she'd been gone for forty-eight hours.

Fuck that. He'd lie.

He dialed 911 again, and when the dispatcher came on the line, he said that his girlfriend had been missing for three days and that he feared something had happened to her. The dispatcher took his name and address and promised that the sheriff would be there within the half hour. Sure enough, a patrol car pulled up in front of his house less than fifteen minutes later, and Russ went out to meet it.

A hard-looking older man emerged from the cruiser, straightening his belt as he walked over. "I'm Sheriff Hitman. Are you Russ Gifford?"

"Yeah. Thank God you're here. My girlfriend's missing."

"Been missing for three days, I hear."

Was that suspicion in the sheriff's voice? Russ frowned. "Yes, she has. Since Monday."

"Mmm-hmm." Hitman fixed him with a hard stare. "Look, Mr. Gifford. There's no man alive that would wait three days to call in a missing persons if his girlfriend disappeared. Why don't you level with me."

"All right. It happened today." He thrust the form forward. "This was on my screen door."

Hitman took the paper.

"I've tried calling her mom, her sister, but no one knows where she is or what's happened to her."

The sheriff looked over the form, handed it back. "I'm sorry," he said. "This is out of my jurisdiction."

Russ stared at him. "What?"

"This is between you and your homeowners' association."

"My girlfriend is missing."

"She is not missing." Hitman nodded toward the pink sheet. "It states very clearly there that she has been removed from Bonita Vista because the homeowners' association does not allow couples to cohabitate."

Russ let out a snort of disbelief. "You're joking, right?"

The sheriff just looked at him.

"You're telling me that if a crime has been committed in Bonita Vista, you won't raise a finger to help out?"

"A crime has *not* been committed," Hitman said patiently. "If you read your C, C, and Rs, you'll find that the homeowners' association has a legal right to enforce its rules and regulations."

"Whose side are you on?"

"I'm not on anybody's side. I'm a law enforcement officer and that's what I do. I enforce the law. Now good day, Mr. Gifford."

Russ stepped after him. "Wait a minute! What am I supposed to do?"

Hitman opened his car door. "If you have any questions, I suggest you address them to your association's board of directors." He got into the cruiser. "Good day."

Russ watched the patrol car back up the driveway, swing around, and head down the street the way it had come.

Board of directors.

He realized that he didn't know who was on the board. He looked down at the form again, but the pink sheet of paper was unsigned and there were no individual names listed, only the name of the association. The officers and their titles could no doubt be found in those damn C, C, and Rs, but he'd tossed the booklet somewhere shortly after receiving it and had no idea where it was. He could ask someone, he supposed, but he and Tammi were not particularly social and hadn't gotten to know many of their neighbors, so he didn't feel comfortable imposing on a virtual stranger.

Ray Dyson would have known. The old man had befriended them and had even invited the two of them to a couple of parties at his house. But Ray was dead.

Maybe his wife. Maybe Liz would know.

He started walking. The Dysons' house was on the street above theirs, and if he cut through the greenbelt it would be faster to hoof it than drive. He crossed the road and started hiking over the pathless dirt.

He'd known that Ray had hated the homeowners' association but he hadn't known why. Now he did. They were a bunch of self-righteous assholes trying to impose their own morality on everyone else. He and Tammi weren't married so she had to go? The two of them had been together for ten years! Probably longer than some of the married couples in Bonita Vista.

Goddamn it, if he had the money, he'd hire a private investigator to check up on those bastards, see how many of them were divorced or had had affairs or somehow did not measure up to the strict standards the homeowners' association required.

Anger felt good. It drove off the despair, kept the self-pity at bay. He walked around an oversized manzanita bush, emerging on the street next to the Dysons' place. Still holding the pink sheet of paper—the Removal Form, as he was starting to think of it—he hurried up the driveway and rang the doorbell.

There was no immediate response, so he rang again. And knocked.

A few seconds later, the door opened a crack and Liz peeked out. "Yes?" she said. She looked awful—no makeup, hair uncombed, dirty bathrobe—but what really threw him was the fact that she didn't seem to know who he was.

"It's me. Russ." He felt obligated to reintroduce himself.

"Yes?"

Her tone was brusque. Either she still didn't recognize him or wasn't in the mood to talk. He pressed on quickly. "I came home from work this afternoon and Tammi was gone. I probably wouldn't've thought anything of it, but I found this in my screen door." He waved the Removal Form at her. "It's from the homeowners' association, and it says that unmarried people cannot live in Bonita Vista and that Tammi has been 'removed.' I don't know what the hell that's supposed to mean—"

Liz opened the door wider, poked her head out, and looked furtively around, as though searching for spies. "They're doing a purge," she said, and her voice was barely above a whisper. "They do that periodically, come down on homeowners who break the rules, get rid of the people they don't like, who offend them."

"But why pick on me? I've never done anything to them. I don't even know who the hell they are."

"I wonder who else is out," Liz mumbled to herself. She looked up at Russ. "Do you know Wayne and Pat? The gay couple?"

"Yeah. I met them at your party."

"Do you know where they live?"

"Around the corner from me. On Oak."

"Check their house. I bet they're gone, too."

Russ realized that the Removal Form was crumpled in his clutched fist. "Well, who's on this damn board? I want to know what happened to Tammi. I want some answers."

"My husband did, too," Liz whispered, and she closed the door on him. He heard the snick of a deadbolt, the rattling of a chain lock.

"Just give me one of their names!" He pounded on the door. "Who's the president?"

But Liz did not reappear, and after several fruitless moments of knocking and waiting and ringing the bell and shouting out pleas, he finally gave up. On the way back, he decided to follow Liz's suggestion, and he stopped by the house Wayne and Pat shared. But no one answered the door, and there was no sign of the couple. Although there were still two cars in the driveway, the place had an air of abandonment.

*Removed.*

The anger was subsiding, and he was filled with an increasing sense of hopelessness, a desperate fear that there was nothing he could do to find Tammi, that he was fated to stand helplessly and impotently by while whatever happened to her happened. He tried to keep the anger alive, wanting the strength it gave him, and he stopped off at the next house over. He didn't know who lived here, but the woman who answered the door seemed nice and neighborly, and he asked her if she could tell him who was on the association's board of directors. He didn't want to burden her with his own problems, so he didn't explain *why* he wanted to know, but she was taken aback by the question and started to shut the door on him.

"Wait!" he said, but the door closed and locked.

It was the same at all the houses he tried. He hit every house on the street, and though a couple of them were vacation homes and a few other people had not yet returned from work, most of the people answered their doors. And none of them would respond to his question about the homeowners' association.

He returned home troubled, depressed, and frightened. The C, C, and Rs were somewhere in the house, and he tore the place apart trying to find them. No luck.

He spent the rest of the evening calling friends and family, seeing if anyone had heard from Tammi, laying out the situation and finding out if anyone had any ideas. No one seemed to believe his story. Hell, if he'd heard this from someone else, he probably wouldn't believe it either.

Liz had spoken of purges, and he wondered what she'd meant by that. He should have asked, although she hadn't exactly been in the most talkative of moods.

In his mind, he saw a group of robed inquisitors tying up Tammi and burning her at a stake in the middle of the forest for living with a man before marriage.

No, that couldn't be the case.

Could it?

*Removed.*

For the first time since childhood, he cried himself to sleep. They were tears of rage and frustration more than of sadness and loss, but his emotions flip-flopped and all of those feelings were somewhere in the mix. He felt as though he should be doing something, as though there *was* something he could do if only he could remember what it was, but that was an emotional response, and he realized intellectually that he was in the same position as any person with a missing loved one. All he could do was wait.

Ordinarily, Russ was a sound sleeper. But the stress of not knowing Tammi's whereabouts and the uncomfortably unfamiliar sensation of having the bed all to himself ensured that he slept only fitfully. He tossed and turned, woke up at eleven-thirty, eleven-forty, eleven fifty-five, midnight. Sometime after one, he finally nodded off and slept for over half an hour straight. He might have made it all the way through the night, but he was awakened by the sound of pounding.

He opened his eyes, automatically looked at the clock— *1:43*—and sat up, trying to determine where the noise originated. The pounding sounded as if it were coming from somewhere in the front of the house. In fact, it sounded as though large rocks were being lobbed at the building. But kids who threw rocks usually tossed only one or two and then fled. He'd heard at least a dozen since being awakened, and there seemed to be no letup in sight. There was, as well, an even regularity to the sounds, as though it were being done by machine, as though some sort of reloading catapult was—

An explosive crash reverberated through the house as the living room window shattered.

Russ was out of bed before the tinkling of broken glass had silenced. He ran out of the bedroom, down the hall, unlocked and yanked open the front door, and flipped on the porch light. "I know who you are, asshole!" He scanned the darkness, unable to see anyone. "I'm calling the fucking cops, you son of a bitch!"

There were rocks at his feet, obviously ones that had been thrown at the house, and he saw others within the circle of illumination provided by the porch light. He felt chilled as he peered into the blackness. "Get the fuck off my property!" he yelled.

There was no response. He could see nothing, hear nothing.

Who was doing this? he wondered. And why?

*Removed.*

He reached down to pick up one of the rocks, and once again the sound of breaking glass shattered the silence of the night.

One of the windows on his car.

Thumping came from all directions as people in the bushes lobbed rocks at all four sides of his house.

Russ shut the door, locked it, hiding inside, the pounding of his heart threatening to drown out even his racing thoughts. He'd wanted to call out, wanted to yell threats, but he was scared and acting on instinct. It was the fact that there was more than one person out there that really frightened him. And the fact that they were so organized.

Who *was* it? And what could they possibly have against him?

The homeowners' association.

Yes.

It didn't make a whole lot of sense—why would grown men be crouched in the bushes in the middle of the night throwing rocks at a house?—but then neither did the whole business of Tammi's "removal." And it followed that if they wanted to remove one of the offending unmarried fornicators, they would want to get rid of both.

Russ had no guns, but he had golf clubs, and he went into the hall closet and pulled out a nine iron, and swung it at shoulder level, hearing the comforting *swish* of sliced air. If any of those motherfuckers tried to get in this house, he'd take off their goddamn heads.

He walked back out to the living room, pulled his recliner against the back wall, and sat down facing the broken window. A cool night breeze blew the curtains in and out, moonlight shimmering on the shattered glass that littered the carpet.

He waited, fingers gripping the golf club until they hurt.

The thumping continued for another hour before stopping abruptly, but he did not sleep again all night.

In the morning, he packed some essentials and enough clothes for a week, locked up the house, and got the hell out of Dodge.

He'd come back later with some friends to get the rest of his stuff—and to put the house up for sale.

# TWENTY-SEVEN

**The Bonita Vista Homeowners' Association Covenants, Conditions, and Restrictions** Article IV, General Provisions, Section 9, Paragraph F:

> *No unmarried resident of Bonita Vista may cohabitate with a member of the same or opposite sex in any residence within the Properties. Unmarried couples may jointly own a lot or residence within the Properties but may not both reside at the location until they are legally wed. Homosexual unions have no legal status and are thus prohibited.*

# TWENTY-EIGHT

They'd been going to sleep a lot earlier here in Utah than they used to in California ("the Mormon influence," Barry said), but their rituals remained the same and, despite the fact that they'd talked about, planned, and fully intended to make love tonight, Barry was dozing by the time Maureen finished taking her shower. The bedroom television was still on—*Politically Incorrect*—and she sat on the edge of the mattress, looking down at him, his features tinted blue by the flickering light of the tube. She'd always envied his ease of sleep. He was one of those people who nodded off shortly after his head hit the pillow and slept through until morning, his face angelically serene no matter what was going on in his life during daylight hours. She, on the other hand, was a tosser and turner, awakened by the slightest shift in his position or the merest change in room temperature.

He smiled in his sleep, and she touched his cheek, gave him a small prod. "Hey."

He frowned, squinted, blinked. "What?"

"You fell asleep."

"So?"

She felt a little hurt. "I thought we were—"

"I'm joking," he told her. He yawned, smiled, pulled her down, and kissed her. She had to work on him a while to get him hard enough, but ever since she'd stopped taking the Pill, she'd had no problem getting aroused; for her, it had given their recent lovemaking an extra edge, had kicked it up a notch, and tonight was no exception. She came quick and hard.

Afterward, she lay in bed, listening to Barry snore beside her, a sound that drowned out the low drone of the television. She looked over at his sleeping face. She wasn't sure how thrilled he was to be trying for a baby. Oh, he said he wanted a family, but actions spoke louder than words as the saying went, and his behavior and attitude clearly indicated that his desire—or at least the intensity of it—was not the same as hers.

Still, she had no doubt he'd be a good dad, no matter how reluctant he might be initially, and she fell asleep looking at him and listening to the comforting sound of his deep, even breaths.

In the morning, they ate breakfast together for the first time in a week, Barry making french toast while she squeezed fresh orange juice. She kissed him at the door before he set off for his office. "Have a nice day, dear."

"What the hell's that about?"

She smiled, patted her abdomen. "We have to start practicing for family life."

The smile he gave her was unreadable, and Maureen watched him get into the Suburban, waving at him as he pulled out of the driveway.

She closed and locked the door. She had nothing to do today, no meetings scheduled, no work to perform, and this time it was by choice.

As hard as it was to believe, almost against her will, she'd grown fond of free days, of having time off, and she'd started deliberately rearranging her duties and shifting her workload so that she worked only Mondays, Wednesdays, and Fridays.

Tuesdays and Thursdays were free; they were her own.

She hadn't gone back to the tennis courts since her run-in with those teenagers, but she hadn't wanted for things to do. She'd hung around the house, worked in her garden, visited with the new friends she was making in the neighborhood. She was getting used to this life, used to Utah, and if things in Bonita Vista weren't exactly perfect . . . well, what was?

She sat down on the couch, turned on CNN. There'd been an earthquake in the desert outside Los Angeles, and according to Cal Tech seismologists, the temblor measured 6.1 on the Richter scale and could be felt as far away as Phoenix and Las Vegas. No damage reports or injury statistics were yet available, although, in their never-ending quest to put victims on the air, the anchors did talk for over a minute to a Howard Stern caller before realizing that they'd been had.

"Baba Booey!" the caller yelled. "Ef Jackie! Ef Timmy's skull!"

Laughing, Maureen turned off the television. It was going to be a hot day today, and if she wanted to get anything done in the garden, she'd better do it before ten. She went up to the kitchen to pour some water into her sports bottle and went outside, carrying the phone with her in case a client called while she was working. It was a bad habit, she knew, and one reason Barry refused to get a cellular phone, even though he readily acknowledged the practical benefits of having one in the car in case of emergency. He didn't like her need to be constantly tethered to her job. She recognized his concerns, but she also tried to make him understand that his job was unique, that most people's occupations required dealing with clients or customers, and that they could not just hang up a "Gone fishing" sign whenever they didn't feel like working. They had to take and answer calls even if they came at inconvenient and inappropriate times.

The garden was doing well, and she fed her roses, plucking out some morning glories that had sprouted up and were winding their tendrils around some of her more sensitive plants. The phone rang while she was picking her first ripe tomatoes of the season, and Maureen wiped her hands on her jeans and grabbed the phone from the rock on which she'd placed it. "Hello?"

It was Audrey Hodges. Laura Holm had stopped to chat for a second while on her daily powerwalk around the neighborhood, had mentioned that she'd seen Maureen working outside, and Audrey was just calling to see how things were going.

"Fine. I'm taking the day off to do a little work around the house."

"Good, good." Audrey paused. "Actually, this isn't entirely a social call. Frank and I are looking for a tax accountant. We've just gotten an IRS notice saying that we owe an extra five hundred dollars because Frank's numbers didn't gibe with the numbers submitted by his employer and our bank. It's the second year in a row this has happened, and I'm getting pretty sick of it. We had a big fight last night and, well, the upshot is that we decided to have someone do our taxes for us this year.

"*Just* this year," she added quickly. "I don't want you to start counting on us and think you have a permanent client. Frank intends to just use your tax forms as a template and follow the same steps next year. I'd prefer to have you do all our taxes from now on, but getting even this big a concession was like pulling teeth."

Maureen laughed. "No problem. I'll even give you a good neighbor discount."

"Thanks, Mo. Say, would you like to come over for lunch?"

She hesitated. "I don't know. I'm kind of busy . . ."

"Come on. You have to eat anyway. We can catch up on a little neighborhood gossip and you can get some extra exercise in the bargain. Just walk down here around noon, eat, and run. I won't keep you."

"Are you saying I *need* the exercise?"

"After my French onion soup you might."

Maureen laughed. "Okay. I'll see you around noon."

She spent another hour in the garden, watering plants and squishing quite a few snails before heading inside, changing her clothes, and washing up. The computer was beckoning to her, and she was tempted to finish the spreadsheet she'd started yesterday, but she forced herself to sit down on the couch and read the most recent *Los Angeles Times* they'd gotten in the mail.

This was supposed to be a day off.

She finished the paper shortly before noon and quickly went to the bathroom, putting on some lipstick before grabbing her house keys and heading out. A lot of people around here didn't lock their doors, she knew, figuring they were safe in a gated community, but after what had happened to Barney, she and Barry always made sure they locked the place up before leaving.

The day was beautiful, not yet hot but pleasantly warm, the sky filled with the type of fluffy white clouds in which children loved to see shapes. On the way down to Audrey's house, she passed the flat vacant space that had supposedly been put aside for Bonita Vista's future swimming pool and was surprised to see a group of shirtless men working on the property. Five or six of them were clearing brush with clippers and rakes and other hand tools, while several other men were working in tandem, using pickaxes to dig at a spot in the rocky ground. They looked for all the world like a chain-gang, although there were no shackles or fetters in sight.

She walked by, not looking at the men, feeling somewhat self-conscious, expecting at any moment to hear wolf whistles and catcalls, but there was only a loud occasional grunt of exertion, the thwack of shears, and the plinging of metal on rock.

It seemed odd to her that there were no power tools, that no one had a chainsaw or a rototiller, and she wondered if the association had some rule against *that*.

Audrey was setting a table on the side patio of the house, and she waved Maureen over. "Come on up! The food's ready. I was just about to bring out the salad."

The Hodges' house was nice, but it was nestled among the tall pines at the bottom of the hill, in the flat part of Bonita Vista, and had no view. She knew that Frank and Audrey had paid a lot more for their place than she and Barry had, and Maureen was thankful that they'd found such a deal. She walked up the wooden steps and around the side of the house to the patio.

"Have a seat," Audrey said. "You want wine, water, Fresca, or iced tea?"

"Water's fine."

"I'll be right out."

Maureen sat down, and her friend emerged a moment later from the kitchen, two tall glasses of ice water in hand.

Maureen accepted her glass gratefully, took a long sip. "I just saw a bunch of men a few lots up the street digging and clearing brush—"

"Oh, those are the guys who volunteered to help dig out the swimming pool and lay the foundation for the community center. Dex Richards is a contractor, and he's overseeing the project, whipping the rest of those couch potatoes into shape. I think even Frank's going to volunteer some time this weekend."

"We didn't even hear about it."

Audrey waved a dismissive hand. "That's because it's been going on so long that there aren't any formal communications to the membership anymore. The association doesn't want to embarrass itself by making promises it can't keep or deadlines it can't meet. But I think this time we might actually pull this thing off. Dex is a good contractor and he knows what he's doing. It'll probably be too late for this summer, but by next spring we should have a pool."

"What's this community center for?"

"Oh, you know. Block parties or birthday parties or youth group activities. Whatever. The association'll probably hold the annual meeting there. We've been holding it in the cafeteria over at Corban High. It'll be nice to have our own place." Audrey held up a finger. "I'll be back in a sec. I'm just going to bring out the soup and salad."

She went inside, and Maureen stared into the trees. The world was quiet, despite an occasional birdcry, and through the still air she could hear the sounds of the men up the street digging, pounding, chopping.

Audrey returned with the food, sat down, and they started eating, talking about the weather, their husbands, Maureen's job, things in general.

Maureen ate a bite of salad. "So, Kenny Tolkin was a con artist, huh?"

The other woman frowned. "What?"

"Frank told Barry that Kenny was living illegally in someone's house and scammed some people out of their money."

Audrey shook her head. "No," she said slowly. "It was *his* house. From what I understand, he was in arrears because he had not paid his association dues for the year. I think he was put on some type of probation but he skipped out. I don't know why. He could've worked it off. The association isn't completely inflexible." She smiled at Maureen. "Although they're pretty close."

They both laughed.

Audrey speared a tomato with her fork. "I suppose he'll put it up for sale eventually."

The soup and salad were delicious, as was the homemade rosemary bread that was brought out a few moments later after a timer in the kitchen rang. Audrey was quite a cook, and Maureen wished, not for the first time, that she was a little more domestic, that she'd taken some cooking classes or, at the very least, listened more to her mother while growing up. It was not too late, though, and with her new resolve to have more free time, she thought she could probably find the time to sign up for some courses, providing Corban had some type of adult ed program.

"So what do you think about the pamphlet?" Audrey asked.

Maureen frowned. "Pamphlet?"

"The sexual harassment pamphlet. Don't tell me you didn't get one?"

"No."

Audrey laughed. "Well, you're in for a treat. Our old friends at the association are now laying down policy about sexual liaisons between homeowners." She shook her head, chuckled. "Not that it'll stop anything."

Maureen raised an eyebrow. "Anything you want to tell me?"

"No, no, nothing like that."

"Do you have a copy of the pamphlet? I'd like to see it."

"I think Frank tossed it, but I'll see."

She couldn't find the pamphlet, but she did come back with twin bowls of peach sorbet, and they ate dessert and talked about the prudery that seemed to have overtaken the world since their teenage years.

Afterward, Maureen offered to stay and help clean up, but Audrey shooed her off. "Get out of here."

"Next time it's at my place."

"Are you expecting me to help with *your* dishes?"

"Of course not."

"I'll be there."

Maureen walked slowly back up the street toward home. She looked again at the shirtless workers as she passed by the pool site and for some reason was reminded of Kenny

Tolkin. Why, she wondered, had he run away? Because he was behind in paying his dues? It was a bizarre and unbelievable reaction, and the idea didn't sit well with her. People only ran when they were afraid, and she thought of the mysterious appearance of the new gate as well as everything else that had happened, and despite the heat of the day she felt cold.

There was no mail in the box when she checked, but there was a glossy pamphlet. Sure enough, it was titled *Bonita Vista Sexual Harassment Guidelines*, and she opened it as she walked up the driveway, her eye immediately drawn to the subheading "Love Can Wait."

Wait for what?

She glanced down at the bulleted paragraphs.

- Sexual relationships between neighbors are very seldom secret. Others will be watching and judging your behavior, which could lead to disharmony in the community.

- Relationships may end and leave one or both of the individuals with bitter feelings. If this happens, there will be uncomfortable and awkward social situations as well as the possibility for retaliation by one or both parties.

- Sex between neighbors, even consensual sex, is considered unprofessional and inappropriate behavior. While there are no current regulations prohibiting such conduct, rules are being drafted and will be put to a vote at the annual meeting in September.

Maureen frowned. There was nothing actually in here about sexual harassment. Like Audrey said, this was simply an unwarranted intrusion into people's personal lives. Not only was the homeowners' association driving off individuals who didn't pay their dues on time, it was also trying to dictate people's sex partners. What was next? Requiring association approval before performing certain sexual acts and positions? This was an audacious and unbelievable invasion of privacy, and she found it both ridiculous and horrifying.

She walked into the house. A small petty part of her considered throwing the pamphlet away, not showing it to Barry, not telling him about it. It was difficult enough to be proved wrong about something without having your face rubbed in it. But this was too egregious to be swept under the rug. Barry and Ray had been right about the association all along, and while the regulations outlined in the pamphlet didn't affect her, the next edict might, and she found herself wondering what the association could possibly try to prohibit next.

# TWENTY-NINE

He was writing again.

Whatever it was that had caused his temporary block was gone, and Barry was grateful. He did not try to analyze it, did not look at it too carefully or think about it overmuch. He was not one to question the whys and wherefores; he simply accepted it when things went well and hoped they continued that way.

He stopped typing, flexed his fingers, and read over the paragraph he'd just finished.

The thought crossed his mind that he'd been corrupted by Hollywood. It sounded melodramatic and probably seemed ludicrous on the face of it, but the truth was that he'd been thinking of filmic possibilities for this new novel even as he was writing it. Always before, plot and characters had served only the story, with real-life considerations having no say in the outcome. But ever since his near brush with movie success, he'd found himself *casting* this novel, trying to figure out the actor or actress best suited for each character. He'd also been unusually aware of visual elements in the story, things that would look good on the screen.

Was this influencing the work itself?

He didn't think so, but he wasn't sure, and the possibility worried him.

Still, things were sailing along. He'd finished twelve

pages this morning alone, and he saved what he'd written, turned off the computer, and stood, stretching. It was lunchtime, a little later than usual, actually, and he closed up his office and walked across the field to the coffee shop to grab some grub.

All of the regulars were there, in place and eating. They were unusually quiet when he walked in, and he had the unsettling feeling that they had halted their conversations as a result of his presence.

"Howdy, all!" he called out, smiling too broadly as he passed by the tables nearest the door.

Hank offered a curt "Hello," not bothering to look up from his plate. Behind the counter, Bert merely nodded, and Barry sat down at his usual table, ordering his usual lunch from an uncharacteristically silent Lurlene.

He sipped his water and tried to catch the eye of one of his buddies, but no one was looking in his direction and they seemed to be making a concerted effort to ignore him. He felt the way he had that first day—unwanted and out of place—and it was all he could do to remain in his seat and not tell Bert to wrap up his food to go.

Gradually, conversation started up again, first over on the opposite side of the room, then at the tables closer to his wall seat. He wasn't listening exactly, didn't want to eavesdrop on other people's business, but when he heard Joe mention the phrase "Bonita Vista," his ears pricked up.

"This time they've gone too far," Lyle was saying.

Someone else agreed.

"And you know they're not going to be held responsible," Joe said loudly. "Nothing's going to happen to them. No one's going to get punished."

Lurlene brought over Barry's order. "His sister found him," she said, ignoring him and addressing Lyle's table. "She was going out to feed the dog, and he was next to the doggie bowl."

Hank cleared his throat. "You guys're talkin' like he's

dead. I thought they didn't know if he was going to be okay yet or not."

"They don't," Joe said. "But it don't look good. A chopper airlifted him to the Cedar City hospital. They got a good poison unit there. But last I heard, he was in a coma and they don't expect him to come out of it."

Ralph spoke loudly. "That homeowners' association killed him just as surely as if they'd put a gun to his head."

Barry focused on his food. The conversation had obviously been pitched at such a level for his benefit, but he was at a loss and didn't know how he was supposed to respond. Or *if* he was supposed to respond. He finished his lunch in silence, paid his bill, then nodded good-bye and headed back out to the office.

What was that about? he wondered. They knew about his hatred of the homeowners' association. Hank did, at least. And there was no way they could think he'd be involved in any poisoning scheme. So why the cold shoulder?

He didn't know, but it bothered him, and after sitting in front of his computer for the next two hours and hacking out only a single paragraph, he shut everything off, closed up shop, and went home.

He was watching TV when Maureen arrived home from a meeting with her newest client, some bigwig at the bank, and she gave him a disgusted look as she put down her briefcase. "Afternoon talk shows?"

"How else am I going to keep up with popular slang? I'm isolated out here. This helps me learn what people are talking about and the way they talk about it. This is research." He grinned. "I can take this off my taxes, right?"

"Try to be a person," she said.

He followed her upstairs to the kitchen, where she poured herself a Diet Coke. "I'm not used to all this . . . selling," she admitted. "Back in California, I just had to convince people that I was the best accountant for the job.

I didn't have to convince them that they needed an accountant, period. People are so backward here."

"Yeah, but the scenery's beautiful." Barry pointed out the sliding glass door.

Maureen laughed. "Yes, the scenery's beautiful."

They decided to go for a late afternoon walk, and Barry waited downstairs on the couch, watching two gorgeous women fight over a grotesquely overweight bigamist on TV while Maureen changed her shoes and filled up her sports bottle.

They walked out to the street, and Barry stopped. "Which way?" he asked, looking in both directions. "Up or down?"

"Let's go down the hill," Maureen suggested. "We'll save the hard stuff for last."

They descended the steeply sloping street, walking slowly and holding hands so as not to accelerate unwantedly. They passed a handful of houses set back among the trees and some heavily forested lots before the road finally leveled off. Suddenly, the trees opened up and they were confronted on the right by what looked like nearly half an acre of denuded land.

"Jesus," Barry said. He stopped short to take it all in. "Look at that." He pointed to the edge of the open space, where a group of shirtless men were lined up before a ditch, digging. An incongruously well-dressed man holding a black whip was standing behind the ditch on a raised section of ground, barking orders. It reminded him of a scene from some low-budget biblical epic or a revisionist indie film about the Old South.

But there were no cameras rolling here.

"What the hell's going on?"

"They're digging a pool," Maureen said. "And laying a foundation for a community center. Audrey said they're volunteers."

The man with the whip cracked it. "Faster!" he ordered. "We're falling behind!"

"It doesn't look like they're doing this voluntarily to me."

He realized that they were both talking low, as if afraid of being overheard, and Barry made a conscious effort to raise his voice. "This must be a joke. This can't be real."

"I don't know, they were doing the same thing yesterday, although without the whip hand. And they've sure done a lot of clearing and digging since then. That's a lot of work for a joke."

"I thought the association had all sorts of brush and tree-cutting prohibitions."

"Not for themselves," Maureen said dryly.

They walked slowly past the open area, watching the men work.

Maureen stopped and frowned. "Is that Greg Davidson?"

He followed her pointing finger, saw a young man on the edge of the group who was half-hidden by a still extant manzanita bush. It *did* look like Greg, and Barry squinted at the man, trying to get a better view. "I thought he and his wife were moving out."

"So did I."

"Greg!" he called out, but the man did not turn to look at him, did not respond at all, simply kept digging.

"Maybe it's not him," Barry said. But he knew better. Obscured sightline or not, he recognized the man, and his gut confirmed what his eyes could not.

There was something wrong here. Greg Davidson was not only supposed to have sold his house and moved to Arizona, but he had been as fiercely anti-association as Ray or Barry himself—and had more of a reason to be so than either of them. So why was he still here, volunteering his time to help the association build a swimming pool?

He wasn't volunteering, Barry thought, and the idea made him shiver.

The overseer cracked the whip once again.

One of the other men looked familiar as well, a skinny guy with short brown hair, but Barry could not seem to place him.

There was no reason they could not walk onto the property and look around, find out if it really was Greg Davidson, ask the man with the whip what the hell he was doing. This was association land, owned jointly by all, and they had as much right to be on it as anyone else.

But they kept walking. Rights were different from reality, and without speaking they each knew that they were not welcome here, that there was something odd and decidedly threatening about this supposedly benign and communally beneficial volunteer effort.

They did not talk until they were well past the site and the road had rounded a copse of tall trees, and even then it was only to say, "That was weird," and "Yeah." What they had seen, what they'd felt, was not something that lent itself to casual discussion, and to say any more than that would invest it with a power neither of them wanted it to have.

Barry filed away the entire experience, as well as their reactions, in his mind, knowing that, like his introduction to Stumpy, it would one day come out in his fiction.

They continued walking, spotting a deer eating the azaleas that lined someone's driveway, seeing some sort of bright orange bird land on the dead limb of a juniper. It was like a different world, a perfect place where everyone and everything lived in harmony, and only the far-off plinking of shovels behind them told him otherwise.

They took a cross-street to the section of Bonita Vista on the other side of their hill, and met Mike halfway up Sycamore Drive. He was standing by the side of the road, bent over and holding his side, breathing deeply. He smiled sheepishly when he saw them. "That slope's a mother."

Maureen laughed. "Come on! If Barry can do it, anyone can do it."

"I resent that," Barry said. He looked over at Mike, who was still breathing hard. "I thought you were supposed to be in shape. You said you played tennis."

"Well, I stand there and hit the ball over the net. I don't *run* or anything. That's why Tina has me exercising out here. She doesn't think I do enough physical activity. By the way, if she asks, you saw me jogging out here, not gasping for air by the side of the road."

Maureen laughed. "Your secret's safe with us."

"Where're you guys headed?"

Barry shrugged. "Around the loop and back home."

"Mind if I join you?"

"Be our guest."

They continued up the street. Like Mike, Barry could already feel himself getting winded, but he refused to acknowledge it or let on, and he took long, slow, deep breaths in order to keep himself from panting.

The road came down the side of a small rise before sloping up again, and at the low point of the depression another street snaked off to the left.

"Shortcut," Mike said, pointing.

Barry read the sign as they approached. "Ponderosa Circle?"

"It's misnamed. It's not really a circle. Halfway through, it turns into Pinion, which opens onto your street."

Barry took one look at the steep road before them. "We'll take it."

"Cowards," Maureen told them.

"I don't see you objecting."

They turned left. The narrow street hugged the side of the hill before dipping into a hollow. There weren't many

houses in this section of Bonita Vista, only occasional dirt
driveways on the right that led up to stilted vacation homes.
The flat ground to their left remained heavily wooded and
wildly overgrown, small metal stakes with lot numbers on
them the only indication that the land had been subdivided
at all.

And then they saw the house.

It was the biggest home Barry had seen in Bonita Vista,
and it sat on an immaculately groomed lot, surrounded on
three sides by a virtual wall of dense vegetation. Two, possibly three stories high, it was painted gray, with black trim
and a black slate roof. The walls were solid save for two
small slits to either side of the door. There were no windows. A wraparound porch seemed an afterthought, an effort to humanize the house, but there was something
off-putting about the iron-gray structure, with its lack of
windows and its intimidating bulk, something that resisted
any and all attempts to soften its appearance.

In the adjacent carport was a silver Lexus.

A localized breeze sprang up, ruffling his hair, blowing
cold against his sweaty skin, but leaving the trees and
bushes untouched. Barry suddenly knew where'd he'd seen
that other volunteer before. He was the nameless Jimmy
driver who'd been forced off the road by the Lexus on his
way home from Salt Lake City, the fellow Bonita Vista resident whom he'd given a ride.

"Remember I told you about that accident on my way
back from Salt Lake City, the Lexus that ran the guy off the
road?"

Maureen nodded. "Yeah."

He pointed toward the carport. "That's it," he told her.
"That's the car." He turned toward Mike. "Whose house is
that? Who lives there?"

"Calhoun," Mike said, and there was something in his
voice that made Barry feel cold.

The world was suddenly silent save for the rustle of the

breeze and the sound of a metal pulley banging against the empty flagpole in the center of the grassy lawn.

"Calhoun?"

Mike nodded. "Jasper Calhoun. The president of the homeowners' association."

# THIRTY

Saturday.

They spent the morning puttering around the yard: Barry scraping from the driveway dirt and debris that had been washed onto their property from yesterday's storm, Maureen trimming, feeding, and watering the plants in her garden.

In the afternoon, Maureen concentrated on building a web page, sitting in front of a blank screen on her computer as she pored through the twin textbooks she'd recently received in the mail. Although she had picked up a few clients, her search for local business wasn't going quite as well as she'd hoped, and if she couldn't take over the town of Corban, then she was bound and determined to become a cyber-accountant and turn her business into an on-line global corporation. "E-accounting," she told Barry. "It's the wave of the future, and I'm on the ground floor."

"That's a mixed metaphor," he told her.

"I guess I'll let you proofread my prospectus when I take my corporation public."

Barry was at loose ends. He'd been cheating the past week, writing at home—as though anyone would be able to prove he hadn't composed certain paragraphs at his office—but he didn't feel like writing today, and he didn't feel much like doing anything else. He tried to get into a book, but found himself daydreaming and reading the same sentence over and over. He turned on the television but there was nothing good on, and when he perused the video titles in their library he could not find anything that looked interesting.

Maureen finally got tired of his restlessness and gave him an assignment.

"Audrey put together her and Frank's tax returns for the past four years, and I promised I'd go over them. They've had to pay twice now, and she wants to make sure there aren't any surprises coming up in the immediate future. She's afraid they're red-flagged and the IRS will go back and get them for other years. Why don't you walk over to their place and pick them up for me."

"Am I being that annoying?"

"Yes. Now go make yourself useful."

Despite his token protest, he was grateful to have something to do, and he went into the bedroom, where he kicked off his thongs and put on tennis shoes. The logical thing to do would have been to call first and make sure Audrey or Frank was home, but he wanted to walk, and he kissed the top of Maureen's head before heading out. "Be back soon, boss."

The weather was hot and muggy. There would be no storm this afternoon, but the air carried enough moisture that it upped the humidity to swamp conditions. Theirs was not the only house that had been deluged by runoff from yesterday's monsoon, and as he walked down the hill he saw several empty vacation homes with driveways full of mud and branches. He found himself wondering what Stumpy did when it rained. Did the limbless man hide under someone's porch or huddle beneath the branches of a tree? Did he have some sort of lean-to out there in the woods? Or was he so brain-damaged that he didn't notice and didn't care, sitting out in the torrential downpour and howling into the wind, wiggling through the mud, oblivious?

Barry walked around the curve of the road and saw the site of the pool and community center. There'd been no one working either this morning or now, but the volunteers had already made significant strides toward their goal, and on the cleared land he could see the partially dug building foundation and the Olympic-sized pit that would be the pool.

He was glad no one was working now. It was broad daylight and he was a grown man, but he was a grown man with a dark and overactive imagination, and the thought of seeing those zombielike diggers and their harsh taskmaster scared him.

He reached the Hodges' house. Frank's pickup was not in the driveway, which meant that he and Audrey were probably in town shopping or something, but he walked between the tall pines and up the porch nonetheless, and rang the bell. To his surprise, Audrey answered the door. "Hi, Barry."

"I didn't think anyone was home."

"I'm here, but Frank's out fishing. Once a month, I let him out of my sight and allow him to spend the day at his secret spot on the creek. He never catches anything, but it seems to lighten his load a bit. If you're looking for him, he should be back around three or four."

"Actually, I came to see you. Mo sent me over to pick up some tax forms."

"That's right! Come in, come in." She stepped aside to allow him entrance, and he walked into the living room.

She motioned him toward the couch. "You in a hurry or do you have time to stay and chat a little?"

He shrugged, looked at his watch. "There's nothing pressing. I can stay a while."

"Good. I want to talk to you about Liz. Frank and I are both worried sick about her."

"So are we."

"I stopped by yesterday afternoon to invite her over for

lunch today, and she wouldn't even open the door. Just shouted at me from inside the house."

"The same thing happened to us. We paid her a visit this morning after tennis, and she wouldn't come out. She told us she wasn't feeling well and would call on us when she felt better."

"We have to do something. I know Ray's death was a big blow, but she has to try and get on with her life. I was thinking we could do some sort of intervention, gather all her friends together and march over there en masse, camp out if we have to and not leave until we have a chance to sit down and talk to her."

Barry nodded. "It's worth a try."

Audrey shook her head as though she'd just remembered something. "Oh, where are my manners! Do you want something to drink? Coffee? A beer?"

"No thank you," Barry said.

Audrey stood anyway. "Well, make yourself at home," she said. "I'll be back in a sec. I have to tinkle." She smiled sweetly at him, holding his gaze for a beat longer than was comfortable, and he looked away, embarrassed.

She walked down the hall to the back of the house, and he leaned forward, sorting through the magazines on the coffee table: *Bondage, Rough Sex, S&M Quarterly, Contemporary Torture Play.* Hair prickled on the back of his neck.

There was something wrong here.

It was a feeling he'd experienced so often lately that it was beginning to seem like his normal state of being, this constant lurking dread, this condition of being always caught off guard, always worried that some new and horrible problem was just around the corner.

He debated whether to leave right now or hang around and wait, but quickly decided that to leave would be not only rude but cowardly. Besides, he might be overreacting. So Frank and Audrey were into some kinky stuff. What they did in the privacy of their own bedroom was none of his business. He glanced around the room, saw nothing else out of the ordinary: an entertainment center against one wall, the stuffed head of a moose that Frank shot hanging over the fireplace, typical middle American furniture and framed art prints adorning the remaining space.

There were only the magazines.

*Contemporary Torture Play.*

He waited.

She emerged from the hallway a few moments later wearing nothing but a chastity belt—a gothic-looking metal contraption that wrapped around her thighs and hips and fit snugly over her crotch and buttocks. Her face was slightly flushed, but not from shame or embarrassment.

From excitement.

Her nipples, he noticed, had been sliced off. Only scar tissue remained.

She opened her mouth, stuck out her tongue, and on it was a key.

Already he was standing, instinctively moving away. "I . . ." he began, but he didn't finish. He didn't know what to say.

She removed the key with thumb and forefinger, holding it out to him. "Unlock my box," she said.

He was still backing up, though the front door was in the opposite direction. He finally found his voice. "Audrey, I don't know if you're drunk or what, but I have to tell you that I'm not interested, I'm not into this—"

She sidled next to him. "You can do anything you want to me," she whispered.

He scrambled, trying to get around her and out of the house.

"Beat me, hurt me, use my mouth for your toilet, give me a boiling oil enema or a hot Tabasco douche."

She reached for him, grabbed between his legs, but he

was not aroused, and she frowned as her fingers kneaded his softness. "What's wrong with you?"

"What's wrong with *me*?" He pushed her hand away. "Jesus Christ!"

Outside, there was the sound of squealing brakes in the driveway, followed closely by the noise of a pickup's door slamming shut.

Barry shoved Audrey aside, the chastity belt clanking as she stumbled, and hurried out of the house.

"I want the pain!" she yelled behind him.

He hit the driveway running, and dashed past Frank, staring at the ground as he sprinted by, afraid to meet his friend's eyes. It occurred to him that he hadn't picked up the tax forms Maureen had sent him to collect, but there was no way he was going back in that house. He ran past the empty pool site and made it halfway home before the hill became too steep and he had to stop, breathing heavily.

What was happening back at the Hodges'? There was no way Audrey could have gotten out of that contraption and back into clothes before Frank walked into the house. Was he screaming at her now, outraged at her attempted betrayal, mortified that she had exposed their kinky sex habits to an outsider? Or—and this is what made the sweat turn cold on his skin—was he not surprised, was he in on it, had he come home early on purpose, in order to join in the fun?

No, that was impossible. He hadn't planned to walk down to the Hodges'. Maureen had sent him out at the last minute to give him something to do and get him out of the house. No one could have known ahead of time that he would be there.

But Audrey had asked Maureen to come over and pick up the forms. Maybe the whole setup had been meant for her.

*Just because you're paranoid doesn't mean they're not after you.*

He looked behind him to make sure Frank was not following in the truck, then picked up his speed and walked briskly up the road.

Maureen was still downstairs at her computer when he arrived home, and he ran a hand through his hair, wiping the sweat off his forehead as he entered her office. "Jesus," he said. "Where's that sexual harassment pamphlet?"

She looked up. "Why?"

He told her everything. From the beginning. His invitation in, the innocuous conversation about Liz, then the "tinkle" announcement, the uncomfortably long look, the chastity belt, the demand for pain.

Maureen was disbelieving at first, apparently thinking he was joking, but halfway through his story her demeanor changed, and when he finished she asked, "She actually touched you there?"

"Squeezed it."

They looked at each other, obviously unsure of what to say. Aside from Liz and Mike and Tina, Frank and Audrey were the only real friends they had here in Utah.

Maureen shook her head. "I can't believe it. Audrey?"

"Audrey. Believe it." He sat down heavily on the room's lone extra chair. "God, I miss Ray. That man was like the last bastion of sanity in this asylum."

"Maybe we should move."

He didn't respond, didn't say anything, but for the first time he conceded to himself that that might be a viable option.

# THIRTY-ONE

The phone.

Two rings. Four. Eight.

It stopped.

Liz allowed herself to breathe again. The third time this afternoon, the sixth today.

She told herself that it could be friends, could be Tina or Moira or Audrey or Maureen, could be someone selling something, but she knew better than that. She knew who'd been trying to get a hold of her all this time, who'd been calling six or seven times a day.

The board.

Carefully, she pulled open a curtain, peeked out. The driveway was clear, and there were no people or vehicles on the road. Looks could be deceiving, though. There were bushes to hide behind, boulders that blocked sight lines. She wouldn't put anything past those bastards.

"I'm sorry, Ray," she sobbed. And not for the first time she begged her husband's forgiveness, asked him to absolve her for not listening to him all those years, not believing.

She wiped the tears away, embarrassed by her weakness though there was no one there to see it.

Outside, the sun was going down, shadows lengthening and darkening on the hill, and she shivered, letting the curtains fall. She quickly went through the house, turning on all of the lights in each of the rooms, but even with every corner of the dwelling brightly illuminated, she was still filled with fear and a bone-deep dread. She returned to the now well-lit living room where she'd started, and slowly, gingerly, as though handling something that was radioactive, picked up the telephone receiver and took it off the hook.

It was worse at night.

It was always worse at night.

She turned on the television for noise and companionship and went into the kitchen to make dinner. Before, she would have prepared a real meal—pan-blackened swordfish or chicken fajitas or turkey casserole—but now she simply melted some cheese on toast and washed it down with a can of Coke. She told herself that she would not drink tonight, she would remain sober and go to sleep clear-eyed and clear-headed, but by eight o'clock there was a bottle in her hand, and by the time she rolled into bed at ten, she was pretty well hammered.

She fell asleep with all of the lights on, and both the living room and bedroom television sets blaring.

She awoke in silence to find all of the lights turned off.

The house was dark and her first panicked thought was that someone had sneaked into her home and flipped the switches to frighten her. But a quick look toward the digital alarm clock on the bedstand told her that it was not just the lights and television. The power was out.

. They'd shut off her electricity.

She swung her feet off the bed, felt for the wall and guided herself over to the window, where she opened the curtains and peered out, looking down the hill where she knew there were other homes. She wanted to see only darkness, only night, but through the trees came the faint yellow sparkle of occasional porch lights.

The other houses had power.

It was just her.

She felt her way back to the bed and crawled in quickly, closing her eyes and willing herself to fall asleep.

But sleep would not come. Instead, she remained wide awake, her mind racing, trying to remember all of the things Ray had told her, all of the details, wishing he had written them down so she'd have a reference, corroboration, proof.

No, not proof. They were too good for that.

Her mind was going in circles, but at least it kept her from thinking about the power and why it had been turned off and the fact that there was someone on her property, snooping around her house, probably trying to get in.

There'd been other incidents on previous nights but none of them had ever escalated to anything dangerous or physically threatening, and she prayed that such would be the case tonight.

She tried to stop thinking, tried to count sheep, tried to think of black nothingness, but no matter what she did she remained wide awake.

She heard noises in the dark: the house creaking; the outside cries of nocturnal birds; coyote howls; crickets; an occasional tapping that could have been tree branches in the wind, could have been . . . something else. Gradually, all of these sounds seemed to coalesce, some disappearing, others gaining in strength, until she heard—

A voice.

At first she thought it was her imagination. It sounded like a young boy, but it was speaking gibberish, not making any sense. Just as the cacophony of night sounds had blended to form the voice, so too did the unintelligible syllables differentiate themselves into recognizable words.

Her name.

"Liz!" the voice called playfully. "Lizzy!"

It came from everywhere, came from nowhere, and she could not tell if it originated outside the house or inside.

"Lizzy! Lizzy! Lizzy!"

Now it didn't sound so much like a little boy. Instead, it had the odd high-pitched timbre of a midget or speech that had been electronically altered. She pulled the covers up over her head, the way she'd done as a child, but that didn't block out the sound, and she tucked the edges of the blanket under her body, under her head, leaving her hands free to plug her ears and keep out the voice.

She knew it was there, though, even if she couldn't hear it, and she remained unwillingly awake until morning, her arms, hands, and fingers falling asleep and tingling but remaining glued to her ears until a hint of dawn light could be discerned through the material of the covers.

At six o'clock, the power came back on, lights suddenly blazing, televisions blasting out morning news programs, and it was then that she knew it was finally safe to get out of bed. She quickly threw on a robe and rushed from room to room, checking windows, checking doors, but everything seemed to be secure and in place. No one had gotten in during the night.

She was not brave enough to go out on the deck and look around, but through the windows she saw no impaled cats or decapitated dogs or any signs of vandalism, and she assumed that all was right.

"Thank God," she breathed.

She was eating breakfast—more cheese on toast, this time with coffee—when she heard a knock at the front door.

She jumped, startled, and nearly dropped her cup. She considered hiding, not answering the door, pretending she was asleep or in the shower, but the knock came again. Louder this time, more insistent.

She put down her coffee cup and walked out to the foyer. Closing one eye, she looked through the door's peephole.

Jasper Calhoun.

Liz sucked in her breath. She could not remember ever seeing the association president outside of an official function—the annual meeting or one of the numerous disciplinary hearings—and to find him standing on her porch this early in the morning, dressed in his robes, was more than a little disconcerting.

Was he the one who had been playing with her power last night?

He looked straight at the peephole, smiling. "I see you Elizabeth. Open up."

That was impossible, she knew. The peephole was a security device, visibility only went one way, and for that, one had to place an eye almost directly on the tiny glass circle. There was no way he could even know she was on the other side of this door. Still, her instinctive reaction was to pull away, move back, retreat into the house.

"Come on, Elizabeth. I want to talk to you."

There seemed something odd about his face, as though he were wearing makeup or a mask, and a shiver passed through her as she studied him through the convex glass.

"You know I've been trying to call you," he said. "I know you're not answering your phone."

She held her breath, willing him to go away, afraid of moving, afraid of making any sound that would confirm her presence.

"I'm not leaving until you open that door and speak to me."

She'd been planning to remain here forever if need be, safe inside her fortress, but suddenly she unlocked and unbolted the door, yanking it open. "Get the hell off my property!" she demanded.

He spread his hands benignly in a gesture of tolerance that was no doubt meant to seem sincere but that came across as parody. "Elizabeth, Elizabeth."

"Stop harassing me and get the hell off my porch!"

"Harassing you?" He chuckled as if the idea had never before occurred to him, as though such an intention were the furthest thing from his mind. "I just came to ask you a question. A very important question on behalf of the board."

"Whatever it is, the answer's no. Now go away and leave me alone."

"We met earlier this week in closed executive session, and unanimously decided that we would like to extend you an offer to join our august body."

She blinked, caught off guard. "What?"

Calhoun smiled, and once again she shivered, unnerved by the odd appearance of his face, by the thick layer of flesh-colored makeup that here, outside in the open air, lent him a weirdly unnatural aspect. Had he always looked this way? Either she couldn't remember or she hadn't noticed. She was reminded of the time she'd seen the filming of a car commercial back in New Jersey. The commercial announcer had looked perfectly normal on television, but in real life the amount of pancake makeup he'd been wearing made him appear grotesque. Perhaps Calhoun did the same thing, tailoring his appearance so he would look regal and magisterial conducting a meeting on the dais of a room with dim lighting, even though it had the exact opposite effect in direct sunlight.

But why would he be wearing makeup? What was he trying to hide under there? Her chill refused to go away.

"We would be very grateful if you would accept our offer to join the Bonita Vista Homeowners' Association Board of Directors."

"Why?"

Calhoun put on what he no doubt thought was a friendly, inviting expression. "You're a full-time resident, you've been here a long time, you know and are friendly with a lot of the newer, younger homeowners. You also have time enough to handle the workload. Frankly, we can't think of a better or more appropriate candidate."

This made no sense. What were they trying to do? Buy

her off? She took a deep breath, tried to think this through logically, but she'd barely slept for the past week, had been under constant pressure, and her thought processes were scrambled.

What would Ray do?

"How about it, Elizabeth? What do you say?"

She spoke slowly. "Let me get this straight. You killed my husband, and now you want me to join your tea party?"

Calhoun's smile disappeared, the expression on his face hardening. "That is a false and scurrilous accusation, one that will not be tolerated. I am sorry for the loss of your husband, as are we all, and we are prepared to allow you a certain amount of leeway. But there is no way that we can allow you to go around spreading lies and vicious rumors—"

"I'm the best candidate, huh?" She snorted. "I don't know the real reason you're asking me to join, the real motive behind this farce, but I know you, Jasper Calhoun. I know all of you. Now get off my property and don't come back."

The smile had returned. "You're making a mistake, Elizabeth."

"It's mine to make."

They stared at each other.

Had she made the right decision? Her heart said yes but her head said no, and she closed the door on the president, hooking the chain lock and turning the deadbolt with trembling fingers, not daring to look through the peephole until she heard the old man's engine start up in the driveway, heard the clatter of gravel from underneath tires, heard the sound of Calhoun's Lexus fade away and disappear.

# THIRTY-TWO

Barry finished the new novel in a weeklong frenzy of activity.

He sent off the manuscript via the post office's Overnight Express, and they celebrated the way they always did by getting ice cream sundaes, a ritual left over from their earlier, poorer days. The teenaged waitress who worked at Dairy King, the local Dairy Queen knockoff, either didn't know or didn't care that they were from Bonita Vista, and when Barry asked for extra nuts, the girl heaped them on. They ate outside on rickety metal tables under unadjustable umbrellas that completely failed to block out the midafternoon sun, but the ice cream tasted all the better for the rough and uncomfortable surroundings.

On the way back, the Suburban's left rear tire blew out, and Barry crouched by the side of the highway for the better part of an hour, sweating and swearing, trying to loosen the undersized spare from the bottom of the vehicle and unscrew the seemingly cemented lug nuts from the blown tire's rim.

He finally finished putting on the spare, and he stood up, getting ready to toss the flat in the back of the vehicle, when a beer can tossed from a speeding El Camino nearly hit his head, missing by inches and splattering against the side of the Suburban. His clothes and hair were soaked with warm sticky liquid, and he heard a joyfully honked horn as the El Camino sped around a curve.

"Goddamn it!" he yelled. He angrily tossed the tire into the back and tried to wipe off his face, hands, and clothes with leftover napkins from Dairy King.

At home, the upstairs toilet had overflowed, although neither of them had been in that bathroom today. He used the plunger, and when he flushed everything was fine, but he worried that this might be the harbinger of septic tank difficulties, the first sign that they had a plumbing problem.

"Maybe you should call Mike or someone," Maureen suggested. "See if they know anything about this."

"Yeah," he said absently, but he wasn't really in the mood. He spent the rest of the afternoon mopping up the bathroom floor and washing the throw rug, leaving it on the upper deck to dry out.

It was a hot day and it segued into a hot night, and when they went to bed they left the windows open and turned on a fan.

They were undressing on their respective sides of the bed when, from the road outside, there came the sound of screeching brakes.

And a muffled thump.

"Jesus shit! Is this day ever going to end?" Barry pulled his pants back up, threw on his shirt, and stormed up the stairs.

He assumed that someone had hit a deer or javelina, and he expected to find a worried driver out of his car and checking the grill and front bumper for dents while an animal corpse lay on the asphalt illuminated by headlights, but that was not the sight that greeted him when he stepped outside.

It was a hit and run. The vehicle—whatever it was—was speeding away, down the hill, already lost in the pines, but in the last faint vestiges of red taillight glow, Barry saw a small crumpled form on the road. His first thought was that a child had been hit, and he ran down the driveway, legs pumping as fast as they could.

But halfway there, he knew it wasn't a child.

It was Stumpy.

Barry reached the street. The deformed man lay unmoving in the center of the roadway, his limbless body twisted into a shape that caused Barry's breath to catch in his throat.

He looked back toward the house and was grateful to see Maureen standing on the porch. "Call 911!" he screamed. "Stumpy's been run over!"

He felt for a pulse, placing his fingers on the clammy and heavily corded neck, but that was something he'd written about and seen in movies, not something he actually knew how to do, and though he felt nothing he was not sure if that was because Stumpy was dead or if it was due to his own medical ineptitude. He leaned down, placed his ear next to the open mouth, listening for the sound of breathing, but could not hear anything.

He knew enough not to move the body, but he didn't know CPR or any resuscitative techniques, and it wasn't until Maureen came out with her flashlight that he was certain Stumpy had been killed.

"He's dead," she told him. "There's no way he could've survived being run over like that. You can see where the tires went over him."

Indeed, now that he looked more closely, Barry saw blood seeping from beneath the body, saw pieces of intestine poking through rips and tears in the side of the callused torso. The eyes were staring glassily at nothing.

Just in case, Maureen bent down and felt the neck, touched the lips, pressed an ear to the chest, but in answer to Barry's quizzical look, she shook her head.

They were expecting a platoon of people: sheriff, deputies, firemen, ambulance drivers, medics, the whole gamut of emergency workers that such an incident would have brought out in a civilized area of the country. But ten minutes later a single ambulance pulled up, lights and siren off, and Sheriff Hitman emerged from the vehicle alone. Hitman walked toward them with a not particularly hurried gait, a notebook in his hand.

Barry pointed an accusing finger at Stumpy's body. "He's dead!"

The sheriff nodded curtly. "Yeah."

"You took your goddamn time getting here! And why aren't there any paramedics? How did you expect to revive him or treat him or . . . or stabilize him?"

"I knew he was dead," Hitman said simply.

Barry wanted to punch the sheriff's reptilian face. He was filled with anger, but he knew that anger was only partially directed at the sheriff's dereliction of duty.

"I didn't say that he was dead when I called 911," Maureen pointed out.

"Yours wasn't the only call."

Barry looked over at Maureen, and they shared the same thought without saying a word. No one else was out this late, there were no other homes on this immediate section of the street, no crowd had gathered or onlookers had come by. The only other person who could have called it in was the driver who had hit him.

They told this to the sheriff and he dutifully took the information down, promising to trace the call and find out where it came from, but Barry had the feeling that Hitman would do no such thing. After describing how they'd heard the accident from inside the house and rushed out to find the body, the two of them stood next to each other and watched the sheriff lift Stumpy and deposit him into the rear of the ambulance. There was no stretcher, no body bag, just the naked battered corpse crumpled on the metal floor of the vehicle.

Hitman shut the double doors. "Thanks for all your help," he said without looking at them. He strode to the front of the ambulance, got in, and drove away.

"That was weird," Maureen said, stunned.

"No shit."

"He didn't even take photos of the crime scene or anything. Don't you think that stuff is pretty standard in any kind of investigation?"

"I don't know what to think," Barry admitted.

"What kind of sheriff is he?"

They walked back into the house, shutting and locking the door behind them. Once again, they undressed and got into bed, but as much as he tried to divert his mind to other subjects, Barry kept seeing Stumpy's broken body and dead staring eyes, kept feeling the clamminess of the man's rough skin, and it was a long, long time before he fell asleep.

They'd arranged several days earlier to play tennis with Mike and Tina in the morning, and after a quick breakfast of Total and orange juice, they walked down to the courts, rackets in hand. It was a Sunday and it was early, but the Stewarts were already there and had obviously been warming up for some time. Mike's light blue shirt had a huge sweat stain on the back, and the court was littered with fluorescent balls.

"Practicing," Maureen whispered. "They're afraid we'll beat 'em."

"Yeah." Barry smiled thinly. Playing tennis was the last thing on his mind right now, and he was here only because Maureen had said it would be rude to cancel. "We need all the friends we can get," she told him.

They walked past the Stewarts' Acura and Barry opened the metal chain-link gate.

"Howdy neighbor!" Mike raised his racket in greeting.

"Good morning!" Maureen answered.

They stepped onto the court, the two women hugging, the men shaking hands. Barry had not yet told Mike about his encounter with Audrey, and he'd asked Maureen not to tell Tina anything either. The Stewarts and Hodges seemed to be closer to each other than either of them were to Barry and Maureen, and he could not be certain where their loyalties lay. He did not think either Mike or Tina were into anything kinky or were aware of Audrey's proclivities, but their friendship with the other couple might make them predisposed to believe any alternate version or explanation, no matter how far-fetched. And at this point, the last thing Barry needed was an eroding of his reputation.

They decided to volley first, and they split up: men on one side, women on the other. It was an easy, nontaxing back-and-forth, allowing them to talk as they warmed up, and Barry described the night's excitement, explaining how Stumpy had been run over in front of their house and how the sheriff had made little effort to disguise the fact that there wouldn't be an investigation.

Mike looked taken aback. "What?"

"That's what happened. Then Hitman drove away . . ." He shrugged, leaving the sentence unfinished.

"That's not possible," Mike said. "I just saw Stumpy less than an hour ago."

Barry felt a familiar tingle at the back of his neck. "Stumpy's dead."

"No, he's not. I saw him."

"Where?"

"I was running the loop. You know, the same way *we* ran that time?" He gave Barry a warning look. "And I saw him sitting by the side of the road off Ponderosa Circle. Well, not sitting exactly. Lying. Or whatever the hell he does. Anyway, he was there and making those retard noises—"

"Mike!" Tina admonished.

"Well, they are! And, as usual, I said hi to him, pretended to be polite, and ran on by. That was it."

Mike obviously believed what he was saying, did not appear to be lying, and that was what was so disturbing. Both of them couldn't be right. And if neither was wrong . . .

A man passed by. He smiled and waved.

"Hey, Travis!" Mike called out. "You heard anything about Stumpy being killed in a hit-and-run accident?"

"Killed? I don't think so! That geek was rootin' around in Merl's compost pile this mornin'! I had to chase him out with a shovel!"

"Thanks!" Mike called out.

The other man nodded and kept walking.

"I know what I saw," Barry insisted.

"I saw it, too," Maureen added.

Mike shrugged. "Well, I know what *I* saw." He shook his head. "Let's just forget about it. You two get your butts on the other side of that net. Me and Tina are in the mood to whip 'em."

But Barry could not forget about it. His distraction probably cost them the match, but he didn't care, and after they said their good-byes and walked back up the hill to home, he told Maureen he was going for a walk.

"Oh no you're not," she said.

"What are you talking about?"

"You think you're tricky? I know what you're planning to do."

"What?"

"Look for Stumpy."

"How do you do that?" he demanded, caught.

"I know you. I've lived with you all these years, and I know the way you think."

He tried to explain. "Look, we both know Stumpy's dead. We both saw it. I just want to confirm the fact."

"Why don't you call the sheriff?"

"Yeah, like we'd get an honest answer from him."

"Well . . ."

"You're welcome to come if you want."

Maureen shook her head. "I've had enough exercise for one day. I'm going to take a nice cool shower and read a good magazine. You can play Hardy Boys by yourself."

"Wish me luck."

"Luck."

He walked down to the bridle trail and headed up the path toward where he had first seen Stumpy. The trail ran through the forest just below Ponderosa Circle, where Mike claimed to have spotted him this morning. He had no idea what Mike and that other guy had seen, but no matter what they thought, it had not been Stumpy, and he was going to prove it.

The dirt pathway wound through a copse of manzanitas and dipped into a muddy runoff channel. Barry avoided the mud by stepping on a series of half-protruding rocks, then followed the trail between an oversized boulder and an exposed section of hillside before it once again leveled off and continued through the trees and foliage.

He'd gone much farther than he had that first time, and he stopped for a moment to rest. As he'd expected, as he'd known, there was no sign of Stumpy. He had no idea what was going on, why anyone would try to fool others into thinking Stumpy was alive, how they could actually *do* such a thing, how they could physically accomplish the deception, but he had no doubt that the association was mixed up in it somehow. The motives were murky, and he couldn't figure out what anyone could hope to gain from such a ruse, but it appeared to be what was happening nonetheless.

He was about to turn back and make that call to the sheriff when he heard a noise off to the left. A heavy rustling in the bushes. Barry's heart leapt in his chest. It could have been a bird, could have been a javelina, could have been a mountain lion, could have been a hundred other things. But he knew it wasn't. He'd heard that sound before. He recognized it.

No, he told himself. It wasn't possible. Stumpy was dead. He'd seen the broken body. Maureen had checked it. Hitman had confirmed it.

A branch snapped, leaves soughed.

This really was something out of one of his novels, and in his mind he saw the sheriff dropping the body off at the coroner's, saw Stumpy resurrected, saw the limbless body snaking out of the morgue, flopping up the highway in the dead of night, inching through the underbrush to get back to Bonita Vista.

There was the sound of moaning coming from somewhere around ground level, and he turned, got ready to run. What if Stumpy was a zombie? Or a vampire? Or something worse? It was broad daylight, but he felt like a little boy confronted with the prospect of walking down a dark alley after seeing a scary movie.

Stumpy flopped onto the path, crying out.

Only . . .

It wasn't Stumpy. It was someone else. Another dirty naked man with no arms or legs who forced himself forward with spastic thrashing movements, head and chest bobbing up and down, bloody genitals scraping dirt and twigs. Burrs and bristles were caught in the wild hair, and the face had only one eye, that one clouded and opaque. The other was a deeply hollowed out hole. Two cracked teeth were all that was left in the bruised and puffy mouth.

There was something familiar about that mutilated face, and though he was seized with panic and the instinctive urge to flee, Barry remained rooted in place, staring. He knew why Mike and that other man had been fooled. At a casual glance, even at a not-so-casual glance, this looked like Stumpy. But the differences were there if one bothered to take a look, and as the limbless man squirmed across the path toward a thicket of ferns, screaming incoherently while jagged stones scraped underbelly skin, it came to him.

Kenny Tolkin.

He squinted, staring, imagining a blue patch over the missing eye. He recognized those features, distorted as they were, and his mouth was suddenly dry.

"Kenny?" he said.

The new Stumpy looked up at him blankly and howled in tongueless impotent rage.

Barry finished off another beer and dropped the can on the wooden floor of the deck with the others. He was living in a horror novel. His life had become his work—only he wasn't sure he could actually sell such oddball shit to readers and have them buy it. Psychotic friends, yes. Ghosts and ageless demons, sure. But a malevolent homeowners' association that dismembered members for being late with their dues? It was too close to reality to be truly fantastic and thus allow readers to suspend disbelief, yet not realistic enough to be taken seriously on any sort of naturalistic level.

He grabbed another can from the ice chest, popped the top, took a swig.

He ran down a list of titles in his mind. Horror fiction was his reference point, and if he could just ascribe a cause to what was happening, if he could just determine a source, he could at least start to think about strategies, at least know what he was up against and plan for it. But there didn't seem to be a ready explanation. Bonita Vista was not built atop burial grounds to his knowledge, it wasn't the scene of some heinous murder or historic wholesale butchery. He doubted that the homeowners' association was an ancient fertility cult a la *Harvest Home* or *The Ceremonies*, and the likelihood that Satan was behind it all was practically nonexistent.

So what did that leave?

He didn't know, and that was what frustrated him.

Thinking about Kenny Tolkin squirming along the ground with his newly cauterized stumps dragging his damaged genitals, it occurred to him that the homeowners' association had killed Stumpy and that they had done so in order to hide what they'd done to Kenny. Hitman was obviously in on it, and their plan to quietly dispose of the deformed man's corpse and substitute the other, pretend as though nothing had happened, probably would have worked had Stumpy not been hit in front of Barry's house. They'd screwed up there. That had been a miscalculation. The new Stumpy had obviously fooled Mike, and he would probably pass muster with everyone else as well. But he and Maureen had *seen*. They'd been there when it happened.

Despite what Ray had said about the courts siding in favor of homeowners' associations and ruling against the rights of individuals, a lot of this shit was illegal. It had to be. There was no way that mutilation and murder would be sanctioned by any law enforcement agency or member of the judiciary.

Except, of course, for Corban's beloved sheriff.

He tried to think this through logically. If he called the FBI or some outside law, would they be able to prove that what he said was true? Kenny had no fingerprints to match, no teeth to correspond with dental records. If his DNA was on file somewhere, that might work. Or his blood type. But chances of that were pretty damn slim.

Hell, would they even be able to find Kenny, or would the association have him hidden away by then?

Or killed?

And what were the chances of finding Stumpy's corpse? It was no doubt scattered ashes by now with no paper trail documenting the steps.

Barry finished the beer, dropped the can on the pile, his brain starting to throb.

And what if he did turn them in, what if he did report the association? Would that make him and Maureen targets? Would that put a price on their heads?

He tried to think about the situation from a novelist's perspective, tried to figure out what he would do, how he would have his protagonist get out of this predicament if this happened in one of his books, but he could not seem to come up with anything remotely helpful. The alternative—sitting on his ass and saying nothing—was morally repugnant. As was the thought of flight, escaping under the cover of darkness or anonymity and disappearing into the outside world, never to return to or think about Bonita Vista ever again.

So what were their choices?

He wished Ray were here. The old man could always be counted on to offer a balanced view of any situation and to come up with plausible courses of action. He also had a knowledge of Bonita Vista and the association that came with history. He'd possessed insider insights, something that Barry would never have and that was irreplaceable.

But Ray was dead.

They'd killed him, too.

Barry sat alone on the deck, staring out at the canyonlands as the sun went down, watching the shadows of the pines lengthen and take over the land.

And from somewhere in the trees, he heard Kenny howl.

# THIRTY-THREE

The meatloaf was nearly done, Grandma Mary had already arrived, and the rest of the family was moving chairs and pulling out the leaves of the table for Sunday dinner, but there was still no sign of Weston. Laura Lynn looked out the dusty glass of the kitchen window, but the yard was empty: the swing set deserted, the tree house vacant. The boy had been gone since just after breakfast, off with that no-good Tarley Spooner no doubt, and she wasn't too surprised that he was late.

She was angry.

But not surprised.

She turned off the oven, stirred the string beans on the stove. Weston knew everyone was coming over for dinner today. She'd made it very clear to him that he could only play outside if he promised to be back well before noon, and he'd assured her that this time he would not forget. She'd believed him, so sincere were his promises, and she thought now that she should have been firmer with him, less trusting, less lenient.

Claude walked into the kitchen, looking for a preview of the meal as always. "Somethin' sure smells good!" he said.

She hit his hand before he could dip a finger in the mashed potatoes. "I swear, you're worse than the kids!"

He tried to steal a roll from the plate on the countertop, and she pulled the plate out of his way.

"Speaking of kids," he said, "have you seen Wes?"

"I was just going to talk to you about that."

"Don't worry. I'll find him." Claude quickly grabbed a spoon and took a bit of Jell-O from the bowl on the sideboard before walking over to the screen door.

"Claude Richards!"

"I'm starving!" He opened the screen and yelled into the backyard: "Wes!"

No answer.

He waited a moment, called out again. "Weston! It's time to eat!"

"Go find him," Laura Lynn said.

"I'll find him all right." Claude pushed open the screen, let it slam shut behind him.

She watched through the window as he checked the tree house, the storage shed, all of the boy's usual haunts.

*Haunts.*

Claude disappeared around the side of the house, and Laura Lynn suddenly had a bad feeling about where this was heading. It wasn't like Weston to lie, to disobey her once he'd specifically promised not to do so. He might be a little rambunctious, a little headstrong, but he was basically a good kid, and the feeling in her gut told her that he had promised her he'd be back in time for lunch and he *would* have been back in time for lunch—if he could have.

She wiped her hands on a dishrag, hurried outside after Claude.

"Weston!" she called. "Weston Richards!"

They were in the front yard now, and the rest of the family was filing onto the porch, having heard the commotion.

"What is it?" Grandma Mary asked.

"We can't find Weston!"

Claude turned to look at her, frowning. "What are you

overreacting for? He's probably playing with Tarley somewhere."

"No." Laura Lynn shook her head firmly, afraid that by giving voice to her fear she was ensuring its inevitability, but unable to keep from speaking her mind. "Something's happened to him. I know it."

Ford, Charley, and Emma came immediately down off the porch, while Grandma Mary herded Rachel and the little ones inside.

"Weston!" Ford called out.

"Weston!"

"Weston!"

"I'm going to check Tarley's house," Claude announced.

Laura Lynn looked around, and her gaze was drawn to the empty field on the east side of their property. She started walking in that direction. "Weston!" she yelled, quickening her stride. "Weston Richards!"

Then she saw it.

A small, unmoving form lying in the dead weeds next to a scraggly black oak tree.

Laura Lynn sucked in her breath. "Weston?" She was running before the whisper was completely out of her mouth, her legs pumping with a fury and purpose that they had never known before. She was dimly aware that the others were following her—Claude and Ford and Charley and Emma—but her focus was on the still, small body in the weeds ahead of her. She knew even before she reached it that it was Wes, and she prayed to God and the Lord Jesus Christ that he was only sleeping or only injured or only knocked out, that he was not dead.

Her prayers went unanswered.

It was indeed Weston. His head was crushed. Blood, some dried, most still wet, puddled in the broken indentation that had been the side of his skull. She could see a cockeyed ear dangling at the edge of the break, and in the midst of the liquid red were fatty flashes of white that could only be brain.

But that was not all of it.

For there was foam coming out of his mouth, a thick peachy froth that looked like bubble bath suds or shaving cream.

She looked up, looked away. Something sparkled, and on the hills north of town, she saw the noonday sun reflected off the windows of the big houses in Bonita Vista, like flecks of mica on a granite rock.

She looked back down at her son's still form and fell to her knees, registering but not really feeling the pain as her kneecap hit a jagged pebble. She touched the blood, touched the foam.

Claude grabbed her from behind. "Laura Lynn! Laura Lynn!"

And she started to wail.

# THIRTY-FOUR

There was something wrong, and Maureen sensed it the second she walked through the door of the title company. It was nothing she could put her finger on—they weren't all staring at her, conversations were still being conducted at normal levels—but she was suddenly uncomfortable, the warm acceptance she'd experienced in previous visits nowhere in evidence now. She passed the secretary, made her way past the agents' desks. She was an intruder here, an outsider, and though there were no overt gestures, though nothing was said, the fact was brought home to her in subtle, almost imperceptible ways as she walked through the office: the slight turning away of a chair, a quickly averted glance, an overemphasis on busywork.

She'd been assigned a temporary cubicle in the far corner, a desk surrounded by three modular walls, and she headed toward it, nodding hello and smiling at the people she saw, pretending not to notice that the return nods were nearly nonexistent and that there were no smiles for her. She was intercepted on the way to her desk by Harland Souther, the title company's manager, and he asked her if she would step into his office, prefacing his request with a nervous cough that she knew did not bode well.

He closed the door behind them after they'd stepped into

the room. "Have a seat," he offered, moving behind his desk.

Maureen sat down warily. "What is it?" she asked. "What's the matter?"

"I'm sorry," he said, "but we will not be able to use your services."

"You're contracted to have me audit your payroll records."

"I understand that. And, as you know, there is an out clause that enables us to rescind the contract and pay you a kill fee. We will be exercising that option."

She faced him squarely. "May I ask why?"

Harland shifted uneasily in his seat. "It's this whole controversy. We've decided not to do business with anyone from Bonita Vista. It's nothing against you personally," he added quickly. "You seem like a nice woman, and I know you're good at what you do. You're new here, and it's not really fair that you've gotten caught in the middle of all this, but . . ." He shrugged helplessly.

"I don't understand."

"You know . . ."

She shook her head. "What?"

"Oh." An expression like surprise crossed his features, and it was replaced almost instantly by a sheepish, embarrassed look. "There's . . ." He trailed off, coughed nervously, obviously unsure of how to begin. "There have been some poisonings in town. Of pets. No one knows who's behind it, but a lot of people seem to think it's the Bonita Vista Homeowners' Association because . . . well, for a lot of reasons. Last week, a little boy accidentally ate some poisoned dog food and now he's in a coma in the hospital in Cedar City. Yesterday . . ." He looked away, sighed heavily. "Yesterday, another little boy's body was found in the vacant lot next to his house. He was poisoned and his head was bashed in. Now I'm not saying who did it, and for

all I know the sheriff already caught someone who's in custody right now. But because of all this, the decision's been
made to cut off all business with Bonita Vista. There's nothing I can do about it. My hands are tied." This last was said
quickly, without pause, almost as though he feared her reaction and was trying to stave off a return assault.

Maureen sat there, stunned. She was tempted to argue
with him, to point out that such a policy was discriminatory and probably illegal, but she understood the feelings
of the people in town, and to a large extent shared them
herself.

She thought of the gate, thought of Ray, thought of all
the reasons she and Barry distrusted the homeowners' association, and she could not fault the people of Corban for
hating and fearing Bonita Vista.

"I know you're caught in the middle of this," Harland repeated, "and, like I said, this really has nothing to do with
you—"

Maureen stood, nodded tiredly. "I understand."

"We'll pay you your kill fee—"

"I understand."

Back at home, she checked her E-mail, scrolling down to
view the list of messages she'd received that morning. The
subject headings were all over the map, but though the specific names were different, the substance of each was the
same.

All of her local clients had dropped her.

It was not totally unexpected, not after what had happened at the title company, but it was still overwhelming to
see it laid out like this, to witness in cold, flat type such
complete rejection.

She didn't even have Frank and Audrey anymore.

She would have laughed if it wasn't so sad, would have
cried if it wasn't so infuriating, but instead she just sat there
blankly staring at her screen.

\*       \*       \*

He hadn't eaten at the coffee shop for over a week. Barry told himself that it wasn't intentional, that he wasn't avoiding the place, that he'd simply had errands to run and leftovers to get rid of and that a legitimate series of circumstances had led to him eating at home or in his office or even skipping lunch entirely.

But he knew that wasn't the truth.

Today, though, he was determined to return. Things had to have cooled off since last time, and he doubted that there'd be the same tension. There was no way Hank could stay angry for this long. Joe maybe. Or Lyle. But Hank was more reasonable, more sensible, and since he was their ringleader, Barry knew that the old man would exert a tempering influence and calm everyone down, remind them that Barry was on their side and was one of the good guys.

But he was wrong.

He sensed it the second he walked through the door. A coldness that had nothing to do with the air-conditioning hit him the instant he stepped into the coffee shop, and he didn't need to look around to know that all eyes were upon him. The only noise was the muted sizzling of the grill back in the kitchen and the plinking of fork on plate as someone at one of the tables continued eating.

He walked self-consciously over to his usual table and sat down, trying not to notice the complete lack of conversation, the air of hostility that overhung the eatery. Lurlene looked over at her father first, getting his okay before angrily slamming down a menu and a glass of water. The water splashed over the table and onto Barry's lap, but he forced himself to smile and keep his voice calm as he picked up the menu and handed it back to the waitress. "I don't need this, Lurlene. I'll just have the usual."

She grabbed the laminated menu from his hand and stormed off without saying a word.

Something had happened since the last time he'd been here. He had no idea what it was, but it had to have been big to engender this kind of anger, and he only wished he knew so he could fight against it.

He used his napkin to wipe up the spilled water and took a sip from the half-filled glass. He was thinking about approaching Hank, just walking over to the old man's table, coming right out and asking what was the matter, when Joe stood up from his place near the counter and strode purposefully over to Barry's table.

Barry wasn't sure how to react, so he just remained where he was, took another sip of water, and watched the other man coming.

Joe faced him squarely. "Didn't think you'd have the nerve to show your face in here."

There was anger in his voice. No. Not just anger. Rage.

Barry's heart was pounding. He could not remember the last time he'd gotten into any sort of physical altercation, but he had the feeling that Joe was going to try and goad him into one right here, right now, although he still had no idea why.

He stood but tried to remain relaxed and friendly, though that was getting increasingly hard to do. "I don't know what you're talking about, Joe. Whatever's happened . . ." He spread his hands in a gesture of innocence. ". . . I'm out of the loop. You're going to have to clue me in."

"Weston Richards," Joe said, practically spitting out the name.

The man stared at him for a long moment, and Barry shook his head, still unaware of the intended meaning.

"I don't know what this Weston's done," he said, "but—"

"Weston didn't do nuthin'!" Lyle shouted from his table near the door. "He was killed. You guys poisoned him!"

Barry looked toward Hank. "There was *another* accident?"

"This weren't no accident," Hank said, and Barry could see the fury in the old man's eyes. "They killed that boy on purpose. The Richardses didn't have no dog."

"And his head was bashed in!" Lurlene glared at him.

There was a sinking feeling in the pit of Barry's stomach. "I don't know anything about this. This is the first I've heard about it."

Hank nodded. "That's the problem. *No one* knows anything about it."

"But we know who's responsible," Ralph said from his seat at Lyle's table.

"Look—" Barry tried to be reasonable. "—I hate that stupid homeowners' association as much as you do. More probably because I have to put up with their shit and abide by their damn rules."

"But you're still a part of it," Lyle pointed out. "You're still a member."

"I have no choice! If I live there, I *have* to pay dues!"

"You have a snowplow!" a woman near the window shouted.

Barry looked over at her. She was someone he had not seen before, an overweight woman with an overbite and too-large breasts, and he didn't understand either her reference to the snowplow or the anger he saw in her eyes. "What?" he asked her.

"In the winter. You have a snowplow up there. But it's only for Bonita Vista. Our plow broke down last year and we were snowed in for nearly a week. Snowed in! But you wouldn't help us, wouldn't let us use your plow, wouldn't clear off any of our roads!"

"What about the water?" Ralph said quietly.

There were nods all around.

"Look, I wasn't even living here last winter. I'm not involved with the water. I have nothing to do with this Weston thing—"

"Our utility rates went up in town because of all the electricity you use!"

"The runoff from your carved-up hills is contaminating the crik!"

"I just live there," Barry said defensively. "I don't—"

"Weston's head was bashed in," Lurlene repeated. "He was poisoned and frothing at the mouth and the top of his head was bashed in. I *knew* that little boy."

"I didn't do it!" Barry said.

"No," Hank said, and his voice was loud enough and grave enough to silence all the others. "But you didn't do nothin' to stop it neither."

They stared at each other, and Barry realized that there was no way he was going to ever win here, no way he was going to change any opinions or convince anyone that he should not be tarred with the same brush as his neighbors.

"They're trying to kill off our kids," the woman near the window said. "They're mad that we won't go along with their plans, and now they're trying to kill off our kids."

Joe's voice was seething. "Pets . . . kids . . . Who knows what's next."

Barry wanted to be able to argue with this, wanted to be able to fight back, but he couldn't. Such an idea might seem ludicrous, but he couldn't dismiss it out of hand, and there was no way he would stoop to defending the homeowners' association.

"I think you'd best get your food to go," Bert said to him from behind the counter, and it was clear from his tone of voice that this was an order, not a suggestion.

Barry's eyes focused on the small white sign propped up on top of the cash register: WE RESERVE THE RIGHT TO REFUSE SERVICE TO ANYONE.

He had the feeling that this was going to be the last meal he would ever order from this place. Or be *allowed* to order.

He stood, finished off the last of his water, and walked over to the cash register.

He would not be surprised if Bert kicked him out of the office as well. And if the sentiment of the coffee shop regulars was any indication of the local attitude toward Bonita

Vista, he doubted he'd be able to find another office very soon.

With the association banning him from writing in his own house, it'd be the old rock and a hard place dilemma.

Maybe he'd just stake out a campsite in the forest, get himself a generator to power the computer, and write out there.

With a frown, Bert handed him the greasy bag of food and took his money, silently proffering change. Barry did not look at anyone as he walked straight through the center of the coffee shop to the door. His footsteps sounded embarrassingly loud in the stillness.

Once outside, he breathed a little easier. The claustrophobic tension that had been pressing in on him dissipated in the open air, and he walked back to his office across the open field, feeling as though he'd awakened from a paranoid dream and was back in the real world.

Fifteen minutes later, he had finished his lunch, abandoned the real world, and was in the realm of death and supernatural horror, the unpleasantness at the coffee shop pushed to the back of his brain, existing for the moment only as a possible element he could add to his new novel.

He was in the middle of a monster-POV chapter, flying along, his fingers barely able to keep up with his mind, when the silence of the office was suddenly shattered by the crash of glass. A baseball flew through the window next to his desk, sending shards flying inward, and Barry instinctively ducked. It could have been kids, a foul ball hit in the wrong direction during a pickup game, but somehow he knew that it wasn't. When there was no follow-up, he quickly sprang to his feet and sprinted the three steps to the front of the office. He yanked open the door, saw a man running across the field back toward the coffee shop, but could not tell who it was.

Was this merely a warning, he wondered, or the begin-

ning of regular organized attacks against him? He didn't
know, but neither possibility was promising, and he backed
up his files on diskette and took the diskette with him as he
locked up the office.

It was nearly midnight, and they lay in bed, not speaking, listening to the soft murmur of the television.

"Maybe we should move," Maureen said softly.

"No." Barry could feel the resolve stiffening within him
as he spoke. "I'm not giving those bastards the satisfaction."

She answered in an exaggerated western drawl. "No
one's gonna run us out of town before sundown."

"That's right."

"But it's cutting off your nose to spite your face. No one
in town will hire me. I'm not exaggerating. No one."

"We don't need these assholes. I'm making enough for
us to live comfortably."

"Yes, but I have a career, too, and I don't want to give it
up for some stubborn, misguided pissing contest you feel
you have to win."

"What about your old clients from California?"

"There are a few," she admitted, "but that's not the point.
If we were *back* in California, I could triple that number."

"You have your e-accounting empire."

"I could do that better in California, too."

"I don't want to turn tail and run. And I resent being
blamed for something we had no part of."

"We're getting it on all sides, from the association *and*
the association's enemies. I don't see any reason for us to
stay."

"Because we like our house. Because we like the area.
The reasons to stay are the same reasons we moved here in
the first place. Nothing's changed. So we have a few less
friends. Big deal."

Maureen sighed. "If we'd bought property in town instead of up here, none of this would be happening."

"We wouldn't've bought property in town," he said. "Ray was right. We're only here because we like the view and the paved streets and the nice homes. We wanted to live in a sanitized, movie version of rural America and now we're paying the price." He looked at her. "Can you honestly say you'd be happy living in a trailer or one of those rundown shacks that the townies live in?"

"We could've built our own house."

"And lived down there with the rednecks and the wife beaters, staring up at Bonita Vista?" He shook his head.

"So it's a class thing, huh?"

"Yeah," he said. "I guess it is. No one likes to talk about that anymore, we all pretend it doesn't exist, but it does. There's a gulf. We're educated and fairly well off, and these are people who've graduated from high school at best and have probably never even left the state. We're not like them, and we wouldn't fit in." He thought of the day he'd invited the guys from the coffee shop up here, and it scared him that his attitude toward them seemed to coincide with that of the association.

"We don't fit in here either," she said.

He smiled at her sweetly and batted his eyelashes. "But we have each other."

Maureen was silent for a moment. "I'm not putting up with this forever," she told him. "You can write anywhere, a house in California or an apartment in New York as well as here. But I don't work on my own. I'm an accountant. I need people for my business. I'll see what I can do with conference calls and faxes and E-mails, but I'm not promising anything. If I start going stir crazy, we're out of here, we're gone."

She was wrong, though. He couldn't write anywhere. He was not allowed to write in Bonita Vista, and there was a good likelihood he would soon be evicted from his little teapot museum office. That *would* be cutting off his nose to spite his face, but, to throw another cliché into the mix, he'd cross that bridge when he came to it.

Neither of them said any more after that. Maureen scooted down on her pillow, put her arm around his mid-section, snuggled next to him, and they both fell asleep listening to the quiet, comforting murmur of the television.

# THIRTY-FIVE

"Barry?"

He opened his eyes groggily.

"Barry?"

There was a hint of panic, a touch of fear, in Maureen's voice that drove away the sleepiness and caused him to sit up instantly, wide awake. The sun was streaming through a part in the curtains, and when he looked at the clock, he saw that it was after nine. He'd been asleep nearly twelve hours.

He glanced over to see Maureen standing by the side of the bed, holding up a copy of the *Corban Weekly Standard*. Her hands were shaking, and the rustle of the newspaper sounded strangely amplified in the silent house.

He was filled with a sense of dread, and he reached out and took the paper from her, reading the banner headline:

CHILD POISONED, BONITA VISTA BLAMED

"It says there's going to be a rally tonight. The people of Corban, the *parents* of Corban, are planning to meet outside the gates of Bonita Vista at eight to protest the poisonings."

Barry read through the article. The rally was being organized by Claude Richards, the father of Weston, and it was his goal to intimidate the guilty parties within Bonita

Vista—the people who had made the decision to lay out the poison and the people who had actually done the deed—into giving themselves up. He wanted to put pressure on the homeowners' association and all of the residents, a tactic that each of the individuals quoted in the article as well as the newspaper itself seemed to support wholeheartedly.

Surprisingly, there was no quote from the sheriff, and Barry wondered where Hitman would stand on this, whose side he would take. No matter how great his loyalty to Bonita Vista, no matter how much he was being paid off, there was no way he could turn a blind eye to a killing. Not of a child. Not in a small town. Not if he wanted to keep his job.

"I don't like the sound of this 'rally,'" he said, handing back the paper.

"Me either. I see a bunch of drunk bubbas bringing their shotguns and talking themselves into mob violence."

"There's nothing scarier than groupthink," Barry agreed.

"So what should we do?"

"What *can* we do?"

Maureen sat down on the bed next to him. "I thought we could take a trip. There's probably more national parks within driving distance of this place than anywhere else in the country, and we haven't been to any of them. Why don't we drive out, find someplace to stay in Cedar City, and go to Bryce or Zion or Cedar Breaks."

"You've really been thinking about this."

"I've been looking through our Triple A book," she admitted. She took his hand. "I don't want to be here tonight. I have a bad feeling about it."

He leaned over and gave her a quick kiss.

"I'm serious. There's the potential for danger here."

"From which side?"

"I don't know. It doesn't matter. I just don't want to be here when it happens."

Barry sighed. "I don't think anything *will* happen—"

"How can you say that!"

"We have a gate with an armed guard. And even Hitman can't ignore something like this. The sheriff'll make sure things don't get out of hand."

Maureen laughed shortly. "Right."

He was about to argue that their home was far enough up the hill that even if the Corban protesters got through the gate and went on some kind of rampage, the mob would probably be stopped or spent by the time they reached their place—

*Rampage?*

—but he stopped himself. What the hell was he doing? What was he thinking? After everything he'd seen, after everything he knew or suspected, was he honestly arguing for the probability of normalcy reasserting itself? This wasn't a normal situation, this wasn't a normal place. Normal logic did not apply. Shit, if he didn't know better, he'd think that he'd been influenced or corrupted, bombarded with association mind rays or magical spells to make him more complacent and compliant and agreeable to the party line.

"You're right," Barry admitted.

"So we'll go?"

"Yeah," he said. "After breakfast, after I take a shower. Just pack enough for overnight, though. We're coming back tomorrow."

"To survey the damage?"

"Hopefully not."

She kissed him. "You're a good man, Charlie Brown." She stood up. "Go take your shower."

"Want to join me?"

"Tonight," she promised.

Barry had finished his shower and was up in the kitchen pouring himself some coffee when he heard a loud knock at the front door. Maureen, already downstairs, answered it and a moment later called his name.

He moved around the corner and looked over the railing

to see Mike enter the living room, newspaper in hand. "Hey!" Barry called, walking downstairs. "How's it going?"

Mike held up a copy of the *Standard*. "I assume you saw this?"

Barry nodded.

"They're calling it a 'rally,'" Mike said angrily, "trying to make it sound like some sort of happy high school thing. It's a planned assault is what it is, an attack on us. They want to get enough people together so that they can storm the gates and . . . I don't know what."

"That's why we're leaving," Barry said. "Mo wants us to spend the night in Cedar City just in case things get too hairy."

"I don't . . ." Mike shook his head, confused. "What are you talking about?"

"I have a bad feeling about this," Maureen said. "I don't claim to be psychic or anything, but I just think we need to get out of here. Something's wrong. Something's going to happen."

"Yeah, something's going to happen. They're going to vandalize our property. You'll come back to smashed windows and shot-up car tires and . . . who knows what all."

"Exactly. That's why we don't want to be here when it happens."

Mike turned toward Barry. "What's the matter with you?" he asked. "This is your home. This is your property. You can't tell me you wouldn't stay and fight a fire to save your house. Hell, we'd all be up on our roofs with hoses, wetting down everything in sight."

Barry nodded reluctantly.

"Same thing here. I know the association is fucked up, but we have no choice but to back them on this. Besides, this is what the association is *supposed* to be doing. Protecting Bonita Vista, standing up for the residents."

"There wouldn't even be this rally if the association

hadn't . . ." He looked into Mike's eyes. "If those kids hadn't been poisoned."

"It's a deal with the devil," Mike admitted. "But we have no choice. Whether we like it or not, those Corbanites see this as an us-versus-them situation. And we're 'them.'"

Barry tried to smile. "What do you think they'll do? Burn down our houses?"

"Vigilante justice is not exactly unheard of in this part of the world, and, yes, that is something I think they might try to do."

"Me, too," Maureen said. "That's why I don't want to be here. You can't fight a mob, you can't reason with a horde of angry stirred-up people, particularly ones whose children have been killed."

"I understand your feelings," Mike said to her. He turned to Barry. "But why are *you* going? Because you fear for your personal safety? That's okay if it is; that's a legitimate reason. But if you're doing this to get back at the association, because you think it'll somehow hurt them, then you're wrong. You read that article. They blame us, all of us, not just the association, and I don't think the rest of us should suffer collateral damage because of it."

It was the fire analogy that had gotten to him. As much as Barry hated to admit it, as much as he wanted to stick with Maureen and the promise he'd made to her, Mike's argument made sense. He should stay with his house, make sure his home was safe. It was his duty.

And there was something else.

"We can't leave," he told her.

"Not this macho bullshit!"

"Who's going to protect our house—"

"What, you're going to buy a gun and sit on the porch to shoot at intruders? Come on! This is craziness! If there *is* any damage, our homeowners' insurance will cover it. Half the homes here are unoccupied! They're vacation homes! What about those people? They're not rushing back for the last stand at the O.K. Corral." She looked into his eyes. "There's no reason to do this."

"What if it's a test?" he said quietly.

"What?"

"What if the association just wants to know who's willing to stay and fight?"

"Fight?" she practically screamed.

"Figuratively, not literally. What if they're just trying to gauge the mettle of their opponents? Us."

"I'll let you two discuss it," Mike said, backing off toward the door. "I think you should stay, though. There's strength in numbers, and we need all the bodies we can get. Like she said, there aren't a lot of full-timers up here, and we don't have a newspaper recruiting people for our side like they do." He stepped outside, and carefully closed the screen. "It's something to think about."

She slammed the door behind him. "It's not something to think about."

"Mo . . ."

"You promised me we'd leave."

"I know."

"What is this? The great iconoclastic horror writer Barry Welch is afraid of what his neighbors will say about him? Fuck them! If you want to show someone that you have balls, show me, your wife, and stand down this peer pressure and get the hell out of here for the night."

That was the problem with being a writer, Barry thought. He could see things from both sides. It was his job to get into characters' heads, to articulate the thought processes behind opposing points of view. Maureen was right, but Mike was right, too. He spent each day engaging in such schizophrenic empathy, and it was why he was always aware of the duality in any given situation.

But he'd never seen things from the association's side.

That was true. And that was why his logic broke down when it came to the homeowners' association.

It was still not inconceivable to him that the association wanted him to agonize over this choice, that they were behind this entire scenario and had placed him in this position in order to observe him and study his reaction, like scientists examining the behavior of a lab rat. Such Byzantine deviousness might seem absurd, the product of an overactive imagination, but when all of the events since their arrival here were viewed as part of a continuum, it was a conclusion that did not seem at all far-fetched.

"What if this is all part of some elaborate scheme on the part of the association?" he asked. "I'm serious about this. What if it *is* a test?"

"Now you *are* being paranoid. Get real. They poisoned pets and children because they knew it would get the populace up in arms and they'd descend on Bonita Vista with baseball bats and guns and then Barry Welch would be forced to decide whether or not to remain home for the evening? You don't think that's being just a little egocentric and self-absorbed?"

He grimaced. "Well, when you put it that way . . ."

"It's about time you came to your senses. Now let's get out of here before some other version of Satan tries to tempt you away from the path."

"Mike's Satan?"

"Just get ready to go."

Barry nodded. "Okay." He happened to glance over at the television. "Wait a minute. Let's check out the Weather Channel, see what the weather's going to be like." He picked up the remote from the coffee table and started flipping through channels, trying to find the station.

"Hey," Maureen said. "What's . . . what's that?"

"What?"

"Flip it back a few."

He pressed the down button and the channels reversed. "There!"

Barry frowned. What was this, some kind of community

access station? A fuzzy, nearly colorless videotape of a tennis match, seen from above, was being broadcast. There was no sound, only the bird's-eye view of an elderly couple in matching whites stumblingly attempting to dash about the court despite an obvious lack of athletic ability.

"That's the tennis court!" Maureen pointed. "Our tennis court!" She picked up the list of cable channels from the top of the television. "Sixteen," she said, her finger running down the station lineup. "BVTV." She frowned. "BVTV? What's . . ." But the expression on her face said that she'd already figured it out.

"Bonita Vista Television." Barry stared at the match onscreen. "So *that's* what that camera's for." He looked triumphantly at Maureen. "I knew it wasn't just security."

"My God."

They watched the man awkwardly try but fail to return the woman's serves.

"I've seen those two before," Maureen said. "I think they live down by Audrey."

"What else do you think they're taping?" Barry asked quietly.

As if in answer to his question, the scene shifted. Now it was a live video feed from inside someone's house, the camera focused on the movements of a lone woman.

Liz.

She was not doing anything, merely sitting on the white living room couch, hands in her lap, head looking up, sobbing, but the scene was so intimate, so invasive, that Barry immediately shut off the television. He could not watch. After only those few seconds of unsolicited voyeurism, he felt dirty and guilty. It was uncomfortable to see a person in so private a moment.

He wondered if the board members were watching on their own televisions.

And if they were smiling.

The thought filled him with white-hot rage, a righteous

anger. He had never hated the homeowners' association more than he did at that moment. He thought of that weasel Neil Campbell, of the prissy seriousness of that unrepentant toady, and he realized that to him Campbell was the face of the association because he had never actually seen a member of the board. He'd seen Jasper Calhoun's car and his house, but he'd never seen Calhoun himself. And he'd never seen any of the others, either. Hell, he didn't even know their names.

A tear snaked down Maureen's cheek, and she drew in a ragged breath. "How could they do something like this?"

"Liz told you the board was after her."

"I'm going to call, let her know about this." Maureen ran upstairs, picked up the phone from the dining room table where they'd left it, and punched in Liz's number as she walked back down the steps. It obviously took several rings for Liz to answer because Maureen was at the bottom of the steps before she started talking, and Barry imagined the old woman pulling herself together, wiping the tears from her face, breathing deeply before picking up the phone.

And doing it all on camera for the amusement of her neighbors.

"You're on BVTV right now," Maureen said. "There's some kind of hidden camera in your house. We turned on the TV and saw you sitting on the couch . . . crying. There's no sound, so we can talk, but get away from the couch, get away from the living room, they can see you."

There was a long pause as Maureen listened to her friend. "Uh-huh . . . Yeah . . . No . . . No . . . I understand . . . Yes we are . . . Same to you. Bye." Maureen hung up the phone, looking stunned. "She says she knows."

"She knows?"

"She saw herself on TV last night." Maureen's jaw tightened. "Going to the bathroom."

"But how—"

"It's not live. It's edited, on tape. She wasn't crying just now, she said that was probably taken last week sometime. She was in the kitchen, cleaning. She was up half the night trying to find where the camera in the bathroom was hidden, but couldn't find a thing. Now she thinks her whole house is probably under surveillance."

"What's she going to do?"

"File a complaint."

"That's it?"

"Keep looking for the cameras, I guess. And try to ignore them until she does."

"Jesus."

"Let's get out of here," Maureen said. "Let's go to Cedar City."

Ten minutes later, their bags were in the Suburban and they were ready to go. Maureen looked back at the house. "Do you think we should board up the windows first, just in case?"

Barry shook his head. "I don't want to show fear. I don't want the association to think we scare easily. As far as they're concerned, we just decided to take a little trip for a few days because we wanted to see the country."

"Okay."

"Besides, we'd have to go down to the lumber yard, buy some plywood, nail it up. I don't know how I'd reach those top windows—"

"I said okay."

"Okay."

They got into the SUV and Barry pulled out of the driveway onto the road.

They were stopped at the gate. "I'm sorry," the guard said, walking out of the kiosk. "No one is allowed to enter or leave Bonita Vista."

He was wearing an expression of grim determination. The olive garb was gone, replaced by a crisp black uniform, the shirt adorned with silver epaulets and insignias, feet clad in knee-high black boots. His usual clipboard was nowhere in evidence, and his right hand rested on the holstered pistol at his side.

"What?" Barry said.

"You may not leave Bonita Vista. It's been deemed a security risk, and I'm afraid that for your own safety, you are not allowed to depart the premises."

"What the fuck is this? The association's declaring martial law?"

The guard met his gaze. "Exactly."

He'd meant it as a joke. Well, not a joke exactly, but a cutting barb, an exaggeration intended to embarrass the guard and draw attention to the absurdity of such a situation. Instead, he was confronted with a flat acknowledgment that his sarcastic overstatement was the truth.

He looked over at Maureen in the passenger seat. Her face was red, livid with anger, and she leaned around him to address the guard. "Listen, you! *We* are the homeowners' association and you work for us! Our dues pay your salary! Now open that goddamn gate and let us through!"

The guard looked at her coldly, then turned his attention to Barry. "I suggest you back up and turn this vehicle around."

"What is your name?" Maureen demanded. "I'll have your job, you insolent son of a bitch!"

"My name is Curtis. And as you know, I also live in Bonita Vista." He leaned forward, resting an arm on the open window frame of the Suburban, letting the tip of his face cross over the invisible boundary that separated the inside of the vehicle from the outside. "And I'd appreciate a little respect from you, you insolent cunt."

He smiled, pulled away, tipped the black cap that covered his blond brush cut. "Good day, ma'am, sir."

Barry put the transmission into reverse and backed up the way they'd come. At the tennis court, he swung into the small parking lot, turned around, and headed up the hill.

"We're trapped," Maureen said incredulously. "We're trapped here and we can't escape."

"Let me think," Barry told her. "We'll go back home for a minute and try to figure something out."

"There's nothing to figure out. I suppose we could walk out of here, but it's a half-hour hike to town and that's the only place we could get to. Besides, that would be going into the lion's den."

He smiled. "We could pull a C.W. McCall."

"Huh?"

"Crash the gate doing ninety-eight."

"Don't think it's not tempting."

Barry pulled into the driveway, turned off the ignition. "He had a gun. Did you notice that?"

"Yes," she said quietly.

They sat in silence for a moment.

"So what do we do?" Barry asked. "Do you have any ideas?"

"No." She sighed. "God, I can't believe this is happening."

"Let's go inside. Maybe we'll think of something."

They got out of the Suburban, walked around the Toyota, but even before they'd started up the porch steps they saw a notice on the screen door. They'd been gone five minutes, eight at the most, but somehow someone had managed to come onto their property and leave a message from the homeowners' association.

"Are we under surveillance?" Maureen asked. "Do they spy on us and wait until we leave so they can rush in and put this crap on our door? This can't be coincidence."

"Nothing's coincidence." He remembered the note they'd found in the closet.

*They're doing it. They're keeping track of it. Don't think they aren't.*

Barry freed the paper from the grating and read it. "It's

an order for all residents to attend the Bonita Vista *anti*-rally at eight o'clock tonight."

"Order?"

"That's what it says." He handed her the notice, then used his key to unlock the door. They walked inside.

"According to this, they'll fine us if we don't show up. Is that legal?"

"I don't know. I have a feeling that it is, though. That's one thing they don't seem to screw up on. However outrageous their actions, they always seem to come down on this side of the law."

"According to Sheriff Hitman. Not exactly an unimpeachable source in my mind."

"I'll call Jeremy. He'll be able to tell us." He locked the door behind them, threw the deadbolt.

Barry went downstairs and dialed Jeremy's number, but midway through the first ring, a robotic female voice came on the line and said, "I'm sorry. Due to a heavy call volume, all circuits are busy. Please try again."

The call was cut off, leaving only a dial tone.

He tried again.

And again.

And again and again and again. Over an hour period, he must have dialed Jeremy's number thirty times, but in each instance he received the same recorded message. He finally gave up, throwing the phone across the room in frustration. It bounced harmlessly on the carpet. Not only couldn't they leave, but they could not contact the outside world. They were cut off here, effectively isolated, and he could not help thinking that it was entirely intentional, that it was part of the association's goal. He would not be surprised to learn that Bonita Vista had its own switchboard and that all incoming and outgoing calls were routed through there, giving the association the power to censor and monitor all of its residents' phone messages.

Neither he nor Maureen could think of any way to get past the armed guard save the *Convoy* option, and they soon tired of staring at each other across the living room as they fruitlessly tried to brainstorm. Maureen finally went downstairs to work on her web page while Barry headed upstairs to make himself an early lunch.

Mike called just after noon. "Did you get the notice?"

"You're the one who left that for me?"

"No. I got one, too. I was just wondering what your plans are."

"I don't know yet."

"They can level a fine against you. And if you don't pay it, they can put a lien on your house."

"I'm so glad we live in a democracy."

"We live in a gated community," Mike corrected him. "The two are mutually exclusive."

"What are you going to do?"

"Go."

"Me, too, I suppose."

"I've got an extra baseball bat if you want one," Mike said.

Baseball bat? Barry felt an unfamiliar shudder pass through him as he thought of wielding a weapon against another person. "You really think there's going to be trouble?"

"I have no idea, but I want to be prepared. Better safe than sorry, as they say."

Barry hung up and told Maureen that he was going to attend the anti-rally, explaining that if there was any hope of preventing violence it would be through a show of strength, a display of numbers. He'd expected an argument, but she was defeated and resigned and said that she'd go, too, that since they'd been forced into this situation and there was no way they could avoid it, they might as well face it head on.

They spent the afternoon restlessly, trying to find tasks

with which to occupy their minds and take up time, but the hours crept by slowly as they shifted desultorily from one unfinished household chore to another. Maureen finally ended up reading a magazine on the couch, while Barry watched Court TV and then a political talk show on CNBC.

Neither of them was hungry, but they forced themselves to eat an early dinner and then wash the dishes together.

They watched the local news, the national news, *Entertainment Tonight.*

And then it was time to go.

There'd been only a half hour of rain in the late afternoon, but the temperature had not returned to the high heat of midday and the evening was unusually cool. Maureen put on a jacket, Barry changed into a long-sleeved shirt. They locked up the house and started walking.

The sun had gone down only recently and they'd been able to see from the house before they left that the western sky still carried a tinge of orange, but it was dark down here among the pines. Night arrived early on the forest floor.

There were others on the road ahead of them: two couples and a family of four. Barry could see their silhouetted forms in the occasional swatches of porch light that spread out from the driveways of the dispersed houses. Neither he nor Maureen spoke, but there was a low-grade murmur audible through the trees and bushes at the bottom of the hill. The sounds of a crowd.

The noise grew louder as they rounded the curve in the road. From a side street, another couple emerged, carrying flashlights trained on the pavement before them. Barry was tempted to say hello, to try and talk with them, find out if they knew anything more about what was happening than he did, but they were not people he recognized and for all he knew they could be association supporters.

He and Maureen were walking hand in hand, and he

squeezed her fingers and slowed the pace, holding back until the other couple moved far enough ahead.

She understood without him having to say a word.

"You can't tell who's on which side," she said quietly after the couple pulled away.

He nodded. "It's best to be careful."

The trees on the left disappeared, the land flattening out as they came to the cleared site of communal property. The pool was done, Barry saw, and filled, the water reflecting back the blackness of the sky above. To the right of the pool, a rough wood frame and cement foundation were already in place for the community center.

The volunteers had been busy.

They walked quickly past the site. In horror fiction, even his own, evil was usually ascribed to locations that were old, that had troubled histories, not to places that were not even finished, that had only a future and not a past or present. But everything was bassackwards here, and the newly completed pool and partially constructed community center seemed imbued with malevolence and engendered within him a shivery sense of revulsion.

They passed Frank and Audrey's house, passed the lighted tennis courts. The street straightened out.

Here was the crowd.

There must have been close to a hundred people milling around. Powerful halogens atop the guard shack illuminated a large section of road and gave the surrounding trees a flat, painted look. Although most of the residents had walked down, there were quite a few cars and trucks—the people who lived on the other side of the hills, no doubt. They were parked in rows in front of the gate, as though to buttress the defenses. The sheriff's cruiser was behind the kiosk, by itself.

It looked like a block party. People were laughing, talking, drinking beer. The only indication that anything was out of the ordinary was the strict line of demarcation, the gate, beyond which was dark, empty silence. And the fact that nearly everyone was armed. He saw no guns, other than those being examined by the sheriff and the guard inside the kiosk, but people were carrying hammers and bats and tire irons. He saw a woman with a carving knife talking to a man wielding a pool cue.

"I don't like this," Maureen whispered.

Barry didn't either. There was something unsettling about seeing ordinary people, upscale neighbors and casual acquaintances, gathered together for the purpose of fighting an opposition mob from the wrong side of the tracks.

"Here they come!" someone yelled.

Barry looked south, over the vehicles, through the interstices of the gate. There was a line of headlights visible through the trees, snaking up the road toward Bonita Vista. He was reminded of Universal's *Frankenstein* films and the hoary cliché of angry villagers storming the mad scientist's castle, pitchforks and torches held aloft.

There'd be no pitchforks or torches this time, though.

Flashlights, maybe.

Possibly guns.

The crowd grew momentarily silent, as though the gravity of the situation had suddenly and simultaneously sunk in with all of them, as though they realized that there was a very realistic possibility of violence. Barry felt a knot of dread forming in the pit of his stomach.

Pickups and old Chevys, boatlike Buicks and battered Jeeps began parking along the dirt shoulder abutting the ditch outside Bonita Vista and quickly became so numerous that succeeding vehicles were forced to spread out into the middle of the street.

He looked over at Hitman standing next to the guard, the two of them loading their weapons, and he wondered again why the sheriff was so pro–Bonita Vista, why he would sac-

rifice the integrity of his job to do the bidding of the homeowners' association. It didn't make any sense. He didn't
even live here.

Did he?

The thought had never occurred to him before, and
Barry was surprised at himself for overlooking so obvious
a connection. Greg Davidson was a local boy made good
who'd moved up into the environs of Bonita Vista. Maybe
the same was true for Hitman. It would account for a lot,
and he thought it was more than possible that Hitman had
been *lured* to Bonita Vista, that the sheriff had been actively
solicited by the association's board and perhaps given a
deal on financing and annual dues in order to recruit him to
their side.

Beyond the gate, car doors were being slammed, engines
were shutting off, though no one was stepping forward. A
buzz passed through the crowd of Bonita Vistans, a repeated phrase that did not quite make it to where Barry and
Maureen stood.

Moments later, the Corbanites started marching en masse,
a ragtag group of angry ranchers, construction workers, me-
chanics, and business owners who appeared ready to storm
the gates. Barry recognized some of the people in the crowd.
Hank. Joe. Lyle. Bert. He felt sick to his stomach, but self-
preservation trumped loyalty and social conscience any day
of the week, and he was prepared to help fend off an assault.
Mike was right. He couldn't stand idly by while his home
was under attack.

He just hoped there wouldn't be any injuries.

Or deaths.

He took Maureen's hand, squeezed it. Her fingers were
cold, her body shivering. To his right was the ruddy-faced
redneck who'd harassed the Mexican handyman. The fat
bastard was in his element, grinning from ear to ear as he
pulled a crossbow from the back of his pickup.

"My old buddies," Maureen said, nodding to her left,

and Barry saw Chuck Shea and Terry Abbey walking purposefully forward, swinging bats.

In his mind, he'd considered the Bonita Vista people soft compared to the townies, rich, pampered, slumming cityfolk as opposed to rough, tough, hardscrabble manual laborers, but he saw now that that was an incorrect generalization. If anything, the Corbanites, despite their very visible and understandable anger, seemed awkward and amateurish, unorganized in their opposition, while the Bonita Vistans seemed prepared, methodical, and capable.

Was it the association's influence?

Barry thought not, and that was the frightening thing. They were this way on their own.

The sheriff and the guard aligned themselves near the stone pillars at each end of the gate, many of the more gung ho and enthusiastic residents filling the space in between.

All of a sudden, the crowd grew completely silent, individuals stopping in place, their attention drawn to someone or something in the pines behind him. Barry turned and saw a line of six old men in black robes standing at the edge of the lighted area, next to the trees. Odd gold stripes and insignia decorated the formal garb, and for some reason he thought of that jackass William Rehnquist during Bill Clinton's impeachment trial, decked out in the robes of a Supreme Court Justice that were desecrated by ridiculous homemade gold stripes supposedly inspired by Gilbert and Sullivan. There was the same sort of absurdity here, only there was also an element of menace, a hint of something dark, dangerous, and fundamentally wrong.

All eyes remained on the six figures. He thought the men would move forward and take charge, but they remained in place and there was something odd about that, too. The one in the middle appeared to be the leader, and Barry had no doubt that this was the president, the famous Jasper Calhoun. Liz had told Maureen something about

Calhoun's peculiar appearance, had said there was something unnatural in the way he looked, and while it could have been the angle of the lights, could have been the fault of distance, Barry thought that *all* of the board members seemed strange, each of their too-white faces bizarre and abnormal.

The townspeople had reached the gate and were massing behind the giant iron barrier.

"You killed our son!" a woman screamed, her face red and teary, features distorted by rage.

Another man grabbed one of the ornamental crosspieces and started shaking the gate. "Murderers!" he cried. "Murderers!"

Other voices were raised, threats and epithets were shouted.

"Call out the volunteers," the president said in a loud stentorian voice, and his speech overrode all competing sounds. He raised his right hand. There was the faint noise of a whip cracking, and from the trees behind the board members emerged three rows of shirtless men. The volunteers marched onto the road and pressed past Barry and Maureen, heading toward the gate. They were the same men who had been working on the pool and the community center, and this close he saw that some were missing hands. Others had serious facial scars or walked with limps. He thought of Kenny Tolkin's eye patch.

Greg Davidson passed by him, staring blankly, the right side of his head shaved, that ear gone.

The crowd parted before the volunteers, allowing them through. They carried no weapons, bore no clubs or guns or blades, but there was about them the hard, unyielding purpose of those who would stop at nothing to achieve their goal. They were Bonita Vista's army, Barry thought, and he wondered if their appearance was as big a surprise to everyone else as it was to him. Nearly all of the residents had brought weapons of some sort, obviously assuming they would be needed, but it appeared now that they would only be a last-ditch backup. The volunteers would be the first line of defense.

Barry watched them go past, far more than he and Maureen had seen before.

"Why are they acting like that?" Maureen said, a quiver in her voice betraying the fear she felt.

"I don't know," he admitted.

"They look like they're . . . hypnotized or something."

Unseen, Frank Hodges had moved next to her. "They're indentured," he said shortly. "They couldn't pay their dues."

Neil Campbell, ever-present clipboard in hand, was suddenly on the other side of Barry. "Read your handbook. It explains all about indenture."

"Open the gates!" the president commanded, and the twin metal doors swung slowly outward, pushing protesting townspeople out of the way.

"You bastards can't treat us like this!" a woman screamed.

Bert from the coffee shop raised a shotgun. "You know what you did! *We* know what you did! And we won't stand for it!"

The volunteers marched through the open gateway.

And the fighting started.

There was a sick feeling in Barry's guts as he watched the shirtless men remorselessly punch grieving mothers in the stomach, watched them grab rifles from townspeople and use them to club the owners' heads. It felt odd to be standing here like this, overseeing the battlefield like generals while others fought on their behalf, and he was suddenly disgusted by his neighbors, by himself, by everyone involved with this travesty.

Surprisingly, thankfully, there were no shots fired, but the conflict was brutal nonetheless, with both sides actively attempting to maim and injure their opponents, and his hor-

ror intensified as he saw an one-armed volunteer use his
one hand to gouge at the eyes of an elderly man in rancher's
overalls.

He'd wondered where Hitman's deputies were, and just
as the volunteers appeared to be gaining the upper hand, the
lawmen drove up, sirens blaring, lights on. They were
forced to park behind the townies' vehicles, which were
blocking the road. The flashing lights of their cruisers reflected off metal roofs and shone through glass wind-
shields, bathing the entire area in garishly surrealistic circus
colors, while a deep, distorted voice boomed through a
megaphone: "Break it up! Break it up!"

Uniformed deputies ran between the cars and pickups,
nightsticks raised, and began to disperse the crowd, collar-
ing and arresting those who refused to obey the orders to
cease and desist. Unmolested, undisturbed, the shirtless
volunteers, many of them battered and bleeding, turned and
walked back through the gateway into Bonita Vista. Barry
looked over at Hitman, and in the strobing red and blue of
the lights, he saw the sheriff smile.

Frank had moved between Maureen and Barry. "I heard
you tried to fuck my wife," he whispered.

"Elizabeth Dyson's filing a complaint against you with
the board," Neil Campbell said on the other side of him.
"Claims you forced her into giving you a BJ after Ray's funeral."

"That's a lie!" Barry yelled. "You're both lying!"

The men moved away, laughing, disappearing into the
crowd. Someone passed by, bumped him. Another shoved a
hand in his back. The scene was becoming more chaotic,
and though there weren't nearly as many people here, he
was reminded of the climax of *Day of the Locust*.

He looked desperately around for a friendly face. Mike
or one of those anti-association people from Ray's parties.
But there were only antagonistic glares from unfamiliar individuals, and the uniformity of this response made him

think that perhaps it was dictated, perhaps it had been ordered.

"Stay here," he told Maureen. He started toward the trees, toward the board. The robed men were watching him, their wrinkled faces serious but their eyes mirthful.

It hadn't been distance or a trick of the light, he realized as he approached. Something about them did look peculiar. Liz was right. Something was off.

"You must be Barry Welch," the president said as he came closer.

Barry pointed a finger at him. "Don't fuck with me!" he ordered.

Jasper Calhoun smiled slightly, nodded.

Someone bumped him, and he turned to look at the gathered residents and the milling volunteers, but he could not see who'd done it. He again faced the board.

They were gone.

Simultaneously, the lights of the guard shack winked off, and the strobing red and blue of the cruiser lights diminished as several deputies drove their vehicles and prisoners away. Around him, individual flashlights were turning down toward the pavement, moving up the road as homeowners started to disperse. The old men had faded into the woods, and he did not understand how they'd been able to disappear so quickly. Had they turned and run, dashing through the trees, their robes flapping behind them? He couldn't imagine such a retreat by those pompous old men, but the only alternatives were scenarios more appropriate for one of his novels, and those he didn't want to think about.

"They're watching you," a woman said to him as he passed by, and Barry recognized the old lady who lived across from the tennis court. He didn't know if it was a friendly warning or an intimidating threat.

Barry strode angrily back toward where Maureen stood, now talking to Mike and Tina. The people before him moved sullenly aside, strangers casting suspicious and hostile glances in his direction.

"Is everything okay?" Mike asked worriedly.

Barry shook his head.

"What did you do?" Maureen asked. "What did you say to them?"

"It's war," he told her.

# THIRTY-SIX

Maureen finished answering the five measly E-mails that her web page had generated over the past three days, knowing even as she typed them that their senders would not engage her services. It was disheartening to realize that something on which she had spent so much time and for which she'd had such high hopes was simply not panning out.

Thank God for her California clients.

She leaned back in her chair, postponing leaving the room. In here, she was cushioned from the realities of the outside world. She could pretend that she was not in Bonita Vista, that she was merely an accountant in an office, and that the things happening on the other side of these walls did not affect or concern her in any way.

Barry was still angry, still stubbornly defiant, but he was worried as well.

Maybe it was time to give up, she'd told him, maybe they should return to California.

That was the wrong thing to say.

"Who's going to fight them if not us?" he demanded. "Would you just abandon Liz and all the other people terrorized by these murderous bastards? We're not just doing this for us! This is our chance to make a difference, to stand up and be counted!"

She'd nodded, raised her hands in acquiescence. She knew better than to press the issue and paint him into a corner. If she left him an out, he might eventually take it, might eventually see that it was the smartest of all possible options, and that they could always continue their Quixotic battle from afar.

She shut off her computer, switched off the monitor. The strangest thing, the most unsettling thing, was their temporary alliance with the association. It felt wrong to her. And to Barry, too, she knew. The association *had* poisoned dogs in town and, intentionally or unintentionally, two children had been killed as well. The sheriff had refused to do anything about it, so families, friends, and neighbors had taken matters into their own hands and staged a rally to draw attention to the problem and intimidate the guilty into giving themselves up. It was a just cause, a moral purpose, and she and Barry and all of their neighbors had only opposed it because they were concerned for their own safety and for the condition of their houses. They were practicing self-defense, went the rationalization, the most natural and legitimate reaction a human could have. But it did not feel that way to her. It felt as though they were shallow, self-absorbed assholes more concerned about their own real estate values than the lives of other people's children.

She and Barry had participated unwillingly, as a result of a threat, but they had participated nonetheless, and that made them morally culpable. She felt guilty about that, and she wished to Christ that they'd defied the association, that they'd at least attempted to stay neutral by remaining home and sitting it out—even if they'd had to pay a fine. They should not have lent their support or given their tacit approval to anything the association had done.

To her surprise, they were still able to shop at the market in Corban. Even after all that had happened. It had been a nerve-racking trip for groceries yesterday when they'd made their first post-rally trek into town, and they'd invited Mike and Tina, and the Stewarts' friends Lou and Stacy, to go with them in case there was trouble, but neither the clerk at the checkout stand nor the store's two other customers had said a word. They'd bought enough groceries for the next two weeks with no problem.

Perhaps the sheriff's deputy stationed by the cash register had something to do with it.

Even if it was only Wally Addison.

They were already making contingency plans, though. Mule Park was the closest town to Corban, and while it was forty miles to the south, they could easily make the trip there and back in the space of a morning and stock up enough food and necessities for a month. The people of Corban had to be resentful of Bonita Vista residents and of the sheriff's obvious partiality, and it was only a matter of time before that resentment bubbled up and boiled over.

She stared at the blank monitor and found herself wondering if she and Barry weren't barking up the wrong tree by attributing everything to the homeowners' association. It seemed to her that Hitman was the real power behind the throne. He was the one straddling the two communities, enforcing the laws as he saw fit, allowing Bonita Vista to run roughshod over the town. He could have—and *should* have—sided with the families of the victims and investigated the poisonings and brought the perpetrators up on charges, but instead he'd ignored the situation, allowed it to fester, and when people had tried to take the law into their own hands, he'd reasserted his authority, allowing them to be beaten by the volunteers before he had them arrested. Now he'd stationed a deputy at the market to ensure that Bonita Vistans could purchase groceries and assigned another deputy to guard the gas station and make sure they were unmolested and able to buy gas.

It was as if the sheriff had declared martial law in Corban, and it occurred to her that he could have accomplished all of this without the association.

That was wishful thinking, though. The sheriff was just a pawn. He was the muscle. The association was the brains.

No, he was not even the muscle. Or not all of it. She remembered those shirtless volunteers with their missing fingers and hands and ears beating the hell out of local farmers and ranchers, using the Corbanites' own weapons against them, and she shivered.

Hitman might be keeping Corban safe for Bonita Vista residents, but Barry had not returned to his office. Not yet. For all they knew, it had been ransacked and vandalized, his computer smashed, but he was not ready to see for himself. His landlord and his old pals from the coffee shop had been in the forefront of the skirmish at the gate, and it did not seem prudent to provoke them.

He'd write on her computer for a while, Barry told her. He'd go back, pick up his equipment, and clear out his office after the furor died down a bit.

Mike was still working at the Cablevision office, and his friend Lou at the telephone company, but it was tense, they said. Several Bonita Vistans worked in town, and Maureen wondered how the rest of them were handling it. No doubt there'd be more than a few fights during breaks and lunches as tensions spilled over, and she just prayed that no one got seriously hurt.

She looked out the window, saw green pines against a clear blue sky.

God, she wished that they'd never driven through Utah, never found this place.

She stood, left her office, and walked upstairs to where Barry was lying on the couch watching a political talk show. On the coffee table beside him was the pen he'd planned to use to jot down notes for a new novel, and a spiral notebook turned to an empty first page.

"Doesn't look like you got much done," she said.

"My brain's not working."

"I'm not working either. No one wants my e-services. Want to sit here with me and watch some BVTV?"

"Very funny," Barry said. "Very funny."

They went to bed early, both of them tired and fatigued not from any physical exertion but from stress.

They were awakened in the middle of the night by banging, thumping, and heavy scraping that sounded as though furniture was being moved. The bedroom door was closed, but from underneath the door shone a strip of yellow light.

Someone was upstairs.

Maureen sat up quickly, looking into Barry's face and seeing there an expression that mirrored the way she felt. "What do you think they want?" she whispered.

*Who do you think it is?* was what she'd originally intended to ask, but she already knew the answer to that and so did he. These weren't burglars who had broken into their home. And while she didn't know the specific identity of the individuals who were searching the house, she knew what they represented, she knew where they were from.

The homeowners' association.

"I'm going to find out," Barry said grimly. He threw the covers off, grabbed his bathrobe, and angrily opened the bedroom door.

She quickly picked up her own bathrobe and put it on over her nightgown, and the two of them walked into the lighted hallway and up the stairs to the living room.

They should have brought along some type of weapon, she thought. A heavy blunt object. Just in case it *was* a prowler. But their first instincts had been correct. The man who stood in the center of the well-lit room, smiling at them, was obviously not a criminal. He looked more like a stockbroker.

"Sorry to disturb you," the man said cheerfully. "We were trying to be quiet."

There were five men all together, each of them dressed in identical business suits, each with a pen and clipboard. Two of them were in the living room, reading the titles of books on the bookshelf, examining the artwork on the walls. The three others were upstairs in the kitchen, loudly opening cupboards and digging through drawers.

"What the hell is this?" Barry said.

"It's time for your four-month inspection."

"How did you get in here?" Maureen demanded. She felt vulnerable, violated, more exposed than she ever had in her life. Upstairs, a familiar click-squeak told her that someone had opened the refrigerator.

"The association has the master keys to all locks in Bonita Vista." The man continued to smile at her, and she thought now that there was something not nice about that smile. He was looking at her as though he could see through her bathrobe, and she instinctively looked down to check, to make sure nothing was being exposed.

Barry stepped forward, crowding the man. "Who are you?"

"My name's Bill." He held out a hand.

Barry's voice was calm, even, and all the more threatening for it. "Get the fuck out of my house, Bill. Now."

The man smiled, nodded. "I think we've seen enough, Mr. Welch." He started scribbling on the paper clipped onto his board. "Let's hit it, boys!" he called out.

The three men upstairs came down the steps, writing on their own clipboards, unclasping the forms and handing them to Bill. The other man by the bookcase did the same.

Bill finished with a flourish, tore off the top sheet, and handed a pink piece of paper to Barry. Maureen looked over his shoulder, reading along.

"It should be self-explanatory. You are required to place out of sight all photographs and personal keepsakes. This includes but is not limited to souvenirs from vacation spots, family heirlooms, and knicknacks that serve no functional purpose." Bill's voice was all business, and there was a coldness to it that belied the happy, hearty act he'd put on for their benefit. Behind him, the other men were filing out of the house silently. "You must have a minimum of three bare walls in each room, and the fourth wall may only have artwork that has been approved by the association's interior design committee. All walls must be white or off-white, and sheets, pillowcases, and bedspreads must be solid colors, preferably earth tones." He smiled again. "But as I said, it's all pretty self-explanatory."

Maureen now understood the lack of a personal touch in Liz's house, the general sparseness in the interiors of the other homes she'd seen. She could not recall reading anything about this in the sacred C, C, and Rs, but she had no doubt that they would find it in the document if they looked through it right now. She stared at the short-haired yuppie's falsely friendly face and was filled with anger and the type of stubborn rage that Barry must have been experiencing. There was no way on God's earth that she was going to rearrange her house according to the dictates of the association. No one could tell her how to decorate her own home, and she'd be damned if an impersonal document created by a cabal of her most fascistic neighbors was going to impose some type of lunatic standards on her taste.

Barry was on the exact same wavelength. "What gives you the right to come into our house and pry into our private life and tell us what we can and can't do in our own fucking home?" He started out speaking at a normal volume, but by the end of the question he was shouting.

"I'm chairman of the inspection committee," Bill said brightly, walking away from them. He nodded as he stepped out the door. "Good night to you." He closed the door behind him and they heard the lock turn.

"Didn't we have the deadbolt and chain hooked up?" Maureen said, turning toward Barry.

He nodded. "I was thinking the same thing."

"How did they—"

"I don't know."

Every light in the house had been turned on. Downstairs, lights in the hall, bathroom, and Maureen's office were blazing, and the thought that those men had been snooping through her belongings while she was asleep in the next room chilled her to the bone. But she was far more angry than scared, and she remembered a horror movie Barry had forced her to watch in which parents had booby-trapped their house to catch their daughter's murderers, and she wished she could do the same thing here. Right now, the thought of Bill and his smug little looka-likes speared on some makeshift shiv sounded mighty appealing.

Neither of them had bothered to look at the time, but as they went from room to room, checking to make sure nothing was broken or stolen, turning off the lights, she saw by the clock in the kitchen that it was two-thirty.

It was another ten minutes before they were back in bed, and although Barry was snoring almost instantly, it was a long time before she was able to fall asleep.

As early as was polite, she called Liz.

Barry was taking his shower, and she poured herself a cup of coffee while she dialed her friend's number.

The voice that answered halfway through the first ring was wary and suspicious. "Yes?"

"Hello, Liz? It's me, Maureen."

"Maureen." Her name was repeated in a disassociated monotone that raised the hackles on her neck and set off alarm bells in her head.

"Liz? Are you all right?"

"Fine. I'm fine." But the monotone remained, her friend's voice drained of its usual life.

"What happened? What did they do?"

Liz didn't answer.

Maureen spoke quickly before her friend hung up. "It's the association," she said. "That's why I'm calling. They've come down on us for . . . for . . . shit, for our interior decorating. We woke up in the middle of the night and five of those assholes had broken into our house to 'inspect' it. They told us we had to get rid of family photos and personal effects, and we had to rearrange our entire house."

Liz's voice exhibited its first sign of emotion.

Fear.

"The middle of the night?"

"Yes."

"They always come in the middle of the night." Again the monotone.

"What happened to you?" Maureen asked once more. "No. Don't say anything. I understand that you can't talk over the phone. I'll come up—"

"No!" her friend said sharply.

"Liz . . ."

"Do. Not. Come. To. See. Me." The words were bitten off.

"I know you're—"

"It's not safe."

The old woman's voice was replaced by a dial tone. She'd hung up, and Maureen stared blankly down at the phone for a moment, unsure of what to do. If she called back, Liz probably wouldn't answer—and if she did answer, she'd be angry. She'd been specifically ordered not to go to Liz's house, so that was out of the question.

Tina.

Maureen found the other woman's number and called.

Mike answered the phone, and she asked to speak to his wife. A minute later, Tina was on the line, sounding sleepy. "Hello?"

"This is Maureen. Did I wake you up?"

"Sort of."

"Sorry, but it's kind of an emergency." She explained about their nighttime visitors and about her unsettling call to Liz. "First things first," she said. "What do we do about Liz?"

"What can we do? You know what happened last time. We all tried to help her, but she just shut us out. I'll call her myself later, go up there if she'll let me, and maybe call Audrey and Moira, too. But I'll tell you true, I have a feeling it's going to be the same situation. There may be nothing we can do. She might have to just work it out herself."

"And if she can't?"

Tina didn't answer.

"What about our situation?"

Tina sighed. "I wondered when they were going to crack down on you."

"You knew about this?"

"I guess."

"Why didn't you say anything? Why didn't you tell me?"

"I thought maybe you'd squeaked by, maybe they hadn't seen the inside of your house or for some reason didn't want to make you conform. I didn't want to worry you unnecessarily or draw attention and let them know that you'd escaped them. But . . . but I guess in the back of my mind I knew it would happen."

"You should have told me about this," Maureen said.

"You're right. I'm sorry." Her voice was wistful. "But it was nice seeing family photos again. And more than one wall of pictures and hangings. And all those collectibles and antiques you have."

"You're still going to see them," Maureen told her. "We're not changing anything."

There was a pause, as if Tina did not know how to respond to that. "But you have to."

"What if we don't?"

Tina's voice grew lower. "The fines will start. And you don't want to get into that cycle. Believe me."

"Then what can we do?"

"There's nothing you can do," Tina said. "It's something we all have to put up with."

"Middle of the night inspections?"

"Well," she admitted, "ours have never been in the middle of the night. Probably they just wanted to rattle you."

"That's selective enforcement right there, then. They're treating us differently than they treat everyone else."

"I don't know if I'd say that," Tina added quickly. "*We've* escaped it, but that doesn't mean other people have."

"But you'd stand up for us? You'd tell the truth? You'd sign a statement saying that your inspections have all been at reasonable hours?"

More backpedaling. "Sign a statement? I'd have to talk to Mike about that."

Tina obviously wasn't going to be much help. And if *she* wasn't brave enough to stand up to the association, Maureen was sure no one else would be. Rather than tempering her anger, the disappointment she felt only fueled it further, and she said a quick good-bye.

She and Barry were in this alone; they'd have to face down the association by themselves.

But that was okay. They didn't need anybody else.

When Barry came out of the shower, she was sitting at the dining room table, staring out the window at the trees, nibbling on a piece of cold toast.

"Did you call Liz?" he asked.

"And Tina."

"And?" he prodded when she didn't elaborate.

She told him about both conversations, about Liz's frightened paranoia and Tina's ineffectual support.

"What do you want to do?" Barry asked. "Do you still want to go back to California?"

"Hell no."

"That's the spirit."

"Fuck 'em," Maureen said, and the words felt good. "We're not going anywhere. We're staying here just long enough to wipe our asses with those damn C, C, and Rs."

# THIRTY-SEVEN

It was another fine.

He had paid none of them yet, but they'd been arriving daily, signed by the association's treasurer—someone named Thompson Hughes. They were all ridiculously inflated, and although he hadn't kept track, the total they owed must be well over three thousand dollars by now. It was ludicrous that they were being penalized in such a way for minor infractions of unreasonable rules, and he'd saved each of the notices for a future court case.

Barry dropped the rest of the mail on the coffee table and tore open the unstamped envelope. This one was levied against them for failure to park both of their vehicles facing in the same direction. For that offense, the association was docking them seven hundred and fifty dollars.

"Seven hundred and fifty this time," he said.

Maureen looked up from her book. "Losers."

With the fine notice was another form, and he unfolded the paper and scanned its contents.

"Jesus," he breathed.

"What's it say?"

"The title is 'Bath and Toilet Violations.' Does that give you some clue?"

"Let me see that!"

He handed her the paper. "Someone has apparently been

monitoring our bathroom habits. It says that you do not have the right number of tampons or maxipads, that a certain surplus number is required, which you have failed to maintain, and that we are discharging three gallons more effluent than is allowable for a domestic residence with two people."

Her face paled as she read. "My God." She looked at him. "You think they have a camera in there?"

"It's possible—and I'm going to get some wallpaper and cover over every square inch of the wall and ceiling just in case—but that maxipad/tampon thing is not something that you could find out with a camera. Someone's been snooping, someone's been in the house."

"But when? We've been home all the time."

"While we were sleeping," he said, and the thought of it curdled his blood. Bill and his inspectors were one thing. As invasive and intrusive as that had been, at least they'd been open about it, at least they had made their presence known. But the idea of people breaking into their home and sneaking around in the dark, checking on Maureen's feminine hygiene products and God knew what else, made his skin crawl. Who were they? And how many of them? The scenario conjured by his writer's imagination had Kenny and the most disfigured volunteers creeping, crawling, and limping silently through the rooms of the house, peeking at and examining their most intimate items: fingering his condoms, sniffing Maureen's dirty panties.

And the scary thing was that he was probably not that far off the mark.

He did indeed put wallpaper over the walls and ceiling, rounding off the corners so there would be no cracks or gaps through which miniature devices could peer. They had several rolls left over from their initial renovation, and it occurred to him that perhaps he should re-wallpaper the entire house—or at least those rooms where they'd painted rather than papered the walls—but the thought was intimidating, He recalled how much work they'd done that first month, and he didn't want to go through that again unless he absolutely had to. Besides, there was no indication that any other rooms were under surveillance.

Maybe they needed to watch BVTV more often.

As he should have expected, the next day they received a notice alerting them that they had made unauthorized changes to a room's appearance without getting approval from the interior design committee. They were required to both pay an eight-hundred-and-twenty-dollar fine *and* remove the wallpaper.

"Fuck that," he said.

"I wonder how the people before us survived," Maureen said. "This place was like a bat cave when we bought it. They must have broken at least as many decorating rules as we have."

"Maybe they *didn't* survive."

She looked at him quizzically.

"Did you notice on all those papers we signed when we bought this place that it said Jordan and Sara Gardner *Trust*? I wondered about that at the time. I assume it meant that the owners were dead and their relatives were selling off the house."

"Probably to pay the fines."

They spent the afternoon at Mike and Tina's. Liz was still avoiding contact with everyone, hiding reclusively in her house, keeping her door locked and her drapes drawn, and they were all worried for her, though none of them had any ideas of how to help. Maureen had sent her a long letter through the mail, trying to appeal to the old woman's logical side and assuring her that she had a lot of allies and didn't have to face anything alone, no matter what it was, but no one was even sure if Liz was collecting her mail these days.

"I'll tell you one thing," Mike said. "This wouldn't have happened if Ray was still here."

"A lot of things wouldn't have happened if Ray was still here," Barry agreed.

Indeed, Ray's death seemed to have been the catalyst for much of what had occurred since. He had been a sort of unofficial opposition leader, the only person with enough influence and gravitas to counteract the association's monopolization, and once he was out of the way, once that domino had fallen, everything else had started to come undone.

Barry wanted to get the names of the people who had attended the Dysons' parties, all of Ray's anti-association acquaintances. "We can put together a petition," he said, "try to get a recall."

"First of all," Mike told him, "there are no recalls. It's disallowed. There's no such thing here. Secondly, the annual meeting is coming up on Labor Day weekend. That's when they vote for officers, make amendments to the C, C, and Rs, conduct all that sort of association business. It's when they allow us mortals to see the man behind the curtain."

"So that's our big chance."

"Yeah."

"If I can talk to enough people, get them to propose, second, and vote for a number of different initiatives, we can institute some of our *own* reforms."

"In theory."

"You don't think it's possible?"

"Let's just say I've been to these meetings before. I know how they go."

"Is it true that on the ballot you can only approve the existing board, there's no other choices?"

"Oh yeah."

"You also have to bring your federal income tax forms to the meeting," Tina said. "The ones from last year. That's when we turn them in."

Maureen frowned. "Why is that?"

"It's required," Mike said. "As crazy as it sounds, the courts have upheld this. It's perfectly legal. I would've thought it was an invasion of privacy, but an association can require full financial disclosure from any homeowner who belongs to it. And of course our association does."

Maureen turned toward Barry. "That's how they learned about the precariousness of the Davidsons' finances, why they knew that an increase in property taxes would force them to move."

Mike nodded. "Yep."

"About Greg Davidson . . ." Barry said.

"What?"

"At Ray's party, he said they were going to sell their house and move. His brother or someone had found him a job in Arizona."

"Yeah."

"But they didn't move. I saw Greg. He's one of the volunteers. I don't know what happened to Wynona, but Greg was helping to dig the pool and he was at the gate the night of the rally."

Mike and Tina exchanged a look. Barry caught it, but he didn't know what it meant, and suddenly he wasn't sure if he should say any more. He thought about Frank and Audrey—

*Open my box*

—and realized that he really didn't know Mike and Tina any better. His gut said they were okay, and they seemed to have all the right ideas, but in Bonita Vista you could never tell.

Maureen seemed to have caught the same vibe. "You don't want to talk about the volunteers."

"It's not that," Tina said. "It's just . . ." She looked over at her husband.

"We didn't find out about them for a long time ourselves," Mike offered. "And, you're right. They're not something that people talk about. Everyone knows they're there, and they help clear the roads after big storms and stuff, but we like to pretend like we don't know anything about them."

Barry shook his head. "I don't understand why you—"

"I volunteered for a week myself."

They were stunned, silent. If Mike had said he'd murdered his first wife and met Tina after his release from prison, it could not have been more shocking, and Barry marveled at how sinister such a mundane concept had become in this wacked-out world.

"I truly did volunteer," Mike said. "I was fined a hundred dollars for violating Article Eight, going outside in the morning to pick up my newspaper while wearing a bathrobe. You're not supposed to appear outside the house wearing a robe. We could've paid the fine, but our refrigerator was going, we'd been saving up for a new one, and this would've put us back another month. I'd heard through the grapevine that you could volunteer, that you could work off your fine instead of pay it, and I approached the board and they said okay. I was assigned to pick up trash on the roads and in the ditches for a week."

"And that was it?" Barry asked.

"Not exactly. On Saturday, the last day, I was told to help clear dried brush from one of the greenbelts, and I found out for the first time that there were . . . gradations of volunteers. There were people like me, who were assigned specific tasks for a specific amount of time, and there were people who weren't trying to work off anything. They were just volunteering to help out, and they could pretty much do whatever they wanted to on whatever needed to be done." He licked his lips. "Then there were the indentureds, and I'm pretty sure that's what Greg is. They're the ones who've lost their homes but owe so much that even that doesn't cover it. They pretty much sign away their lives, forfeit their rights and are at the association's beck and call until their debts are paid off. They supposedly live together in a bunkhouse somewhere, although I still don't know where that is. I've never asked."

Barry was expecting more, but apparently Mike was through. "That's it?" he said. "There has to be more to it than that. You were at the gate that night. You saw them. Greg and the rest of them were like robots. They looked like they were drugged or hypnotized or something."

"It's not that," Mike insisted. "I can't explain it, but there's nothing truly coercive involved, no magic or drugs or brainwashing or anything. They really can walk away if they want to, although I have no doubt that they'd have their asses sued off if they did. But they're in so deep to the association that they stay. They'll do anything to get themselves out from underneath that rock." Another of those looks at Tina. "*Anything.*"

"But—" Maureen looked at Barry. "—they all seem to be . . . mutilated in some way. There's something wrong with all of them. They're missing ears or fingers or hands."

"Volunteering is not the only way to pay off debts," Tina said through tight lips.

That was as detailed as either of them would get, and Barry wasn't inclined to push them further. There was something else there, but while Mike and Tina were being evasive, it was out of fear, not malice, and he understood their apprehension. Mike, in particular, had to walk a thin line. Although he worked for a national corporation, his office *was* in town. And while he disagreed with and resented the association, they pretty much left him alone. It was not in his best interest to rock any boats.

After some innocuous chitchat that allowed them all to depressurize a bit, Barry and Maureen finally took their leave, making tentative plans to play tennis with the Stewarts next weekend.

They returned home to find Maureen's garden gone.

They'd only been away for a few hours, but in that time someone—

*the volunteers?*

—had not only torn out and disposed of every bush, vine, sapling, flower, and vegetable that Maureen had planted but had packed down the dirt and placed in it dozens of dead and dying manzanita bushes.

"What is *this*?" Maureen asked incredulously.

The land on the north side of the house looked like a cruel parody of the property as it had appeared when they bought the house, as though a blight had descended on native shrubs, killed most of them off, and left a few weakened specimens in its wake.

"Guess what?" Barry said. He pointed toward the screen door.

A pink sheet of paper.

"Oh no."

Maureen reached the door first and ripped off the form. Barry read over her shoulder. They were being fined for noncompliance with regulations and would also be charged for the labor and materials supplied by the gardening enterprise, which replaced the offending plants with acceptable local vegetation.

"'Acceptable local vegetation'?" Maureen fumed. "They stuck some dead twigs in the ground!"

"Don't worry. We're not paying it."

"That's not the point. They destroyed my garden. My tomatoes still had blooms, and another batch was about to ripen. I had zucchini that was ready to pick."

"I wonder if there's some sort of grievance committee, someplace we could go to complain about an action like this."

"Fat chance."

"They should have to take responsibility for this. We were told specifically, after that first time with Barney, that we were allowed to have a garden and to landscape our property."

"That's not all. Look."

He read the line to which she was pointing. It stated that all flowers and houseplants had to be removed from the inside of the residence within forty-eight hours. Otherwise, additional fines would be imposed. The amount was unspecified.

They were both agreed that no changes would be made; their plants would be neither moved nor removed. Since the inspection, they'd been tilting dining room chairs and placing them under the doorknobs in order to discourage intruders, but Bill and his buddies had somehow found a way to unhook a chain latch and throw back a keyless deadbolt, so this extra precaution probably hadn't amounted to much. Still, Barry vowed that tonight he would also duct tape the edges of the doors. At the very least, it might tell them if someone had broken in while they were sleeping.

Maureen decided to walk through where her garden *used* to be and see if any of her plants had been spared. Barry went inside. He had an idea. He was pretty sure that Maureen would not approve, so he waited until she came back in and told her that he was going to walk around the property and do his own inspection "Our homeowners' insurance might cover this," he told her. "So after I look around, I'm going to take some photos and call them to file a claim, see what comes of it."

She thought it was a good idea.

He did intend to take pictures and file an insurance claim, but he also had more immediate plans. From underneath the bottom deck where he stored their gardening implements, tools, and leftover renovation materials, he found what he was looking for: a large cardboard box. Using a pair of clippers, he raggedly cut off one side and then placed it on the ground, and painted a short, crude message. The only color of paint they had was white, but against the dark brown of the cardboard, the letters stood out and were clearly visible.

Barry positioned the sign at the base of a scrub oak,

using a large rock to hold it in place, and walked out to the street to make sure his message was legible and could be read by passing cars.

FUCK THE HOMEOWNERS' ASSOCIATION

It was legible all right. He grinned. This would show those bastards. He'd be fined, but it was worth it to him to make sure that they were aware of his defiance, that they knew he was willing to take his dissatisfaction public.

Besides, he'd just throw the fine notice in a drawer with the others.

He walked back inside, still smiling, and got the camera out. He took pictures of the damage from different directions, then, just for fun, took a picture of the sign.

He was cheered up for about ten minutes, but then he started thinking about all the time he'd wasted on this crap, all of the hours spent worrying and responding and thinking and brooding that could have been used for more productive purposes, and suddenly, he no longer felt so good. His thoughts turned to those creepy old men of the board and the futility of fighting against such entrenched institutionalized power.

Maureen was lying on the couch, watching the Home and Garden channel, mourning her lost plants. She, too, seemed drained. She'd been all fired up after their nighttime inspection, ready to go to war with the entire world if need be, but subsequent harassment had taken its toll, and now she looked positively beaten down.

Was any of this really worth it?

Maureen must have been thinking along the same lines because she sat up, using the remote to mute the television's sound. "Maybe we should move," she said.

He didn't respond.

"We can leave and still save face. We didn't buckle, we didn't cave, we stayed. We showed them. Now let's sell this place and put this hell behind us." There was a quaver in her voice. "Please?"

Barry nodded tiredly. "Okay."

"Thank God," Maureen said. "Thank God."

And he found that he felt the same way—off the hook, filled with relief.

It's over, he thought. It's finally over.

# THIRTY-EIGHT

Barry sat in Doris' office, enduring the hostile stares of her coworkers. The real estate agent was on the phone, discussing a seller's willingness to carry with an obviously jittery buyer, but the fat man and the skinny woman who worked for her had nothing to do and behind her back were fixing him with the type of glare usually reserved for disciples of Adolf Hitler.

He was pretty sure he'd seen both of them at the rally.

Doris hung up and fixed him with a bright smile. "Sorry about that. What can I do for you?"

"Well . . ."

"It's not Bert, is it? He's not causing you any problems?"

"I'd . . . we want to sell our house."

"Oh." The real estate agent nodded, stood. "Come on. Let's go into the conference room." She led him into the other half of the trailer, closed the door behind them, and pulled out two adjoining chairs from the table. "Have a seat."

He followed her lead. "Your agents don't seem too thrilled to see me here."

"Don't you worry about that. They'll do what I tell them to do and they'll think what I tell them to think, or they'll be fired."

"I understand their feelings. Been running into a lot of it

lately. We're not exactly the most popular people in town right now."

"I don't care what other people say," Doris told him. "I understand Bonita Vista. I've sold enough homes there." She smiled at him, leaned over, and patted his leg reassuringly. But the hand remained in place a beat too long, and when she finally moved it away, her fingers brushed his crotch.

He looked out the room's small window, afraid to meet her eyes. He was pretty sure she was coming on to him, but he didn't want to encourage her and tried to think of some way to make it clear that he was not interested, that this was strictly a business meeting.

"I've found that the people in Bonita Vista are *very* nice," she said. He turned to face her, and she lowered her eyes in a way that she probably thought was sexy but instead seemed crude and embarrassingly obvious.

It *was* a class thing, he realized. It was terrible to admit, even to himself, but as much as he hated that damn homeowners' association, he felt more at ease with the residents of Bonita Vista than he did with the people of Corban. He wanted to be a conscientious liberal, to be one with the masses and all that good shit, but when it came down to it, he had money, he was educated, and he just didn't belong with these people.

He looked at Doris with her big hair and loud clothes and overlarge jewelry and there was not even a flicker of interest, no temptation whatsoever. The fact that she was sympathetic to Bonita Vista turned him off even more, and he wondered if everyone who had dealings with Bonita Vista was automatically corrupted. The sheriff. Doris. It seemed like whoever came in contact with the gated community and the association was . . . influenced somehow.

He'd been reading and writing too many horror novels.

No.

He wished that was the case, but it wasn't.

"Where do you live?" he asked.

"Out on Barr's Ranch Road." She leaned forward, confiding in him. He smelled too-strong perfume. "But I own a lot in Bonita Vista and I'm going to build a house there in a few years."

The hairs on the back of his neck prickled.

"Well, we want to *sell* our house," he told her.

"I'm sorry to hear that. I really am. Corban is situated in the most beautiful section of the state. We have four full seasons—"

"I know. You don't have to sell me on the area. We've been living here for over five months now. It's a beautiful place. But we're not happy with the antagonism between Bonita Vista and the town, and to tell you the truth we've been having a few problems with the homeowners' association."

"I understand," Doris said. Again, she touched his leg. "You had a thirty-year fixed, right? Why don't I just go out and get your file, and we can talk this over."

He was glad to be away from her, if only for a moment, and he took a deep cleansing breath, only now realizing how tense her unwanted attention had made him. He moved his chair back, away from hers to give himself some space. He wished there was another real estate agency in Corban, but he was stuck. Doris was the only game in town.

She returned with a manila file folder, closed the door behind her, and sat down in her chair, scooting it forward until they were again right next to each other.

"Do you have any idea what we could sell it for?" he asked. "We'll let it go for the same price we paid if we have to, but if we could make a profit, that would be even better."

"I'm sorry," she said brightly. "You can't sell your house."

"What?"

"Your homeowners' association has invoked a bylaw

that allows it to freeze assets—in this case your house and property—should you be involved in any disagreement or dispute with the association. Apparently, you have refused to pay numerous fines and charges levied against you."

"They can't do that!"

"They've done it. I have a note attached here to your file."

"What if I don't acknowledge that? What if we sell it anyway?"

She laughed. "Oh, sugar! It's in the agreement you signed."

"What agreement?"

"Why, your homeowners' association agreement." She sorted through the sheaf of papers. "Hold on. I have it right here."

She handed him a legal-sized sheet of densely packed type. Buried in the reams of contracts and documents they'd signed when initially buying the house was an agreement to abide by all of the bylaws, rules, regulations, covenants, conditions, and restrictions of the Bonita Vista Homeowners' Association. Barry read through the carefully written legalese. They had effectively ceded to the association rights and powers that no sane or halfway intelligent person would ever grant anyone else. How could he and Maureen have signed such a thing? He didn't remember the document at all and couldn't imagine he would put his signature on an agreement without reading it, but there it was in black and white.

"Here," she said, "I'll make you a Xerox."

He nodded, acting calmer than he felt. "Thank you."

Five minutes later, he was outside, holding his copy, blinking in the hot August sun. If before he'd felt paranoid about living in Bonita Vista, now he felt positively trapped. There was no way out. They were doomed to remain here unless they caved in and forked over money for the excessive and unjust fines imposed by the association. He drove back to Bonita Vista distressed, unhappy, and filled with a bleak resignation.

At the gate, the guard smirked at him, as if knowing exactly what had occurred.

He parked the Suburban in the driveway and sat for a moment. He sighed heavily. Maybe they *should* pay off their fines. Such a thought would have been inconceivable even an hour ago, but principles no longer seemed quite so important. If they could pay off their fines and then sell the house at a profit, they might emerge from this mess at least no worse off than when they started.

He unbuckled his seatbelt and got out of the vehicle, walking over to check the mail before going back inside the house. In the mailbox, in addition to bills and a horror newsletter, was a homeowners' association form ordering them to trim and/or replace all dead manzanita bushes on their property or face a stiff fine of up to five hundred dollars for each day the problem was not rectified.

Something snapped within him.

"Fuck!" he yelled. "Fuck! Fuck!" He tore up the notice, ripping the sheet into ever-smaller pieces. They were the ones who put in those dead manzanitas! *They* had purposely replaced Maureen's plants with sick and dying bushes and now they were blaming the two of them for the manzanitas' unacceptable condition, using it as a pretense for imposing even more unwarranted fines. "Fuck!"

"Barry?"

He must have been yelling louder than he thought, because Maureen was on the porch steps looking worriedly in his direction.

"They're fining us for the dead manzanitas!" he shouted. "Those fuckers ripped out our plants and charged us for it, replaced them with dead bushes, and charged us for it, now they're fining us five hundred fucking dollars a day!"

She walked over to him, took his hands. "Don't worry.

We're getting out. We don't have to put up with this lunacy anymore."

"No, we're not."

"We're not what?"

"Getting out. Doris said they have some type of lien on our house. We can't sell it or rent it out or do anything with it until we pay off the money we supposedly owe the association."

Maureen paled. "You're kidding."

"No. We're stuck here until we pay the fines. Unless we want to just bail and take a loss on this place, leave it here and let the fines pile up."

"We can't afford that. I mean, we could afford it—barely—but it would be financially irresponsible and self-destructive." The accountant in her had kicked in. "The fines *would* pile up. And all of this would go on our credit record."

"I'm not paying them a dime," he said.

"I know how you feel, but—"

"I would have!" he shouted, in case someone was listening in. "But I'll be damned if I'll let those monkey dicks pull this kind of stunt."

"Then what are we going to do?"

"Nothing. We're staying right here and we're not paying a fucking dime. Let the fines accumulate!" he yelled. "We don't care!"

"What if they try to collect?" Her voice lowered. "What if they send volunteers?"

"Bring 'em on!" Barry shouted out as loud as he could. "You hear me, assholes? Bring 'em on!"

The next morning, the manzanita bushes were gone, replaced with an assortment of thorny, rough-looking shrubs. A notification form stated that the deteriorated condition of their property was unacceptable and that voluntary entreaties had been ignored at this address in the past, so the association had taken upon itself the job of bringing the yard up to code. A bill for both the plants and the labor would be sent to them within two working days.

His anger had faded, and in its place was a familiar sense of hopelessness. He'd been seesawing between those emotions far too often lately, and he had no rational explanation for it. Was it this place doing it to him? He could not dismiss the possibility. He recalled a theory he'd once read about the Superstition Mountains in Arizona. Prospectors looking for the Lost Dutchman invariably went crazy searching for the mythical mine, becoming paranoid and murderous. According to this hypothesis, the mountains were magnetic and it affected the brains of anyone who stayed within their borders for too long. Maybe something like that was happening here.

Maybe not.

Days passed, and Barry felt as though they were not only under siege but isolated and completely alone. Neighbors waved to them on the street when they walked; Mike and Tina came over with a list of all the anti-association people they could remember from Ray's parties and stayed for dinner; they played a pickup game of tennis with another couple they met on the court. But everything seemed false and superficial. He and Maureen were putting on public faces that masked the real feelings underneath, and he had the sneaking suspicion that everyone else was doing the same.

Maureen at least was keeping busy, doing work for her California clients, but he himself was lost. Although he'd made token efforts, he had not yet started writing again. Not even a short story. Each time he broke out his pen and notebook and sat down to write, he drew a blank.

Maybe he could sue the association for loss of wages due to pain and suffering.

A week after his trip to the real estate office, they were

eating lunch on the deck and the painters showed up. He didn't know who they were at first, assumed they were some type of inspector sent by the association to snoop around their yard. He intended to ignore their existence the same way he ignored the endless stream of fines and notices, but when the four men unrolled a massive plastic dropcloth on the driveway, quickly pulled paint guns out of the back of the truck, turned on a compressor, and started spraying the front of the house, he threw down his sandwich. "That's it!" He pulled open the sliding glass door and ran downstairs and outside. "What the hell are you doing?" he demanded. "This is my house!"

The three men painting the windowless section of the front wall with a coat of brown ignored him completely. But the oldest man, a bald fellow applying masking tape to the windows, looked over as he approached. "We've been hired to repaint this residence," he said. "The work order's in my truck. You want to see it?"

"I don't give a damn about your work order!" Barry yelled. "This is my house and I don't want it painted! Now you stop where you are and make that section the same color it was!"

"Can't do it, Mac." The old man continued taping up the window. "I got a work order from your homeowners' association. You got a beef, take it up with them. But the way I understand it is they asked you to change the color and conform, you wouldn't do it, so they called us."

"I don't believe this shit!"

"I'm sorry," the old man said. "But, like I said, you gotta take it up with them. They're the ones paying the bill." He gave Barry a sympathetic look. "That's why I wouldn't live in no neighborhood with a homeowners' association."

Who were these men? Were they from Corban? They had to be. After his experience at the coffee shop, and especially after the rally, he'd assumed that the townspeople were of one mind and were all antagonistic toward Bonita

Vista. But he realized that there was a whole class of workers whose livings were intertwined with the gated community and whose livelihoods depended on it.

Economics made strange bedfellows.

Again, he thought that everyone Bonita Vista touched
was somehow corrupted.

"I don't want my house painted," Barry said, and this
time it sounded more like a plea than a demand.

"Sorry," the old man said again. "Nothing I can do. I got
my work order."

They slept that night with all of the windows closed, but
the house still smelled like paint.

The next day, they received a Request for Reimburse-
ment from the homeowners' association for the amount
owed the painters: five thousand dollars.

He was sitting on the deck, staring drunkenly at the sunset, when Maureen quietly slid open the door and sat down
next to him. In her hand was a stack of pink association
forms and a computer printout. "I've been adding up all of
our fines and charges," she said.

"And?"

"It's almost a hundred thousand dollars."

He practically spit out his beer. "What?"

"I know. I couldn't believe it either. But it's over twenty-
five thousand for the initial landscaping—"

"Twenty-five—"

"Let me finish." She ran down a list of overcharged services and exorbitant fines.

"Well, we're not paying them anything."

"They'll take our house."

"We're going to owe more than the house is worth!"

Maureen's eyes widened. "That's their plan," she said
wonderingly. "That's exactly what they want. They want to
take our home and drive us into bankruptcy. Jesus, why

didn't I see it before?" She looked at him. "The fines? Okay, they might be settled by taking the house. But the work? The painting, the landscaping, materials, and labor? Those involve tradespeople who have to be paid. Do you honestly think that the association is going to let us off the hook for those charges? Hell no. They'll take us to court, and we'll lose because the work was done, the services were provided, and we *owe*." She took a deep breath. "They're going to ruin us."

"Should've listened to Greg Davidson," Barry said. "Hey, maybe I could *volunteer* to work it off."

"Don't even joke about that," Maureen scolded him.

She was right. It wasn't very funny. He wished he had something else to say, wished he had some sort of plan to get them out from under this, but he didn't, and he drank his beer and stared out at the sunset in silence.

# THIRTY-NINE

She couldn't take it any more.

Liz stared at the phone in her hand for a long while, then took a deep breath, and dialed the number of Jasper Calhoun.

A chill passed through her as the old man answered. "Hello, Elizabeth."

How had he known it was her? Caller ID, she told herself. A lot of people had it these days. There was nothing unusual or mysterious about it. Still, she thought of his odd face with its unnatural complexion, and the cold within her grew.

"What can I do for you?" he asked.

Even after all that had happened, she had too much pride to beg. She refused to give Calhoun the satisfaction of pleading for mercy. But they'd broken her. For all her tough talk and firm intentions, she had not been able to hold up under the constant onslaught. Maureen and Tina and Audrey and Moira could say they supported her and offer her friendship and hope, but they weren't with her at night.

They weren't there in the house when the bad things happened.

Last night had been the last straw.

She'd heard voices calling her from outside, seen lights

shining on various windows even through the drapes, and she turned on the television to distract her. What she saw took her breath away and caused her to fall back onto the couch.

On BVTV, for all to see, was the death of Ray.

It was a re-enactment. She knew that. But, damn it, the man looked a lot like her husband, and she watched as he slipped in the shower and hit his head on the hard porcelain. He lay there for a few moments, head bleeding, then got groggily to his feet and staggered out of the bathroom to the kitchen, where he attempted to pick up the phone. The show was depicting the association's version of events, the story they wanted everyone to believe, and though Liz knew it wasn't true, she wanted to believe it, too.

She *could* believe it, she decided.

She just wanted all this to stop.

The man who looked like Ray stumbled onto the deck, then fell over the railing to the hard ground below, his already bleeding head landing sickeningly atop an irregularly shaped rock. The camera cut to a scene inside the house where Liz saw herself—her real self, not an impersonator—sobbing on the couch.

She let out an anguished cry, unable to endure this cruel indignity, a whole host of hurtful emotions churning within her. Immediately, the scene switched to a live feed, and she saw and heard herself wailing in real time.

She shut off the television, ran into the bedroom, jumped on the bed, and hid under the covers, pulling in arms and legs and head so no part of her was exposed. There might be a camera in this room, too, but it wouldn't be able to capture her. The camera could focus on her blanket and bedspread all night as far as she was concerned. They would not get another shot of her.

She was filled with bleak despair and a crushing sense of loss. She replayed in her mind the scenes she'd just wit-

nessed on TV. Ray's re-enacted death had been filmed
here, at her home, and she wondered when and how that
had occurred. She'd left the house only briefly and infre-
quently since the funeral, and it was impossible for them to
have staged such elaborate setups in those brief snatches of
time.

At night, she thought. They filmed it at night. That's
what she'd heard. That's what the noises were.

But filming those scenes only accounted for *some* of the
noises. What else was going on? What else were they doing
here?

She felt even more violated than she had before. Having
her suspicions confirmed, knowing with certainty that others had been in her house, gave her not only a feeling of
powerlessness but hopelessness. She did not know how
much longer she could put up with this. She did not know
how much longer she could survive this constant barrage.

So she'd decided to meet the association halfway.

"Elizabeth?" Calhoun prodded.

"I'd like to talk," she said.

The president chuckled. "I knew you'd come around."

"I don't want to be on the board," she insisted. "I just
want to—"

"Talk," he said. "I know. Why don't you open up your
door and let me in. We'll discuss the best way to handle this
situation."

Open her door? Liz hurried out of the kitchen and into
the entryway, where she looked through the peephole. He
was on the porch! Standing on the welcome mat, talking to
her on his cell phone.

*Don't let him in*, a voice inside her said, and the voice
spoke in Ray's dulcet tones.

But she could not endure any more of this. She was not
as strong as Ray had been, and alone, without his unflag-
ging self-confidence and dogged determination, she could
not stand up to their harassment.

*Don't . . .*

Taking a deep breath, she unlocked and opened the door.

The president stepped inside, smiling, and she shivered as he touched her shoulder. "It'll be all right now," he told her. "Everything's all right. Everything will be fine."

# FORTY

"I guess we weren't invited."

Barry and Maureen stood in the darkened guest bedroom, staring out the open window. The cool breeze, a preview of approaching autumn, carried with it the sound of
revelers. Through the trees, a concentration of lights at the
community center created an irregular dome of illumination
in the moonless night sky.

They'd seen cars driving down earlier. And people walking. He knew from previous flyers that the community center would be having its grand unveiling this week, but
they'd never been told a specific date and had received no
invitation to the gala.

Other people obviously had.

He moved over to the east window and looked out. He
saw more lights than usual twinkling through the pine
branches: people had left their porch lights on while they'd
gone down to see the new center.

"It looks like almost everyone went," he said.

"You can't tell that by looking out the window."

"Call it a hunch."

"I doubt if Liz went," Maureen offered helpfully.

He snorted. "Yeah, that makes me feel better."

"Come on. Do you honestly think they're all going to turn
into rabid association supporters just because they went to a

party? Most of them probably only showed up for the free food and drink. "

"Maybe."

"What's that mean?"

"You know damn well what it means." He turned to face her, seeing only an impressionistic version of her features in the darkness. "They get their way, the association. I don't know if it's . . . it's magic or . . . I don't know what it is. But these people are on their side! Look at the sheriff. Look at everyone who showed up to head off that rally! We were there under duress, but most of our beloved neighbors were there on their own, happily brandishing their weapons and longing for a fight."

"Then maybe it's a good thing we're ostracized. Maybe they'd convert us, too."

"No," he said firmly. "That could never happen."

"And the same goes for other people. Not all of them, maybe. But some of them. Mike and Tina. A few of the others we met."

He remembered the party at Ray's when Greg Davidson had announced his intention to leave Bonita Vista and everyone had gathered around swapping anti-association stories. "Maybe," he said. "Hopefully." He moved next to her, and they stood at the window, staring into the darkness, listening to the party.

"Labor Day's only a week away," Maureen said softly.

"I know."

"Are we going to go to the meeting?"

"Of course. This is our chance to make everything public. According to the rules, each homeowner gets three minutes to say whatever they want. I'm going to write a speech, and I'm going to suggest amendments, and by the end of it, at the very least, we'll find out who stands where. I'm taking those bastards to task, and we'll see who's with me or against me."

"You? What about me?"

"Us," he amended.

"No, I mean what about me? Do I get to speak, too?"

He was surprised. "Do you want to?"

"No. But is it three minutes for me and three minutes for you, or three minutes total? If we can stretch our time out to six, I'll take up where you leave off and keep talking."

"It's three minutes per lot."

"Then the floor's all yours."

"I have to start working on this now, time myself, try to cram in as much as I can. The annual meeting is the one time a year they even make the pretext that this is a democracy. It's our only shot. We've got to make it count."

A lone skyrocket exploded in the air above the community center, purple sparkles falling down on the trees. A loud cheer went up.

"What do you think will happen?" Maureen asked.

Barry was silent for a moment. "I don't know," he said finally. "I don't know."

The painters returned in the morning. This time, Barry and Maureen were both in the driveway before the men had emerged from their truck.

"What do you think you're doing here?" Maureen demanded as the painters got out of the cab and walked around to the rear of the vehicle.

They ignored her.

"You just painted our house a week ago."

The three younger men pulled out their tarp and started spreading it on the driveway.

Barry walked up to the old man. "Let me guess," he said. "This color is no longer acceptable. They want you to paint it a different shade."

The painter pulled a roll of masking tape from the bed of the truck. "Yep."

"Have you done this before? Painted the same house over and over again until the owners go bankrupt?"

He paused for a moment, as if hesitant to answer, then

nodded his head. "Yep." He pushed past Barry and started taping up the nearest window.

They left before the painting started, closing up the house and driving out to the lake, where they spent the day hiking and picnicking and pretending that they were a normal couple having a normal day. When they arrived home late in the afternoon, the painters were gone, but their tarp remained draped over bushes on the south side of the house and only half of the building was completed.

"I guess they're coming back tomorrow," Maureen said. Barry nodded.

They'd slept with the windows closed last time and that hadn't worked, so this time they left the windows open and the fan on, but the smell of paint still permeated everything, and they both awoke in the morning with headaches.

The job took two days. The painters were clearly being more thorough than before, which made Barry think that this sequence had been thoroughly planned in advance. This would turn out to be a more expensive job, he was sure, and while a part of him wanted to physically throw the painters off his property and burn their truck, he knew they were only following orders and would merely be replaced by someone else.

He thought of another idea, though, and he talked to Maureen, told her of his plan. To his surprise, she agreed.

They waited until the painters were done. After they left, he and Maureen took the white interior latex left over from their remodeling and painted a gigantic happy face on the wall of the house facing the street. On the north wall of the house, they painted a frowning face.

The next day, the workers were back. This time, they were not merely uncommunicative, they were openly hostile. When Barry met them in the driveway, drinking his morning coffee and offering them a hearty hello, they gave him dirty looks and muttered obscenities. "Who does he think he is?" one of the younger painters asked another.

"Stupid fuck," the old man muttered.

His plan had worked. He and Maureen had thrown a monkey-wrench into the association's schedule, had reset the agenda on their terms.

The painters taped off the windows, put down their dropcloth, hooked up the sprayers, and obliterated the left half of the happy face. After they moved to another section of wall, Barry put down his coffee, took out his white paint and started brushing it on the recently completed area, making a series of X's in a random pattern.

The old man stormed over to him. "Just what do you think you're doing?"

"It's my house," Barry told him. "And I'm painting it."

"You can't—"

"It's my house. I can do anything I damn well please, and if you don't get out of my face, I'm going to kick your fucking ass, strip you naked, and paint you yellow like the coward you are."

He expected the old man to threaten him, to tell him that there were four of them and only one of him. He was even prepared for a fight right then and there should the bald asshole rush him. But the painter turned and walked away, spoke to his coworkers, and a few minutes later the four of them packed up their gear and left.

A victory.

The painters did not return, no others took their place, and there was not even any sign of Neil Campbell and his ubiquitous clipboard. No one called, no notices were left in their mailbox or on their door. The half a happy face and random Xs remained on the wall.

That night they made love, and in the middle of it, the phone rang. He wanted to let it ring, but Maureen insisted that he answer, it might be important, so he reached over to the nightstand, picked up the phone, and pressed the Talk button. "Hello?"

The voice on the line was harsh yet whispery. "Throw her another hump for me!"

*Click.*

Someone was watching them. They were being monitored. He pulled the sheets over their bodies and looked frantically around the room, searching for a hidden camera.

"What are you doing?" Maureen demanded, squirming uncomfortably beneath him.

He rolled off her. His erection was gone. Still hidden by the blanket, he reached down to the floor for his underwear. He pulled on his briefs and ran over to the television, turning it on.

On BVTV was a video of him and Maureen making love. Maureen was on top, and the camera zoomed in on her buttocks as his hand slid down and into her crack.

"Sons of bitches!" Barry yelled. "Sons of bitches!"

The phone rang again, but this time neither of them answered it.

In the morning their house had been painted black.

# FORTY-ONE

**The Bonita Vista Homeowners' Association Covenants, Conditions, and Restrictions** Article V, Security and Control, Section 9, Paragraph A:

> *The Association and any of its committees or subcommittees has the right to monitor residents on any section of the Community properties or on any jointly owned right-of-way in any manner it deems appropriate using any means at its disposal. Residents whose dues are in arrears or who are involved in disputes with the Board may be monitored anywhere at any time including in their private residences.*

# FORTY-TWO

It was hard writing a speech. He was used to creating dialogue, having two characters express ideas and points of view through conversation, but coming up with a stirring, rabble-rousing address in the real world was quite a bit different from doing so within the boundaries of a fictional universe in which he controlled all of the variables and all of the reactions. He was not and never had been a public speaker, so the fact that he would be performing this himself—and before a hostile audience no less—brought additional pressure.

His first draft clocked in at a whopping fifteen minutes. He pared it down as much as he could, read it to Maureen, and it still came in at twelve.

He would have to be selective, and he would have to be merciless. It was impossible to fit in everything he wanted to say, so he would be able to address only his most important concerns and use the most egregious examples of the association's transgressions.

But he was having a hard time figuring out what those were.

He scrolled down the computer screen, reread his words for the hundredth time.

"Tape!" Maureen called from the living room.

He hurried upstairs. He'd been videotaping BVTV all

day and night, fast-forwarding and reviewing the tapes every six hours as they filled up, looking for anything filmed in their house. He had figured out where the camera in the bedroom was from the angle of the shot he'd seen on the television, and he'd torn out that section of wall until he found the device, which he'd immediately smashed. How someone had gotten the camera into that spot was a mystery, and the only thing he could figure was that it had been built into the house during initial construction and had been there ever since.

They'd patched over the hole in the wall as best as two amateurs could, but it still looked like hell and Maureen had hung a framed Georgia O'Keeffe poster over the space to hide the bulging spackle.

So far, they'd seen no indication that any of the other rooms in the house were under surveillance, but he wouldn't put anything past Calhoun and his cronies, and he continued his close monitoring of BVTV.

The day before the association's annual meeting, Barry finally had a speech he was happy with. It still ran long— four minutes instead of three, even speaking fast—but he figured he could keep talking while they told him his time was up and get the last little bit in before he was cut off completely. Celebrities did it on award shows all the time. It was a legitimate tactic.

They went to bed early, both of them exhausted from stress. They made love for the first time since discovering the camera and talked for a while about what they would do and where they would go when they finally escaped Bonita Vista. Gradually, the pauses between their sentences grew longer and their voices slowed as they started to drift off.

He wasn't sure when he finally slipped into sleep, but at some point he was no longer lying in his bed. He was sitting on a hard metal folding chair with all of his neighbors. At a table on a raised stage, Jasper Calhoun and the rest of the be-robed board were gazing imperiously out at the tightly packed crowd.

The president announced in a strong clear tone: "Additions to the C, C, and Rs include a provision declaring that all men may butt fuck Maureen Welch at their convenience, without her permission or the permission of her husband, Barry. All those in favor?"

A sea of hands shot up with Nuremberg precision.

"All those opposed?"

Only Barry's hand was raised.

"Passed!"

He awoke in the morning looking across the pillow into Maureen's open eyes. "Meeting today," she said.

The room was packed. Most of the people he did not recognize, but there were others he did: Mike and Tina; Frank and Audrey; Lou and Stacy; Neil, Chuck, and Terry; individuals from Ray's parties; homeowners he'd seen at the rally. They were seated on metal folding chairs and there must have been over a hundred of them.

In the front of the room was the board.

In the back were the volunteers.

The layout was remarkably similar to that of his dream, and he experienced an uncomfortable feeling of déjà vu as he and Maureen walked into the community center. There should have been voices, should have been talking, the large room should have been filled with the buzz of numerous conversations. But everyone was quiet, each of them glancing through enormous black-bound books that lay in their laps. To the right of the doorway, Barry saw, was a table piled high with dozens of identical volumes.

A man standing next to the table, dressed absurdly in livery, motioned them over. "Please pick up your revised copy of *The Bonita Vista Homeowners' Association Declaration of Covenants, Conditions, and Restrictions,*" he said. "Ratification is the first item on today's agenda."

He handed Barry a book. It weighed a ton and was the size of the oversized family Bible that his grandmother used to keep on her dining room table.

"We're supposed to read through this entire thing in, what, five or ten minutes?" Barry asked.

"It's just a formality," the man said.

"How can we make an informed decision if we don't know what's in there?"

The man laughed. "That's a good one." The laugh was genuine, and it made Barry uneasy. The idea that the votes of the homeowners were important and actually meant something struck this man as legitimately funny. An ominous sign.

Liz was seated near the closest aisle, and she waved them over. She'd saved the two seats next to her, and he and Maureen exchanged a glance as they walked up.

It was as if nothing unusual had ever happened, as if she had not been a paranoid recluse for the better part of two months, and her normality was disconcerting. Liz smiled as they sat down and said she was glad they'd come, she hadn't been sure they would. She spoke in whispers, and though Barry wanted to talk in a normal tone of voice, wanted to demonstrate that he was unintimidated and unafraid, he found himself whispering back, daunted by the silence of everyone around him. "There's no way we'd miss this," he said. "I finally have an opportunity to give that board a piece of my mind."

"Please pick up your revised copy of *The Bonita Vista Homeowners' Association Declaration of Covenants, Conditions, and Restrictions,*" the man in livery said from his post near the table as someone new walked in. His voice sounded absurdly loud in the stillness. "Ratification is the first item on today's agenda."

Barry placed the massive volume on his lap and opened it up. Liz's copy, he noticed, was on the floor next to her. Several of the people around them had also laid their books on the floor, though some were attempting to read through the amended regulations.

He turned pages randomly. There was a rule disallowing the cooking of Asian food at any residence, another stating that all homeowners must own an American flag, although the flag could not be displayed either in or outside the house. He flipped quickly through the book. The regulations grew wackier and wackier. Only Number 2 pencils could be used to write grocery lists; residents were required to wash their hair daily and use conditioner; baldness was not acceptable in public, and homeowners who were losing their hair had to wear toupees outside the privacy of their homes. He was certain that there were dangerous edicts hidden among the frivolous ridiculous ordinances, but there was no time to find them, and he was glad that he'd prepared a speech ahead of time. If people were going to automatically ratify regulations with which they were completely unfamiliar, they needed to hear what he had to say.

He'd told Mike about his planned speech, asked his friend to spread the word, and Barry could only hope that he had. He glanced around the silent crowd. If everything went well, people would respond to his questioning of the board with questions of their own and those old men would find themselves under attack, forced to defend policies and procedures that until this point had been taken for granted. Even the best laid plans went astray—and this was a half-baked scheme to begin with—but he had faith that he might be able to at least stir things up here today.

The president's gavel fell on the table with the sharp suddenness of a gunshot, and Barry jumped along with everyone else. All eyes turned toward the raised platform on which sat the board of directors.

"Hear ye! Hear ye!" the man in livery announced from the back of the room. "The annual meeting of the Bonita Vista Homeowners' Association will now come to order!"

Jasper Calhoun, seated at the center of the table, stood and smiled munificently. "Welcome neighbors," he said.

A huge cheer went up, the people around them began clapping wildly, and Barry looked at Maureen. He'd been sitting there waiting for a follow-up sentence, having no idea that the president's simple greeting would be an applause cue, and the response of his fellow homeowners was as startling and unexpected as the rap of the gavel had been. He had a sudden uneasy suspicion that this was part of some ritual, like a church service, with programmed cues and responses.

Leaning over Maureen, he spoke to Liz. "How long do these meetings usually last?" he whispered.

"Two or three hours," she whispered back.

*Two or three hours?*

The president beamed at the crowd, and his smile grew even wider, though that was not something Barry would have thought physically possible. The disproportionate breadth of his mouth gave Calhoun's face a creepy, wolflike appearance. "We will begin this meeting with the most important task facing us today: voting on our Covenants, Conditions, and Restrictions."

Another cheer.

"You've all had time to look over the amended declaration. All those in favor of accepting the revisions raise your hands."

Arms shot into the air.

Barry was thrown off guard. "Wait!" he yelled, leaping to his feet. "Aren't we going to discuss this? We—"

"Opposed?" the president said.

The gavel was rapped on the table before Barry even had a chance to raise his hand or finish his sentence.

"The amendments are accepted," Calhoun announced.

Barry stood there dumbly, looking around at his seated neighbors, all of whom seemed to be eagerly awaiting the next word from the president's lips. *They're all hypnotized,* he thought, it's the only explanation. But he knew that wasn't true.

He glanced down at Maureen. She, too, seemed stunned. The idea that such a massive revision of a document affecting the lives and property of everyone here could be approved in a single vote and without any discussion, without time to even fully comprehend all the changes, was unbelievable.

Barry was still standing, and Calhoun pointed at him with the gavel. "Mr. Welch, would you please have a seat?"

He faced the president. "I want to know why there wasn't any discussion about these revisions. Isn't it normal to vote on amendments individually, after people have a chance to give their opinions?"

"This is Bonita Vista," Calhoun said, as if that explained everything. "Please sit down so we may continue our meeting."

Barry was aware of the hostile stares directed at him from some of the other homeowners, and he felt Maureen tugging on his shirtsleeve. He still had his speech to give, but this apparently wasn't the time for member comment and since he wanted to win over the crowd and not alienate them, he sat down. He had not expected the other residents to be so in sync with the board, and it worried him.

On the platform, one of the other board members handed the president a slip of paper.

Calhoun nodded at the man, then faced the audience. "A motion has been made to do away with all cats in the town of Corban. As you know, we have begun our process of eliminating dogs, but as the eradication of all pets is our ultimate goal and part of our ongoing effort to bring Corban into the Bonita Vista family, it has been suggested that we begin killing cats. Shall we put this to a vote?"

"Yes!" the crowd shouted.

Again Barry thought of the church analogy. There was definitely a ritualistic element to this meeting that he and

Maureen were not privy to and that did not sit well with
him. Even more unnerving was the subject matter. He had
known the association was behind the dog poisonings, but
he'd assumed that it was a decision made by the board. The
idea that the entire membership had voted on and approved
such a horrific and inhuman policy threw him for a loop.

Had they approved the child murders as well?

Goose bumps rippled down his skin.

"All those in favor of expanding the pet eradication to
include cats and kittens raise your hands."

Arms shot up all around him.

Barry looked about wildly. Mike's hand was not raised
but Tina's was, and with a sickening drop in his stomach he
realized that his neighbors, even the ones he'd considered
his friends, even the nice men and women he'd met at Ray's
parties, *were* the homeowners' association. He'd been
blaming the board of directors for everything, as though
they were solely responsible for it all, as though the organization was not comprised of himself and his fellow homeowners but was something separate and apart. He knew
now that was not the case. The board members did not op-
erate in a vacuum, and the people who elected and supported them were the ones validating the hatred, racism
and intolerance they espoused.

He could attribute some of it to peer pressure, but peer
pressure only went so far, and the enthusiasm with which
his neighbors were taking part in this meeting made him realize that despite what they said in public, their true feelings came out here, where they were together with others of
their kind. It was the dark side of democracy that allowed a
person to actively endorse reprehensible policies and behavior by disappearing into the anonymity of a group.

He understood now why Hank and Lyle and all of his ex-
buddies at the coffee shop had been so angry. Because, in
some sense, he *was* a part of this. They all were. Perhaps especially those like himself or Maureen or Tina who voted

gainst specific proposals but allowed them to stand, who
uckled under to the will of the majority and lent legiti-
nacy to the illegitimate by not refusing to recognize those
ules.

"All opposed?" Calhoun said.

Barry and Maureen raised their hands, but Tina, Liz, and
he few others who had not voted for the motion were not
trong enough to vote against it.

"Passed!" the president announced. He chuckled
ovially. "We're on a roll today, people. We will now con-
luct our formal election for the board of directors. As you
now, this will be done by secret ballot, so none of you
eed feel ashamed if you're not happy with the way Mr.
Jehring here has been doing his job."

The board member next to Calhoun gave a halfhearted
mile and wave, and the president slapped him on the back.
Just kidding, buddy."

Two teenage girls dressed in bikinis or underwear—it
vas hard to tell which—walked from the back of the room,
p the center aisle, handing out stacks of ballots and rubber-
anded bundles of small pencils to the individuals at the
nd of each row. "Pass them down."

Maureen took the stack from Liz, peeled off a sheet and
assed it on to Barry. As Ray had warned him, there was
nly one word printed next to the six names on the piece of
aper: *Approve*. Next to each was a box.

Barry immediately wrote *Disapprove,* next to every
ame, as did Maureen.

Calhoun banged his gavel. "We will now open the floor
o comments. Anyone?"

Barry stood.

"The board recognizes Mr. Welch."

"I have a statement I wish to read."

"Go right ahead, sir."

"I have three minutes, right?"

Calhoun smiled. "That is correct."

"The purpose of a homeowners' association," Barry read, "is to provide for the common good of the community, not to penalize members of that community for failure to abide by unfair, discriminatory, and illegal rules and regulations. I personally—"

"Time!" one of the board members called.

Barry looked up angrily. "I'm entitled to three minutes."

"Time!"

"I personally have been subject to harassment—" he continued reading.

"*Time! Time! Time! Time!*" He was drowned out by the shouting of the seated homeowners. Except for Maureen and Liz, everyone around him—including Mike and Tina— was chanting in unison, smiling as though this were all one big joke or part of a game.

Barry pointed at the board members, tried to make himself heard above the clamor. "You're killing animals and killing kids and mutilating dues-paying homeowners you disagree with!"

They were all chuckling tolerantly, and he wanted to lash out at them, wanted to rush the stage and slap the shit out of those strangely formed faces, but instead he kept yelling. "Why aren't there any real elections? Why are you afraid to let people actually run for office and let us have a real choice?"

Calhoun pointed toward the rear of the room. "I'd like to introduce Paul Henri, our sergeant at arms!"

A huge cheer went up.

"Paul? Will you please escort Mr. Welch from the meeting?"

The liveried man from the back table strode up, pushed past Liz and Maureen, and grabbed Barry's arm. Barry tried to pull away, but the sergeant's grip was surprisingly strong. Fingers dug painfully into his muscles, and he felt himself being dragged out to the main aisle.

"This is against the rules!" Barry yelled. "You can't shut

me up just because you disagree with me! I refuse to be silenced! The C, C, and Rs don't allow this!"

"The amended ones do," Calhoun said calmly.

There was laughter all around.

Barry tried to punch the sergeant at arms, tried to pry the vicelike grip from his forearm, but the man was unbelievably strong, and he was pulled toward the exit.

"Let's hear it for Paul Henri!" the president called.

The audience joined him in a chant: "Hip hip hurray! Hip hip hurray!"

Barry was shoved outside, the door slamming shut behind him. He turned around, pounding on the door, demanding to be let in, but to no avail. Looking up at the windowless building, he tried to hear what was going on inside, but the community center was soundproof.

What was going on in there now? Almost everything of importance had been decided and only ten minutes had passed. What were they going to do for the next two hours?

He wasn't able to find out because a moment after his eviction, Maureen was forced out of the meeting as well.

# FORTY-THREE

"Jeremy?"

"Dude!"

Barry switched the phone to his other ear, looked grimly over at Maureen. "We're, uh, having a little problem here."

"The same one we talked about?"

"Yeah." He felt better already. Jeremy was automatically being circumspect, not mentioning anything directly in case the phone was bugged. His friend might be paranoid and overcautious, but sometimes that was a good thing. He smiled reassuringly at Maureen. "Remember you offered to . . . to come out here if I needed some help?"

"I'm there, dude. We all are. When do you want us?"

It was as if a great responsibility had just been taken from him. As a writer, as someone who sat by himself in a room all day and typed, he was by nature and necessity something of a loner, an individualist who preferred to handle problems on his own, who saw himself as a solitary warrior against stupidity, hypocrisy, and all of the usual abstract ideals that writers loved so well, a staunch defender of truth, justice, and the American way. He had never been a team player, had never liked committees or collectives. He would rather deal with adversity on his own. But sometimes, he had to admit, it was nice to be part of a group.

Sometimes it was necessary.

He told Jeremy the situation without spelling things out, promising details later, and his friend said that he'd gather Dylan and Chuck and that the three of them would be on the road as soon as humanly possible.

Sure enough, he and Maureen were eating breakfast the next morning when the phone rang. It was the guard at the gate. "Mr. Welch?" the guard said in an unctuous, disapproving voice. "I have detained the occupants of two vehicles at the gate who claim to be friends of yours—"

"They are," Barry told him. "Let them in."

"I have a Mister Jeremy—"

"I know who they are, and I told you, let them in."

"This is highly irregular at this—"

"You are the guard," Barry interrupted, his voice equally disapproving, anger just below the surface. "You work for us. Now do your job and obey me."

He pressed the Talk button on the phone, cutting off the conversation, smiling as he put it down on the kitchen table. "They're here," he told Maureen.

Several minutes later there came the shave-and-a-haircut honks of two distinctly different car horns. Barry shoved the last forkful of hash browns in his mouth, hurried downstairs, and found his friends getting out of their cars and stretching.

"Long night!" Jeremy called out. "We've been driving since yesterday afternoon!"

Dylan emerged from the Saturn's back seat. "With a short stop off in Vegas."

Maureen had followed him downstairs, and she grinned when she saw that Jeremy and Chuck had brought their wives. She greeted both Lupe and Danna with warm, grateful hugs.

Lupe glanced around at the house, the yard, the trees. "It doesn't *look* like hell," she said.

"Seems like a beautiful place," Danna agreed.

"Looks can be deceiving." Maureen led them into the house. "As I'm sure you've heard before."

Dylan had come stag, hitching a ride with Jeremy and Lupe, and he walked over to the mailbox and back, stretching his legs. "Things have changed a bit since last I was here. Who was that dickwad guarding the castle?"

Barry smiled. "You like that? That's the famous gate I told you about. And he's our personal twenty-four-hour-a-day guard, making sure that the great unwashed don't try to drive down our streets and look at our homes."

Jeremy walked up. "Things are getting bad, huh?"

"You don't know the half of it."

Barry spent the next half hour describing the situation to them in detail, from the moment he returned from his California trip and saw the board president force the Jimmy driver off the road to the surreal annual meeting and his ceremonious expulsion. More than once, Maureen called for them to come inside, get something to drink, but as sexist as it was, he felt more comfortable talking outside here, away from the wives, and he laid things out in a blunter, more honest way than he would have if the women were present.

Chuck shook his head. "What the hell have you gotten yourself into?"

"This is kind of cool in a way." Dylan looked sheepish as all eyes turned disapprovingly toward him. "Well, not cool maybe, but . . ." His voice trailed off.

"Trust me," Barry said. "It's not 'cool' at all if you have to live here."

"But do you have to?" Chuck asked. "Can't you just move back?"

"We wanted to," he admitted.

"So what's the problem?"

He explained about the fines and the frozen assets and the very real possibility of bankruptcy. "Besides," he said, "I can't let those bastards think they ran me off. I can't let them win."

"They won't win," Jeremy told him. "We're here."

Dylan grinned. "All right!" he said, pumping a fist into the air. "Time to kick some ass!"

They went inside finally, joining the women, and talk turned to other things, personal things: work, families, lives. Both Barry and Maureen found that they were hungry for news of the outside world, happy to lose themselves in the minutiae of their friends' existence, to receive updates on the southern California lifestyle they'd given up and left behind. All seven of them crammed into the Suburban, and Barry took them on a tour of Bonita Vista and then the town of Corban, including his teapot museum office. They had a greasy and unsatisfying lunch at Dairy King—Chuck had suggested the coffee shop, but Barry vetoed that idea, reminding them why—then did a little touristy sightseeing, taking in nearby Pinetop Lake and walking off a few calories with a short hike along the lake's nature trail.

They returned home between two and three, the hottest part of the day, and continued to catch up on gossip, moving from the living room to the upper deck and then back into the living room when the sun started to go down and the bugs came out.

Lupe suggested that they go get a pizza, but Barry said dryly that they weren't really leaving the house after dark these days, and Maureen said that she'd planned on making tacos.

"That's even better," Lupe said.

Maureen cut tomatoes and onions, while Lupe shredded the lettuce. Danna grated cheese. Maureen sent everyone out of the kitchen while she cooked the meat and fried the tortillas, and then it was time to eat.

Talk of the association was banned at the dinner table, and to Barry it felt almost as though none of that insanity had ever happened. They were cocooned in their own little world here, safe from the harsh and twisted realities of

Bonita Vista, and for the first time in a long while he wen
for over an hour without thinking once about the home
owners' association.

They had wine with dinner and a few beers afterward
and they noisily talked politics and celebrity scandal as the
made their way down to the living room. Barry sat down o
the floor, motioning for the two couples to take the couch
Maureen settled into the chair, and after looking around an
ascertaining that there was no other place to sit, Dyla
plopped down on the floor by the fireplace.

"So what about sleeping arrangements?" Danna asked
"I saw only one guest room."

"Two of you take the room," Maureen explained. "Tw
of you can sleep up here; the couch turns into a bed." Sh
smiled. "Dylan? I'm afraid you're stuck with a feather mat
tress on the floor of my office."

"That's okay. Can I look up porn on the Internet whil
the rest of you are asleep?"

Maureen heaved a throw pillow at him.

"That'll be fine." Dylan chuckled. "No problem."

They'd caught each other up on almost everything, an
for the first time since their friends had arrived this morn
ing, there was a protracted silence.

"It's too quiet here," Dylan said. "All this nature an
stuff. I find it very disturbing. Don't you have some tune
or something?" He pointed toward the television. "Yo
guys got cable or satellite?"

Barry reached up to the TV table and tossed him the re
mote. "Go wild. Make yourself happy."

There was nothing decent on any of the broadcast o
cable channels, so Barry read through his list of videotape
until they found one they all could agree on: *Youn
Frankenstein*.

Jeremy cleared his throat, spoke up. "Bare? Do you hav
a copy of those famous C, C, and Rs?"

"Sure. Hold on a sec." Barry went downstairs, grabbe

the massive book from Maureen's computer desk, and hurried back up, handing it to Jeremy. "Here you go."

While the rest of them watched the movie, Jeremy pored through the document. "Jesus!" he'd exclaim periodically, but when anyone asked what he'd found, he waved them away.

Finally, he put the book down. The movie had ended some time ago, and they were watching a Dennis Miller rerun on HBO. "I can't believe this is real," he said.

"Tell me about it."

"Did you know that homosexual couples are banned from your little utopia here? And unmarried couples?" He looked over at Lupe. "And minorities. Which I assume means anyone who isn't white."

Dylan laughed. "I guess you two won't be retiring here in bee-yoo-tee-full Utah then, huh?"

"I need to go through this with a highlighter. I'm not even halfway through it, and I can't even remember all of the craziness I read." He shook his head. "This is one densely shit-packed document."

Barry grimaced. "I'll bet you believe me now, don't you?"

"I always believed you. I just didn't think they'd be so obvious about it. They're not only trying to impose their values on the membership, to legislate morality in a blatant way that no federal or local government would even attempt to do, but they're codifying shit that isn't even legal, apparently intending to use the courts' previous upholdings of homeowners' association bylaws as a shield."

"I was hoping you'd say that. I thought so myself, but you're the lawyer, and I figured you could make an informed judgment."

"Jesus."

Using the remote, Dylan had been flipping through channels. "Hey," he said. "What's this? Some kind of community access station?"

"BVTV," Barry and Maureen said in unison.

On the screen, a young woman was jogging on one of the bridle trails. The camera zoomed in on her jiggling breasts.

"BVTV?"

"Bonita Vista Television," Barry explained. "I guess I forgot to tell you about that. There are security cameras all over this place. They use them to videotape people and broadcast it on their station."

"Sometimes," Maureen added quietly, "they tape people in their own homes."

"My God."

"Don't worry," Barry said. "I've gone over this place with a fine-tooth comb. We're safe in here."

"In here, maybe," Jeremy said. "But outside this house, we all have to be on our guard, watch what we say, put on a happy face. The streets, the greenbelts, the empty lots— it's all theirs, enemy territory."

That cast a pall on the evening, and they broke up soon after, Maureen bringing out fresh linen to make up the sofa bed for Chuck and Danna, then taking Jeremy and Lupe to the guest bedroom. Barry pulled the feather mattress out of the closet and set it up on the office floor for Dylan, tossing him a blanket. He went into their bedroom, closed the door, took off his clothes, and got under the covers to wait for Maureen, but he was more tired than he thought because by the time she returned he was dead asleep.

Liz called during breakfast,

It would have been a minor blip on the day's radar under normal circumstances, but considering the present state of affairs, it was a big deal and a cause for celebration. Maureen answered the phone and took the call, and she motioned frantically for Barry to take over the pancakes while she went downstairs to the master bedroom to talk in private.

She hadn't spoken to Liz since the meeting, and the few

words they'd exchanged at that time had been stilted and impersonal, but Liz sounded stronger than she had at any time since Ray's funeral. There was a renewed feistiness in her attitude and a welcome wryness in the older woman's voice as she said, "Sorry I haven't called lately, but I was temporarily overcome with grief, despair, and unbearable self-pity."

"How are you?" Maureen asked, sitting down on the bed.

"As well as can be expected, I suppose. Nothing's ever going to be the way it was, but I think I'm learning to accept that. I'm sorry I've been so out of it lately."

"That's okay. I understand."

"Part of it is lack of sleep. They've been keeping me up every night, trying to break me down, calling me at all hours with weird threatening phone calls, turning my power on and off, throwing things at my house. It's psychological warfare, and it obviously worked. It cut me off from my friends and made me so nervous and jumpy I was afraid to answer the phone or step out of the house."

Anyplace else, at any other time, Maureen would have thought that, far from the crisis being over, it had kicked into high gear, Liz exhibiting alarming signs of acute paranoia. But she had no doubt that her friend's feelings were justified. "You lost your husband. We didn't expect you to be the life of the party."

"Yes, but we both know my behavior went a little beyond that. And I want to thank you, all of you, for not giving up on me, for being there when I needed you even if I didn't take advantage of it."

"We're your friends," Maureen said.

"Well, I'm grateful, and I'm sorry for the way I acted. I thought I could try and make it up to you. I thought maybe you and Tina and Audrey could come up this afternoon for drinks and . . . well, just to talk."

"I'd love to," Maureen said. "We have some friends up

from California, though." She hesitated, not wanting to decline the invitation for fear of throwing a wet towel on her friend's tentative efforts to pull her life back together, but not sure she'd feel right about abandoning Lupe and Danna for half the day. "If it wouldn't be too much of an imposition, and if you felt you were up to it—"

"Sure," Liz said, and she sounded like her old self. "Bring them along."

"And, uh, Audrey . . ." Maureen let the words trail off. She didn't want to burden Liz with additional problems, not now.

"You had a falling out," the older woman said intuitively.

"Yeah, kind of."

"Consider her uninvited."

"But that's not fair. You've known Audrey a lot longer than you've known me."

"I trust you," Liz said.

It was a vote of confidence that made her feel happy and privileged. "What time do you want us there?" she asked.

A wry chuckle. "Whenever's convenient for you. I'm certainly not going anywhere. I'll be here all day."

"One o'clock?"

"One o'clock would be fine."

Maureen walked back upstairs and saw that Barry had given Danna and Lupe the two pancakes that had been cooking and now had two others on the frying pan. He greeted her with a quizzical raising of eyebrows.

"Liz," she explained.

"Everything's okay, isn't it?"

"Yeah. She invited me over this afternoon." Maureen's glance took in Lupe and Danna. "All three of us. Seems she's feeling better."

"A friend of yours?" Danna asked, sipping orange juice.

"One of our only friends up here. Her husband was the one who was killed."

"Oh."

Barry nodded. "She's one of us."

"Their house has a really spectacular view," Maureen couldn't help adding. "It's worth a trip up there just to see that."

Barry handed her the spatula, relinquishing his role as cook. "So you think she's okay?"

"I think so. I hope so." There was a pause. "She disinvited Audrey, but I think Tina's going to be there."

"Are you okay with that?"

"I don't know. We'll see."

The seven of them spent the morning walking the neighborhood, Barry and Maureen pointing out the pool and community center as well as the home of the association president. Chuck brought along his palmcorder, videotaping everything they saw, zooming in on the president's house in particular and recording it in detail. "We need to find out where the other board members live," he said. "Then we tape their houses and go over everything with a fine-tooth comb, make sure they're not breaking even minor rules. Any infraction and we'll nail their asses to the wall, sue them for singling out some people and not others."

Maureen laughed. "I'm glad you guys are here."

"Seven heads are better than two."

After a lunch of sandwiches and salad, Maureen charged Barry with cleaning the dishes and went downstairs to comb her hair and put on some lipstick.

"You sure you want us to go?" Danna asked. "We could just stay here . . ."

"It'll be fun. And we won't stay too long. Don't worry."

"But we're going to *walk* again?"

"This is like a spa vacation," Lupe told her. "Sun and exercise. We'll return home to California tanned and fit."

"That's one way to look at it."

They kissed their husbands good-bye, Barry told Mau-

reen to say hello for him, and they started off. All three
were breathing heavily by the time they reached the crest of
the hill, where Tina was waiting, standing in the intermittent shadows of Liz's willow tree in a vain effort to stay out
of the hot sun. "I saw you walking up," she said.

Maureen wasn't sure how she felt about seeing Tina
again. At the annual meeting, she'd been right there with
the crowd, part of it, putting the lie to everything she'd ever
said regarding the association. And Tina hadn't said a thing
when she and Barry had been ejected from the building.

Still, she was here, being friendly, making overtures, and
it was clear that she was ready to stand by Liz in her hour
of need. That should count for something.

Maybe she'd just been caught up in the moment.

Maureen nodded hello. "Have you seen Liz yet?"

"I thought we could all go in together."

"Kind of scary, isn't it?"

"It was a surprise when she called," Tina admitted. "And
she sounded perfectly normal, like she's back to her old self
again."

"I thought so, too."

"She seemed okay at the meeting, too, but I didn't get a
chance to talk to her and she disappeared right afterward . . ."
Tina trailed off, obviously feeling awkward. She cleared her
throat and smiled a greeting at Lupe and Danna. "Hello."

"I'm sorry. Where are my manners?" Maureen introduced her friends. "Tina, this is Lupe Mullens and Danna
Carlin, our friends from California. And this is Tina Stewart."

There were greetings all around, and Maureen was about
to suggest that they go in and see Liz when their hostess
came out herself to meet them. It was a surprise to see Liz
out of doors after hiding so long in the house, but it was a
welcome surprise, and Maureen impulsively rushed over
and threw her arms around the other woman, hugging her
tightly. "I'm glad you're back," she whispered.

Liz laughed. "I didn't go that far."

Introductions were repeated.

"Let's go inside before we melt," Liz said. "I've made some Red Zinger iced tea. Or there's wine if anyone is so inclined." She paused. "I'm a little off wine myself at the moment."

Maureen's surprise must have shown on her face.

"I'll tell you all about it when we get inside."

The interior of the house looked exactly the same as it always had. Maureen wasn't sure what she'd expected, but ordinarily after the death of a spouse mementos were hidden or highlighted, objects and photos with special meaning either put away so as not to cause pain or moved to places of respect in order to honor the deceased. There'd been no need for that here.

Liz poured iced tea for all of them, and she did indeed tell them why she was not drinking wine these days. She described the hell into which she'd descended, dealing with the anguish of her husband's unexpected death and then with the escalating harassment of the homeowners' association that kept her from working through her grief in any sort of natural way. She'd get drunk to numb the pain, to shut out not only the memories of Ray's gruesome demise but the voices and noises she heard at night, and it was only in the past few days that she'd been able to pull herself out of despair.

The rest of them were silent after that, and Maureen reached over and grabbed her friend's hand, squeezing tightly.

Liz looked from Tina to Maureen. "You two have been great. Audrey and Moira, too. I know I didn't act like it, but it meant a lot to me each time you stopped by or called, and knowing you were there for me helped give me the strength to climb out of that hole I'd dug myself into."

Danna looked embarrassed, but Lupe was smiling sympathetically.

Liz wiped her tearing eyes. "Enough of this self-pity," she said. "Catch me up on gossip and current events. I want to know what's going on out there."

Tina was full of news about which neighbor was feuding with whom, about men and women who'd lost or changed jobs, about a new house that was being built over on Fir Street, but as it always did, the talk naturally shifted back again to the association, and it was Tina who brought up Bonita Vista's ever-deteriorating relationship with the town of Corban. Maureen was surprised when the other woman placed the blame squarely on the board, and she couldn't help recalling Tina at the annual meeting, her hand enthusiastically shooting into the air to support Jasper Calhoun's edicts and approve the revised C, C, and Rs.

Actions spoke louder than words, as the saying went, and while Tina might speak out against the association with them here in private, she was not divorced from it, not separate from it, she was a *part* of it.

And she supported its actions.

Maybe this was all part of some plot, Maureen reasoned, maybe the only reason Tina was here was to spy, to listen to what they said and report back on it. Hell, maybe she was even wearing a wire.

Or maybe the association's hidden cameras were recording all this for posterity.

Maureen knew she was being as paranoid as she'd accused Barry and Ray of being, but she knew also that her feelings were totally justified.

Liz grimaced. "Pretty soon, we'll be cut off from the town entirely. What then? Is the association planning to open its own grocery store and gas station, build a power plant?"

"They're ambitious," Tina said. "I'll give them that. But I don't think they'd go that far."

"But what do they hope to gain by angering the town?"

It was a question Maureen had been wondering herself, and it was one for which none of them seemed to have an answer.

There was a significant pause in the conversation.

Maureen broke the silence. "Speaking of the association," she said, "wasn't there a gay couple at one of your parties? I think one of the guys was named Pat?"

Liz nodded soberly. "Wayne and Pat. They're gone."

"That's what I was wondering about. We were going through the C, C, and Rs last night and saw an antigay rule and an anti-living-together rule."

"Yes."

"Gone?" Maureen said, the word finally sinking in.

"They disappeared. I'm sure their house is untouched and all of their clothes are in the closets, but . . . they're gone." Her voice dropped, as though she were afraid of being overheard. "It happens around here."

Maureen thought of all the empty houses in Bonita Vista, the ones she'd assumed were vacation homes with absentee owners. In her mind, she saw fully stocked refrigerators filled with rotting food, place settings at dining room tables covered with dust, and suddenly their calm, quiet neighborhood no longer seemed so benign.

"As for not allowing couples to live together, that's resulted in more than one enforced marriage."

"You're kidding."

Both Liz and Tina shook their heads.

"It's true," Tina said. "Jeannie and Skylar Wells moved here from Phoenix where they'd been living together forever. They got a little nudge from the association, and the next day—the next *day*—they went down to the justice of the peace and got hitched."

"A 'nudge'?" Maureen said.

Liz looked at her. "They won't talk about it."

Lupe cleared her throat. "I want to know about this anti-

minority rule. How strictly is that enforced? I'm Hispanic."
She smiled. "As I'm sure you can tell. Say I wanted to retire up here."

"You want the truth?" Liz asked.

"Of course."

"There's no way I would buy a home in Bonita Vista if I
were you. Discrimination is illegal and, who knows, maybe
if someone took them to court over that provision, it'd be
struck down." She leaned forward in her chair. "But no one
has."

The statement had an ominous ring to it, and Maureen
felt an unwanted shiver tickle her spine. Her mouth felt dry,
and she sipped her iced tea. "You mean this place wasn't always all white? There've been minority homeowners in the
past?"

"There was a single man, white man, had a place up
here, over on Blue Spruce Circle. A vacation home. He
came maybe every other summer, stayed for two weeks or
so. Usually to paint his house, clear brush, comply with
whatever warning the association sent to him. One year he
showed up with his new wife, a Vietnamese woman. Two
days later, he'd cleared out, and a week after that, the house
went up for sale. We never saw him again."

"What do you think they did?" Lupe asked. "Threaten
him with a fine or something?"

"More than that, I'm sure. But what it was specifically I
can't say."

"And that's it?" Maureen asked. "There's never been another nonwhite person up here?"

"That rule keeps them out. They don't buy here. And in
case you haven't noticed, Utah is not exactly a hotbed of di-
versity to begin with."

Everyone laughed, everyone except Liz, who grew even
more serious. "The thing is," she said, addressing Lupe,
"they've used that rule on guests as well as residents. I
don't want to scare you or anything—"

"I don't scare easily," Lupe insisted.

"—but apparently in their minds, this provision applies to visitors. Some friends of ours—the Marottas," she said to Maureen. "I think you met them at one of our parties—had a brother or cousin or something who'd married a black woman. They all came up for Thanksgiving a couple of years ago, and the wife was found naked and crying the next morning in the ditch in front of the Marottas' house, half frozen in the snow. I don't know exactly what happened, but Tony and Julia still won't talk about it. They refuse. And they've never had Thanksgiving here again."

"They try anything with me and Jeremy, they're going to be sorry they were ever born." Lupe's voice was firm, her expression set.

"That's a good attitude," Liz said, nodding. "But I'm not sure attitude is enough. Not with the association."

Twenty minutes later, Maureen, Lupe, and Danna were walking back home. Though they had a lot to talk about, the mood was considerably more somber than it had been on the way over, and the optimism Maureen had felt knowing that Liz had stood up to Jasper Calhoun and was once again her normal, feisty self had completely dissipated, replaced with a demoralized resignation that left her feeling empty and cold.

# FORTY-FOUR

Liz stood next to Tina in the darkened community center feeling guilty and deeply ashamed. On the monitor facing Jasper Calhoun and the board ran a replay of their afternoon meeting with Maureen and her California friends.

"You did good," Calhoun commended them. "You are assets to Bonita Vista, both of you."

"Thank you," Tina said, obviously pleased.

Liz said nothing.

"Elizabeth?" Calhoun prompted.

"Thank you," she whispered.

She was glad that the room was dark and the board could not see the tears rolling down her cheeks.

And she was glad that Ray was dead and had never lived to see this day.

# FORTY-FIVE

Barry had been looking through the revised C, C, and Rs, following Jeremy's lead. He'd perused them before, of course. Several times since the meeting. Looking for loopholes.

But now they were different.

He'd been trying to reconcile that for over an hour. He pored over regulations he didn't remember, unsuccessfully attempting to convince himself that his memory was going, or that he had too much on his mind, or that a person could not remember every single paragraph in a document this size, but he knew that those excuses were just that—excuses.

The C, C, and Rs had changed.

That was impossible, though. It meant that either someone had been sneaking into his house and replacing his old book with revisions, or that the pages were revising themselves, new rules magically appearing on formerly blank space.

Neither option was believable, neither was possible.

But, tellingly, he did not reject either one.

The ELP record they'd been listening to ended, and Chuck hurried outside to his car. "Hold on a minute," he said. He'd brought along a cache of new CDs, among them a Tom Waits album that Barry had read about but not yet heard, and he returned a few moments later, tossing a dark jewel case into Barry's lap.

"All right."

"There was a guy out front," Chuck reported. "Tall, skinny, wimp-looking sucker with a clipboard, writing notes. He walked away when he saw me, pretended he wasn't spying on us."

"Neil Campbell," Barry said, picking up the CD. "Association lackey."

"They know we're here," Jeremy said dryly.

Dylan grinned. "Good." He opened the door, stuck out his head. "We're kicking ass and taking names, motherfuckers!"

"That was mature," Barry told him, but secretly he was pleased. It felt good to have allies, people from the outside world who could say and do whatever they wanted with impunity.

They'd already watched Chuck's video of the neighborhood twice, looking for anything that appeared to be a gross violation of the association rules, but in his examination of the C, C, and Rs, he'd found nothing, and he shut off the television as he walked over to the stereo. Switching the tuner from Phono to CD, he popped in the Tom Waits and cranked up the volume, smiling as he heard the singer's familiar baritone growl.

He turned back toward the others. "Why are we sitting in the house?" he asked. "Let's go upstairs, sit out on the deck and plan our strategy there. Mo and I bought this place for the view, why don't we take advantage of it?"

"Yeah. Right. Sounds like a party." Dylan yawned, stretched. "So where's this bridle trail where the freak hangs out?"

"Stumpy?"

"Yeah."

"Follow me." Barry led the way up the steps and across

the open space adjacent to the dining room. He opened the sliding glass door and walked onto the deck. "Around that area," he said, pointing. "You take the road to the first street on the right, then walk down a bit. The trailhead's on the right. It's pretty well marked."

Dylan nodded, grinned. "I think I'll go for a walk."

Barry hesitated, not sure how to articulate what he was thinking. "It's not . . . fun," he said. "Stumpy—uh, Kenny—is . . ." He sighed. "Well, he's spooky, to be honest with you."

"You think I'm a pussy?"

Barry had to smile. "Always."

Dylan laughed. "Don't worry, bud."

"I'm serious, Dyl. It may sound interesting and neat while you're up here, but when you're down there by yourself in the woods, all alone, and you hear Stumpy—Kenny—coming toward you through the bushes, it's creepy."

"Cool."

"Take Jeremy with you. Or Chuck."

"Hell no. And you can't come either." He patted Barry's shoulder. "Don't worry. I brought a change of underwear in case I brown my shorts."

Dylan walked back inside to put on his hiking shoes, and Barry leaned on the rail, looking out over the trees, listening to the music. The glass door slid open, and Chuck and Jeremy came onto the deck.

"Good CD," Barry said.

Chuck nodded.

Downstairs, the front door slammed. A moment later, they saw Dylan on the road, heading down the hill. They each yelled obscenities at him and received the finger in return.

"You think Pussy Boy's hiding in the bushes and writing this down on his clipboard?" Chuck asked, grinning.

Barry laughed, nodded. "I'm sure I'll get a full report

and a recommendation to attend a language etiquette course."

"Recommendation?" Jeremy said, eyebrow raised.

"Order," Barry amended. "Hell, I already got a warning about my music being too loud." He snorted. "And I was listening to Joni Mitchell."

"Joni Mitchell?" Chuck laughed. "They're going to love Tom Waits."

"Don't worry. I'll hear about it."

The women returned soon after—Barry could tell because the music was suddenly turned off—and he, Jeremy, and Chuck went back inside, where Maureen filled him in on what she'd learned from Liz and Tina. "They're like a law unto themselves here," she said. "They're judge, jury, and executioner."

Jeremy nodded solemnly. "They seem to think they're a minigovernment and that they have all the rights and powers that entails. I don't care how many courts have upheld homeowners' associations' restrictions, that does not allow them to assault and harass people."

"Or kill people," Barry said.

"That goes without saying. What I'm thinking we should do is put together a chronology of events, lodge a criminal complaint with the local authorities—"

"A lot of good that will do."

"Let me finish. Then we go up the chain all the way to federal law enforcement. Justice Department. File discrimination complaints. Simultaneously, we hit them with a civil suit, a class action on behalf of all current and former homeowners who have been psychologically intimidated or physically threatened."

Lupe was nodding, and Barry had to admit that it made a kind of sense.

"We'll attack these assholes from all sides, and I'll be throwing so many briefs at them they won't know what hit them." He held up the copy of the C, C, and Rs that he'd brought in with him. "But we need to map out a specific sequence and strategy. This Kenny Tolkin who got his arms and legs chopped off. You think we could get him out of here, show the FBI or whatever law enforcement agency we approach what's been done to him?"

Barry nodded grimly. "If worse came to worst, the four of us could track him down, pick him up, and put him in a car."

"He wouldn't come voluntarily?"

"I don't think he'd understand. His . . . something's happened to his mind as well. Shock I suppose. And he can't communicate because he has no tongue. It's . . . I don't know of any other way to do it."

"We can't just kidnap him."

"I have my palmcorder," Chuck said. "We'll tape him."

Jeremy nodded. "Not a bad idea. And this is exactly what we have to do over the next few days. Figure out everything the association's done and find a concrete way to document it, plan out both our criminal and civil cases against them."

Barry looked over at Maureen and saw in her face the same hope he felt himself. In addition to being more than a little paranoid, Jeremy was obsessive and thorough; good qualities in both a lawyer and an adversary.

Lupe headed toward the bathroom. "A lot of iced tea," she explained.

"Yes it was," Danna agreed. She went downstairs to the other bathroom.

"Can we use your computer?" Barry asked Maureen.

"Go right ahead." She smiled. "Anything for the cause."

"Jeremy," Barry said. "Why don't you put together an outline of what we need? I'll tell you what I can, and we'll fill in the blanks later."

The three men headed down to Maureen's office, while she waited upstairs for Lupe to get out of the bathroom. "It *was* a lot of iced tea," she said.

# FORTY-SIX

Barry's directions were easy enough to follow, and Dylan soon found himself heading down a narrow footpath between tall trees and high bushes.

What was this? A hollow? A gulch? He wasn't up on his nature lingo, but the trail wound down between two close and heavily wooded hills, and whatever it was, it was pretty damn cool. Ahead, an obnoxious bird cawed in one of the trees and at his approach flew noisily into the air. A blue jay.

He had no idea where this path went or how far into the woods it extended, but it seemed to be heading away from Barry's hill and the roads where the houses were, into uncharted territory.

Where was the freak?

He should have asked Barry how far in he needed to go. He'd been walking—what?—five or six minutes. Was he supposed to go ten? Twenty? Thirty? The trail dipped again, passed over what looked like a dry creek bed, then followed the bottom edge of a dark rock bluff. In a section of forest where the pine trees grew between huge standing boulders, the path forked.

Dylan stopped. He was getting tired. And bored.

"Stumpy!" he yelled.

A bird called out, but otherwise the woods were silent.

"Anybody out here?"

Nothing.

"I got a big dick!" he shouted at the top of his lungs.

He studied the diverging paths. The one to the right seemed to head up a hillside and into the hot sunlight. The one to the left sloped down into another hollow or gulch or whatever. He considered turning back, but he wanted to see the freak and he figured he should give it another ten minutes. Besides, he didn't exactly feel like spending the entire afternoon listening to Barry and Jeremy try to pick apart obscure rules and regulations.

He started down the left trail and was rewarded with an immediate drop in temperature as the trees and bushes closed in around him, blocking out nearly all of the afternoon sun and throwing the area ahead of him into shadow. He began jogging over the hard-packed dirt, hoping to cover more territory, yelling "Hello!" every few seconds in order to flush out Stumpy or Kenny or whatever his name was.

Ahead, he thought he saw a building through the trees, and Dylan slowed down. He was out of breath already—not used to this high altitude—and he stopped for a moment, inhaling and exhaling deeply.

It *was* a building, he could see now, a long low structure made of wood and rock that corresponded to that of the forest and effectively camouflaged the place from anyone who wasn't almost on top of it. Something about that didn't sit well with him. He thought of everything Barry had told them, and it suddenly seemed mighty suspicious that there was a secret hideout here in the middle of the woods where Stumpy was supposed to be.

Maybe it was where he lived.

*Maybe it was where he was made.*

His first gut reaction had been to turn tail and run, but as Dylan peered through the dark foliage at the equally dark building, his adrenaline started pumping. This was why he'd come out here, this was what he'd come to see.

He approached slowly, keeping a watchful eye out for any signs of life. He had stopped shouting, having determined that the best course of action would be not to announce his presence but to sneak in and out with no one the wiser. Leaving the trail, he crept through the bushes toward the building, trying not to step on twigs or leaves, trying not to make any noise. The wall ahead of him appeared to be windowless, so he swung around, making a wide arc, and was gratified to see that on the side of the building was an open doorway.

He pushed his way through a series of interlocked bushes, managing not to cry out when a stray broken branch dug into his ankle, and then he was standing in the cleared space next to the building. This close, the similarity between the structure and the surrounding forest seemed even creepier. There was something *organic* about it, and Dylan was suddenly aware of the fact that there was no noise here. The distant sound of bird cry and the underbrush scuttling of lizards that had accompanied his trek down the path had disappeared, replaced by silence.

He stepped forward carefully, intensely aware of the too-loud sound his shoes made on the gravelly ground.

It looked like a bunkhouse, he thought, seeing it this close. He half-expected Stumpy—or Kenny—to come lurching out of the darkened doorway, shrieking at him, but the place seemed to be abandoned, and he appeared to be the only one here. He was grateful for that, and his reaction made him wonder what he was doing here in the first place, why he didn't just turn around and head back up the path to Barry's. He didn't know. But he did know that he needed to look inside that building, that even if he didn't see the freak, he still had to find out what was inside there.

He walked up to the doorway. The building obviously had no windows, but at the far end of what appeared to be a single large room that took up the entire interior of the structure, he saw the dim yellowish glow of an old kerosene lantern. He squinted into the darkness but was unable to make out any specific features, so he stepped inside, stopping just past the entrance to let his eyes adjust.

It *was* a bunkhouse, and he could see that the small cots lining both sides of the long room were occupied. He whirled around, intending to flee, but strong hands grabbed his right arm. He swiveled to see a tall elderly gentleman staring blankly at him,

The man had no ears.

Other hands grabbed his left arm, clamped around his neck, and then the people in the cots were rising, standing, walking toward him.

Or some of them were walking. Others were limping, and while they were not Stumpy, Dylan could see in the far-off light from the lantern and the dim illumination from outside that they all appeared to be handicapped, missing arms or hands or legs or feet.

He tried to free himself from the grip of those who held him, but his captors held him tight.

*Captors?*

He struggled mightily, lashed out with his feet, tried a backward head butt, attempted to jerk his right arm free and throw a roundhouse punch at the tall man before him. No one had yet spoken, the only sounds in the bunkhouse were his own grunts and exhalations and the shuffling/clopping of feet on wooden floor, and he was starting to get seriously scared.

The grip on his left arm weakened for a moment as the man holding onto it was bumped by a fingerless figure approaching from the side, and Dylan took advantage of the opportunity, yanking his arm away and using it to claw the face of the tall man. For a brief second, he was almost free, then the hands on his neck tightened, and he slipped, almost fell. "Fuck!" he managed to get out.

And then they were beating him.

*       *       *

When Dylan came to, he was gagged and restrained, strapped down with chains and bands of leather to what felt like a metal table. He was no longer in the bunkhouse, he knew that, but exactly where he'd been taken was not yet clear. He was able to move his head, and he turned it first to the left and then to the right, seeing only dark blurriness from between his puffy eyelids. Gradually, his brain adjusted to this altered vision, deciphering the scrambled signals and reformulating them into a more coherent picture. He saw a grimy stone wall, although his brain must have been having trouble judging distances because it looked as though it were several yards from where he lay. Next to him, on the table, was an old and obviously well-used machete, a hammer and a pack of nails, and a portable band saw with a rusted blade. Above, high and far away, was a black ceiling.

A woman walked up, dressed in dirty jeans and a torn, bloody T-shirt, a pair of yellowed plastic goggles hanging around her neck.

"One of the guests?" she asked.

An old man appeared next to her, a strange-looking individual with dry, crinkly skin and a face that owed more to the makeup wizardry of horror films than the biology of real life. "Yes," he said, his voice deep and filled with the offhanded authoritarianism of someone in power.

"What's the plan?" the woman asked.

The old man looked at Dylan dismissively. "Do the hands and feet first," he told the woman. "We'll figure out where to go after that."

"Roger wilco." The woman lowered her goggles.

Behind his gag, Dylan screamed as the band saw started to buzz.

# FORTY-SEVEN

When an hour had passed and Dylan wasn't back, Barry felt a slight twinge of unease.

When two hours had passed and Dylan still hadn't returned, he was filled with fear and a horribly familiar sense of panic. He gathered together Jeremy and Chuck, and the three of them headed out to the bridle trail to search for their friend.

They walked up and down the trail, following each fork, encountering only a pair of yuppie joggers and an old woman.

No Dylan.

It was nearly dark when they finally returned to the house, tired, angry, discouraged, and worried. The wives met them on the porch, and one look at their faces told Barry that Dylan had still not come back. They went into the house, closing and locking the door behind them. Maureen hurried upstairs to get drinks.

"You think the association got to him?" Jeremy asked, voicing the thought that was on all of their minds.

Danna turned toward Barry. "He was off to see that armless, legless guy, right?"

But Barry was already shaking his head. "Stumpy— Kenny—couldn't've done this. He's scary, but when you get down to it, all he could do is gum someone to death. He certainly couldn't take down a big guy like Dylan."

Jeremy nodded. "So it was someone else. Or several someone elses."

"Whatever it was, we're not going to find out by guessing about it in the living room." Barry looked at him. "You want to call Sheriff Hitman or do you want me to?"

"I'll talk to that bastard." Jeremy picked up the phone from the table, dialed 911, and waited.

And waited.

He hung up, dialed again, and this time someone answered. He asked to speak with the sheriff, and when the person on the other end of the line began asking questions about the nature of the emergency, Jeremy turned on the legalese and in his most serious and officious voice began berating and intimidating the person into transferring the call to the sheriff.

Barry had to smile. An angry and belligerent Jeremy was something to behold, and not for the first time he was glad the man was on his side.

But Jeremy's verbal pyrotechnics did not work on Hitman. Even listening to only one side of the conversation, Barry could tell where it was going. He'd been there before himself: Hitman was not empowered to intervene in association business, this was clearly an association dispute, and if he had any problems, Jeremy should address them to the board.

"God *damn*!" Jeremy said, clicking off the phone and slamming it down on the coffee table. "What do they have on this sheriff? Video of him in bed with a pig? Jesus Christ! How can a law enforcement officer totally ignore his responsibilities like that? He's not doing his fucking job! And he's not even embarrassed or sorry about it!"

"That's what we've been wondering," Maureen said.

"I'm definitely going to other agencies with this. Hitman's either completely corrupt or grossly incompetent, and if I have to sue his ass for malfeasance and dereliction of duty, then, goddamn it, that's what I'll do. There's no way he's getting away with this."

Barry was silent, his faint hopes dimming. Jeremy was a resourceful opponent, but the association was a juggernaut, willing and able to flatten any obstacle in its path.

"What next, then?" Chuck asked.

Barry took a deep breath. "I guess we wait for morning."

He stood by the window, looking out at the road as if expecting Dylan to return any second, while a BMW filled with teenagers sped by, the driver honking his horn and yelling, "Your mama sucks cocks in hell!"

Barry awoke at six, before Maureen and, from what his ears told him, before anyone else. He'd slept through the night as usual, but there'd been dreams, bad dreams, and he was glad to wake up. He slipped out of bed slowly, carefully, one foot at a time so as not to disturb Maureen, and put on his robe and slippers before opening the bedroom door and padding upstairs.

He was quiet. He intended to sneak silently up to the kitchen so as not to disturb Chuck and Danna, but he could see by the early morning light seeping through the mini-blinds that the sofa bed had been folded up. The living room looked unused, the linens and pillows untouched. He turned on a lamp, frowning, and made a quick tour of the house. The door to the guest bedroom was closed and locked, Jeremy and Lupe obviously inside, but both the upstairs and downstairs bathrooms were empty, doors open. No dishes had been used in the kitchen, not even a water glass, and through the windows there was no sign of anyone in the yard.

Chuck and Danna had disappeared.

They've probably gone for a walk, he told himself. They'd made the sofa bed, refolded the linen, and sneaked outside for an early morning constitutional. But there was a gnawing doubt in his gut, and part of him wanted to wake up everyone else in the house, rush outside, and start an immediate search.

He pushed those thoughts aside, did not allow his mind to proceed in that direction. To acknowledge that something bad had befallen them would be to acknowledge that some-one—

*something*

—had broken into their house and that he could not do. The possibilities were just too far-reaching, the implications too terrifyingly intimidating. Especially after yesterday.

It was an ostrich attitude, with its irrationally rational appeal, but something seemed to have shut down inside him, some sense of justice or outrage or responsibility, and he found that he *could* believe nothing untoward had occurred. He could honestly say that he thought it likely his friends had simply awoken early and gone out for a stroll around the neighborhood.

One by one, the others awoke, and Barry, who'd been sitting silently in the living room, stood, went upstairs, and busied himself in the kitchen making coffee. Maureen came up first, then Jeremy, then Lupe. All of them asked about Chuck and Danna, and Barry shrugged off the questions, saying that he didn't know where they were, they'd been gone when he awoke, but that they were probably just taking a morning walk to clear their heads after yesterday's drama.

"Oh yeah," Maureen said sarcastically. "They're probably out looking for Dylan."

He did not bother to respond.

They ate breakfast in silence, the only noise in the house the false cheer of a morning news show on TV and the chomping of cereal.

"Who are we fooling?" Jeremy said, setting down his

spoon. "How long are we going to pretend that they're coming back?"

"We don't know that they're not," Barry stressed. "We can't just go jumping to conclusions."

"After Dylan, it's not such a big jump," Maureen told him.

"They wouldn't just go without telling us," Jeremy insisted. "Something's happened to them."

Lupe stood, looked over the railing into the living room. "Their luggage is gone," she pointed out.

Barry moved next to her. She was right. Chuck's overnight bag was missing and Danna's two small suitcases were nowhere to be seen. How could he have missed something so obvious?

"Then I guess they took off," Barry said without conviction, "headed home."

"How could they leave without their car? And why would they? If they wanted to leave, they would've told us, and we all would've driven out together. They wouldn't . . . what? Hike back to California? Call a cab?"

He looked over the railing at the untouched sofa bed.

First Dylan.

Now Chuck and Danna.

They were picking off his friends one by one.

"Maybe *we* should get out of here," Lupe suggested.

Barry nodded in agreement, though he felt torn up inside. Three days. It had only taken three days for Bonita Vista to break down and decimate his best and strongest line of defense.

Still, there remained a core of iron within him, a resolute unwillingness to concede defeat that, if anything, was growing stronger. He was reminded of the tag line for a movie: *This time it's personal.*

But it had always been personal. He thought of their cat Barney, thought of the murder of the man who had harassed

Maureen, thought of Ray. His opposition to the homeowners' association had never been anything *but* personal.

Jeremy shook his head. "I'm not leaving until we find out what happened to them. If I have to stay here a fucking year, I will, but there's no way I'm going to abandon my friends."

"Let's head out," Barry said, "take a look around Bonita Vista, see if we can find something."

Jeremy nodded grimly. "We'll start with the president's house."

"Do you want to go with them?" Maureen asked Lupe. The other woman looked over at her husband, then shook her head and started digging into her cereal. "I'll stay with her," Maureen told Barry.

He nodded, came back to the table to quickly finish off his coffee, then went down to the bedroom and put on his shoes. Jeremy was ready to go by the time he came up to the living room, and Barry unlocked, unbolted, and opened the front door.

And saw a pink sheet of paper affixed to the outside of the screen.

Jeremy pushed open the screen door, reached around the metal frame, and grabbed the paper.

"It's a form," he said, and his voice was flat. "Or your 'recipient's copy' of a form. A *Regulation Compliance* form, to be exact. And there's a 'Violation' box checked. 'Unauthorized Presence of Minority.'"

"Shit," Barry said. He thought of the sealed letter they'd found in the closet that first week.

*They're doing it. They're keeping track of it. Don't think they aren't.*

They'd been talking quietly, but the quiet must have carried its own weight because he saw movement out of the corner of his eye and looked up to see Maureen and Lupe standing on the edge of the stairs gazing down on them, both of their faces registering the same expression.

Jeremy looked up at his wife, reading aloud. " 'Hispanic female and husband staying at residence. If violation continues, offending couple will be removed.' "

"Removed," Barry repeated.

"What do you think they mean by that?"

Barry looked at him. "What do *you* think?"

"My God," Lupe said, and her voice was shaking. He thought she was about to cry, but when he looked up at her he saw lines of anger hardening her face. It was rage that was making her voice quiver, not fear. "Someone has to teach those racists a lesson."

"I have the will and the way," Jeremy said. He looked at Barry, the form crumpled in his fist. He dropped the paper on the floor. "Let's go. Let's pay a little visit to Mr. Jasper Calhoun."

Calhoun's house looked even more fortresslike than it had before, its intimidating size and dark gray walls contrasting sharply with a green expanse of sloping lawn—an artificial imposition on the natural landscape that the C, C, and Rs should have prohibited. As before, a cold breeze blew here, ruffling his hair, and if he had not known that it was impossible, he'd have sworn it originated from the windowless residence.

They stood for a moment on the road.

"God, that's a monstrous house," Jeremy said.

"In more ways than one."

"That, too. But I'm just shocked it's so big. If I recall correctly, there are size limitations on structures in Bonita Vista. Although maybe this thing was grandfathered in."

"Mike Stewart said that Calhoun lives alone. He has no family."

"Why does he need all that space, then? What could he possibly use it for?"

Barry didn't answer. It was a question he didn't want to think about.

They walked down the perfectly maintained path past an

apple tree, past a plum tree, past a birdbath. The silver Lexus was not in the carport, so there was a good chance the president wasn't home, but they continued on anyway, up the wooden steps of the wraparound porch to the door. Jeremy rang the bell, and a muffled gong sounded from somewhere deep in the house.

Barry turned his head slowly, looking around. The yard was silent, empty.

Jeremy rang the bell again, but after another minute it seemed obvious that no one was home.

The slits to either side of the door were narrow windows, and Barry cupped his hands to shield the glare, pressing his face against the one on the right, but the smoked glass was so dark he could barely see the outline of the closed mini-blinds inside.

What *did* Calhoun need all that space for?

They walked back up the path to the street, and Barry sensed the weight of the house behind him. It felt as though he was being watched, as though the house were some sort of giant sentient creature all hunkered down and waiting to pounce, and he had to fight the urge to run back up the lawn to the street.

He did not notice until they reached the pavement that neither of them had spoken since stepping onto Calhoun's property, and he wondered if Jeremy had been as anxious as he himself had been. He felt better now that they'd reached the street, but he was sweating, as though he'd just had a particularly close encounter with some sort of predator.

They started walking back toward Barry's. Jeremy was the first to speak. "You know me," he said. "I'm not one of these touchy-feely guys. But I'm telling you that place gave me the creeps."

Barry nodded.

"You think they could be in there? Dylan? Chuck and Danna?"

"I don't think they are," Barry said, and he found that it was true. He could easily imagine his friends chained to the wall in some dungeonlike room within that monstrosity, but it didn't feel right to him. He had no doubt that there were things within that building that were equally horrific, that he would prefer not to know about or see, but he didn't think Chuck and Danna were there, and for that he was grateful.

Where did he think they were, then?

His gut instinct was that they *were* gone, that they *had* left Bonita Vista, either on their own or via some forced evacuation, and though he had no evidence to back him up, he told Jeremy his feeling.

"I've been thinking that, too," his friend admitted. "They drove Dylan off, and they might've done the same to Chuck and Danna; although what could have happened between bedtime and morning that would make them just pack their things and go, without telling any of us, is a mystery. I personally think it's more likely that they were kidnapped or dragged off or somehow forced to leave. But you're right. The association probably wouldn't want to keep them here. Their goal would be to get rid of them." He paused. "Get rid of us."

"Maybe Lupe's right," Barry said. "Maybe you two should go back to California. Before something bad happens to you."

"I hate the idea of letting them run me off." Jeremy looked over at him. "Besides, we came out here to help you."

But he didn't rule out the possibility.

They walked the rest of the way home in silence, each lost in private thoughts.

"I still think the best way to attack them is with lawsuits," Jeremy said as they reached the driveway. "Because even if they win, it's a nuisance. They have to hire a lawyer, have to make the effort to fight the allegations. It takes time and money and resources, and maybe it takes the pressure off the people here a little bit."

"It might also give us other ideas and help us find some chinks in the armor."

"That, too."

They were halfway to the house when Mike pulled up in his pickup. He got out of the truck, leaving the engine running, and handed Barry a large manila envelope. "I was told to give this to you." He held up his hands in a gesture of innocence. "I'm just the messenger here. I don't know what's in it."

"Told by whom?" Jeremy asked.

"I'm just the messenger." He shrugged, gave Barry an apologetic look, and retreated back to his pickup. Maureen and Lupe were coming out of the house, walking down the porch steps, and before anyone could say anything more, Mike drove off without another word.

"What's that?" Maureen asked, walking up.

"I don't know."

Barry spread open the clasp and opened the envelope's flap, pulling out an eight-by-ten sheet. It was a photograph. A photograph of a dark-skinned man being tortured by unseen assailants. The picture had clearly been taken in Bonita Vista—the sweep of pines leading south to the canyonlands could be seen in the background—and had been taken fairly recently: there was the hood and front end of a new Honda Accord visible on the left half of the photo.

The man was being flayed alive.

Barry stared at the picture in horror. A section of the man's shoulder had been peeled away, and the deep flowing crimson beneath a perfectly square flap of exposed musculature contrasted horribly with the dull darkness of his skin. The man's eyes were wide and crazed, his mouth open in a twisted, agonized scream, and there was blood dripping from his lips.

All of his teeth had been knocked out.

The only signs of the individuals performing this atrocity were two pairs of gloved hands holding the victim's bare arms and the blurrily silhouetted head and shoulders of another man facing away from the camera and holding up an exceptionally long pair of shears.

Barry's salivary glands had stopped working, his mouth was cotton dry. Both Jeremy and Lupe looked sick.

He turned the picture over. Stamped on the back in red ink was a description of the photo: "Punishment Administered for Violation of Article IV, Section 8, Paragraph D."

Lupe started crying.

Jeremy rushed to put his arms around her.

"I'm sorry," she sobbed. "It's just . . . I'm sorry."

"It's okay," Maureen reassured her. "We understand."

"I guess I'm not as tough as I thought."

"It's okay," Jeremy told her. "Don't worry." He glanced over at Barry. "Sorry, dude. The war's won. We're leaving, we're out of here, we're gone. And if you're smart, you'll do the same."

# FORTY-EIGHT

**The Bonita Vista Homeowners' Association Covenants, Conditions, and Restrictions** Article IV, General Provisions, Section 8, Paragraph D:

> *Non-Caucasian individuals, due to their propensity for engaging in crimes against both person and property, are not allowed to reside or stay within the boundaries of Bonita Vista.*

# FORTY-NINE

Jeremy was *good*.

He and Lupe had left midmorning, and by early afternoon, he was calling Barry from his cell phone on his way back to California, telling Barry to expect a visit from the FBI. While Lupe drove, he'd been making constant calls, cashing in favors, exploiting contacts, all the time filled with the white-hot rage that had become Barry's second nature and that only the homeowners' association seemed able to elicit. He'd convinced the FBI to investigate not only Dylan's, Chuck's, and Danna's disappearance but also local law enforcement's unwillingness to even look into the situation.

"Now for our ace in the hole."

Unreasonably, Barry felt a surge of hope and optimism. "What?" he asked.

"Your boy Kenny Tolkin. He wasn't talking out of his ass, he really was a player. I've learned that there was an article in the *Times* this morning about how he was AWOL and quite a few big-name celebrities were worried. He was apparently supposed to meet with Madonna last week but he never showed, something that was totally unlike him. Tom Cruise was stood up on Monday, and there's a quote from Tolkin's L.A. office where they admit that they haven't heard from him and can't seem to get in touch with him. You have to read this."

"We get the *Times*. We still subscribe. It just comes in the mail two days late."

"Too long to wait. I'll fax it to you as soon as we get back. Suffice it to say that when someone of this stature is missing, no effort is spared to find him. The big guns'll be coming down on Bonita Vista. Hard."

"Good."

"I'm also going to fax you a questionnaire that I want you to fill out and, if possible, get notarized. What I'm going to do is use it as part of a packet for the law enforcement agencies working on Tolkin's case. With your testimony as to probable cause, they should be able to obtain a search warrant for the open lands in Bonita Vista."

It was not like Jeremy to be so explicit over the phone. His enthusiasm was overriding his usually overcautious phone habits, and this time it was Barry who had to shoulder the paranoia. "You know this is not a secure line," he said.

"Shit! You're right, dude. I'm sorry. I just got carried away. I'll fax you the rest of my ideas along with the article. Any news at your end?"

"No."

"All right then. Expect to hear back from me in a couple of hours."

There was a pause.

"What is it?" Barry asked.

"It may be nothing, and I don't really want to worry you—"

"Not a secure line, remember."

"I know, I know. But a car almost hit us back in St George. Maybe it was nothing, maybe coincidence, but i came right *at* us. An Infiniti." There was a second of si lence. "We were passing a new subdivision, a gated com munity. It sped out of the driveway, headed right for us, then sped off when Lupe slammed on the brakes."

"Oh my God."

"Draw your own conclusions. We shouldn't say more. I'll call when we get back home."

Barry turned off the phone, sat down hard on the couch. Jeremy was right, it *could* be a coincidence. But his mind was already racing. What scared him the most was the idea that the association could reach all the way to other cities, maybe all the way to California in order to impose its will, to carry out its plans. In his mind, Bonita Vista had always been an isolated community, and he'd assumed that once they got away from here they'd be free from the tyranny of these local yokels. But now he imagined a network of homeowners' associations spread across the country, each doing the others' dirty work, tracking and punishing individuals who crossed them or their brethren. He hoped to God that this was all a gross overreaction and that Jeremy and Lupe's close call with the car was perfectly innocent and understandable.

But he didn't think that was the case.

And neither, he knew, did Jeremy.

"So what's he say?" Maureen asked.

Barry took a deep breath, and told her.

The FBI agent, Thom Geddes, arrived the next morning after calling ahead an hour, then a half hour, and then fifteen minutes before. Both Barry and Maureen were pacing nervously, awaiting his arrival, and as soon as he pulled into the driveway they were unlocking the front door.

Introductions were short, formal, businesslike. The agent clearly wanted to get started on his investigation and to complete it as soon as possible. He seemed capable, competent, and above all, a legitimate representative of the United States' premier law enforcement agency, with unlimited power and resources at his disposal—which gave Barry a feeling of relief and renewed hope.

Geddes looked down at the electronic notebook in his hand. "As I understand it, Dylan Andrews, Chuck Carlin, and Danna Carlin were guests of yours. Two days ago, Mr. Andrews went missing, and Mr. and Mrs. Carlin disappeared sometime between that night and the following morning. Because of various incidents and confrontations that you have had with the Bonita Vista Homeowners' Association, you suspect that this organization is behind the disappearances. Is this correct?"

Barry looked at Maureen, then nodded. "Yes, it is."

"Good. I will pay a visit to—" He looked at his notebook. "—Jasper Calhoun, and interview Mr. Calhoun about these disappearances."

Barry didn't know what he was expecting, but it wasn't this immediate and straightforward course of action, and the blunt honesty of the agent threw him for a moment. "Can I . . . come with you?" he asked.

"No!" Maureen said.

"If you wish," Geddes replied, turning off his notebook.

Barry looked over at Maureen. "I need to be there."

"Like hell!"

He put his hands on her shoulders, looked into her eyes. "They're not going to kill or kidnap an FBI agent. I'll be perfectly safe. This is my opportunity to confront that bastard."

"I just—"

"I know."

Geddes pretended to ignore them.

"I need to hear what he says," Barry told her. "I need to see his face. These are our friends. I can't just . . . abandon them. I have to be there."

Maureen took a deep breath, nodded. "Okay."

The agent cleared his throat. "I will be conducting the interview. You—" He looked at Barry. "—may observe."

"Gotcha."

Maureen kissed him. "Find out where they are," she said.

He let her go, moved away, motioned toward the door. "I know where Calhoun lives," he told the agent. "I can take you there."

"I'll drive," Geddes said in a flat voice. "And we'll take my car. You can direct me to the house."

The phone rang, and Maureen answered it. Barry and the FBI agent were just about to walk outside when she shoved the phone at him. Her hand was trembling, her face pale. "It's for you," she said. "It's *him*."

Barry stopped, put the phone to his ear. "Hello?"

"Barry." He recognized the stentorian tones of Jasper Calhoun. "Our man at the gate told me that a federal law enforcement agent has come to visit you. I assume this is in regard to your missing friends."

No one had told Calhoun about his missing friends. How had he—?

*Hitman.*

"Yes," he said, keeping his voice calm. "That is correct."

"Well, the homeowners' association would like to cooperate in any way possible. I'm at the community center right now. If the agent would like to speak with me for any reason, I will be at this location for the next hour or so."

*For any reason?* Calhoun knew damn well why they wanted to talk to him, and Barry thought of those comic-book villains who tried to play mind games with the men who were trying to capture them, who considered life some sort of elaborate chess game.

"We're on our way," Barry said shortly, and hung up. He looked from Maureen to Geddes. "He's at the community center at the bottom of the hill."

The agent nodded. "Let's go."

Calhoun was indeed at the community center, seated in front of the hall at the same table he had occupied during the annual meeting, looking as though he had never left. The room was empty and dark, all of the chairs gone, a pasty gray light filtering in through a small square of skylight in the middle of the ceiling. The president faced the deserted clubhouse, and Barry could not for the life of him figure out why the man was here or what he could possibly be doing all alone in the building.

The lights switched on before they were halfway across the floor, and Calhoun was standing, moving out from in back of the table, stepping off the platform. He was smiling broadly, an expression of false cheer on his face, and he led with an outstretched hand. "I'm Jasper Calhoun, president of the Bonita Vista Homeowners' Association."

He and Geddes shook, and once again Barry was struck by the man's odd, almost inhuman, appearance. He hoped that the agent had taken note of it as well.

As before, Geddes was all business. There was no small talk, only a few introductory remarks, and then his electronic notebook was open and he was asking questions.

Calhoun had come prepared. Barry had to give him that. After denying knowledge of everything the FBI agent asked, after accounting for his whereabouts and the whereabouts of the other board members during the disputed time periods and offering to provide surveillance videotapes to back up his claims, after effectively blunting all possible suspicions, the president picked up a series of charts and graphs from the table at which he'd been sitting and started quoting the remarkably low crime rates consistently posted by Bonita Vista.

"I'm as anxious as you are to have this situation resolved," Calhoun said earnestly. "Any crime, especially an unsolved crime, reflects badly on Bonita Vista and is a blot on our sterling record. To be perfectly frank, one of my duties as a board member is damage control, public relations, and this is a nightmare for us. As I'm sure Mr. Welch will confirm, we are very concerned about our image and take extraordinary measures to make sure that our community is not only safe but *perceived* as safe by both residents and nonresidents. In fact, I believe Mr. Welch and his wife had some personal experience with the efficient way in which we deal with lawbreakers and troublemakers. Mrs. Welch was harassed by a disgruntled ex-employee, and two members of our security committee detained him until the sheriff could arrive to arrest him. The association was willing to press charges and to make sure that Mrs. Welch never had to testify in court or see the man again." He spread his hands. "This is an example of the service we provide for our residents and the extent to which we will go in order to preserve and protect our reputation."

He sounded good, Barry admitted. Hell, if he didn't know better, *he'd* probably believe the story.

"It wasn't just one lone criminal. We have also been harassed by the association," Barry said. He pointed at Calhoun. "You and your cronies have fined us and intimidated us and repainted our house and relandscaped our property."

The president smiled sympathetically.

"Do you deny citing us for violating a rule that bans minorities from staying in Bonita Vista?"

"Homeowners' associations do necessarily have rules and regulations that all of its residents must follow."

"Illegal, discriminatory rules?"

Calhoun looked at Geddes. "Life is a little different within a gated community, particularly one that is located in an unincorporated area, where the homeowners' association must furnish the sort of services and protection ordinarily provided by government agencies. Are you familiar with homeowners' associations at all, Agent Geddes?"

"I live in a gated community," Geddes admitted.

"And do you like it?"

"I wouldn't live anywhere else."

Calhoun nodded. "Then you know what I'm talking about." He gave Barry a tolerant smile. "I'll be the first one to admit that they're not for everyone. Some individuals don't respond well to the stringent requirements for membership. But associations maintain standards that are necessary for the good of the community. That is what we do here. But to extrapolate from that that we are involved in kidnapping or other illegal activities is frankly ludicrous."

There was a lot more that Barry wanted to say, but Geddes was already closing his notebook. He raised a silencing hand as Barry started to speak, then thanked Calhoun for the interview and started toward the door, indicating that Barry was to follow.

The lights went off as they reached the exit, and he turned to see Calhoun seated at the table in exactly the same position as when they'd arrived.

He shivered.

"So?" Barry prodded as the door closed behind them. He knew the answer already but felt obligated to ask.

"I'm sorry," Geddes said as they walked back out to the car, "but I'll be recommending that we concentrate our efforts on searching for an outside suspect, a person or persons with a specific grudge against your friends. I do not believe that Mr. Calhoun is in any way involved in these disappearances—if they *are* disappearances—and I don't think that your homeowners' association is responsible for or complicitous in whatever crime may have occurred."

"They—"

The agent held up a hand. "I understand your antipathy toward the organization, but I think you have allowed it to cloud your judgment. The idea that your homeowners' association is behind the kidnapping of your friends makes no logical sense and there is absolutely no evidence to support it. As Mr. Calhoun said, the proposition is ludicrous. This doesn't mean that we won't make every effort to locate your friends. Of course we will. The majority of our cases are missing persons, and it's very rare that we do not close our cases. This branch of the Bureau in particular has a stellar record in this area." He stopped walking. "We know our job, Mr. Welch. And we're good at what we do. We'll also keep you apprised of any and all developments in the case. But I have to be honest, and I'm telling you right here and now that you're barking up the wrong tree."

*I wouldn't live anywhere else.*

Barry looked at the agent, then nodded and started toward the car. "I understand," he said.

# FIFTY

And then it was all over.

Or at least it seemed to be. No progress was made in finding their friends, but a week went by with no fines or charges or intrusive action. And then another. And another. It was as though things had gone back to the way they were that first month, and Maureen found it easy to pretend that all was well. She helped Barry repaint the house brown with forest green trim, and they went into town and cleaned out his office, where, miraculously, everything was as he had left it. She also picked up a few clients from her E-accountant web page.

And she was pregnant.

She was not positive at first. Her period always varied a day or two, and once it had even been a week late. But when two weeks had gone by and there were not even any signs of imminent menstruation—no bloating, no oily skin, no PMS—she knew that she was pregnant.

She'd had a feeling from the beginning that this time it was the real deal, but she didn't want to jinx it so she'd said nothing to Barry. She was still not certain what his reaction would be. Irrespective of the chaos around them, she was not sure he was ready to be a father, not sure, despite his protestations to the contrary, that he ever wanted to be a father.

But she told him in bed on the night of the fourteenth day.

"I have news."

"Good or bad?"

"Under the circumstances, I'm not sure." She looked at him. "I'm pregnant."

"Are you positive?"

She nodded. "My period's two weeks late."

"That's great!"

He hugged her tightly. She hadn't realized how anxious she'd been, wondering and worrying about his reaction, and she was filled with a deep grateful joy at his obvious excitement. They ended up talking far into the night and, afterward, making love.

Corban had only one doctor, a general practitioner, and even if there hadn't been animosity between Bonita Vista and the town, neither of them would have been willing to entrust the health of their baby to him. So the next morning Maureen got on the Internet, did some research, and found the name of a respected obstetrician over in Cedar City. It was a long drive, but it was worth it, and they made an appointment to see Dr. Holm two days later.

Everything went well. Because of her age, she was technically in the high-risk group, but the doctor said she was healthy, practiced good nutrition, and had been taking the proper vitamins even before conceiving. She would have to have ultrasounds and an amnio, but he didn't foresee any problems. The only worry he had was that she was not immunized for rubella. German measles was known to cause serious birth defects, and he advised her to stay away from crowds, to not fly in airplanes, to not attend movie theaters or amusement parks, and to steer clear of recent immigrants who might carry the virus.

She called all her friends from California, then dragged Barry up to see Liz.

When she answered the door, their friend looked old and

tired. She'd seemed fine when Maureen had gone up to the house with Lupe and Danna, but now all of the life seemed to be drained out of her. With Barry's arm around her midsection, Maureen put on a cheerful front and gave the glad tidings. She'd hoped Liz would be happy for them, excited by the news, but the dour expression that seemed to have been permanently etched on the old woman's face did not change. "What are you going to do about it?" she asked shortly.

Maureen frowned, uncomprehending. "What?"

Liz gestured around the hillside. "Couples are not allowed to have children in Bonita Vista."

"That's not true. The Williamses have kids. And I've seen teenagers at the tennis courts."

"The no-children rule is fairly new and those people were grandfathered in. But everyone who moved here within the past three years is forbidden to either procreate or adopt."

"I never saw that rule in there," Barry said, his arm tightening around her.

Maureen hadn't either, but the case of the ever-changing document had never been solved, and they still hadn't had time to go through the massive volume that housed the revised C, C, and Rs. She had no doubt that Liz was telling the truth.

"There was a man here a couple years back," the old woman said, her voice flat and unemotional. "Dent Rolsheim. He had two kids by his first wife back in Phoenix but she had full custody. He'd remarried and moved here and was fighting it, pouring every cent he had into trying to get his kids back. Finally, the case went to court and he was granted joint custody, with the wife taking them for the school year and Dent taking them for summers and holidays. The day after he picked up the kids and brought them back here, they disappeared. All of them. Dent, the kids, the second wife. Gone. No one ever heard from them again."

Maureen felt the grip of panic around her heart. "What if the association tries something like that when our little guy's born?"

Barry's jaw tightened. "Don't worry," he said. "We won't let them."

"Them?" Liz said, raising an eyebrow. "*Us.*"

She slammed the door in their faces.

# FIFTY-ONE

**The Bonita Vista Homeowners' Association Covenants, Conditions, and Restrictions** Article VI, Membership Rights, Section 3, Paragraph D:

> *Children are not permitted to live within the boundaries of Bonita Vista or on any of the Properties herein, the sole exception being those persons under age eighteen who were already living with their families prior to the institution of this restriction. Should any couple decline to take suitable steps to resolve the conflict between an unapproved adoption or pregnancy and this Declaration, the Board has the authority to void the adoption or terminate the pregnancy in the manner it deems most appropriate.*

# FIFTY-TWO

They were awakened in the middle of the night by the phone ringing, and Barry grabbed it angrily, sure it was someone from the association attempting to harass them.

But it wasn't.

The voice on the other end of the line belonged to his brother-in-law, Brian, who was calling because Sheri had been in a serious accident and was in Intensive Care. Barry's sister and her husband lived in Philadelphia, where both of them worked the night shift at the post office's distribution center. Less than an hour ago, Sheri had gone out to get some sandwiches at an all-night deli and had been struck by a car while walking across the street. The driver had neither slowed nor stopped, and it was only the fact that the deli cashier had seen the accident and called 911 that she was alive at all. As it stood, she was in critical condition and her prognosis was not good.

"Get over here," Brian sobbed. "She needs you, man."

"I'll be there as quick as I can."

He clicked off the phone and looked over at Maureen, stunned. "Sheri was in an accident. Hit and run. Brian says it's bad. There might be brain damage. She also might need a kidney and I'm the only family member with matching blood type. They want me to fly over for tests."

It hadn't hit him until he spelled everything out for Maureen, and he suddenly felt as though he couldn't breathe. Tears welled in his eyes, and he concentrated hard so as not to cry, knowing that if he started he would not be able to stop.

He wiped his eyes. "Pack enough for a week," he said. "I don't know how long we'll be there, but it's better to be prepared. We'll drive up to Salt Lake and see what's available, wait for standby if we have to."

Maureen was already shaking her head. "You heard what the doctor said. I have no immunization for rubella. I can't fly on a plane with all that recycled air. Who knows what kind of passengers will be on there? I'm not going to jeopardize the baby."

He nodded in acknowledgment, though the meaning of her words was only now filtering through. It was as if everything was on delay, as though words had to travel great distances to reach his brain.

In the back of his mind was the idea that the association was responsible, that they were behind the accident and had planned this all out in order to separate him from Maureen, but he knew that was not possible.

Was it?

"You're going to stay here?" he said.

"Yes. But don't worry about it. Get ready and go. Sheri needs you."

"I don't think—"

"I'll be fine. Nothing'll happen to me."

"At least stay inside," he told her. "Don't even go out in the yard. Keep everything locked up and barricade the doors until I get back. Put a towel over your lap when you go to the bathroom in case they've installed new cameras and make sure you sleep in pajamas. Change and take your showers in the dark and do it quick in case they have infrared."

"I thought they stopped taping us after you took out the camera."

"Maybe they did and maybe they didn't. But just to be on the safe side, act as though your every move is being watched." He took a deep breath, looked at her. "Maybe we should drive. Then we could both go."

"To Philadelphia?" Her voice softened. "She might not make it, Bare. I don't want to upset you, but you need to get out there now."

"You're right," he said numbly. "You're right." He thought for a moment. "Why don't you come with me up to Salt Lake? You can stay in a hotel until I get back. That way you won't have to be here alone."

"I'll be fine."

"Maybe not. You said—"

"I'll be fine," she repeated. She kissed him. "Get ready. Go."

He called her from the airport and then from the hospital when he got there. Things were looking up a little, he said. Not much, but a little. There'd be no need for a kidney, and it appeared likely that she'd pull through—the crucial period had passed—but the doctors were still uncertain as to whether or not she had suffered brain damage.

For Maureen, the day was long. She recalculated an estimated tax schedule for a client in California whose used-record store income was below the initial projection, but that was it for real work. She spent the rest of the morning and the afternoon listening to music and rereading an old Philip Roth novel, waiting for another call from Barry. He phoned again that night. Sheri's condition was unchanged. They talked for nearly an hour before Maureen gently told him he should go to bed, it was ten o'clock on the east coast and he needed the rest. He hung up, after promising to call again in the morning after he visited the hospital.

She hadn't done much today, but she was tired, and Maureen went to bed after checking all of the locks and placing a chair under the knob of the front door. Despite what she'd told Barry, she did not feel comfortable remaining here alone, and she wished now that she had agreed to go to Salt Lake City. Why had she stayed? What had made her do such a stupid thing?

Made her?

Now she was thinking like him.

*Made her.*

The thought was impossible to dislodge once it had crept into her brain. It really had been a stupid decision, and she could not for the life of her recall the logic or reasoning behind her choice.

Barry was the one who liked noise, who needed to fall asleep with the television on. By herself, she would have ordinarily gone to bed in a silent house. But tonight she was grateful for the voices and the light, and she fell asleep listening to the canned laughter of an unfunny TV show.

She was awakened after midnight by noises. The timer had long since turned off the television, but the house was not silent. From upstairs came loud taps and creaks and a subtle, persistent rattling. She wanted to pretend she didn't hear them, to pull the covers over her head, plug her ears, and force herself back to sleep. But she couldn't feign ignorance knowing that someone might be creeping through her house. She was responsible for two now, and it was her job to protect her home and child.

She reached over, flipped on the lamp atop the nightstand.

A man stood in the doorway holding a coat hanger.

The scream that tore from her lips seared her throat with its intensity and she could not suck in enough air to sustain it, but she continued screaming nonetheless.

In three quick strides, he was next to the bed.

And he was smiling.

Still screaming, Maureen shoved off the covers and scrambled to the other side of the mattress. She intended to throw open the window and jump out through the screen but a strong hand grabbed her left ankle before she had even made it off the bed. She kicked out with both legs, trying to hurt him, trying to connect, but her feet hit only open air, and then she was flipped onto her back.

The man was wearing a business suit. He was not someone she recognized or had ever seen before, and the impersonality of the attack made it that much more frightening. She knew why he was here and who had sent him, and she also knew who had informed on her.

*Liz.*

She tried to sit up, ready to scratch his face and claw out his eyes, but he punched her in the stomach, and as she gasped for air and clutched at her midsection, he straightened out the coat hanger. "Article six," he said. "Section three, paragraph D."

"No-o-o-o!" she screamed.

Grinning, he shoved her legs apart.

And a crimson blotch exploded on his chest.

His eyes widened, and he straightened up, twisting around as he tried to clutch at his back, making a sickening gurgling noise deep in his throat. He'd dropped his coat hanger, but he made no attempt to retrieve it. Instead, he lurched to the side as a high, keening whine escaped from his mouth.

Liz stood behind him. She pulled out the knife she'd plunged into his back and shoved it in again, higher. No blood bloomed on his shirt this time, but Maureen could see it spraying behind him, coating Liz's arms, soaking the dresser and carpet. He fell on the bed next to her, jerking spasmodically. Maureen pushed herself over the foot of the bed, rolling onto the floor, and when she looked up again he was still.

Liz remained in place, covered with blood, hands at her side. "I'm sorry," she said, and she started to cry. "It's my fault. I'm sorry."

Maureen stood and hugged her friend.

"I was weak. I couldn't help it. I went to them." By now she was sobbing. "I just wanted it to stop."

Maureen looked at the body on the bed, Liz's knife still protruding from the back of his suit jacket.

"I didn't tell them," Liz said, wiping her eyes and smearing the blood on her face. "Honest. You have to believe me. I knew they knew, but I wasn't the one who told them."

The knowledge filled Maureen with relief. "I believe you."

"I should've done something, though. I should've . . ." She trailed off, then took a deep breath. "I knew they'd send someone, and I waited outside your house and followed him in when he showed up."

"Thank God you did." Maureen could not seem to take her eyes off the would-be abortionist's body. "But they'll be after both of us now."

"Not me," Liz said. "I *went* to them."

Maureen knew that was supposed to mean something to her, knew she was supposed to understand its implications, but she did not.

Liz seemed to straighten, to find some untapped reserve of strength within her. "But they'll be doubly anxious to get to you now. You'd better get out of here. Where's Barry?"

"At his sister's in Pennsylvania."

"Then go to a hotel somewhere, in some other town." She held up a hand. "Don't tell me where."

"But . . ." Maureen gestured toward the body. ". . . but you killed him. And he's one of theirs. They won't let you get away with that."

"Don't worry about it."

"I can't just leave you."

"Get out of here," Liz ordered.

"But—"

"I'll take care of this. Just grab what you need and go. Now."

# FIFTY-THREE

**The Bonita Vista Homeowners' Association Covenants, Conditions, and Restrictions** Article VI, Membership Rights, Section 8, Paragraph G:

> *A homeowner may justifiably use deadly force on any of the Properties whenever he or she deems it appropriate.*

# FIFTY-FOUR

Maureen called him from a hotel in Cedar City.

Barry had just come back to his sister's house from the hospital and was bone tired, but he was wide awake as Maureen described the attack on her and Liz's last-minute rescue. At the old woman's behest, she'd packed what she thought she'd need into the Toyota and took off, ending up in Cedar City at dawn. She'd been trying to get a hold of him ever since, calling every five minutes for the last hour.

"They were trying to stop us from having a baby," she whispered, and the words sent a shiver down his spine. "They were trying to abort it."

There was nothing more he could do for Sheri—and Brian had his own sister, Margot, and her family there for support—so Barry caught the next plane west, an AA flight to St. Louis. He waited only an hour at the St. Louis terminal for a standby coach seat on a plane flying to Salt Lake City, and by late afternoon, Utah time, he and Maureen were hugging in her room at the Holiday Inn.

She told him again what happened, this time in more detail. After she finished, he tried to call Liz, but twenty rings later there was no answer and he finally hung up. He made a quick call to Brian at the hospital in Philadelphia to see if Sheri's condition had improved—it was unchanged—

then turned toward Maureen, sitting next to him on the bed.

"We'll both stay here tonight," he said. "But tomorrow I'm going back home. I want you to stay here for a few days while I . . . straighten things out."

"No!" she said, clutching his arm. "Don't go back there! We're through with that place. Just sell it, sell the house, sell everything."

"We can't, remember? There's a lien."

"Fuck it. Write it off then. We'll survive. We'll find a little tract home. We'll rent an apartment if we have to."

"Like you said, it would follow us around. We can't just walk away and pretend it didn't happen. There's a record. It'd be financial suicide—"

"Don't give me that. Since when have you given a damn about finances?"

He met her eyes. "You're right," he said. "I just . . . can't let them win. I can't do it. I can't walk away from this."

She squinted suspiciously. "What did you mean, 'straighten things out'?"

"I don't expect you to understand—"

"Oh, it's a guy thing, huh?"

"No, not that."

"A man's gotta do what a man's gotta do?"

He grabbed her shoulders, held them tight. "Someone has to take a stand."

She pulled away from him, stood. "What does that mean? What does any of this mean? You're talking like someone in a bad western movie. They tried to abort our baby!"

"That's why I'm going back."

"Goddamn it, Barry!"

"I'm going back."

"I won't let you!"

"You have no choice." He looked at her. "*I* have no choice."

*     *     *

By the time he reached Bonita Vista it was nearly noon.
At the gate, the guard smirked at him, forced him to show
his driver's license, and took an inordinately long time
looking up his name on the list of residents. Finally, his
admission approved, the gate swung open. Barry threw
the melted ice from his Subway cup out the window and
into the face of the guard as he drove past. "Asshole!" he
said.

He stepped on the gas and sped up the hill.

Their home had been desecrated. The property had been
relandscaped yet again, this time with a rolling green lawn
that defied the natural aesthetics of the hillside and looked
as though it had been transplanted from a golf course. One
lone tree remained, but all shrubs and bushes were gone,
the irregular ground smoothed over and planted with bright
green grass.

The house looked like something out of Dr. Seuss.

Their shingled roof had been redecorated with black and
white zigzag stripes. The side of the house facing the street
was bright yellow, the upstairs window red, the two bottom
windows blue. The door was not only pink but had been
padded with some sort of fuzzy material.

Inside, much of the furniture had been removed and the
walls were blank, all of Maureen's artwork and groupings
taken down. There was only one couch, the coffee table,
and his stereo system in the living room; only the bed,
dresser, and television set in the still-bloodstained bedroom. He had no idea where the rest of their stuff had gone,
but he had the feeling that it was not safely packed away in
storage.

The mailbox was crammed with dozens of fines and notices from the homeowners' association.

First things first. He walked back into the house, got a
book of matches from the junk drawer in the kitchen, and
strode down to the end of the driveway, where he very ob-

viously and dramatically dumped everything out of the mailbox onto the asphalt. He lit a match, touched it to the corner of one envelope, then to the corner of a pink form. In seconds, the entire pile of papers was burning.

As he'd suspected, as he'd hoped, Neil Campbell appeared from up the street, walking briskly, clipboard in hand. The prissy little man looked positively apoplectic. "You can't do that!" he shouted, turning in at the driveway.

"Can't do what?"

"Those are official notices from the Bonita Vista Homeowners' Association, and you are required to respond to them! You cannot—" He pointed with his clipboard, his arm shaking in disbelief. "—burn them!"

"Get off of my property," Barry said.

"What?"

"You heard me."

"There is a clause allowing board members and committee—"

"If you're not off my property in one minute, I'll throw you off myself." Barry pushed up his sleeve. "Do you understand?"

Campbell backed up a step. "You're making a big mistake. I am here as a representative of the Bonita Vista Homeowners' Association."

"Thirty seconds."

He started writing furiously. "I am reporting all of this."

"That's it." Barry grabbed the toady's arm. "Get out of here. Now."

"Don't you touch me!" Campbell jerked away.

Barry punched him. Hard. His fist connected with the man's stomach, and by God it felt good. Campbell doubled over, let out a surprised gasp, then scrambled backward to get out of the driveway.

"Don't you ever set foot on my property again!" Barry kicked the pile of burning papers, sending a half-blackened piece of envelope skittering out into the road.

Campbell ran off.

"And tell your friends, too," Barry shouted after him.

He smiled as he watched the forms and notices burn themselves out.

In the morning, an expensive embossed envelope waited for him in the mailbox. There was nothing on the front, no return address, not even his name. It was blank.

Inside was an invitation for dinner at Jasper Calhoun's house.

His first instinct was to throw the invitation away and not go, but he realized that was only because he was afraid. He recalled the ominous dread he felt when he and Jeremy had walked up to the president's home. It would be simpler and safer to stay at home tonight, watch TV, listen to his stereo, read a book. But he had returned to Bonita Vista for a confrontation, and while he would prefer that confrontation to happen at his house, on his own turf, he was not about to run from it no matter where it occurred.

There was no RSVP on the invitation, and he assumed that was intentional. Calhoun wanted him to worry about this, wanted him to fret over it until the very last minute.

He did spend the afternoon worrying, but it was not over whether he should accept the invitation. It was over what he should bring with him. He had no gun, but he considered hiding a knife in his boot or sticking an array of screwdrivers in his belt buckle or even walking in wielding a nail-studded two-by-four. He was pretty sure this was a trap, and he would be a fool not to protect himself.

In the end, however, he decided not to bring a weapon. There would doubtless be others present at the dinner—henchmen, board members, friends, supporters, followers—and it would be impossible for him to fight them all no matter what he was carrying. Besides, there'd probably be some sort of frisk or body search or metal detector. The best idea was to go in clean.

He debated whether to tell Maureen, and eventually decided he would not. He did not want to worry her, but he did call, and they talked about trivial things, innocuous things. Without saying so specifically, he led her to believe that he was merely cleaning up the house and yard while poring through the revised C, C, and Rs looking for ways to attack the association by using its own rules and regulations.

"When are you coming back?" she asked.

"Soon, I hope."

There was a pause.

"I don't suppose you're going to tell me what's really going on there?"

He should have known she was too smart to be fooled by his crude attempts at misdirection. "No," he admitted. "I'm not."

"It's not just me anymore," she told him. "There are two of us who need you."

"I'm not going anywhere."

"I'm sure Dylan, Chuck, and Danna thought the same thing. I don't know what you're doing, and maybe I don't want to know, but be careful. This isn't a game. Those people are dangerous. I don't want to send out a private investigator a year from now and find out that my new baby's father has been turned into a Stumpy."

Barry didn't respond, but the idea was one that had already occurred to him, and he felt cold.

"Come home to us," Maureen said. "Nothing is worth your life."

"I know that. Don't worry. I won't do anything stupid."

The dinner was scheduled for eight, and though he could have walked, Barry decided to drive. He might need to make a quick getaway. And if . . . something . . . happened to him, at least the disposal of his Suburban would cause them trouble and inconvenience.

He parked on the street rather than in the driveway so other people could see his vehicle. Walking up the path, he was filled with the same sense of trepidation he had experienced before, magnified by the fact that it was night. Calhoun had strong lights illuminating his grassy lawn, but they only served to make the surrounding woods seem darker.

A servant met him at the door. No, not a servant. A *volunteer*. Barry recognized the man. Ralph Hieberg. He'd been introduced to him at one of Ray's parties.

"Come in, Mr. Welch. You are expected."

Barry stepped into the vestibule. "Ralph," he said. "What are you doing here?"

The man's eyes darted furtively to the left and then the right. Barry thought he was actually going to answer, but he said, "Just come with me. Please. I only have a month to go. I don't want to get in trouble."

Barry nodded, understanding, and allowed himself to be led through another doorway into what appeared to be the living room.

He'd been expecting a building of dank dark corridors, a maze of passageways that led to some horrible inner sanctum, but instead the interior of the house was bright and airy. The room into which they walked was decorated in a Japanese motif, with bamboo-framed paper walls, low tables, and mats and cushions on the floor. There were no lights or lamps but illumination seeped through the translucent paper from all sides, ensuring that there were no shadows.

Ralph walked around the tables to the opposite wall and pulled aside a section, which slid open to reveal another room beyond. He stood to the left and motioned for Barry to enter.

There was writing on the walls, Barry noticed as he followed the volunteer. He looked carefully at the wall as he

passed into the next room and shivered as he realized that
the bamboo frames held not traditional blank rice paper but
blown-up pages from Bonita Vista's *Covenants, Conditions, and Restrictions*.

They went from this room to another . . . and then another . . . and another. Each looked exactly like the one before it. He saw no couches, no television, no bookcase, no
kitchen, no bathroom, only an endless series of living
rooms with low tables and mats and cushions and C, C, and
R walls. Until finally they were in a room with no furniture,
only an empty wooden floor and walls that did not glow
with that sourceless illumination but were dim and dull.
Ahead, the translucent paper was red and there was no writing on it. From behind the red wall he heard moaning and
occasional sharp yelps. Barry found it hard to swallow; it
felt as though his heart was in his throat.

"This way, Mr. Welch." The volunteer pushed aside a
section of the red wall and the two of them walked into the
chamber beyond.

*This* was what he had expected.

The room was massive, bigger than the entire bottom
floor of his own house, with a high black ceiling from
which hung dirty irregularly spaced lightbulbs. The walls
were stone, the floor worn, unpainted wood that was
stained with drops and splotches of what could only be old
blood. There was a large pit in the center of the chamber, its
sides made of burnished steel, its bottom covered with
straw. Rusted metal tables stuck out at odd angles around
the edge of the pit, like broken wheel spokes.

On the tables were blades and saws and what looked like
medical instruments.

In the pit were Stumpies.

They were moaning and wailing, although whether in
pain or some desperate effort to communicate, he had no
idea. There were six men and one woman, and thankfully
Barry didn't know any of them. He'd expected in that first

second of comprehension to see Dylan and Chuck and Danna with their limbs cut off, but the poor pathetic wretches who flopped around in the sawdust were not people he had ever seen before.

It was the armless, legless woman who was most disturbing, her bruised and battered nudity reminding him uncomfortably of Maureen. The others were squirming through the straw, jerking their bodies into and over each other. But she lay alone against the rounded steel wall, the wild matted hair of her private parts glistening with wet blood, her swollen mouth open silently, her eyes fixed on one of the dim bare bulbs overhead.

"This way, Mr. Welch."

Numbly, he walked around one of the rusted tables, this one containing a ball peen hammer covered with flecks of flesh and bone, an assortment of filthy screwdrivers, and a long serrated knife. As he followed Ralph past the pit, he could not help looking down. In the straw surrounding the Stumpies, he saw feces and what looked like rotted fish.

The volunteer stopped before a narrow metal door recessed into the stone wall. He did not look at Barry, did not look at the door, but stared down at his feet and seemed to be gathering his strength as he took a deep breath. Quickly, he reached out, grabbed the oversized handle, and pulled the door open. He looked scared as he motioned Barry in.

They stepped through the narrow entryway.

"Mr. Welch!" Ralph announced.

This room was even darker. There were no electric lights here, only smoky, foul-smelling candles held in wrought iron stands placed in the four corners of the chamber. It took a moment for his eyes to adjust, but when they did he saw a dusty display case containing the stuffed bodies of cats and dogs, parrots, and hamsters—the pets outlawed by the association. Other damaged, discarded remnants of normal life that were not permitted in Bonita Vista were ar ranged haphazardly around the room: dead houseplants in broken pots lying atop a cracked and listing knickknack shelf, split birdhouses hanging from a battered clothesline pole that leaned against a child's playhouse.

At the opposite end of the chamber, Jasper Calhoun was seated at the center of a long oak table, flanked by the other five members of the board. Goblets of dark red liquid and plates of strange, unappetizing meat sat on the table in front of them. The tableaux reminded Barry of the Last Supper, with the transubstantiation made horribly literal.

"Welcome to our boardroom," Calhoun said. To the sides of him, the others nodded. The strangeness of their oddly shaped, too-white faces did not seem out of place here, Barry thought. This was the environment in which they belonged, this was their home.

Underneath the table, he could see naked women chained to the floor, servicing the six men.

Calhoun saw the direction of his gaze and smiled. "Our female volunteers," he said. He nodded down at his lap. "That's Ralph's wife. Right, Ralph?"

The volunteer nodded stoically.

"You could have had Maureen work off your debts this way."

Barry pretended to be thinking thoughtfully. "I read your sexual harassment pamphlet, and as I understand it, this would be classified as harassment under association rules. Am I correct?"

Calhoun stood, his face flushing. Underneath the table, Ralph's wife scurried to the side. "I will not have the rules quoted to me in my own house!"

"I take it that's a yes?"

The president took a deep breath, and forced himself to smile. "Too bad about your friends," he said. "I wonder whatever happened to them." He looked down at the slab of strange meat on his plate and very deliberately peeled off a stringy section, eating it.

He was bluffing. He had to be. This was all show, a performance put on for his benefit, but Barry had to admit that the technique was effective. He was way out of his depth, and fear had overtaken anger as the dominant emotion within him.

"What do you want?" Barry said shortly. "Why did you invite me here?"

Calhoun sat down again, steepled his fingers. "We seem to have reached a stalemate. As far as the bylaws are concerned, you are a squatter. You no longer hold any rights to your house or property, yet you continue to reside there and seemingly have no intention of moving out."

"What's your point?"

"You said at the annual meeting that you wanted a real election. I take that to mean that you would like to have yourself or someone handpicked by you elected to the board."

"Yeah?"

"I think it's time to invoke Article Ninety." The wall behind the table was suddenly illuminated by a spotlight hidden in the ceiling, and Barry saw that there was writing on the stone. Elaborate calligraphic script, with red letters nearly a foot high, covered the space from floor to ceiling. He could read the words "Article Ninety"—there was no title, no section number, no paragraph designation—but that was it. The rest appeared to be gibberish.

"It is the one article that you will not find in your printed version of the C, C, and Rs," the president said.

"Why is that?" Barry asked.

Calhoun leaned forward over the table, and there was an intensity in his expression that caused Barry to back up a step. "Because it cannot be captured or caught or frozen in time. It cannot be diminished by being limited to a single meaning. It is forever changing, adaptable to any circumstance that arises, and it is at the very heart of our home owners' association. It is what grants us our authority and

power, what allows you and everyone else to enjoy the per-
fection that is life in Bonita Vista."

Barry stood there, not knowing what to say or how to respond. He could not recall hearing the door behind him
close, and he casually turned his head to the side, pretending as though he was surveying the room but actually
checking to see if the doorway was clear and he could haul
ass out of here.

No such luck. The metal door was securely shut.

He faced forward again, filled with a growing dread and
feeling of claustrophobia. The chamber smelled to him of
sweat and blood and bodily fluids. He had to suppress the
very real urge to vomit.

"It is the responsibility of the minister of information to
address Article Ninety," Calhoun said. He nodded toward
the old man seated directly to his right. "Fenton?"

The other man shooed away the woman working on his
lap and stood. If possible, he looked even more peculiar
than the president, his too-perfect and off-center nose appearing to have been placed on his face in order to imitate
an element of normalcy that simply was not there.

"Article Ninety," he intoned. "We ask thee for thy words
of wisdom."

"Thy wisdom is infinite," the other board members
chanted.

"Provide us with the knowledge to deal with this as with
all matters."

"Thy rules and regulations are as blessings to us all."

Fenton closed his eyes, turned and bowed to the wall.
"Article Ninety, Barry Welch wishes to mount a challenge
to appear on the ballot for the Bonita Vista Homeowners'
Association board of directors. How is he to be accommo-
dated and how are we to determine his eligibility?"

Abruptly, the gibberish disappeared. The words on the
wall were still in that elaborate archaic calligraphy, but they
were suddenly readable, understandable. The resulting dec-

laration was not couched in the pseudolegalese that made up the rest of the C, C, and Rs but in a stilted quasireligious formality that sounded no less odd. Fenton straightened from his bow and read the words aloud: "Whosoever desires to place his name upon the ballot must first engage in battle with a current member of the board of directors. This must of necessity be a fight to the finish, the death of one ensuring the position of the other on the sacred ballot. Have mercy on the soul of this combatant for he knows not what he does."

The six old men turned to look at him. Barry was already shaking his head. "I don't know what's going on here, but I want no part of it."

"It's too late for that," Calhoun told him.

"I'm not fighting anybody." But at the same time, he was thinking that this was why he had come, this was the confrontation he had been seeking. He had not expected anything so simplistic or crudely literal, but he now had the opportunity he'd been seeking to combat the board. He thought of Barney the cat, thought of Ray, thought of Kenny Tolkin, thought of Dylan and Chuck and Danna, thought of Maureen and their baby, and he allowed the anger to seep in, allowed the rage to build.

Calhoun grinned, and as before his smile seemed far too wide. "Barry Welch," he thundered. "I hereby challenge you to battle! In front of all and sundry neighbors! Hand-to-hand combat to the death!"

A cheer went up from the other members of the board and from the volunteer women underneath the table. Behind them, the wall grew dark as the spotlight cut out, the room once again receiving only the dim illumination of sooty candies.

Yes, Barry thought. *I could fight any of these assholes. I could kill all of these sons of bitches.*

Calhoun's grin was positively feral. "Do you accept the challenge?"

"I accept!"

"Excellent," the president said. "Excellent." He sat down, his smile disappearing instantly. A cold stoniness hardened his features as he nodded imperiously at Ralph. "Now get this piece of shit prepared for battle."

# FIFTY-FIVE

Barry was led through a narrow doorway to the side of the taxidermy display case and then down a long corridor with rusted metal walls that looked and smelled like the inside of a disused sewer pipe. At the end was a filthy, low-ceilinged room filled with volunteers who grabbed him and stripped off his clothes. They made no sound, and that was the eerie thing. They simply yanked open his shirt, pulled at the sleeves, took off his shoes, unbuckled his belt, tugged down his pants, passing him from one to the other, the only noise in the claustrophobic chamber his own startled grunts and protestations.

He was left with only his underwear, smudged with mud and grease by dirty hands. The volunteers backed off, fanning around the edges of the room, looking at the floor, at the walls, at the ceiling, at each other, at anything except him. They seemed ashamed of what they'd done to him— of what they'd *had* to do to him—and he had the curious sensation that they were behind him on this, that they were on his side, that they would like to see him win.

Win what?

He didn't know. Was this supposed to be a fistfight? "Hand-to-hand combat" was a broad enough term to encompass a variety of fighting styles, and he had no idea what the rules of the bout would be. Just judging on ap-

pearances, Calhoun was big and flabby and old. He should
be able to kick the president's ass with no problem. But he
thought of the odd, pale skin covering that strange musculature, and the aura of power that surrounded all of the
board members, and he was not at all sure he would be able
to beat the old man in any kind of fight.

He was not even sure Calhoun was human.

He didn't want to think about that.

Barry looked over at Ralph, who was standing impas-
sively next to a square hole in the wall the size of a large
television, a black opening that looked like the entrance to
a crawlspace.

"Am I supposed to go through there?" he asked.

"When you are ready."

"Where does it go?"

He received no answer.

Barry looked around the room at the shuffling volunteers, then back at that ominous opening in the wall. He was
nervous, sweating, filled with a dark dread. He'd been sup-
pressing or avoiding the central truth of the coming fight,
but now it was all he could think about. *Someone was going
to die.* Whether it was himself or Jasper Calhoun, one of
them would be dead within the next hour, killed by the
other.

He didn't know if he would actually be able to murder
the association president in cold blood. He hated him, yes.
And he would probably be very happy if the man suddenly
dropped dead. But could he do the killing? Most likely, if
he won the fight, he would show mercy and let the president live. But if things progressed the way they did in novels and films, at that point Calhoun would turn the tables
and attack, exploiting his weakness, and then he would be
*forced* to kill the old man. And it would be righteous and
justified because it was provoked and he was only acting in
self-defense.

*Someone was going to die.*

That was a truth he could not seem to escape.

Taking a deep breath, he crouched down, looked into the dark hole, then got on his hands and knees. He expected some surreptitious sign of support, a nod, a smile, a whisper of "Good luck," but Ralph remained silent and stone-faced as Barry crawled into the small passageway.

The floor was cold, hard concrete, and periodically, as he crawled, Barry's fingers and knees touched puddles of sticky unidentifiable liquid. There was only darkness at first, an inky black that seemed not merely the absence of light but an entity of its own, and several times he scraped his elbows or bumped his head on the hard walls and ceiling of the crawlway. But gradually he began to discern grayish light up ahead, an upright rectangle that grew closer and closer, and just before he reached the tunnel's exit, the passage opened up and he was able to stand.

He stepped out into an arena.

It threw him for a moment, and for several disorienting seconds he did not know where he was or what he was looking at. Then everything sort of clicked into place. He saw the dirt floor strewn with bloody sawdust, the high surrounding walls, the circle of filled amphitheater seats above. The arena was nearly the size of a football stadium. As big as it was, there was no way Calhoun's house could accommodate something this large, yet here it stood, and as Barry looked up into the stands, he saw that all of his neighbors were here, all of the residents of Bonita Vista, dressed in suits and gowns and formal attire.

The ceiling was some sort of skylight, and through its translucent safety-wired glass Barry could see occasional flashes of far-off lightning. The lightning was accompanied by low rolling thunder. The only illumination within the arena itself came from a series of lanterns and torches lining the curved wall behind the last ring of seats. In the center of the sawdust-covered floor, hanging by a hook from a tall bamboo post, was one additional light, a lantern in the shape of a—

—human head.

His breath catching in his throat, Barry squinted into the dimness. It not only looked like a head, he was pretty sure it *was* a head. He saw flickering flames behind partially parted lips, through the empty sockets of missing eyes. He moved forward, not wanting his suspicions confirmed but needing to know.

It was Dylan.

He could see, as he drew closer, the specific features of his friend's face thrown into silhouette by the orange fire burning inside the hollowed-out skull.

He wanted to scream, wanted to lash out and hurt someone, wanted to blow up this whole fucking building and everyone in it. He looked up into the stands, saw expressions of excitement and anticipation on the faces of women he'd seen jogging by the house, couples he'd seen playing tennis. From a ringside seat off to the side, Mike waved, shouted: "We're all behind you, man." Next to him, Tina nodded.

They were not behind him, he knew. They were not here to show their support.

They wanted to see blood.

The Stewarts had already turned away, were talking to Frank and Audrey and another woman Barry did not recognize. All of them laughed.

He looked again at the lantern made from Dylan's head, remembered all the good times they'd had together, remembered when they'd first met in a junk course on the history of science-fiction films, remembered the nights they'd spent hanging out in Minderbinder's before he'd gotten married, remembered the time they'd double-dated two sisters who'd gotten into a screaming hair-pulling fight with one another in the middle of a Suzanne Vega concert.

"Dylan," he whispered.

There was movement in the darkness beyond, some sort of commotion at the opposite end of the arena. Frowning, Barry stepped past the lantern—

*Dylan's head*

—in order to see more clearly.

And beheld Jasper Calhoun, standing in front of the far wall.

Waiting.

As if on cue, the rumbling thunder intensified, the storm promised by the previously intermittent lightning now arrived.

Calhoun looked over at him, grinning. Sequential bursts of increasingly bright lightning exploded above the thick glass of the skylight ceiling, and during each flash the president's face seemed to . . . change. Briefly. For an instant. Above Calhoun, in box seats lining the north edge of the arena, the other board members also appeared to be temporarily transformed, as though, during their brief seconds of existence, the lightning bolts were somehow able to reveal the true nature of those evil old men.

No, that's what would be happening in one of his novels. That's not what was happening here.

Calhoun's face shifted . . . shifted back.

Barry had to fight the urge to run away. His desire must have been obvious because all of a sudden Mike and Frank and several other men in their section of the stands started chanting, "Article Ninety! Article Ninety!" It was clear that they were urging the combatants to begin the battle, demanding an immediate start to the match, and the cry was taken up around the amphitheater: "Article Ninety! Article Ninety! Article Ninety!" The rounded concrete walls seemed to amplify random crowd conversations above, and beneath the chant he heard bets being made on the fight's outcome, heard hopeful expectations for gruesome bloodletting.

He continued to face the opposite end of the ring. Calhoun was wearing his ridiculous robes, and Barry was glad. The bulky garments would limit the old man's movements, he thought. The president would not be able to move freely either offensively or defensively.

Who was he kidding? Calhoun was a monster. There was no way in hell the two of them were evenly matched. This fight would not be happening if there was even the slightest possibility that Calhoun could lose. It was rigged, the outcome guaranteed. Barry knew that the deck was stacked against him, and if he were to come out of this in one piece, he needed to quickly figure a way out of here.

He turned around, saw volunteers standing in the doorway through which he'd come, blocking that exit. There didn't seem to be any doorway on Calhoun's side of the ring, and the wall surrounding them was too high to scale— assuming he could get through the well-dressed crowd if it wasn't.

For the first time, he wondered what would happen if he was killed, what they would do with his body. Would Maureen be informed? Would he appear to have been the victim of an accident, or would he just disappear, his whereabouts never to be known, leaving Maureen and his unborn son or daughter forever in the dark? Would a lantern made from *his* head decorate this hellish arena?

He should have told her about this, he thought. He should have at least written and mailed a letter so she would know the truth.

Suddenly Jasper Calhoun raised both of his hands, and the activity of the spectators halted, their chanting and myriad conversations stopping instantly. Even the thunder ceased, and though Barry knew that was a coincidence, it still made him feel uneasy. The president smiled at him from across the ring, then clapped his hands twice.

Paul Henri, dressed once again in livery, emerged from between the five board members and stepped to the edge of the wall. He blew on some sort of trumpet whose notes were lost to the air, but his voice, when he spoke, could be heard clearly. "Let the games begin!"

With a roar, Calhoun came at him, robes flapping like the wings of some crazed black bird. Barry felt an instinctive rush of primal fear. His first impulse was to run, to duck left or right, get out of the way, but he held his ground and punched into the oncoming figure, experiencing a grim satisfaction as his fist connected with what felt like the president's stomach.

He hadn't anticipated such an abrupt attack. He'd half-expected to have the ground rules spelled out, to be told beforehand what was and was not acceptable, maybe even to shake hands and count off ten paces before turning to fight, but apparently all was fair in war and an association dispute, and he knew now that he'd better use whatever dirty tricks or underhanded techniques he could—because Calhoun certainly would.

He'd hit the old man with everything he had, putting weight and momentum behind his punch, but the president barely seemed to feel it. He lurched sideways, then turned, lashing out with hands that looked more like claws. Barry was only just able to avoid their reach, and then Calhoun head-butted him hard in the face.

He felt his nose explode. Blood flooded into his throat and shards of bone seemed to shoot under the skin of his cheeks like needles.

He fell backward onto the sawdust and heard rather than felt his head hit the hard-packed dirt below: a sharp whip crack that cut off with a dull solid thud.

He looked up and saw a double ring of faces looking over the edge, all of them yelling and cheering wildly. His gaze happened upon Curtis, the gate guard, and Frank. Both of them were smiling cruelly, happy to see him in pain.

The arena shook as an explosion louder and clearer than the background thunder, a noise that sounded like too-close cannon fire, rocked the building. Lightning had hit the sky-light, cracking the thick safety glass, and through a fracture in the ceiling, rainwater began leaking down in a dripping curtain that bisected the ring, soaked the sawdust, and somehow put out the fire in Dylan's hanging head. Barry grinned crazily. "It's a sign from God!" he yelled at Calhoun. "He's bringing down His wrath on all you mother-fuckers!"

The president remained nonplussed. "There is no God," he said.

Barry felt woozy, warm blood from his shattered nose and the wound at the back of his head mingling with the cold wetness of the rain on his scalp, but he retained enough presence of mind to roll as Calhoun attempted to stomp on his face.

A black boot barely missed his head, and he reached out and grabbed the attached leg, digging his fingers into flesh. He yanked hard, putting all of his weight behind it, and Calhoun was momentarily thrown off balance. Barry staggered to his feet and ran toward the north end of the arena to get away from the president, trying to gain time and formulate a fighting strategy. *Think!* he told himself. He tried to remember a rule or regulation that would prohibit this fight or at least put an end to it. The only thing Calhoun respected was the C, C, and Rs—it was his law, his Bible, and if Barry could come up with an association ordinance that addressed this specific situation, he could get out of it.

Otherwise, he would be killed.

He reached the north wall and turned to face Calhoun. The old man was running, robes flapping, the lightning heightening his expression of demonic glee.

*Robes flapping.*

*Robes.*

That was it! Barry suddenly remembered Mike, volun-teering because he was fined a hundred dollars for going outside in the morning to pick up his newspaper while wearing a bathrobe. It was against the rules, Mike said, for a person to appear outside his house wearing a robe.

But this was inside Calhoun's house, not outside. And he wasn't wearing a bathrobe. It was more like a judge's robe.

Did the rules specify a bathrobe, though, or was the wording vague? Did it simply say "robe," meaning *any* robe? He didn't know. But this was a chance he had to take.

Calhoun was getting closer.

And while the president might not be outside of his house now, he *had* been outside of it in his robes before. By the gate, during the confrontation with the Corbanites. And at the annual meeting, in the community center. And when he'd talked to Barry and the FBI agent.

The old man was almost upon him.

But what regulation prohibited that? What was it Mike had said? He'd mentioned it specifically, spelled out the exact rule he had broken.

*Think!*

Was it Article Three? Article Five?

"Article Eight!" Barry screamed. He stepped aside as the president lunged for him, pointed at the old man. "Article Eight! No one may wear a robe outside his house!" It was a paraphrase, probably a gross generalization, and it was all that he recalled from what Mike had said, but it did the trick. Calhoun stopped as if a switch had suddenly turned off inside his brain. He stood there, clawed hands opening and closing, leaking rainwater dripping onto his head.

"You broke the rules!" Barry said. He looked up at his neighbors in the stands. "He broke the rules! He violated the C, C, and Rs!" He heard distressed murmuring from around the arena, was gratified to see the other board members frantically conferring with one another. "What's the punishment for violating Article Eight?" he asked Calhoun.

"Remain seated!" the president announced, and though his voice was as deep and resonant as ever, it contained a welcome note of unease.

"He's outside in his robes all the time! He's never without his robes! And it's against the rules!"

"Article Eight!" someone yelled.

The cry was taken up by a man across the ring. "Article Eight!"

Barry's heart was pounding. "Article Eight!" he shouted. He started chanting, trying to prod the crowd, desperate, knowing this was his one and only chance. "Article Eight! Article Eight! Article Eight!"

Calhoun's expression was one of rage and hate. He advanced on Barry. "The battle will continue!" he declared. "Article Ninety."

Barry ran away, cutting a wide swath around the pole and Dylan's dark hanging head. "Article Eight!" he continued to shout. He raised his hands, trying to get the crowd to chant along with him. "Article Eight!"

There was still that disgruntled murmuring, but only a few individuals were chanting along with him.

The old man ran after him, then leaped, wet robes whipping back, reminding Barry once again of some huge bird of prey. It looked for a second as though Calhoun was going to be able to fly, to glide through the air and swoop down on him. But the president landed a few feet away, then took two long, quick strides toward him.

They were at the south end of the ring, where Barry had come in, Ralph and the volunteers still blocking the exit. There was nowhere for him to go, and Barry ducked left as Calhoun swung at him. He reached out to defend himself, and his hand connected with the top of the president's head.

Calhoun's hair slipped off. It was a wig, and underneath, the old man was not bald but . . . something else. Barry saw pulsing black tendrils beneath nearly transparent skin, saw the hint of another form under the mask of makeup, and though he'd imagined such scenarios numerous times as a writer, to experience it firsthand caused his heart to accelerate with terror.

But he was still levelheaded enough to remember one of
the revised C, C, and Rs he had read in passing at the annual meeting. "No baldness in public!" he shouted.

Calhoun stopped, shrank back.

"Article Fifteen!" Liz yelled.

Barry looked up, saw her standing proud and tall in the
center of the crowd above him. She caught his eye, nodded,
smiled.

*For Ray,* he thought.

"Article Fifteen!" he echoed.

He sensed a shift in the mood of the crowd, a shift in his
direction, but there was an ugliness to it, an unpleasant un-
dercurrent he did not like. The people had been unsure before, unwilling to commit one way or the other, afraid to
take a stand for fear of future retaliation, but they were with
him now.

Calhoun obviously sensed it as well, because he turned
around in a slow circle, stunned, looking up at the crowd,
his fellow members of the association. "Wait!" he ordered.

But the residents of Bonita Vista were all standing,
pointing down into the ring, pointing at him.

"Article Eight!" the men yelled.

"Article Fifteen!" the women countered.

Calhoun seemed to wither visibly under this verbal onslaught, as though the words took a physical toll on his
body.

At the north end of the arena, the other board members
were trying to leave, attempting to get out of their seats and
make their way up the aisle to escape the growing wrath of
the mob, but gowned women and tuxedoed men were
streaming into that section of the stands, pushing them
down, blocking their way.

People began dropping over the wall into the sawdust.
Barry backed against the concrete, glancing around warily
unsure of where this was going, unnerved by the chaos

around him. From above, a shoe came sailing down, hitting Calhoun in the face. A thrown wine glass shattered against his arm.

The president laughed, a deep, booming chuckle that sounded far too loud. Makeup had smeared away from the section of cheek struck by the shoe, and again Barry saw that transparent skin, those pulsating black tendrils. If this had been a movie or a novel, Calhoun would have been revealed as an alien. Or some type of creature from another dimension. But Barry somehow knew that neither of these were the case. The old man was not a distinct and separate being. He had been born human.

He had *become* this way.

From being on the association's board of directors.

Calhoun turned easily in one fluid movement. He was still chuckling, and he spread out one now definitely taloned hand and pressed it against Barry's bare chest, pushing hard.

Barry felt ribs cracking, found it suddenly hard to breathe. His own hands reached out frantically, trying to find purchase and keep himself from toppling backward. His fingers touched the soft silky material of the old man's robes. He latched on, desperately clutching the fabric even as he tumbled. The material did not rip, and the slight tethering of the robes helped break his fall, allowed him to land sitting on his butt rather than flat on his back.

Calhoun whirled to face him.

And then they were upon him.

There must have been a dozen men on the floor of the arena now, fists clenched, faces filled with anger. More were dropping from the wall. Some were carrying weapons—pocketknives, keys, champagne bottles—and they attacked the president. "No robes!" Curtis the gate guard screamed, swinging the butt of his revolver at that strange head.

An elderly man stabbed Calhoun's back with a pen. "Article Eight!" he yelled. He pulled the pen out, stabbed again. "Article Fifteen!"

A handful of men were grabbing at Calhoun's robe, and though Barry could not hear the sound over the thunder and the screaming crowd, he saw the material rip, saw the black cloth tear lengthwise, rending the garment. Calhoun let out an ear-splitting howl. From beneath the ripped material, what looked like diseased and blackened organs came tumbling out, still leashed to the body and to each other by clumps of bile-covered ligaments. They sizzled where the leaking rain water hit them, small jets of steam shooting up from hundreds of pinpoint fissures that erupted on the strange, dark viscera.

Calhoun seemed to have no skin or muscle on his body. Barry didn't see how that was possible with the robes so loose and flowing, but it was as though the president were some type of mummy and the garments had protected him, acted like a bandage and kept in the disparate elements that made up that loathsome form.

Twitching spastically, crying out in rage and pain and hate, Calhoun dropped to his knees, then fell flat onto his face. He managed to turn himself over, all trace of makeup gone now, his head a throbbing sac of black wormlike growths, and then he was still, the hole that had once been his mouth wide open and collecting rain.

He lay there for only a moment.

Then they tore him apart.

Barry grimaced and finally had to look away. The killing itself was bad enough, but this crazed animal savagery sickened and frightened him. He could not believe that his mild-mannered neighbors were capable of such barbarism, and he struggled painfully to his feet, then crept along the edge of the curved wall.

At the opposite end of the arena, the nude, lifeless body of one of the other board members was tossed into the ring to the sound of cheers. There was no sign of the other old men of the board, but somewhere in the middle of the crowd a shred of black robe flew into the air.

Barry reached the doorway through which he'd entered the ring. Ralph, still standing in front of the other volunteers, knelt down before him. Barry frowned.

"Hail to the president!" Paul Henri announced from somewhere up above.

The crowd was suddenly still, silent. Holding his chest, trying not to jostle his hurt ribs, Barry looked up. Paul Henri blew on his trumpet, and this time the notes were clear and audible: some sort of fanfare. From above, a group of women solemnly lowered a ladder. His head felt numb, his ribs hurt like a son of a bitch, but the pain was not crippling and he was able to climb.

At the top, he was met by Frank, Audrey, and several other men and women whose faces looked vaguely familiar but whom he did not recognize. He looked around for Liz but did not see her. There were open doors at the top of the stands where couples, families, and individuals were exiting, hurrying out into the rain, lightning throwing their scurrying forms into silhouette.

"Congratulations." Frank bowed to him.

"What do you want?"

"You have earned your place on the Bonita Vista Homeowners' Association board of directors." He held out a new black robe.

Barry knocked it away, though the action made his ribs ache with agony. "Go to hell." He pushed through the line of his neighbors, starting up the steps toward the exit. Glancing to his left, he saw the crumpled body of the nude board member on the bloody sawdust, the shredded bits and pieces of Jasper Calhoun.

This was something he would not tell Maureen, could not tell Maureen.

"You're free!" he called out to Ralph and the volunteers, still down in the ring. "Go home!"

But they looked at him blankly, made no move to leave, showed no expression on their faces.

Barry turned toward Frank. "Tell them it's over. Calhoun's dead, the board's gone, there are no more volunteers."

Frank met his eyes, and Barry understood. It wasn't over. The association was not simply a group of people, it could not be eliminated by killing its members. It was a system, a series of rules and regulations that existed apart from and above the individuals who made up its membership. It could only be stopped if those rules were rejected, if people refused to join or participate. He looked down at Ralph and the volunteers. Even *they* were not victims. They were part of the problem.

He elbowed his way past Frank and the others, walked up the steps, and out the door. The arena exits came out on the east side of Calhoun's house. Logically, there was no way such a huge structure could physically be located within a residence even as large as Calhoun's, but Barry did not want to think about that. On the wide stretch of lawn, scores of people were running about, many of them heading for the road.

There was no rain, but the storm was still raging, thunder sounding and lightning flashing, wind whipping the surrounding trees into a frenzy. Separating themselves from a nearby group of people talking animatedly among themselves, Mike and Tina came hurrying up to him, trailed by another older couple. "The top of the hill's on fire!" Tina said. "It's spreading down toward the houses on Spruce! What should we do?"

Barry shook his head, tried to push his way past them.

"Lightning hit the gate!" someone on the road yelled. "It's open and they're getting in! Where's the president?"

"He's over here!" Mike shouted.

"No!" Barry said.

People came running toward him.

"The townies! They're on a rampage!"

"They're going to riot! Call out the volunteers!"

He kept walking, ignoring them, striding purposefully toward his car. He could see from a strange glow at the top of the hill that the lightning fire was spreading quickly, fanned by the wildly blowing winds. It was as if the surrounding forest was filled with nothing but dry tinder, despite the recent monsoons. Behind him, he heard cries of panic, calls for someone to alert the fire department. A woman yelled that lightning had also struck over on Poplar Street and that a partially constructed house was burning, the fire racing through the greenbelt. Several people shouted into cell phones.

There were no fire hydrants here, he remembered. Even if Corban's volunteer firefighters wanted to put out the blaze and save the homes of Bonita Vista—a *very* big if— there was no water with which to do it. The whole place was going to burn to the ground, and Barry felt like laughing. It served those bastards right. So smug and self-satisfied, so convinced of their infallibility. Now they'd been brought down by their own shortsightedness, by not doing one of the few things that homeowners' associations were legitimately supposed to do—maintain the community's infrastructure.

No one chased after him, tried to stop him or even spoke to him, and he felt good, strong as he strode away from the house and through the disintegrating crowd. He could smell the smoke, and he was glad the wind was fanning the flames.

He hoped the fire consumed Calhoun's house. Especially that evil boardroom and its horrid wall of ever-changing words.

*Article Ninety.*

He had the feeling that if that could be destroyed, all would be well.

What about the Stumpies?

They would probably be killed—unless one of the volunteers in the house rescued them—but Barry found that he could live with that. They had already given most of their lives for the homeowners' association, and he had no doubt they would willingly sacrifice the rest if it would put an end to the excesses of the organization once and for all.

The people who only moments before had been trying to congratulate him were fleeing, running back to their homes in order to gather valuables or fight off fires. A fight broke out near Calhoun's flagpole. It was a free-for-all. Barry heard a loud, inhuman screech behind him, and he turned to see a well-coifed woman go down, shoved by an angry man in a suit and tie.

"Mr. Welch! Mr. Welch!" That despicable little toady Neil Campbell was running after him, without his clipboard for once, and Barry stopped to face the association flunky.

"I can help you," Campbell said breathlessly.

"With what?"

"Anything! I'm at the board's service! I'll be your right-hand man! Any investigations you want conducted, any houses you want kept under surveillance, any—"

"Neil?" Barry said.

"What?"

"Eat shit and bark at the moon."

Barry turned away, unable to keep the smile from his face as he walked purposefully out to the road. A pickup barreled by and seconds later rammed into a Jeep. From somewhere down the hill, a car alarm sounded. Flickering flames could be seen through the trees, and the smell of smoke was everywhere.

Burn, baby, burn, Barry thought.

Still smiling, happier than he'd been for a long long time, he jogged up the lawn toward the road. Where the Suburban waited that would take him to Cedar City. And Maureen.

# EPILOGUE

The insurance company had paid off on both the house and the property, taking the burned land off their hands. Barry had no idea whether the company planned to sell the lot as is or put up a new house and rent it out. He didn't care. He never wanted to see or think about Bonita Vista again.

They were moving on.

The red Acura hugged the curves as Jim J. Johnson drove through downtown Willis and onto a side street that wound up the ridge. Barry reached for Maureen's hand and squeezed it.

"This is the most remote neighborhood in town," the real estate agent said, turning onto a narrow dirt road that passed through a copse of scrub oak, pinion pine, and juniper. "They're still on the sewer system, but there's no cable out here. Strictly satellite dish." Two empty lots separated by an abandoned half-finished A-frame popped up on the right. A one-room log cabin was set far back from the road on the left.

"See what I mean?"

They looked through the car window at an old dented trailer, two dirty kids fighting over a spraying hose in the yard.

"Like I said, I'm not sure you'll be happy here," the agent told them. "You look like the kind of people who would appreciate more, shall we say, *refined* surroundings. Now we have a gated community here in Willis, a new planned neighborhood with two manmade lakes and a private golf course. The views are spectacular, the best in town, and strict zoning ordinances ensure that you'll never have to put up with trashy neighbors. What do you say I drive you out to Rancho de Willis and let you see for yourselves?"

Barry stared out at a poorly constructed patio attached to a rundown shack, saw a child's broken Big Wheel lying upside down in a patch of weeds.

"No," he said, looking at Maureen.

She smiled.

"This will be perfect. This will be fine."

# PENGUIN PUTNAM INC.
## Online

Your Internet gateway to a virtual environment with
hundreds of entertaining and enlightening books
from Penguin Putnam Inc.

*While you're there, get the latest buzz on
the best authors and books around—*

Tom Clancy, Patricia Cornwell, W.E.B. Griffin,
Nora Roberts, William Gibson, Robin Cook,
Brian Jacques, Catherine Coulter, Stephen King,
Ken Follett, Terry McMillan, and many more!

**Penguin Putnam Online is located at
http://www.penguinputnam.com**

## PENGUIN PUTNAM NEWS

Every month you'll get an inside look at our upcoming books and new features on our site. This is an
ongoing effort to provide you with the most
up-to-date information about
our books and authors.

Subscribe to Penguin Putnam News at
http://www.penguinputnam.com/newsletters